CHASING THE WIND

THE DOUGLAS FILES: BOOK FIVE

NATHAN BIRR

Beacon Books LLC

Published by BEACON BOOKS, LLC

Cover Image Copyright ©
burnsboxco/iStock/Thinkstock

ISBN: 978-0-9981813-2-5 (hc)
ISBN: 978-0-9981813-3-2 (sc)

www.nathanbirr.com

Also by Nathan Birr

Overnight Delivery
The Douglas Files: Book One

Black Male
A Douglas Files Short

Three's a Crowd
The Douglas Files: Book Two

WinterKill
A Douglas Files Short

All an Illusion
The Douglas Files: Book Three

Shot List
The Douglas Files: Book Four

God, Girls, Golf & the Gridiron
(Not Always in That Order)
. . . A Love Story

All is Calm?

The Book of Levi

*To all along the way (especially Mom and Dad)
who have taught and modeled the Scriptures to me . . .*

An eternal thank you!

Chapter One

Sunday, January 13, 2013
3:33 p.m.

"YOU WANT ME to steal a Bible?"

Jackson Douglas studied his potential client from across the table as she slowly nodded.

"Yes."

He sat back and took a deep breath.

Her name was Abigail Vanderbilt, but she had told him to call her Abby. The nickname fit her better. She was in her early thirties, he guessed, average height and weight, not a knockout but not unattractive either. Blond-brown hair in a shoulder-length bob, small mouth, wide brown eyes that studied him over a cup of tea. She wore jeans and a mauve Henley top, faint makeup, no jewelry, and only a dash of perfume. Missing were the air of superiority and the tall, rigid posture that should go with a regal name such as Abigail Vanderbilt.

Then again, she didn't have the angry scowl and dark gaze, the abundant leather, and the chopped, belligerent speech of a Bible-stealer either. So maybe Jackson didn't have Abby pegged quite as well as he thought.

He reached for his coffee, warranted on a gray, drizzly day, and took a slow drink, allowing him time to formulate his line of questioning. If he was going to consider making Abby's case his first of the new year, he had to know what he was getting into.

"Whose Bible is it?" he finally settled on, feeling as if it was the question Jesus might ask. Not why she wanted to steal the Bible, but who the rightful owner was. That would determine a lot—about her and about whether Jackson was soon to be employed.

"It was my stepfather Alec's," she said, lowering her cup and dabbing the corner of her mouth with her thumb.

"Alec Vanderbilt?"

1

"You know him?"

Jackson shook his head. "Should I?"

"Only if you're familiar with the art world. Or the CIA."

Jackson frowned. His intrigue meter rose at the same time his internal alarm bells sounded their first warning.

"Was," he said, again honing in on what he deemed the salient point. "Whose is it now?"

"That's the thing," Abby said. "I think it should be mine."

"Obviously, or you wouldn't have asked me to steal it. But whose is it?"

She locked eyes with him. He waited for a Clintonesque debate over the meaning of the word "is." Instead, Abby sighed. "Technically, my stepbrother Desmond has possession of it. You see, when Alec passed away, his inheritance was supposed to be equally divided between me, Desmond, and Noah."

"Who is . . . ?"

"Our half-brother. Desmond was Alec's son from his first marriage. Noah was his son from his second marriage, to my mom, who had me before meeting Alec. When they got married, Alec adopted me, and we were one family . . . no step-this or half-that."

"So what happened?"

Abby looked down at the teabag she was bobbing in her cup. "Mom died a month before my sixteenth birthday."

Jackson swallowed. He could empathize. His parents and brother had died in a restaurant explosion twenty months ago tomorrow.

"Desmond is eleven years older than me and was out of the house by then. Plus he was never all that close to Mom, so it didn't affect him as much as the rest of us. Noah was only ten and was crushed. He went into a shell for the rest of his childhood. And I," she said, looking up, "relied on the one person I had left."

"Alec."

She nodded. "From the moment he married Mom, he became my dad. I never knew my biological father—he died when I was two. So Alec filled the void. After Mom's death, we both filled the void for each other, and our bond was . . . It was special."

Jackson looked up as a waitress with a pot of coffee stopped by. He let her top off his cup, trying to place the face. His friend Reggie owned the restaurant, and, as a result, Jackson spent a lot of time there. But Cameron's had experienced a lot of staff turnover lately, and he couldn't place her.

"So how does all this genealogy link back to a Bible, right?" Abby asked.

Jackson nodded.

"Like I said, Alec's inheritance was supposed to be divided three ways. But Desmond's lawyers strung the whole thing out in probate. I don't know how they did it, but they got him almost everything—the house, most of the artwork, and two-thirds of the money. I tried to fight them, but . . . my lawyers weren't in the same league."

"What about Noah?"

"Indifferent. He moved to Europe a few months later."

"How long ago was this?"

"Ten years this December," she said, nodding over her shoulder as if December was in the booth behind them. The movement caused Jackson's eyes to flicker to a TV screen over the bar, a TV screen showing an AFC Divisional playoff game. It reminded him that he had things to do unless Abby could provide a compelling reason why he should risk his recently reacquired private investigator's license to steal a Bible.

Abby took a drink before continuing. "At the time, Desmond claimed the Bible had disappeared, that it wasn't part of the inheritance. He insisted he didn't have it, and Noah and I didn't. That happens, I suppose, stuff gets lost in the mess, but I always knew he was lying."

"Why would he lie about it?" Jackson asked. "What's so special about this Bible?"

"For one thing, it's over three hundred fifty years old."

Jackson whistled.

"According to family lore, the Bible originally belonged to Jan Aertson when he immigrated to New Netherland as an indentured servant in 1650."

"Who is Jan Aertson?"

"The great-great-great grandfather of Cornelius Vanderbilt."

"You're . . . Wait, you're related to those Vanderbilts?"

"Technically," Abby said with a sigh. "But the family tree would have to be a forest to trace it. You pretty much have to go back to Jan. Anyhow, I don't know if the legend is true or not, but I do know this Bible has been in the family for generations, and it's old enough to have come with Jan from the Netherlands. I've done the research and, in good condition, it would be worth up to a quarter of a million dollars."

Jackson whistled again.

"But it's not in good condition. This was Alec's Bible all his life, after having been passed down for centuries. It's also full of his markings and notations. But considering his prestige in the art world, it would probably still fetch up to a hundred thousand dollars."

"Still a good reason to hide it from the inheritance if you're Desmond," Jackson said.

"And that's only half of it. In addition to being a collector of fine art, Alec also worked for the CIA. He started out of college and retired . . . well, nobody really knows when. Some claimed he worked there until the day he died. And legend has it that some of the notations in his Bible are actually CIA code."

"Hold it," Jackson said. "When you say legend, you mean like the legend of Paul Revere or *The Legend of the Seeker?*"

"I don't know. But Alec's life was full of secrets. He was always meeting people late at night or in clandestine places, disappearing unexpectedly, having strange guests show up. Art people are a little eccentric, which I'm sure explains some of it. But I always wondered if the rumors were true, that he was—at least partially in some capacity—still working for the CIA."

Jackson raised his eyebrows.

"After he died, I believed it even more. There were two guys in suits and shades—straight out of *Men in Black*—at his funeral. They even bugged me after the reading of the will, snooping around. I think they were CIA spooks after the Bible."

Jackson wasn't convinced. But he wasn't ready to discount the theory either.

"So which are you," he asked, "a treasure hunter or a codebreaker?"

"Neither," Abby replied. "I want the Bible because it's a link to my father, to the person I cared about more than anyone and was closer to than anyone after my mother died. I don't care if what he wrote was CIA secrets or his reflections on the 23rd Psalm. I just want this Bible because it was his."

"Why would Desmond want it?"

"Money. Doesn't matter who's paying."

"He's not a collector."

She huffed, almost a snort. "No. He already sold half of Alec's art collection, and the rest he keeps for image and prestige."

"What does he do for a living?"

"Makes more money off what Alec left him, hobnobs in the art world as if he actually belongs." She huffed again. "Probably involved in a number of criminal enterprises, although that's just speculation. Technically he's a talent assessor, but I think that's more of a hobby than anything. A way to meet women."

"So what makes you think he still has the Bible? If he's in it just for the money, how do you know he didn't sell it years ago?"

"I talked to him at Christmas. I made the gesture to go see him since we are still related. I was hoping to bury the hatchet, lay the groundwork for a peaceful inquiry about the Bible. Instead, he told me he'd just found it and was going to sell it to the highest bidder. I think he had it all along, keeping it just to spite me, not having a clue how much it was really worth. Now that he's somehow found out, he's going to sell."

"Why would he tell you about his plans?"

"Because he knew it would get under my skin. Even when we were younger, Desmond always lived to make me miserable, and he always had the power to do so. Alec was many things, but not a great disciplinarian. And as much as he loved me, he would never believe me over Desmond if it came down to it."

"So Desmond is going to sell the Bible, and before he gets the chance, you want me to steal it?"

Abby nodded. "I know that possession is nine-tenths of the law, and in fact, I talked to my lawyer just this week. I thought maybe that since Desmond admitted he had it, I'd have a chance of getting it back legally. Well, to make a long story short, the answer is no. Especially since if I started any legal action, Desmond could just make the Bible 'disappear' again. If he hasn't already sold it by then."

"But since he can't legally own something that doesn't legally exist, our stealing it wouldn't be illegal, is that how you figure it?"

She nodded again. "And I can prove Alec wanted me to have it, if I can just see it."

"How?"

"He wrote me a message in the front, in the dedication area, shortly before he died, bequeathing it to me. Unfortunately, he didn't specify it in his will."

Jackson sat back, furrowed his brow for a moment. "I'm not real familiar with the workings of estate law, but whenever Desmond makes the announcement that he has the Bible and is willing to sell it, won't potential buyers get to look through it?"

"Yeah, so?"

"So, wouldn't you be able to find that dedication page then?"

"Maybe, assuming he doesn't rip it out first. But my lawyer said that still wouldn't be enough legally to get it from him. Plus, you're assuming this is going to be an out-in-the-open Christie's auction."

"It's not?"

"I doubt it. Too many hoops and regulations that way."

"Does anybody else know what he's planning?"

"I don't think he's announced yet. But I'll bet dollars to donuts it's Friday."

"This Friday?"

Abby nodded. "Every year, Desmond throws a masquerade ball, always for some art-related charity. Usually, something trumped up for the snooty Hollywood types, not a legitimate charity like the Red Cross or Doctors Without Borders or something. And he controls the invites, so he can use it as his personal auction service."

He leaned forward. "Any idea where he's keeping the Bible?"

Abby bit her lip and shook her head. "I would guess at the house."

"Security?"

She shook her head again.

"And we only have four days until he auctions it off?"

"Yes, but I have an ace up my sleeve."

"Do tell."

"The ball Friday night. Mostly so he can rub it in my face how much money he has, Desmond always invites me. And a guest."

Jackson turned and tipped his head. "It does get us in the door." He tipped it back. "What about bringing a lawyer? Once Desmond admits to owning the Bible, they could file an injunction and settle this in court."

"Maybe," she said. "But my lawyer said my chances in court after all this time were between slim and none, and that's if the dedication page is still there. And, my gosh, talk about expensive. Do you know what a lawyer charges these days?"

"I don't."

"More than I can pay. I'm an artist, Jackson, making a little here, a little there, living off the interest from the small percentage of Alec's inheritance Desmond didn't get."

He nodded.

"Trust me, I wouldn't resort to this if I thought there was any other way."

By "this," Jackson assumed she meant stealing, not hiring a private investigator.

She continued. "The ball gets us in the door, like you said. And in costume."

"Access to the entire house?"

She nodded.

"Won't he suspect you're planning something?"

"No. He'd never give me enough credit to pull it off . . . or to even attempt to pull it off."

Jackson ran it through his head. If Desmond was the rightful owner—whoever determined rightful—there was no way he would consider taking the case. But if Abby was right and Alec had intended for her to get the Bible . . .

"Don't take this the wrong way," Jackson said, "but I have to be careful. How do I know you're not just trying to avoid Desmond's little auction and get this on the cheap?"

"Because I've seen your rates. They aren't cheap."

"Try the P.I. firms. They bill by the hour."

"I didn't say I wouldn't pay. And you're right, I could be conning you." She leaned forward. "So try this. Take the next four days and research me. I'll give you my Facebook page, names of friends, contacts in the art world. Then research Desmond. Judge for yourself who to believe. And if you think my motives are anything other than what I've told you, you can stand me up Friday night."

"Sounds reasonable."

"That a yes? You'll take the case?"

"Under one condition."

"Which is?"

"I'm not going as Harry Potter or anything from *Twilight*."

Chapter Two

Tuesday, January 15
11:32 a.m.

"FRANKLY, I'VE BEEN worried about you," Zachary said.

"Oh yeah, why's that?"

Jackson's court-ordered psychiatrist looked down his long, pointed nose at Jackson. It added to a look of condescension the man couldn't help. Tall and pasty white, with dark hair in a short ponytail and a matching dark goatee, and prone to hippie dress, Dr. Furman T. Zachary and his socks and sandals looked more like a pot-smoker turned poet than a man with a Ph.D. But despite his appearance and his monthly nibbling at the corners of Jackson's personal pain, Jackson couldn't help but like the man who insisted his patients call him Zach.

"Oh, a couple of reasons," Zachary said in his measured tone. He reached for and lit his pipe. Even a born-again mind doctor was allowed a vice or two, he had explained. "You've had a tumultuous few months, on top of everything that happened in Nevada. And then I hear that you've been shot."

In response, Jackson raised his left arm and rotated it. Without wincing. "That's in just two weeks' time," he said.

"Do you want to talk about any of that?" Zachary said, pausing to inhale. He blew rings toward the ceiling. "When last we spoke, your license was suspended, you had taken up acting as a side job while performing rescue missions in Mexico, and the weight of everything that took place in September was still heavy on your mind."

Jackson nodded.

Nevada. September.

He had gone to Las Vegas with his late brother's fiancée, Hillary, returning a favor by helping her locate a potential witness. He'd found the witness all right, dead on her bathroom floor. From there, things had spiraled out of control, leading to Hillary's kidnapping and culminating with a slaughter in the desert. Jackson had killed twenty members of a militia group called RASER in order to rescue Hillary, and in the process had unveiled a twenty-five-year-old paramilitary mind-control project that involved a three-star general, a U.S. senator, and a millionaire real estate mogul and Vegas casino owner.

Jackson had avoided prison time when the investigation of a twelve-member tribunal composed of members of various government agencies and branches of the military had ruled his actions were justified. It hadn't hurt that he'd also served up the crooked senator on a silver platter and been backed by the casino-owning mogul. But he had temporarily lost his private investigator's license and been put on probation, on top of the mental and emotional strain that had come with taking so many lives.

If that wasn't enough, Jackson had killed five gangsters back in May, witnessed the suicide of a client in July, and been involved in a shootout at thirty thousand feet that had left five more dead in November. And of course, a day didn't go by that he wasn't haunted by the deaths of his parents and brother.

"The weight's still heavy," Jackson said. "But I'm kind of getting used to it."

"You get used to hanging too if you do it long enough," Zachary said.

Jackson looked at him. "Meaning?"

"Meaning, just adding burdens and growing accustomed to them doesn't make things better."

"I don't know, Doc. I think this might be my burden to carry."

Zachary pursed his lips. "How so?"

"It's like everybody's been telling me—you included—that if I don't do what I did in Nevada, Hillary could be dead. Or Ashley last May. Or Maggie in Mexico. So . . . maybe somebody's got to do the dirty work. Society needs garbage men and guys to clean out the sewers, right? Maybe that's me."

Zachary nodded. "What inspired this change in perspective?"

"A cute Air Force JAG lawyer, for one." He smiled for a moment at the memory. "Other things."

Tracing his eyebrow, Zachary said, "Let's explore 'other things.'"

"The reason I got shot," Jackson said. "The actress I told you about, Noelle . . ."

Zachary nodded.

"She had a stalker, and I helped her out by finding him."

"And then he showed up and accosted her. You told me last time. He's the one who shot you?"

"Yeah. He thought I was her boyfriend or something. As soon as he got out of County, he came for me. Then, when she got back from San Diego for the holidays, he was waiting in her apartment." Jackson swallowed. "He was about to rape her when I put the pieces together, figured out what was going on, and showed up." He breathed. "And blew his head off with my shotgun."

Zachary exhaled smoke.

"So, I started to think maybe that was me, the garbage man of society. I'd really rather not kill people for a living, but if it's to save young ladies from rape, torture, and death . . . Somebody's got to do it."

After a pause, Zachary asked, "Are you trying to convince me or yourself?"

"You think I'm wrong?"

"I think you want to be very careful in anointing yourself *The Dark Knight*."

"Nice reference, Doc. I'm impressed. And I know. But maybe this is my calling. Seriously. I'll do the dirty work, suffer the consequences—mental, emotional, spiritual—for the betterment of society."

Zachary nodded, not in agreement but as a way of listening. "What about legally?"

"Yeah, a few hoops to jump through there too."

"Are you through them?"

"LAPD cleared me for the shooting at Noelle's place, and the aforementioned cute JAG lawyer informed me that my probation is over and my license is reinstated. I've got both of my weapons back from the cops, so I'm a full-fledged, gun-toting, baddie-busting P.I. again."

Zachary frowned.

"What?"

"You're rather flippant about all this."

"Flippant's sort of my style," Jackson said.

"I know, but it hasn't been since September."

"So this is a return to normalcy," Jackson said. "Truman'd be proud."

"Harding," Zachary corrected. "Wrong war."

"Both before my time."

The frown remained.

Jackson leaned forward. "Look, Zach, I get what you're saying. And believe me, I'm not really embracing this idea. But . . . if it can keep the bile out of my throat, I'm willing to consider it. I've got nothing to lose anymore." He shrugged. "And as for the glibness, well, that's how I roll."

Zachary rocked in his glider. "How are your friends taking it?"

"Reggie's on your side. Cautionary."

"What about your girl friends?"

Jackson narrowed his eyes. "Why do we always come back to them?"

"They seem to be a major part of your life."

Jackson sighed. "I haven't told them. It's not something I really plan to advertise. And I hope I never have to take another life. But if I do . . . I've got my head around it, I think."

"I hope with you."

"And for what it's worth, my current case shouldn't involve much bloodshed."

"You're working again?"

"Man's got to eat."

"From what you've told me, I thought the man in question usually bummed meals off his best friend."

"If I'm just here to get my chops busted, I can get that for free from said friend."

Zachary very nearly smiled. "What sort of case?"

Jackson waited until the doctor was looking his way. "I'm going to steal a Bible."

Zachary didn't blink as he lifted his pipe to draw on it.

"You've got to at least appreciate the irony," Jackson said.

"Better than stealing a Quran, I guess. You get caught then, you lose a hand."

Jackson dropped his finger toward Zachary. "That is why you get the big bucks. I never would have seen it from that angle."

*   *   *

Wednesday, January 16
7:23 p.m.

"WILL YOU stand still?" Samantha MacRaney mumbled through a mouthful of safety pins.

"This thing itches," Jackson said. "What in the Sam Hill is it made of anyhow, camel's skin?"

Sam reached up and pinched some fabric on his jacket, then used her free hand to pluck a pin from her mouth. She pinned the pinched fabric.

"Ouch!"

Sam removed the pins from her mouth. "Seriously, I can't be poking you every single time."

"I wouldn't have thought so either."

Her hands went to her hips. "Do you want my help or not?"

Jackson hid a smile. Hands on hips meant fake exasperation, not the real thing. And truth be told, having Sam fussing over him was a pretty good way to spend a rainy Wednesday evening. But a guy had to keep up appearances.

"At least tell me we're about finished," he said.

"Two more. Now hold still."

She pinned the jacket in the final two places, then helped him slide the now-smaller garment off his shoulders. He was left in a flowing white shirt with sleeves the size of pant legs and a neckline that would have made Elvis blush. With his jeans, it made him look like an aging European artist. Come Friday, worn under a jacket with Sam's alterations, and with a few more outfit modifications, he'd be ready to clash swords with Captain Kidd.

"We done with this?" Jackson asked.

"Unless you want the sleeves taken in," Sam replied.

"And the accompanying acupuncture? No thanks."

"Ha, ha."

Jackson grinned as he removed the nineteenth-century dueling shirt and replaced it with a Dodgers tee. Feeling like a man again, he picked up a faded brown tricorn hat. "Where'd you find this again?"

"Same place as the jacket, actually," Sam said as she carefully folded the jacket. "Try it on."

He donned the hat, which dwarfed his head.

"It will be fine once we get the dreadlocks," she said. "And I still think you want them with the hat, as one piece."

"Whatever you say, matey."

Sam shot him a look. Her deep blue eyes were normally beautiful and beguiling, but they could shoot some venom when need be. Sam's carefree smile was so appealing that Jackson did his best to keep it on her face. Her good-natured disposition made it pretty easy.

He removed the hat and set it on top of her blond tresses. "You know, there were a few lady pirates."

"I am not playing pirate fantasy with you, Jackson."

"I wasn't asking you to."

She removed the hat. "I would like to go to a costume party, though."

"Masquerade ball."

"Whatever." She tilted her head. "Does an eyepatch count as a mask?"

"I'm dying the beard too," he said.

Sam rummaged through her bag for the Bob Marley rastacap she'd also picked up that afternoon, all on Jackson's tab. Which would become Abby's tab, part of his expense list.

"Are you really going to steal a Bible?" she asked as she worked to remove the rastacap from the dreadlocks attached to it.

"That's the plan."

"Somehow that doesn't seem right."

"Stealing from a thief?"

"Does that justify it?"

"I don't know. It did for Robin Hood."

"Robin Hood isn't listed in Hebrews 11 for his life of faith."

"No, but Rahab is."

Sam sighed. "Always Rahab. Anytime anybody wants to do anything sketchy and justify it biblically, they always point to Rahab."

"Hey, it's better than my last cases, isn't it?"

"We'll see. If thou shalt steal, who's to say the current owner shalt not shoot at you?"

"Maybe I can convince them there's a real musket ball in this thing," Jackson sad, picking up his squirt gun. He'd scoured four different toy stores before finding one that sold a cheap replica of a seventeenth-century pirate pistol. It actually may have been more an eighteenth-century frontiersman pistol, but it would do.

Sam eyed the gun and shook her head. "I can't believe you talked me into this."

"As I recall, you volunteered."

"To help with your costume. I didn't know you were going as Blackbeard."

Jackson reached for his fake cutlass. Made of plastic, it too was obviously a toy, especially when viewed up close, yet made to look like the real thing. He swiped at the air a few times, then extended the blade under Sam's chin. "That be Captain Blackbeard to you, wench."

"Jackson," she groaned, shoving the sword away.

"What, this is how pirates flirted."

"And this is how maidens responded," she said with another stare that could melt stone.

"Maidens were the Middle Ages," he said, lowering the faux blade.

Sam resumed freeing the dreadlocks from the hat. "Have you actually planned this heist?"

"Heist might be a little strong, but yeah," he said, slicing the air with his sword. "Abby sent me floor plans so I could determine the most likely location of the Bible, find safe zones, and plan exit strategies. And she's been to several of these balls, so she knows the format. I've got a custom-made pouch to hide the Bible in under the bulk of that jacket. My sword, if seriously wielded, could actually do some damage, and if I brandish the gun, it might scare people long enough for me to get away. And I've done my homework on Desmond and Abby both. She actually understated his jerkiness. Yeah, I've planned it."

Sam nodded. "I ask because normally you just wing things."

"Winging's always worked."

"So far."

"I'm as prepared as I can be, Sam. Honest."

She sighed. "I really wish you'd get involved in some safe profession like accounting."

"Or being an ER nurse?"

"One of us takes bullets, and one of us takes them out of people. Here, try this on."

"You just glued it."

"And I want to see if it's right before it sets."

"What if it glues to my head?"

"Then I'll wish I'd put it on your mouth."

"You're cute when you're feisty, you know that?" Jackson said as he donned the dreads and tricorn hat.

Sam ignored his comment and stepped closer, adjusting the dreads so they were just right. Then she stepped back to take a look. "I think that will work. Why a pirate, anyhow?"

"Because pirates are cool."

"Pirates were vicious and debauched."

"But cool."

Sam rolled her eyes.

"Careful, lass. Mutineers be known to walk the plank."

She shook her head and smiled. "You are such a dork, you know that?"

"Aye."

"But I have to admit, all this pirate gear sort of becomes you."

"See what I mean? Women dig pirates."

"Except for one thing."

"Mm, what's that, love?" He extended his cutlass around her and gently pulled her closer.

"This," she said, fingering the beaded beard extension (à la Captain Jack Sparrow) that Jackson had forgotten was spirit-gummed to his chin, "looks ridiculous."

She yanked it off.

"Aaagh!" Jackson said, jumping back in reflex. He tripped on the coffee table and fell back onto the couch.

Sam grinned. "What's the matter? Was the great pirate captain felled by a wee bonnie lass?"

Chapter Three

"OH MY GOSH! You look incredible," Abby said when she met Jackson on the patio of her West Los Angeles apartment building. It was only a few blocks from where Jackson's brother Grant had lived.

"Looks can be deceivin', lass," Jackson replied, although he had to agree with her. He wore black combat boots, bought at an Army surplus store; brown buckskin pants; some sort of a scarf-like thing—the end of which hung to his knees—as a belt; the baggy dueling shirt open halfway under the tailored red jacket with gold lining; his dreads and dyed beard; the tricorn hat; a few rings on his fingers; and makeup dirt, scars, and tattoos courtesy of Sam earlier that evening. His cutlass, water pistol, and a spyglass all hung on or were strapped to his belt. If there was a door prize for most authentic, he had a chance.

Jackson dropped his pirate accent. "And wait until you see the eyepatch." He flipped it down temporarily for Abby to admire, then turned it back up onto his forehead. It was somewhat transparent, but not enough that he could drive with it down. Or not go crazy.

"Aren't you hot in that getup? And those dreadlocks?"

"Heat isn't half the trouble itching is. I take it you aren't having either problem?"

Abby wore a white silk gown, sleeveless, with high slits and a plunging neckline. It made room for a collar stretching from shoulder to shoulder and bedecked with gold and turquoise sequins, same as on a belt with ties that draped to her knees. She wore a black wig, straight to the shoulders, strings of gold and rows of beads weaved in with the hair. Sparkling earrings were almost longer than her hair, matched by a gold snake armband and numerous bangles. They were connected to a translucent turquoise cape that flowed behind her like a desert breeze. But the most striking accessory was the glittering Mardi-Gras-style mask covering her eyes. Cleopatra, Nefertiti, Hatshepsut—Jackson wasn't sure. But she was convincing.

"I am actually freezing," Abby replied as they crossed the parking lot. "The weatherman said seventies and balmy tonight."

It was mid-fifties and breezy, with a threat of thunderstorms. Even in SoCal, January brought the bite of winter.

"Just picture yourself in some sand-swept palace overlooking the Nile," Jackson said, holding the door of his Ford Granada for Abby. Well into its fourth decade, the car had originally belonged to Jackson's grandfather. When he'd moved to a houseboat in Marina del Rey, the already old Granada had become Jackson's. He had treasured it ever since, ignoring the looks it drew from almost everyone.

Alec Vanderbilt's historic mansion, now in possession of his son Desmond, was perched on a hillside off Latigo Canyon Road in Malibu. It was a little less than a forty-minute drive, and Jackson and Abby spent it going over their strategy for the evening. As they turned off the Pacific Coast Highway and climbed into the Santa Monica Mountains, Jackson pulled a key from his pocket. He extended it to Abby.

"What's this?"

"Spare car key."

"Why?"

"In case you need to make a getaway. If I get caught or something."

She took the key hesitantly. "You're not instilling me with confidence, Jackson."

"Just covering my bases."

As Jackson turned into the driveway, a distant flash of lightning momentarily illuminated the entire Vanderbilt mansion. It was a rambling, multi-level structure, with staircases and hallways connecting level to level to half-level. It was a maze, according to Abby, and according to the floor plans, she'd shared with Jackson. Built in the 1930s and added onto several times, it was a combination of Mission Colonial and Urban Loft, with a touch of rustic hunting lodge thrown in for good measure. The defining feature was a large great room—or in tonight's case, a ballroom—on the backside of the house. A deck cantilevered over the cliff on the house's west side and winding around the south side to encompass a pool and hot tub surrounded the great room. (No word if any guests were coming as mermaids or wielding tridents.)

From the road, the driveway wound downhill and ended in a loop that circled a fountain in front of the garage and main entrance. Jackson braked to a halt, and immediately a valet in a red vest appeared at his door, while another assisted Abby from her side. After flipping down his eyepatch, Jackson studied the valets while searching his pockets. They were young, just teenagers, not some private security firm's undercover agents.

Jackson pulled three pieces of chocolate wrapped to look like gold coins from his pocket (they had been on clearance at one of the stores he'd visited) and handed them to the valet with his keys. "Keep 'er steady, or it's the plank for ye, savvy?"

A faraway rumble of thunder echoed off the night sky as the valet eyed Jackson suspiciously. But he took the keys and chocolates.

"Aye, that's a good lad," Jackson said as he circled the car. He took Abby's arm, and they headed inside where a butler in a tailed tuxedo—no mask—welcomed them, collected Abby's invitation, and directed them down two short flights of stairs to the main hall. Because he had memorized the layout, Jackson knew that a hallway off the foyer led to the kitchen, dining room, a "smoking room," and several guest bedrooms. A home gym, billiard room, conservatory, and access to the pool were up a half flight of stairs to the left of the main hall. The master suite, library, a mother-in-law suite, and a private kitchen and breakfast nook were all on the second floor and accessible from a stairway at the front of the house or via a loft that overlooked the great hall. Maze didn't begin to describe it.

Ignoring a handful of guests (none of whom had very original costumes) standing off to the side in small conversation circles or seated on elegant couches and chairs that formed three separate enclaves in the main hall, Jackson and Abby headed for the great room—shaped like an upside down home plate—at the far end of the hall. Wide-open French doors allowed soft stringed music and the din of mixed conversation to draw them into the enormous room.

Jackson stopped for a moment just inside the doorway and marveled. A vaulted ceiling rose to at least twenty feet at its peak directly above them, ascending from there so that it towered even higher over the point where the two angled walls came together. Molding in the corners and around the doors and windows revealed spectacular craftsmanship, as did intricate nature carvings in the wood-paneled walls themselves. The walls were broken by an array of windows that looked out over the deck and down the hills to the Malibu coast. At least, in the daylight. Tonight, they just reflected the soft glow of hundreds and hundreds of flickering candles. The candles were accompanied by three magnificent chandeliers, each probably costing more than Jackson's entire house.

"Time?" Abby asked, drawing Jackson back to the task at hand.

He consulted a gold pocket watch, an old piece of junk he'd found at a thrift store for a dollar. "Ten after nine."

She nodded. "We should put in an appearance for a while. We have till midnight. That's when the masks come off to reveal true identities."

"How exciting. You see Desmond?"

"No, but knowing him, he'll make a grand entrance."

Jackson nodded and scanned the crowd. He saw a lot of tuxedos and Zorro masks or evening gowns and Mardi Gras masks. But there were also plenty of people in full costume, from the obligatory Darth Vader, Phantom of the Opera, or the ever-popular superheroes to more creative concepts like a World War II fighter pilot with a leather aviator hat and goggles, a belly dancer with a veil, the catcher for the Angels, a Roman gladiator with a brass helmet, and a woman in pajamas with a sleeping mask that somehow didn't obscure her vision. Sort of like his eyepatch, Jackson guessed.

It being his first masquerade ball, Jackson wasn't sure how things were supposed to work. Normally at swanky parties, one mingled and sipped champagne. But in that case, a guy knew who he was talking to. This was chitchat with a complete stranger—and an unidentifiable one at that. It was like anonymous internet speed-dating.

"There are a few people I should say hello to," Abby announced. "I can introduce you."

"Actually, the lower profile I keep, the better."

"I wasn't going to give your real name."

"Still, I'll just find some grub and grog."

She nodded, and they split. Jackson had no trouble locating servers with ostentatious hors d'oeuvres and long-stemmed glasses of champagne. There was also an open bar in the corner, and although Jackson didn't drink, what self-respecting pirate didn't take advantage of free rum?

"Ahoy there, matey," Jackson called to the bartender, figuring he might as well stay in character. "A pint of your stoutest ale."

The bartender—also no mask—gave him a lopsided half-grin. "Rum, I take it?"

"Aye, just make it strong, lad."

Jackson waited for the drink by downing his last crab cake and eyeing the male partygoers. He'd been able to find a dozen good pictures of Desmond Vanderbilt online but still wasn't sure he'd be able to make him in costume.

"Here you go, Cap'n," the bartender said.

Jackson flipped him a chocolate doubloon with a wink. "Cheers," he said, raising the glass but not drinking. Instead, he headed for a door on the north side of the room. It opened onto the deck, from where Jackson theoretically could see if Desmond had any exterior security Abby didn't know about. He could also get rid of the rum.

His journey took him past a hulking Batman and a very gothic female vampire, complete with blood dripping from the corners of her mouth. And another pirate, this one more in the vein of Smee than a true captain of the seas. They eyed each other for a moment, then Jackson waved him off with a comment about a "scurvy dog."

Cool air greeted him on the deck, as did several sky-coloring flashes of lightning on the western horizon. From the north side of the great room, Jackson could venture to his right to another small garden that spanned the distance between the great room and the upper floor of the mansion or walk left around the point of the great room. Checking to make sure he was alone, he reached for the spyglass. It was just a cheap toy, but Jackson had MacGyvered it into the real thing using a broken pair of binoculars. Too bad they hadn't been night-vision goggles.

He spent several minutes panning his good eye over the walls, roof, and private deck off the master bedroom, using the growingly frequent flashes of lightning to see. There was no way to get from his deck to the private deck— at least not without rock-climbing gear or a tightrope. It was not a valid entry or exit point.

Spotting no cameras or security guards, Jackson lowered the spyglass and walked around to the other side of the great room. Several partiers stood around the pool, their murmurs of conversation drifting to him. A few quick flickers of orange and the scent of tobacco gave away their reason for hanging out poolside. Again seeing nothing in the way of cameras, sensors, or other security equipment, Jackson turned back and retreated to the north side of the house.

With another look to make sure he was unobserved, Jackson drew his pistol and popped the top on it. Very carefully, he poured the rum from his glass into the squirt gun. He spilled a third of it on his hands and the outside of the gun, but a quick test revealed he'd gotten enough in the "chamber" to send a spurt at least fifteen feet forward. In a pinch, if he could aim at the eyes, the toy might serve as a functional weapon. Whether it was the oncoming storm or the vibe from a party where everyone hid their identity, Jackson had a feeling he was going to find himself in a pinch.

He returned to the party, setting his glass on an empties table. Then he looked for Abby. In her gold-trimmed dress, she ought to stand out in a crowd that seemed mostly dark. But there were a few other glittering gowns or brightly ornamented characters. One in particular grabbed his attention. Halfway across the room, in the midst of a conversation with several gentlemen, was a blonde decked head to toe in brilliant white. The gown was resplendent, and she wore it with such poise and stature that it doubled the charm. Her hair was long and luxurious, precisely styled, framing an oval face that looked very familiar. A dazzling white mask blocked Jackson from seeing her eyes and nose, yet he couldn't shake the feeling he knew her.

"There you are," Abby said.

"Any sign of Desmond?"

She shook her head and guided him by the elbow to a spot with a little more seclusion. "See any security?" she whispered.

"None."

"I'm sure he has people here," she said. "But it's like I said before, I don't think he'd hire anyone. Just his personal staff. These are all friends. At least, they're supposed to be."

"You have any idea who the lady in white is?" Jackson asked.

"Where?"

"Two o'clock," he answered. "Lady of the Wood or White Witch of Narnia or something."

Abby glanced for a moment. "No. She's beautiful whoever she is." She looked up. "Do I have to remind you to keep your mind on business?"

"No. I just thought I knew her." He met Abby's gaze. "Honest. I'm dialed in."

A tinkling of glass interrupted further conversation. All eyes in the room turned to the balcony overlooking the entire great room. A tall, lanky man in a tuxedo, top hat, cape—and, of course, mask—held his glass high in the air with his left hand while brandishing in his right the wand with which he had clanked it.

"Desmond the Magnificent?" Jackson asked.

Abby nodded. "Sans magnificence."

"I hate magicians."

When the room quieted, Desmond called out in a booming voice, "Welcome to the eighth annual Vanderbilt Charities Masquerade Ball!"

Polite applause followed. When it died out, Desmond launched into several minutes of flowing prose about all the work his charities were doing, none of which sounded like it was worth two cents. While standing behind the railing and a banner proclaiming the same welcome he had just issued, Desmond lauded several people, praised himself a little, and thanked everyone for coming to his celebration.

"How much of their donations went to fund this party, I wonder," Abby said, leaning into Jackson's shoulder.

Desmond made a few more remarks about his charitable work, complimented the costumers in general, and told everyone to enjoy the food and drink, dancing, and trying to determine who was who behind the mask before the clock struck twelve. Everyone chuckled gaily, as high society people are bred to do. Jackson rolled his eyes as Desmond closed by announcing a surprise he had in store for his guests a little later in the evening.

"Isn't he something?" Abby asked.

"Quite. Do you need to go say hello?"

"I probably should."

"I'm going to see if I can get a better look at Galadriel there."

"Eyes on the prize, Jackson. I'm not paying you to hit on the guests."

"Don't worry. It's not even ten yet. I'll give the party a few more minutes and then get cracking."

"By the way, have you been drinking?"

He shook his head. "I don't drink."

Abby winced. "Funny. Because you smell like rum."

Chapter Four

10:03 p.m.

THE THUNDERSTORMS HAD moved inland. They hadn't yet brought rain, but repeated lightning bolts flashed through the great room windows and thunder seemed to shake the Vanderbilt mansion to its century-old foundation. With everyone in costume and mask, a thunderstorm seemed like the perfect ambiance, and the guests chuckled along with the weather as they ate, drank, conversed, and danced.

After Desmond's introductory speech, Jackson had succeeded in three out of four tasks. He kept a low profile, first and foremost. The last thing he wanted was to be searching the house for the Bible and have someone ask where the gravelly-voiced pirate was. He especially avoided Desmond, who, along with his mask, wore a sneer that made Jackson want to punch him right in his pointy nose.

Second, Jackson scouted the premises. Under the guise of stretching his legs and snacking on more appetizers, he familiarized himself with the lay of the land. It was one thing to study floor plans drawn by Abby, and quite another to see it for himself. He wandered to the balcony, the billiard room, and to one of two powder rooms off the main hall, where he checked his costume. Not bad for a scallywag. He also saw that the majority of the guests weren't straying from the great room or the hall. That was good and bad. He'd stick out if he were spotted roaming, but also wouldn't be likely to be spotted in the first place.

Third, he had a second handful of crab cakes. They really were quite tasty.

The only thing he failed to do was identify the woman in white. She was constantly in a crowd, usually consisting primarily of men, and her mask kept him from getting a good enough look at her to identify her. Still, he could feel the wheels turning in his head.

He found Abby again, the visible portion of her face red and her round jaw set hard. "Trouble?" he asked.

"Desmond is such . . . He just spent five minutes rubbing it in my face that he was going to sell the Bible."

"Did he say anything else about it—where it was, maybe?"

She sighed. "No."

"Where is he now?"

"I don't know."

"Okay. I'm going to make my move."

"You're sure I can't help?"

Jackson shook his head. "It'd be best if you stay visible. You're creating an alibi, remember?"

She nodded.

"Remember," he said, going into his best pirate voice, "stick to the code."

Abby nodded again, and Jackson melted into the crowd. For a moment, he thought the vampire was following him, so he stopped to make a heavy-handed and heavy-tongued pass at Tinker Bell. Content that Vampira had lost interest, he quickly climbed one of two flights of stairs leading from the great room to the balcony.

Stairs at the far end of the balcony led farther upward, toward the master bedroom and library. Guessing them to be the two most likely places for the Bible to be hidden, Jackson checked to make sure he was alone and unobserved, then climbed the north stairs.

At the end of a short hallway, double doors on the left opened, Jackson knew, to the master bedroom. To the right, another hallway led to the library, a pair of spare bedrooms, and a staircase connecting to the main level. Jackson chose the library first as a result of keen detective work: its door was unlocked. He found himself in what could pass for a small college's library, with several rows of fully stocked shelves, a desk with the archetypal green-shaded lamp, and a pillowed bench seat built into a bay window on the far wall. He immediately concluded the room was a reflection of Alec Vanderbilt and not Desmond.

After closing and locking the door behind him and removing his eyepatch, Jackson got to work. If the Vanderbilt Bible was really worth hundreds of thousands of dollars, he doubted it was likely to be filed on a shelf between *Strong's Concordance* and a commentary on the Pauline epistles. But he had to check. He didn't dare turn on the lights, resorting instead to using a small penlight to scan the shelves. The books covered everything from science to history, from art to fiction. Fortunately, they were well organized, and it only took a few minutes to hone in on the theology and religion section. He recognized several titles, saw a few more that piqued his interest, and even spied a couple of Bibles. None of them were centuries old.

For the sake of thoroughness, Jackson also searched the art and history sections, figuring a connoisseur such as Alec may have categorized a valuable Bible as art or—were he not a religious man—as merely a historical work. It wasn't there either. Lastly, he circled through the shelves looking for any obviously old books or novelty sections where it might have been filed or refiled by Desmond. Again, no luck.

Checking his watch, Jackson saw it was almost ten-thirty. Maybe he should have taken Abby up on her offer to help.

He made one more sweep of the library, but the Bible hadn't been filed as fiction, a reference work, or a biography. Starting to sweat through his jacket, Jackson removed it. That's when he felt his phone vibrating in his pants. He quickly fished it out and flipped it open.

"Abby?" he whispered.

"Hmm. Now what should I make of that?" a somewhat husky female voice asked.

"Maggie?"

"Just out of curiosity, how many more names do you have to guess?"

"Sorry, Mags. I was expecting a call."

"Clearly."

"A client."

"Sure."

He sighed. "Something on your mind? I'm kind of busy right now."

"I'm just lonely and bored," she said. "I know how you like a good Friday night that begets Saturday sunrise. Maybe Capitol Burger and the arcade?"

"Arcade? Maggie, very old school."

"Just off the top of my head."

He sighed again. "I would, really, but I'm on a case."

"A real case?"

"Yeah, and I'm kind of in the middle of it right now. Can I call you tomorrow sometime?"

"Sure. I won't keep you. In case Abby's trying to get through."

"Clever as you are impetuous, Maggie," Jackson said, then closed his phone. While talking, he had run his penlight over all the walls and found a portrait of an old, gray-haired man. He appeared dignified, austere, resolute—looking a little like the bad guy in *Minority Report*. Jackson knew him to be Alec Vanderbilt. And an especially vivid flash of lightning confirmed his first hunch that the picture wasn't quite flush with the wall.

As if . . .

Jackson went back to his jacket, retrieved a pair of latex gloves, and with his hands in the gloves, pulled at the edge of the frame. The portrait swung out, revealing a wall safe.

"Blast," Jackson muttered. Despite his successful efforts a few months back in Las Vegas, he was not a safecracker. But as he moved the penlight up close, he saw that the safe door was ajar.

"Curious."

Fearing an alarm was about to go off—or already had and Desmond's goons were on their way to the library—Jackson slowly opened the safe door and shined the light inside.

It was empty.

Had someone beaten him to it?

Or had the Bible never been there to begin with?

Regardless of what had been inside, why would Desmond leave an empty safe ajar when it meant leaving the portrait covering it askew?

Jackson stepped back, thinking, giving Desmond's security team time to reach him. They never came, and he mulled some more. Had the door been left ajar because the contents had recently been removed, only temporarily? Like, say, if Desmond had taken the Bible out of the safe so he could reveal it at the party? Had he not bothered to close it because he doubted anyone would venture to his library, notice the slightly ajar portrait if so, or at worst find anything in an empty safe?

It was a workable theory but left him wondering where the Bible was now.

It wasn't in the library. Not on any of the shelves, not on the desk, not on the window seat, and not in the safe. Either Desmond had it on his person or had stashed it somewhere else where he could quickly retrieve it. Or it had never been in the safe to begin with.

So where was it?

Jackson mentally walked through the house. None of the other rooms made sense, except the master suite, and that didn't make much sense. Why move the Bible from one secure location to another? No, if Jackson's hunch were right, if the Bible had been in the safe, the only logical place for Desmond to move it would be somewhere he could easily access it to show his guests. That brought it back to being on his person, as it wasn't on display in the main hall or great room.

Unless . . .

Jackson pictured Desmond's costume: tux, top hat, cape, wand. A magician.

A particularly close crack of thunder rattled the window and vibrated in the floor beneath Jackson's feet. He retrieved his jacket, lowered his eyepatch back over his eye, and slipped out of the library undetected and walked back to the balcony. Leaning on the heavy oak railing straight out of a ski chalet's loft, he surveyed the great hall beneath him, full of people. Where to hide a Bible so as to make it magically appear?

Jackson willed himself to think, but that wasn't how his mind liked to work. It preferred to observe, ruminate, and deduce. Forced musing wasn't his strong point.

"All you need now is a steering wheel."

Jackson turned to see the lady vampire. Her angular face and thin lips were set in a faint, fang-concealing smile, as might be given to induce a man to tip his head to the side and expose his neck. Her eyes were narrow and piercing, but that could have been attributed to the mask that teased to reveal them. In truth, it wasn't much of a mask, but the pasty makeup and streams of blood coming from the corners of her lips made up for it.

"A steering wheel?"

"Against the railing there, you look like a captain at the helm."

He studied the almost foot-wide railing cap. It was dark mahogany and, like everything else in the house, finely crafted. He could just picture Norm Abrams or Tom Silva on *This Old House* having a lengthy discussion about the history of woodworking and how such a cap was made and installed and so forth.

"I'm Bianca," the vampire said, extending her hand.

"Real name or character name?" Jackson asked.

"Character, until midnight."

"In that case, Bianca," he said, getting into pirate brogue again, "we've got us a wee spot of irony."

"How's that?"

He turned his body so as he could make a slight, arms-outstretched bow. "I'm Captain Blood."

Bianca smiled. "Clever."

"It was that or Captain Crunch."

She moved beside him and leaned on the railing. "Are you here with someone?"

Jackson nodded down at the great room crowd. "Aye, the lovely goddess of the Nile by the pastry table. You?"

"Alone, I'm afraid."

Railing. Suddenly Jackson wanted to get rid of the bloodsucker beside him.

"Well, I'd offer to buy ye a drink, but I'm fresh out of pieces o' eight, and I'd hate to be put under an Egyptian's curse."

Bianca dropped a shoulder slightly. "And yet you're up here by yourself."

"Aye." He lost the accent. "Can I let you in on a secret?"

She nodded.

"I can't stand these artsy types. I should be at home watching the Kings, but my girlfriend dragged me here. I can only stand so much conversation about paintings and sculptures and old relics. And . . ." Lightning fittingly flashed outside the window at that moment. "The deck isn't quite safe."

"Would your thoughts on a drink change if I told you I couldn't stand the artsy types either?"

"Maybe, but not the part about the Egyptian curse. My girlfriend's kind of jealous."

"I understand," Bianca said, batting her insanely long eyelashes. "Maybe another time."

"Aye, lass. Maybe."

Bianca winked and headed toward the stairs. Jackson crossed his eyes over the room below him and, seeing no one looking his way, bent down to retie the laces on his boots. His real motive was to scan the underside of the balcony railing. It was almost a foot wide, dark, with thick balusters every eight inches. It would be the perfect place for . . .

Jackson spotted an anomaly to his right. Peeking over the railing, Jackson again checked the guests below. None seemed to be paying any attention to the balcony, so he ducked back down, hoping his silhouette didn't show through the banner hanging from the railing. It looked almost like canvas, and the lighting in the balcony was low, so he doubted anyone could see him. Just in case, he made a show of tying his other boot while also scooting a few feet to his right.

It stood to reason that Desmond would announce his great surprise from the balcony, where he'd made his earlier speech. And if that surprise were indeed the Bible, having it at hand would be necessary. Fastened to the bottom of the railing, between balusters, hidden by the banner, where only a searching eye could possibly see it? Then, mid-announcement, a whoosh of the wand, a little puff of smoke, and voila!

The anomaly wasn't a Bible attached to the underside of the railing, but a small shelf between two of the balusters. It looked temporary, and Jackson raised his head slightly to see what was on the shelf.

It was a black box, about the size of a hardcover novel. Taking a quick look around, Jackson took hold of the box and slid back the lid. Set inside the felt-lined box was a brown, leather-bound volume engraved only with the words "Holy Bible."

Not daring to touch such an old relic without gloves or the permission of someone more knowledgeable about such matters than himself, Jackson concluded it was the correct Bible. He quickly withdrew the plastic pouch from inside his jacket. Inverting it, he used it like a hot pad to pluck the Bible by the spine from the box and then carefully wrapped the pouch around it. Securing the pouch, he tucked it into the front waistband of his pants. The Word of God hidden like a gangster's piece.

Pulling the jacket closed, Jackson was content the Bible couldn't be spotted. He quickly returned the empty box to its hiding spot, smiling as he thought of Desmond opening it to find air. One more time, he glanced around to make sure he hadn't been observed. Then, after looking down to locate Abby, he headed down the stairs. She was in the corner, chatting with two women in sparkling evening gowns and the woman in pajamas and a sleeping mask. Jackson pushed his way through the crowd and reached for Abby's arm.

"Begging your pardon, ma'am, but I couldn't help noticing all your gold."

"Will you excuse me," Abby said to the other women. When she was clear, she leaned close to Jackson.

"Hoist the main sail," he said before she could ask.

"You're coming, aren't you?"

"Less noticeable if we exit the room separately. Wait for me in the foyer."

Abby nodded and slipped out of the great room. Trying to summon the courage a real pirate would have had to feel, Jackson approached the bartender again.

"Another rum, mate?" the bartender asked.

"Aye. Make it a double."

While the bartender poured, he nodded at Jackson's jacket. "You have any more of those delicious coins?"

Forcing a grin, Jackson retrieved his remaining chocolate doubloons, which had started to melt through the wrapping. "They be a bit tarnished but nevertheless worthwhile." He dropped them on the counter and reached for the glass of rum. "Thank ye kindly, lad."

Jackson took the drink and pushed through the crowd once again, heading for the foyer after Abby. Ignoring the sense that every eye in the room—especially those of Bianca the vampire—was on him, he was almost to the double French doors when a second tinkling of glass stopped him.

Keep going, Douglas!

But for some reason, he stopped. Stopped and looked up to the balcony where Desmond Vanderbilt had just set a glass on the railing. "I trust everyone's having a good time!" he shouted.

The guests applauded and raised their glasses.

"I promised you a surprise, and before the revelation at midnight, I thought I should make good."

Go, Douglas. Now.

He didn't move.

"Many of you knew my father," Desmond continued. "You know how he loved art, loved to possess it. Many of you also have heard the rumors about my father's career in the CIA. I assure you, they aren't all true."

There was some nervous laughter.

Abby appeared at Jackson's elbow. "What are you waiting for?" she whispered. "Let's go."

But Jackson's feet were in concrete.

"My father was a great man who lived a grand, full life. And he left so much of himself behind in his collections. But for many years, one particular item was thought to be missing."

"Jackson," Abby hissed.

He held up a hand.

"Did I misinterpret the code?"

He shook his head.

"My father's Bible, a three hundred-fifty-year-old King James Version that—legend has it—contains confidential CIA codes and memorandums, disappeared around the time of his death."

"Jackson!" This time Abby took his hand and began to pull. He was still rooted in place.

Desmond paused. Opened his mouth to speak and shut it. He stepped back and looked down.

And Jackson regained control of his legs. He and Abby ducked under the balcony and into the foyer. He had to fight his own urge to run and Abby's pulling on his hand, but he kept to a steady walk, depositing his drink on a table as they passed.

Desmond had seen that the Bible was missing. It wouldn't take long before he would lock down the party, start putting pieces together. Jackson hoped Bianca had disappeared into the bathroom for a while.

Once they were through the main hall, Jackson quickened his pace, up the steps through the foyer and out the front door. "Ford Granada, can't miss it," Jackson said to the valet. "And we're kind of in a hurry, if you know what I mean." Then he leaned down toward Abby and whispered in her ear. "Go with me."

She looked up at him hesitantly but nodded slightly. He responded by placing his arm around her waist and pulling her close, then brushing his lips across her cheek. Then he winked at a second valet. Meanwhile, he waited for someone to burst out of the mansion and yell, "Stop them!"

It didn't happen, and the Granada appeared from around the fountain. Giving Abby a quick squeeze, Jackson released her and started around the car as the valet hopped out. That's when a walkie-talkie squawked.

Jackson and Abby both turned to the second valet as he lifted the walkie to his mouth. "Henry here."

The reply was unintelligible, but Henry immediately looked up. "That was Mr. Vanderbilt. He said not to let anyone leave."

Jackson snatched the keys from the valet beside him, at the same time yelling for Abby to get in the car. He gave the valet a shove toward the fountain and looked to see Henry rushing toward Abby's door. Without thinking, Jackson drew his squirt gun and pulled the trigger. A stream of rum splattered first on the roof of the Granada, then on Henry's face, and finally in his eye. He stopped with a scream and dropped backward.

Jackson jumped into the car, cranked the ignition, and floored the gas. With a squeal of tires, he tore around the circle and out of the driveway, nearly scraping bottom as he turned onto the road.

"Tell me you got it," Abby said.

Jackson finally flipped up his eyepatch. His answer was a joyful growl. "Aye."

Chapter Five

11:44 p.m.

NOT UNTIL THEY were back on the Pacific Coast Highway and heading toward L.A. did Jackson relax. Somewhat. This was another time when having a highly recognizable car was a real disadvantage. Especially when it wasn't a Ferrari that could outrun everything on wheels.

Thieves on TV always talked about the "high," the thrill of pulling off a job, that moment when the outcome could go either way. Same for daredevils and adrenaline junkies who risked life and limb to accomplish some death-defying feat on a motorcycle. They were all idiots as far as Jackson was concerned. The real high came from sitting back with an iced tea, enjoying the ocean breeze without a care in the world.

But it had been a long time since he'd experienced such a high.

"What do you think Desmond will do?"

Jackson glanced in the rearview mirror, then turned to Abby. "He's your brother."

"Stepbrother. You think he'll go to the police?"

He shook his head. "He's claimed all along he hasn't had the Bible, so it'd be hard for him to complain that it had been stolen from him."

"Wasn't he going to reveal it at the party?"

"Yes, but he never actually came out and said that he had it. He hinted around it, but if he calls in the police and tells them his Bible was stolen, he has no evidence that he ever actually had it except his own word. Plus, it would be an admission he'd lied previously, which could get him in trouble if you pursued legal options."

"So we're in the clear?"

"Not exactly. Unless he's as stupid as he is mean, he suspects you and I are involved. Why else would we have run?"

"You don't have to worry about him going vigilante or something," she said. "Not Desmond. If his lawyers or accountants can't handle the issue for him, then he's out of luck."

"You called him a criminal the other day."

"White-collar. Strictly."

Jackson nodded. "Well in case I'm wrong, and he does go to the police, our official story is that I was drunk and a little unruly and you wanted to get me home before I caused a bigger scene than I did with the valets. Sorry about that, by the way."

"No worries."

They returned to Abby's building, and Jackson accompanied her up to her third-floor apartment. She tossed her mask and wig aside and stepped out of her sandals, not bothering to change from the Egyptian lady-Pharaoh costume before viewing the Bible, which Jackson had removed from the waistband of his pants shortly after leaving the mansion and which she had anxiously held on her lap, resisting the urge to unwrap it in the car. Now, as Jackson shed his dreadlocks and cap and his jacket, she methodically washed and dried her hands before approaching the counter separating her living room from her kitchen.

She flitted a quick look up at Jackson as she tentatively opened the pouch. With trembling hands, she removed the Bible.

"Oh. My. Gosh."

It did not look like a Bible from the 1600s. For one thing, it wasn't huge, but comparable in size to the Bible on Jackson's nightstand. The brown leather binding was worn and frayed, and the engraving on the cover was as much white as its original gold. But it was, altogether, in reasonably good shape. Not for a collector maybe, but Jackson's grandpa's Bible, for example, was far the worse for wear.

"Should we be wearing gloves or something?" Jackson asked.

"Alec never did."

"Still, if it's a four-hundred-year-old relic . . ."

"Truth be told, I don't think it was much more than that most of the time," she said. "My ancestors weren't always the most spiritual of people. Until Alec had it, I think it sat on a shelf more than anything."

Jackson shrugged and moved around the counter as Abby opened the cover. Blue scrawl covered the entire page, forming several long paragraphs of text.

"Oh my gosh," Abby said, gently stroking the page. "I can't believe it. After all these years." She turned the page. "Oh my gosh! Here it is."

"What?"

"The dedication I told you about." She pointed to the middle of the second page, to another paragraph in the same quasi-legible scrawl. "'*My dearest child,*'" she read. "'*It is the prayer of an old man that you will discover the wonderful treasures hidden in this precious book. I only hope they will bring you as much joy in your life as they have brought me. Forever your father, Alec.*'"

There were tears in Abby's eyes as she finished reading, and Jackson didn't have the heart to tell her that the dedication was kind of ambiguous. Alec had three children, and there was no gender specificity in his note.

"'*Forever your father,*'" she said, sniffing as she wiped tears with her forefinger knuckles. "After Mom died, he took me in his arms and . . . and told me that he would . . ." She took a moment. "That he would forever be my father." She wiped more tears. "It was how he signed the card attached to the steering wheel of the car he gave me for graduation, and all the letters he wrote while I was at college. I . . . I can't believe this."

Jackson smiled. Although he'd taken the case, he'd kind of thought it seemed like much ado about nothing, going through all the risk and hassle to steal the Bible. But now, seeing the emotion on Abby's face and hearing it in her words—no one had ever accused Jackson of being a softie, but it hit him that this was why he had become a private investigator. Not to take down baddies but to help people.

"I should go," he said after a few moments of silence. "This is kind of personal for you."

"No, please stay. Actually, I'm hoping to retain your services."

"For what?"

"Look at this," she said, flipping several pages. She still wasn't to Genesis. "Look at these numbers here, and this . . . this isn't even in English. Say what you will about the legend, but there's something to it."

"I thought you weren't interested in old CIA codes."

"I'm not, not as such. But don't you see," she said, wiping another tear, "they're another link to my father. Anything I can learn about him and what he wrote would just mean the world to me."

"How can I help with that?"

"I did my research before I came to you, Jackson. I've heard how your mind works. I'm hoping you can help me crack Alec's code."

He nodded. "If that's what you want."

"It is. Look, I know it's late, but . . . I'm not going to sleep. I can put on a pot of coffee, or brew some tea . . . And it's Saturday morning by now," she added, looking at the clock. "I'll pay you for a second day."

"You're sure about this?"

"Positive."

"Okay. If you throw in the coffee."

*   *   *

Five and a half years ago . . .
Sunday, September 9
9:26 a.m.

"I HAVE a confession to make," Leroy Douglas said, moving away from the pulpit. For him, it had always been more of a reference point than an anchor. "I've been sandbagging you good folks."

A hundred or so sets of eyes pierced the seventy-year-old-man in a jacket and tie. It was as dressed up as Leroy ever got, and he said he only wore the jacket and tie out of reverence for the house of God and because some of the older members of the congregation wouldn't stand for it if he didn't. Having observed the majority of the people in the small, quaint church building, Jackson didn't doubt it. In jeans and a black button-down, he was one of the least well-dressed people there, certainly in his row.

"For the last few weeks now," Leroy continued, "I've preached from some pretty obscure passages of Scripture. I tested some of you by digging through Leviticus, Habakkuk, and Philemon. And I did it for a reason. I did it with this Sunday in mind."

Leroy burrowed his hands into his pockets and leaned back slightly as if discussing the weather or the Dodgers with the guys outside the hardware store on a Saturday morning. "I've had the privilege of serving as your pastor for the last twenty years. You encouraged me through the darkest time in my life, and you've made these last two decades, cumulatively, some of the happiest. So when I realized this would be my final Sunday, I asked myself, what do I want to leave these people with?"

He had slowly meandered back to the pulpit. "Turn with me to Second Timothy chapter three."

The rustling of pages filled the sanctuary. Jackson, because he had been running late, had forgotten his Bible and was forced to share with Grant as Leroy, in his slow, somewhat croaky style, read eight verses that served as the Apostle Paul's instructions to Timothy. He specifically highlighted verses sixteen and seventeen.

"*All Scripture is God-breathed and is useful for teaching, rebuking, correcting and training in righteousness, so that the man of God may be thoroughly equipped for every good work.*'" He closed the Bible, his finger keeping his place, and again paced away from the pulpit. "I've spent the last month bringing you messages from obscure books because I wanted to drive home the point that this entire book is valuable. Not just the familiar passages. Not just the New Testament. Not just the comfortable stuff. But the parts that step on our toes. The parts that we struggle to understand or reconcile. The parts that frankly are kind of boring. It's all in here for a reason, and that reason is your and my spiritual maturity."

Leroy shuffled to the other side of the pulpit. "I did some math the other day. I figure I've been pastor to about a thousand different people in my fifty years. That's not a lot by some standards, but I think it's pretty significant, because my role as a pastor is to help teach, rebuke, correct, and train. I'm what the Bible calls an overseer. A shepherd. That's not a role I've taken lightly. I've failed many a time, as Hank likes to point out," he said with a wink and a smile toward a man in the back row. Inside joke, apparently, as the room erupted in laughter.

"But seriously, it's a role I'm relinquishing now. I trust the Lord will bring someone else to this church, as He's brought to the other pulpits I've vacated, and I hope you'll end up in better hands than you are in now. That all said, I'd be remiss if I didn't take these minutes to give you a concluding exhortation. An exhortation that I hope will continue to spur you in my absence. An exhortation Paul passed to Timothy under similar circumstances, in what is widely considered his last epistle."

Leroy opened his Bible again. "*But as for you, continue in what you have learned and have become convinced of, because you know those from whom you learned it.*'" He looked up. "I want to be careful here, because we have to have this as our ultimate authority," he said, raising the Bible. "I'm not trying to usurp the

Scripture. But I'm talking to those of you who have been instructed by godly men and women. Maybe it was your pastor. Maybe a Sunday school teacher. For many of you, it was a parent or close family member. They taught you and trained you in the Word of God. They used it as their model for rebuking and correcting you. And so my exhortation to you is simple: Continue."

Jackson looked down the row at his parents, David and Hannah. They'd taught him everything he knew—about God, about life, about becoming a man himself. And the Bible had always been their benchmark.

He thought of their parents. Leroy and his late wife, Marsha. Hannah's parents, now both deceased. All of them were godly people who not only imparted their faith to Jackson but also showed him how to live it. Admittedly, he wasn't living as well as they had taught. But he was still young. Ish.

Leroy was reading again, and Jackson turned his eyes down to the Bible in Grant's hand. His younger brother by two years, Grant was the good son. Not that Jackson was exactly Charlie Sheen, but Grant always made Jackson's wool appear a few shades darker by comparison. And if he weren't so squeaky clean, Jackson would think he did it on purpose. Take today, for example. Jackson might have been dressed a little casually, but were Grant's pressed shirt and paisley tie really necessary?

And yet, Jackson had to admit that for all his brother's one-upmanship—intended or otherwise—Grant was a good kid. A grown kid now, and still a pious pain in the butt sometimes, but another testament to the Douglas family's spiritual lineage. Truth be told, Jackson didn't know a more sincere follower of Christ than his brother.

Sitting there with the family he loved so much and had learned so much from, and listening to the final sermon of his grandpa's fifty years as a minister of the Word, Jackson found himself humbled. Some kids were born to crack addicts and meth dealers. Some were born in the jungles of Cambodia or the projects of Harlem. He lived in San Diego, raised by a family who had never missed a step in his upbringing. He wasn't sure where, but there was a verse in the Bible about much being expected of those to whom much had been given. Well, Jackson had been given much. Now to figure what was expected of him and how exactly to give it.

"The Bible is full of people who pointed the way," Leroy said. "Examples who showed their contemporaries and who still show us today how we are to walk as children of God. For those of you fortunate enough to have such examples in your life, I urge you again to continue in what they have taught you. And that all comes back to this," he said, raising the Bible up beside his head. "It all comes back to God's Word. From the creation account in Genesis to the great culmination in Revelation and everywhere in between, this book you have been blessed with, taught out of, and seen modeled is the answer to it all. So study it. Memorize it. And continue in it and in what you have been taught from it."

He slowly lowered the Bible and looked out over the congregation.

"'*May the grace of the Lord Jesus Christ, and the love of God, and the fellowship of the Holy Spirit be with you all.*' Amen."

Chapter Six

THE SKY WAS clear, and the air warming as Jackson approached Leroy's houseboat in Marina del Rey. He'd bought it almost fifteen years ago when his wife, Marsha, had passed away, originally intending to spend as much time on the water as docked. But *Marsha* the houseboat wasn't real big on mobility, so Leroy spent the majority of his time fishing off piers, listening to opera and baseball, and still studying the Good Book he used to preach from.

Jackson stepped onto the deck of the houseboat and rapped on the door. "Coffee and donuts!"

He wasn't sure, but he thought he heard a quickened pace from inside.

Leroy pulled open the door with an expectant look. Tall, still in good shape, with graying dark brown hair and lively blue eyes, it was hard to believe Leroy Douglas was into his fourth quarter-century of life. He wore jeans and a T-shirt, standard fare. The nut didn't fall far from the tree.

"Tell me those don't have filling in them," Leroy said eyeing the box of donuts in Jackson's hand.

"Prunes," Jackson said, handing the box over. "Happy birthday, Grandpa."

"Wondering if you'd remember," Leroy said as they entered the living room of the houseboat. A chest-high counter separated the living room from the kitchenette, and Leroy set the donuts on the counter.

"How could I forget?" Jackson asked. "I have to say, you don't look a day over seventy-five."

"Ha, ha. You have a preference?"

"Take whichever you like." Jackson set Leroy's coffee by the box. "So, I'm working again."

"As a private eye or as a whatever it was you were for that Hollywood fella?"

"The former."

"Oh?"

"Yeah, and I would have taken you for lunch today, but I wasn't thinking too clearly at two a.m. when I promised my client I'd meet her for lunch."

"Two a.m., huh?"

"All aboveboard."

"Nothing good happens after midnight, bud."

Jackson nodded and opted for a change of subject. "I'll make up for it by taking you for dinner. Today, tomorrow, sometime."

"Whatever," Leroy said with a wave and a swallow of the first third of his donut. "Dates don't matter too much to a man my age. One day is the next." He raised the donut to his mouth again. "What's this case?"

"I stole a Bible."

Leroy paused mid-bite. "Lose yours?"

Jackson grinned and told his grandfather about being hired by Abby Vanderbilt and the party the night before, concluding with the mysterious code they had found, primarily in the front and back fly leafs but also littered throughout the old Bible. "We spent a couple of hours at her place last night, but couldn't make anything of it," Jackson said.

"And this girl hired you to decipher this dead guy's code?"

"Not really a girl. I think she's older than me."

"So how's it coming?"

Jackson reached for a donut. "Take a look," he said, reaching into his back pocket. "Been looking at them all morning, but I can't make heads or tails of Alec's writing." He tossed a couple dozen pictures on the table. "Some of the time he wrote paragraphs that at first seem like exposition of the text, but on closer examination by someone with reasonable biblical knowledge, don't make any sense or have any contextual link. But they're generic enough that somebody who just stumbled upon them and who didn't know more than the Lord's Prayer and the 23rd Psalm wouldn't catch on."

Leroy nodded.

"In other places, the writing is more cryptic. Random words, a few phrases, combinations of numbers and letters. He writes in at least three languages that I can tell. I have no idea what any of it means."

Leroy licked frosting off his thumb and scooped up the photos. "Wow, actual photos. Not some stamp-sized image on a Wi-Fi phone or something?"

Jackson grinned. "Nope, real thing."

"Imagine that. So what's this supposed to be, CIA secrets or something?"

"I don't know. Alec Vanderbilt worked for the CIA from 1961 until question mark. These," he said with a nod at the photos, "are either locations of foreign operatives with their call signs or his version of the Bible code. Or the rantings of a senile old man. No offense."

Leroy harrumphed. "Well, if he worked for the CIA for half a century, I doubt it's going to be as easy as cracking the *Times* cryptoquote."

"Your eagle eye spot anything?"

"Wrong member of the family, kiddo." Leroy looked up. "You know what your father would have given to have a chance at this puzzle?"

"Or me to be able to ask him."

Leroy nodded. David Douglas had served a dozen years in the Office of Naval Intelligence. Among other work, he had cracked codes and encryptions belonging to everyone from the Soviets to al-Qaeda.

"Well, good luck," Leroy said. "It's gibberish to me." He flipped the photos back down. "This how you get to spend your Saturday?"

"I guess. I'm meeting Abby at noon to tell her I have nothing so far and see if she wants me to continue. And since she's paying me by the day, I'd better give her a good day's worth of mental strain. But if I catch a break, I'll give you a call. We can grab dinner."

"I just hope you catch me before I take the bologna out of the freezer."

"Giving the potpies a rest, huh?"

"Have fun, kiddo. Hey, you want these? Brain food?"

Jackson looked back at the donuts. "They're all yours."

*　　　　　*　　　　　*

12:14 p.m.

JACKSON AND Abby sat on opposite sides of a window booth at Café 50's in Santa Monica. Outside, the sidewalk and street were full of midday traffic. Inside, Jerry Lee Lewis rocked the jukebox and Jackson and Abby both dined on burgers while poring over the photos of the Bible.

"Have you figured anything out yet?" Abby asked.

"Not by way of cracking the code," Jackson said.

"But you have figured something out?"

"A few things. Look at the way he wrote," Jackson said, reaching for his milkshake.

"What about it?"

He took a slurp. "It's script. Cursive. And it flows."

"So?"

"So, it means he's intimately familiar with his cipher. He doesn't have to look down at some key every few letters. It's one fluid pen stroke."

"So these numbers and letters are his own special code or something?"

Jackson nodded. "Then there are the paragraphs, some of which are in Greek or Aramaic or something I've never seen, there's some in what looks like French, and the stuff that's in English reads like random study notes."

"That's weird."

"Very. Could be that some of this is code and some isn't. Could be that some of it is dummy code to throw us off. Could be that some of it explains the rest of it." He shrugged. "At this point, it could be anything." He took a hunk out of his cheeseburger.

Abby pursed her lips.

"I also," he said pausing to finish swallowing, "noticed he wrote a lot at the beginning and end, using up blank pages. That's mostly paragraphs of text. But he's got notations and these strings of numbers, letters, and words scattered all throughout. I'm guessing that somehow the numbers correspond to pages or chapters and verses."

Abby sat up. "Well, that's something."

Jackson swallowed. "Yeah, but we don't know what. Without a cipher or a key, we're basically trying to read another language. And actually are sometimes. Seriously, who writes in Greek?"

Abby sighed.

"There's also one other possibility."

"What's that?"

"There really isn't a discreet way to ask this."

Abby leaned forward. "So ask it."

"What was Alec's mental state before he died?"

"You think he was crazy?"

"I think he worked for the CIA for decades. He wouldn't be the first person to have the wealth of knowledge get to him. I'm not saying he was crazy, but maybe all these writings aren't some huge, complicated code. Maybe they're just . . . nonsense, crossed wires."

"Alec was sharp as a tack, Jackson. His body failed, not his brain."

"Okay." He nodded as her eyes bored into him, and repeated himself. "Okay."

Now she nodded. "So will you keep working on it?"

"As long as you're paying, yeah. But it may not be easy." He took another bite of his burger, squirting grease onto his chin. The hallmark of a good burger.

"What'd you do for New Year's Eve?"

"I got shot," he said as he wiped his chin with a napkin.

"What?"

He nodded. "It's a long story."

Abby frowned. "Well, that kind of takes the steam out . . . You were really shot?"

"I'd show you the scar, but it wouldn't be polite in a public setting."

Abby nibbled on a fry.

Jackson wiped his hands on the napkin and tossed it aside. "What were you going to say? About New Year's Eve."

"I spent this New Year's Eve thinking about ten years ago," she said. "The day Alec died. I couldn't believe it—I still can't—It's been ten years. If there's any chance of cracking this code, I'm going to keep at it, even if it's hard and even if it costs me a few days' fees."

"Okay."

"So what's our next step? How do we figure this out?"

"We need to get back to the Bible itself," he said, starting to stack some of the photos. "We're going to make a note of everything he wrote, the page he wrote it on, the book and text it corresponds to. If we can catch some sort of theme or pattern, maybe we can crack the code."

Abby nodded and reached for her backpack on the seat beside her. "I brought the Bible al—"

"You might want to finish your burger first," Jackson said. "You know what grease does to centuries-old books?"

"Yeah, I suppose," she said with a sheepish grin. "I'm just so anxious."

"I know," Jackson said. "But we've got all afternoon. We can take it back to my place, your place, the library, the beach . . . wherever."

"You're right. Sorry, I just kind of get tunnel vision sometimes."

"Tunnel vision's not always bad," Jackson said. "Just watch out for trains."

Abby laughed quietly and picked up her burger.

"So tell me more about Alec," Jackson said as The Coasters started singing "Yakety Yak."

"Like what?"

He shrugged. "His personal life, professional life. Give me the bio of the man whose code I'm trying to crack."

"Well, he was born here in L.A. in 1939," Abby said, reaching for her milkshake. It was strawberry to Jackson's chocolate. "His dad died on Iwo Jima, so his mom and grandparents raised him. They lived in L.A. his whole childhood, and he never really left home until he went to college."

"Whereabouts?"

"Stanford. He graduated in May of '61 and joined the CIA in August."

"And nobody knows when he quit?"

"He officially retired December 31, 1977, ten months after his marriage to Pauline Zeller ended in a mutual separation."

"She Desmond's mother?"

Abby nodded. "They married in June of '64 and Desmond was born three years later."

Jackson reached for an onion ring. "Why'd they split up?"

"Depends who you ask. Work was kind of the official story, but there were rumors Alec was having an affair. And he did have a relationship for a few years with another woman and had another son before marrying Mom in 1982."

"Noah?"

"No."

Jackson gulped the last bite of an onion ring. "He had a fourth child?"

"Tate Archambeau. His mother, Regina, is a bigwig in the Southern California art community. She and Alec were together after he and Pauline divorced, but they never married. When their relationship ended, she made it clear she didn't want him to be a part of raising Tate."

"Was it an ugly breakup?"

"I don't know," she said, going for the milkshake again. "I don't think exceptionally so, but their lives were going in separate directions, and she preferred to raise Tate herself. Alec obliged."

"So that's why he wasn't in the will?"

"Among other reasons. Tate was messed up. While still in high school, he got caught up in drugs and never got out. About a year after Alec died, Tate was found unresponsive in an alley with needle pricks all over his arm. He died before they could admit him to the hospital."

"I'm sorry."

Abby shrugged dispassionately. "He'd been using forever, and I think even Regina had disavowed him by then. But there was no way Alec would have left him a dime."

"Makes sense."

She leaned on her straw and sucked without the straw burping. "After Alec married Mom, things settled down. We were a happy family. No rumors of CIA involvement or affairs or anything. July 3, 1982, was a turning point, like Alec turned over a new leaf and a new life."

"Any idea when he did all this writing in his Bible?" Jackson asked. "The penmanship looked pretty consistent, so I'm assuming it wasn't over the course of years as he aged."

Abby shook her head. "I never really saw the Bible that much. I don't know. I'd guess it was shortly before he died, but that's just a guess, and I can't say as I have a reason for it."

Jackson nodded. "What about the rumors and legends? How long have they been in effect?"

"As long as I can remember. As a kid, I never paid any attention to them. But as I grew older, got into the art community myself, I became aware of them."

Jackson looked up at the door as Frankie Valli started crooning. A young woman stood just inside the doorway, her dirty strawberry blond ponytail bouncing from shoulder to shoulder as she turned her head to look around the café. She was about Abby's height and size, maybe a pinch taller and thinner, with fair skin that contrasted with her dark jacket. She had a pleasant face—Jackson characterized her as good-looking. But in a beach community like Santa Monica, he was accustomed to seeing far prettier. And yet, there was something about her that kept him from pulling his eyes away. Maybe the way she stood searching the café instead of entering it. Maybe the way her baggy khakis and bright blue shirt under the jacket didn't quite mesh with the apparel of the rest of the Café 50's clientele. Or maybe it was the way her eyes narrowed slightly when they passed over Jackson.

"What is it?" Abby asked.

"I don't know. But I'm going to put away the photos," Jackson said, scooping up the rest of them.

"Jackson, what's going on?"

He lifted his eyes again to the door. They never made it there, because he spotted the woman halfway to their booth. Something about her looked familiar.

He tried picturing her with the sunglasses that were in her hair over her eyes instead. Or with her hair down. A different color. Different length? He was close, he could sense it.

So was she. "Abigail Vanderbilt?" she stopped beside their table and asked.

Abby looked to the woman, then to Jackson, then back to the woman. "Yes," she said as the tumblers in Jackson's mind clicked.

The hair was it. It had been longer and darker. Much darker. And the face. It had been even paler. And streaked with blood.

"Bianca," Jackson said.

"Actually, it's Robyn Pearson," she replied, reaching into her pocket. She came out with a wallet containing a badge and credentials and held it open for them to view. "I'm with the FBI. I need to speak with the two of you."

"Wait a second," Abby said. "Bianca who? You two know each other?"

"She was at the party last night."

Abby frowned.

"Vampire," Jackson said. "Very gothic. Can I see that ID again?"

Robyn opened the wallet for him again, at the same time pulling a business card out of her other pocket. She dropped it on the table. "That has my cell as well as the FBI field office in L.A. Give them a call if you'd like."

"I don't understand," Abby said. "Why was an FBI agent at Desmond's masquerade ball?"

"The same reason you were," Robyn answered.

"You have an affinity for seafood-flavored appetizers and role playing?" Jackson asked.

Robyn teased with a quick smile. "I'm here to retrieve the Vanderbilt Bible. It's a matter of national security."

Jackson chuckled

"Something funny?"

"No, it's just . . . I thought that line was only uttered on TV."

"I'm not the one who riffed off Johnny Depp all night long."

"You were a vampire, and you're calling me clichéd?"

Robyn offered a thin-lipped smile in response before turning to Abby. "I need the Bible."

"I . . ." She looked to Jackson.

"Who says we have it?" he said.

Robyn's smile became a smirk. "You just did, by not saying 'We don't have it.' Talk about lines out of TV."

"It's not here," Abby said.

"But you know where it is?"

Abby again looked to Jackson.

"Mind if I search that backpack?" Robyn asked.

"Unless you have a warrant," Jackson said.

She sighed. "I don't need a warrant. Like I said, this is a matter of national security, and I need that Bible and I need it now. So we can either do this the easy way or the hard way."

Jackson would have chuckled at another cliché, but he was too angry. Something in him hated being firmly overruled by authority figures. The fact that the authority figure was a somewhat attractive woman didn't help things. Worst of all, she was right. She had the rank to pull, and while he wasn't sure on the protocol the Bureau had to follow when it came to warrants and probable cause and national security, he knew that one way or the other, the FBI would get the Bible. And his and Abby's resistance would just make things worse in the end.

"You can't," Abby said.

"I can," Robyn answered. "Now please, let me look inside the backpack before I have to make a scene and ruin your lunch."

Reluctantly, with lip trembling and eyes smoldering, Abby slid the backpack across her lap to Robyn. Pulling a pair of black crime scene gloves from another of her jacket pockets, Robyn dug into the backpack and came out with the Bible, in the same pouch in which Jackson had smuggled it out of the Vanderbilt mansion the night before. She gingerly unwrapped the pouch and opened a few pages of the Bible. Satisfied, she closed it and bound it again.

"You can't just take that," Abby said.

"I'm sorry, ma'am. I have no choice. It truly is an urgent matter of national security that this Bible be secured." Tucking the Bible under her arm almost like a football, Robyn turned to leave. But first, her sea-green eyes met both Jackson's and Abby's. "Thank you for your cooperation."

With that, she turned and left, pausing only to flip down her shades before pushing through the door and out into the California sunshine.

Chapter Seven

12:37 p.m.

FOR A FEW moments, Jackson wasn't sure if Abby was going to cry or scream. She did neither. Instead, she closed her eyes and sighed heavily. When she opened them again, they were boiling cauldrons of brown.

"She cannot get away with this."

"I don't know," Jackson answered evenly, hoping Abby's pent-up anger didn't fly out at him.

"I don't care if she is FBI. She doesn't have the right to confiscate private property like that. It's in the Fourth Amendment."

"Well, the Patriot Act might have negated that, and technically, I'm not sure it is private property. If you're not the legal owner . . ."

"So you're on her side?"

"No," Jackson said. "I just don't think we have legal grounds to do anything about it."

Abby furrowed her brow. "Can you find out?"

He furrowed his in return.

She leaned forward. "I paid you to get the Bible for me. I'll keep paying."

"You might be better off with the lawyers."

"No, I want you. Find out if the FBI had legal grounds to take the Bible. If not, then I'll stop paying you and pay my high-priced lawyers until I run out of money."

"And if so?"

Abby sighed. "Then . . . I'll . . ." She sighed again. "We'll cross that bridge when we come to it."

"It's your dime," he said. "I'll look into it."

She sat back. "In the meantime, I guess we still have the photos. Maybe we can unlock the code from them and prove Alec's notes had nothing to do with national security. Then the FBI would have to give it back."

"It's a long shot, but we can try."

"Thank you."

"Abby, there's something else to consider here."

"What's that?"

"The FBI may not want the Bible."

She furrowed her brow again. "What are you talking about? They just took it from us."

"I mean, they may not want to keep it. If they're worried that it contains secrets that concern national security, they might rather—"

"Dispose of it," she finished. Jackson nodded, and she sighed in disgust. "You cannot let that happen, Jackson. I don't care what you have to do, if they want to destroy my father's Bible, I want you to get it back."

"I'll see what I can do. First thing, I'm going to see what I can find out about Robyn Pearson."

"She didn't strike me as the typical government agent."

"Yeah, but neither do Callen and Sam."

"Who?"

He waved his hand, then signaled to their waitress. She arrived just as Johnny Cash started walking the line. "You folks finished?" she asked.

Jackson nodded. "Did you see that woman who stopped by our table a few minutes ago?"

"Tall, blond ponytail, dark jacket?"

"Yeah. You ever seen her before?"

"I see a lot of faces," she said as she picked up their plates. "But hers didn't look familiar."

"Okay, thanks."

"I'll be right back with your check."

Abby frowned. "You think she's a regular here or something?"

"I think it's weird that she found us here, now. Not last night at your apartment, not this morning." He shrugged. "It may be nothing, but it's odd."

"I want to know how she knew about the Bible to begin with," Abby said. "I mean to be at the party last night."

"You didn't tell anyone else?"

"No."

"Could Desmond have?"

"I suppose, but why? The only reason he gave me the scoop was to get under my skin."

The waitress brought the check, and Jackson and Abby paid and headed outside. He kept an eye out as they walked to Abby's car. He doubted Robyn or a theoretical partner had hung around to spy on them after taking the Bible, but he wasn't taking chances.

"Now what?" Abby asked before getting into her car.

"I'll follow you back to your place. I want to go online and see if the number on this card matches the FBI's website," he said, raising the business card Robyn had left on their table.

"You think she's a fake?"

"No."

"Then why?"

"Just checking her out. Like you said, there was something not agency about her."

The drive took only ten minutes, in which time Jackson tried calling Mouse. With his ability to scour the web and scale technological parameters (read: hack), he was one of Jackson's first calls when he needed classified information. Mouse couldn't—Jackson didn't think—hack the FBI database, and he wouldn't ask him to. But as Mouse had often told him, there was stuff on the web that nobody knew about.

It didn't matter. Mouse didn't answer. Working, sleeping, or engrossed in killing aliens on his computer.

"Do you want a drink?" Abby asked when they had settled in at her apartment. The windows were open to allow the ocean breeze inside, and Jackson was seated on the couch with Abby's laptop booting up on the coffee table. "I could use a martini," she added.

"No thanks."

"That's right, you don't drink. You mind if I have one?"

"Suit yourself."

Abby went to fix her martini, and Jackson waited for the signature Windows logon ditty and then pulled up the FBI's Los Angeles field office's web page. As he reached for Robyn's business card in his wallet, Abby's doorbell rang.

From the kitchen, Abby frowned at him as she dropped an olive into her glass. She rubbed her fingers together and moved to the door. On instinct, Jackson closed the laptop and stood.

"Can I help you?" Abby asked.

The voice was thick and husky. "Ma'am, I'm Agent Ellen Andrews. This is Agent Stanley Newton. FBI."

"Stan," he said as Jackson slipped over behind Abby.

"Sir," Agent Andrews said with a curt nod. She was tall and thin, with short blond hair and a chiseled face. In contrast to Robyn, she wore a dark pinstriped pantsuit over a blue blouse, both tight, and heels that put her at Jackson's eye level. Beside her, deep-voiced Agent Newton was, without the heels, the same height, with dark hair instead of blond. His suit was also dark, but sans stripes, and worn with a blue tie and white shirt instead of a blouse. Both looked professional. Neither resembled Robyn Pearson in the least.

"You mind if I see those badges?" Jackson asked.

"Of course," Newton said, withdrawing a wallet from his suit pocket. He handed it to Jackson, who studied the badge on one side of the wallet and the ID on the other. He was not an expert in federal agency badge identification, but it looked similar to Robyn's. He returned it to Newton, cast a cursory glance at Andrews' outstretched badge and credentials, and nodded.

"If you don't mind, you are . . . ?" Andrews asked.

"Jackson Douglas. A friend of Miss Vanderbilt's."

That seemed to satisfy them.

"Is there something I can help you with?" Abby asked.

"I'm sorry," Jackson said, "but would you mind if I called and confirmed your identities?"

Andrews sighed audibly. Newton smiled cockily. "You need the number?" he asked.

"No, I can find it," Jackson said, quickly returning to the laptop. In two minutes, he was on hold with the FBI's L.A. office. He sat in front of the laptop for four more minutes, while Abby and the two fibbies stood around awkwardly, before finally getting to speak with a person. "I need to identify a couple of agents who just knocked on my door," he said.

"Absolutely," the very professional voice answered. "Do you have their names and/or badge numbers?"

"Agent Ellen Andrews and Agent Stanley Newton."

"One moment."

Jackson heard repeated keystrokes. Then, "Sir?"

"Yeah."

"Agent Andrews is a Caucasian female, five-nine, short blond hair, blue eyes, a small mole above her lip."

"That checks," Jackson said, taking a glance to spot the mole. It was there.

"Agent Newton is a Caucasian male, six-foot, close-cropped black hair, blue eyes, a crooked smile."

"That looks like him. Thank you."

Jackson closed the phone and stood. "They're legit. Sorry about that."

Newton displayed his crooked smile again. "Forget it."

Abby stepped back and admitted them to the living room. "What can I do for you?"

"We understand that you are in possession of a Bible previously belonging to Alec Vanderbilt," Andrews said.

Abby narrowed her eyes. "You understand that how?"

"Miss Vanderbilt, do you have the Bible?"

"No."

Andrews glanced at Newton. He glanced back.

"I'm afraid it is a matter of national security," Newton said. "We need that Bible."

"You're in luck," Jackson said. "You have it."

"Excuse me?" Andrews asked.

"It's true, the left hand doesn't know what the right hand is doing, isn't it?"

Andrews shook her head. "Sir, I'm not sure—"

"Less than an hour ago, an Agent Pearson took the Bible from us, citing national security."

"Agent Pearson?" Andrews said. She shook her head.

Jackson shrugged. "That's what she told us."

"She? Did she have a first name?"

"Robyn."

"Agent Robyn Pearson," Andrews said.

Jackson nodded.

"There's no Agent Robyn Pearson with the FBI," Newton said.

"Nowhere or not in Los Angeles?" Abby asked.

Newton held up his phone, showing first Abby then Jackson a "name not found" message on the screen. "Nowhere."

"You just took her word?" Andrews asked.

"She had a badge just like yours," Jackson said.

"It was a fake."

"I didn't know that."

"And FBI agents do not work alone. You should have called to verify her identity."

"Unfortunately, I wasn't suspicious enough of the FBI yet," Jackson said, his frustration at himself for not having done exactly that coming out in anger.

Andrews sighed the mother of all sighs. "When and where did this happen? Here?"

Newton was already tapping away at his phone as Jackson explained that Robyn had found them at Café 50's.

"If she wasn't an FBI agent, who was she?" Abby asked.

"Someone else who wants the Bible, clearly," Andrews replied.

"Can you give us a description?" Newton asked.

Jackson and Abby took turns describing Robyn's appearance, giving Agents Andrews and Newton a fairly comprehensive sketch. They also recounted in exacting detail their interaction with her, covering ground two and sometimes three times.

"Is there anything else you can tell us?" Andrews asked with another sigh.

"I don't know how there could be," Jackson said.

"There is no need for lip, sir. Need I remind you that had you been as diligent with her as you were with us, this would not have happened?"

Jackson planted his tongue in his cheek to keep from saying something stupid.

"If you think of anything else, please let us know," Andrews said. "I believe you know the number, but here's a card with our cells as well."

"Wait," Abby said as they turned to leave. "The Bible . . . You say it's a matter of national security. Why? What do you think is in Alec's Bible?"

"I am sorry, ma'am, but we're not allowed to discuss it."

Newton gave them both a nod as he followed Andrews out the door, which Abby closed sternly behind them.

"Can you believe that?" she asked.

"We should have seen through her," Jackson said. "*I* should have."

"What difference does it make? The Bible's gone."

"Yeah. Although . . ."

"What?"

"If the FBI has the Bible, we're hamstrung. It'll either be tied up in red tape that will cost you thousands in lawyer fees, or we have to resort to stealing it back from the feds. But if Robyn's a fake . . ."

"Then we wouldn't be stealing it from the FBI."

Jackson nodded. "Unfortunately, it puts us behind square one for finding her."

Abby exhaled and set her drink on the counter. "I'm too depressed to drink."

The doorbell rang again.

"If that's a lone male FBI agent, I quit," Jackson said.

Abby took a deep breath as she reached for the door. She opened it and gasped. "Desmond."

"Abigail." He pushed past her into the room and stopped when he saw Jackson. "The pirate."

"Takes one to know one."

Desmond turned back to Abby. "Where's the Bible?"

"I don't have it."

Desmond swore. "I know you stole it from me last night."

"You don't know anything, Desmond. And I don't have the Bible."

"Then what's he doing here?"

"He's my boyfriend. I do have a right to date, don't I?"

"And why was he at the ball last night?"

"Because the invite said 'and guest,'" she replied. "Now would you please leave?"

"No. Not until I search your apartment."

"No. You have no right."

Desmond pushed past her and Jackson stepped into his path. Desmond was tall and thin, and even less impressive without his top hat and cape. Or wand. Unless he was a closet jiu-jitsu guy, Jackson had no doubts he could take him.

"Get out of my way," Desmond said, his voice an octave higher.

"Better yet, you get out of this apartment before I throw you through the window," Jackson said evenly.

Desmond stared at him for several seconds before backing down. Jackson stood his ground and nodded at the door.

"This isn't over," Desmond said over his shoulder to Abby.

"And yet, it feels like it is," she said, literally slamming the door on his heels. She leaned back against it, and Jackson once again wondered if she was about to cry or scream. Once again, she only raised her eyes to meet his. "What's our game plan?"

"Find Robyn before the FBI does," Jackson said. "As far as they're concerned, we're an expired clue. If we can get the Bible from her without them knowing we got it from her, we should be in the clear."

"How do we do that?"

"I don't know. I've got some contacts. Let me see what I can find out."

She nodded.

"In the meantime, we have the photos. We'll keep working and see if we can deduce something that will help us."

"Like what?"

He shrugged. "I don't know. But Robyn knew about the Bible somehow. Maybe she's tied to Alec's past. Or maybe there's an unknown piece in there that will clear things up for us. There's more to this than the 'national security' line everyone's trotting out."

Abby nodded. "I agree."

"I'm going to check in with some people, ask around," Jackson said. "I'll get back to you with an update later today."

She nodded again. "Thank you, Jackson."

"Hang in there."

Back in his car, Jackson first tried Mouse again. There was still no answer, so Jackson set a course for his friend's house. En route, he called Ashley Larson. A detective with LAPD, Ashley had put herself forever in Jackson's debt last year when she had hired him, and he had ended up saving her life. It was a favor Jackson didn't hesitate to call in, and he hoped she'd be agreeable to doing a little research.

Unfortunately, Ashley wasn't at her desk or answering her cell. It was a Saturday, but who knew what sort of schedule a detective kept? He opted against leaving a message.

Jackson's last call was to FBI Special Agent Jamie Joseph. Jackson had met him a few weeks earlier in New York while on another case and had helped Joseph and the Albany branch of the FBI bring down a pair of New York crime families. As a result, Joseph also owed Jackson a favor, and Jackson hoped he could help him track down the fake agent Robyn Pearson.

Agent Joseph wasn't at his desk either, so Jackson left a message. He tried Joseph's cell, again with no luck, again leaving another message. Oh-for-five, but Jackson held out hope that maybe Mouse was at home and too deep into a virtual world to answer the phone. But when neither Mouse nor his overweight and overbearing sister Pam opened the door, Jackson had to concede that he had struck out.

Returning home, Jackson ran the last twenty-four hours in his head. How had Robyn learned about the Bible? And how had the FBI? Had Andrews and Newton or some junior agent been at the masquerade ball too? And just what was in that Bible that made it such a hot commodity?

Jackson returned home and grabbed a cream soda from the refrigerator. He took it out onto his deck, which, from its vantage point in Pacific Palisades, offered a brilliant view of the Pacific Ocean a little over a mile away. It was a posh neighborhood and the house, despite being the smallest on the block, would have been well out of Jackson's price range had it not been in foreclosure when he bought it. Jackson had spent over a year remodeling the place, and now savored afternoons such as this, when he could relax and enjoy the fruits of his labor.

If not for the case weighing on his mind. So between sips of his soda, he took out the photos of the Bible and surveyed them again. Without a key, it was like translating Chinese.

After twenty minutes of fruitless and frustrating efforts, he put away the photos and watched the ocean and the cumulous clouds building on the horizon until his phone rang. It was an unknown number, but Jackson took a chance.

"Hello?"

"Jackson Douglas?"

"Yeah. Who's this?"

"Desmond Vanderbilt."

Jackson sat up. "How do you know my name?"

"Abby told me."

"Where is she?"

"With me. Safe. For now."

Jackson stood. "What—"

"The Bible. I want it. And I think you have it."

"You're wrong. What have you done with Abby?"

"Nothing. Yet. And it will stay that way as long as you get me that Bible."

"Look, pal, I told you, I don't have it."

"Then you'd better get it. And don't involve the police, or you won't be seeing your 'girlfriend' ever again."

Chapter Eight

3:03 p.m.

JACKSON LOWERED THE phone, staring out toward the ocean without seeing it. His first thought was to call Desmond, call him a few names, and threaten him right back. But the *Ransom* move was a risky one, and blowing his top over the phone wouldn't accomplish anything. Desmond already knew that Jackson could kick his tail or he wouldn't have backed down in Abby's apartment, so there was no need to call and tell him that. Threats had their time and place, but this wasn't one of them.

So he called Abby's cell instead. It was stupid, he knew. Desmond wouldn't have called Jackson if he didn't actually have Abby. Still, Jackson had to try.

Abby didn't answer, and Jackson hurried inside and upstairs. He grabbed his Glock 9mm pistol and headed back out the door. He made the drive to Abby's apartment in twenty minutes, good considering the time of day.

On the way, he had tried Mouse and Ashley again, both without success. He'd thought about calling the police outright, despite Desmond's warning. But he doubted any accusation he threw at Desmond would stick, at least not if Jackson didn't have evidence to back up his claim.

After ringing the doorbell produced no results, Jackson found Abby's door unlocked and let himself in.

The place had been tossed.

Couch cushions and pillows were on the middle of the living room floor, along with a tipped over lamp, books and magazines, and the contents of a small writing desk. In the kitchen, empty drawers were stacked on the counter, their contents strewn over the floor and remaining counter space. They were joined by boxes and bags of food and staples, canned goods, and broken plates, cups, and silverware.

Jackson moved to the bedroom and bathroom, both in similar conditions. But there was no sign of Abby. Disregarding Desmond's warning, Jackson dialed 9-1-1.

"Yeah, I'm at 454 Benson Lane in West L.A.," he said when the operator answered. "Somebody's making a ton of noise up in apartment 3C. It sounds like World War III up there."

"Is anyone hurt?"

"I don't know. A single girl lives there, but I don't know if she's home. If she is, she's in trouble."

It took another thirty seconds before the operator agreed to dispatch a unit. Jackson didn't wait around.

The way he figured it, he had two options. He could spend his time trying to recover the Bible or trying to find Abby. Going for Abby cut out the middleman, but unless Desmond had her stashed at his mansion—unlikely— and Jackson could gain admittance without shooting up Malibu—unlikelier since he was sure Desmond had hired help—he would just be wasting time that could be spent getting the Bible back. So he picked option one.

Jackson got into his car and pulled out Robyn's business card. Kicking himself again for not trying it earlier, he dialed the number for the FBI's L.A. field office, the same number that he had found on the website and used to authenticate Andrews and Newton. It took him five minutes to confirm what they had told him—there was no Robyn Pearson with the Federal Bureau of Investigation.

Jackson closed his phone as a police car rolled into the lot. At least their response was prompt.

Robyn had dared Jackson and Abby to call her bluff, not even providing a fake phone number. It wasn't an uncommon tactic among con artists— make a good faith offer that can't be backed, hoping that the offer itself will satisfy the other party. A variant of the old "pig in a poke" scam, and Jackson had fallen for it.

There would be time to punish himself mentally for that later. But now he had one avenue left. There was a good chance it led to a dead end, but it was worth a try. So as he watched two cops hurry into the building, Jackson dialed the other number on the business card. Robyn's cell.

"Yeah?"

"Robyn?" he asked. The voice sounded off.

"Um, yeah."

"It's Jackson Douglas."

A pause. "I'm sorry, who?"

Was she drunk?

"The pirate. Abby Vanderbilt's friend."

"Oh. Right. Is there something . . . I can help you with?"

He almost told her that yeah, she could come clean about who she really was. But she was still in character, meaning she didn't know he knew who she wasn't, and he didn't want her to wriggle off the hook. "Abby's been kidnapped."

"What?"

"Her brother thinks we have the Bible. He's got her and says if I don't return it to him, she's dead."

"Oh no. Desmond? No . . ." She went silent.

"Robyn?"

"Yeah. Um, I don't have it."

"What?"

"I don't have it anymore. It . . . It's a—"

"Do you know who has it?"

"Um, sort of."

"Sort of? What's going on?" Jackson asked, struggling to keep his composure.

"Um, where are you right now?"

"West L.A."

"I'm at a hotel in Hermosa Beach. Why don't you come over?"

That was a start. And it was all he had. "Okay. What's the hotel?"

"The Breakers. Sixteenth and Beach. Room 204."

"I'll be there as soon as I can."

Jackson entrusted the search for Abby to the cops, hoping they could find something in her apartment to lead them to believe she had been kidnapped and that Desmond was the kidnapper. It was doubtful. If anything, they would just find Jackson's prints.

Thirty minutes—and unanswered calls to Mouse and Ashley—later, Jackson arrived in Hermosa Beach near the southern edge of L.A.'s western beachhead. He parked in a public garage and hiked the few blocks to The Breakers. Three stories tall, with peach stucco walls, plenty of windows (most of which overlooked the ocean), and patios and balconies for every room, it wasn't exactly the Hotel del Coronado, but it wasn't a fleabag either.

Room 204 had southwestern exposure, looking out over the Hermosa Beach Pier at the ocean. Jackson rapped on the door, wondering what game Robyn would be running and what game he should run in return.

She opened the door just far enough to peek out at him with her left eye. She quickly closed the door and then reopened it all the way. Acknowledging Jackson with a nod, she stepped back so he could pass. The jacket was gone, but she still wore the blue shirt—a tank top—and khakis. In her right hand, she held an icepack, which she raised to the back of her head as she shut the door.

"Uncle Sam's a tough master, huh?" Jackson said as he walked past her.

"I was assaulted."

"Yeah, by who?" Jackson asked, turning around.

"I don't know," Robyn answered. She used her free hand to pull a gun from the back waistband of her pants. "I was going to ask you that same thing."

Jackson stared at the gun, then down the short barrel at her. "Put that down."

"Not until I get some answers."

"*You* get some answers?"

"Yeah. Like who were the goons that knocked down my door and brained me?"

"How would I know? You think I sent them?"

"You weren't too happy when I took the Bible from you."

"I don't respond well to thieves."

"I told you, it was a matter of na—"

"National security, yeah, I know. Funny, that's what the FBI agents who stopped by Abby's apartment said too. Right before they exposed you."

"What?"

"That's right. They outed you, so can the act. And drop the gun before I take it from you and 'brain' you again."

Her eyes narrowed as if daring him to try it. But then she lowered the gun. "I am with the FBI."

"Then how come when I called that number on your card, they said they'd never heard of you?"

"Because I didn't give you my real name."

"Come again?"

She sighed and tossed the icepack on the bed. "Robyn Pearson is an alias. Apparently, the L.A. office didn't get the memo."

Jackson scoffed.

"My real name is Roberta Pierce. I am with the FBI, I am here to recover the Bible, and it really is a matter of national security."

"Well, how many people does the FBI have after this Bible anyway?"

"As far as I know, one."

He looked incredulously at her.

"So wait," she said. "You believed these agents right away when they said I was a fake but did you ever consider they might be fakes?"

Jackson rolled his eyes.

"Did they show you their badges?"

"Yeah."

"Did they look like this?" she asked as she picked hers off the dresser.

He breathed out a sigh that turned into another. "Yeah."

"Exactly?"

He sighed again and reached for the badge. "Let me see it."

Roberta withdrew the badge. "You can look but not touch."

"What, you a germaphobe?"

"No. I just don't let civilians hold my badge. No FBI agent would."

He nodded.

"Did they?"

Jackson licked his lips.

"How heavy was it?"

"Not very."

She dropped hers on the desk with a clunk. "That heavy?"

"Hard to say."

"Sounds like they were fakes."

Jackson shook his head. "Come on, you expect me to buy this little dog and pony show?"

"It should at least create reasonable doubt."

"Oh, I've got plenty of doubt right now."

"But you're only doubting me?"

He nodded. "Your clunking badge trick is neat, but I called the L.A. office. They authenticated both agents."

"You called the L.A. office?"

"Yep."

"The same number as on my card?"

He nodded.

"And they authenticated them?"

He nodded again.

Roberta shook her head. "That doesn't make sense."

"Makes plenty of sense to me."

"Why would they . . ." She stopped, mid-shake of the head. "Unless . . ."

He bit. "Unless what?"

She turned and paced. "What time did these agents—what were their names?"

"Andrews and Newton."

"What time did they visit you?"

"I don't know, one-thirty, quarter to two."

"I got back here around one-fifteen. I went for lunch about two . . . The timeline fits."

"What timeline, Marcia Clark?"

Still pacing, Roberta turned at the far end of the room. "What'd they look like?"

Jackson sighed and gave her brief descriptions of Agents Andrews and Newton.

"That sounds like them."

"Sounds like who?"

"My attackers. Your descriptions were a little wanting—"

"You think they attacked you?"

"Who else?"

"I don't know, how many people have you conned recently?"

"Think about it, Douglas. I take the Bible from you—"

"So you admit it now?"

Roberta made a sour face. "I take the Bible from you, legally, and then they come to take it, but you tell them I have it. An hour later, I get my door kicked in on me, get knocked over the head, and wake up to see them tearing out of the parking lot and find the Bible gone. I don't know about you, but that's a little too much coincidence for me."

Jackson shook his head. "This doesn't wash. Why would FBI agents attack you, even if they didn't know you were undercover? That's not how the FBI works."

"No, not the FBI."

"Not the FBI," he said, laughing under his breath. "So let me get this straight. I call the L.A. office, and they've never heard of you—"

"I told you, they must not have gotten the memo about my alias."

"Whatever the reason, they've never heard of you. But they do authenticate Andrews and Newton, and I'm supposed to believe they're fakes and you're legit?"

Roberta nodded slightly, a pathetic smile on her face.

"And what, they hacked into the FBI phone system or something?"

"Or your phone. I know it seems crazy, but if they are who I think they are, yeah."

"And who's that?"

Roberta made eye contact. "The CIA."

Jackson raised his eyebrows. "The CIA? Seriously?"

"Either that or foreign operatives, but I'm betting the CIA. No other government agency would have the ability—or the nerve—to hack the FBI phone system, or to fake being FBI agents, for that matter. And they wouldn't need to. NSA or DOD or Treasury Department or Homeland could just flash their actual credentials. And legitimate FBI agents wouldn't do a smash and grab job like that."

Jackson could only shake his head.

"I can see you're still not convinced," Roberta said. "So here, call this number." She walked over to the nightstand and jotted on the hotel stationery. "I know you have to take my word that the number is legit, but if they have hacked into the FBI's system and intercepted phone calls, the entire L.A. office might be compromised."

"And who is this I'm calling?"

"Denver," she replied. "Private line. Think Robin Masters' red phone."

"Rick, T.C., and half the island had that number."

She tipped her head and grinned. "And here I thought I was the only *Magnum* fan of my generation."

With a sigh, Jackson pulled out his phone and dialed the number on the pad. After three rings, a perky female voice answered. "Federal Bureau of Investigation, Denver Office. This is Kristi."

"Kristi, I need to authenticate an agent from your office."

"One moment."

He lowered the phone from his mouth. "What makes you think they haven't hacked the Denver office too? Or the entire FBI? Do you believe in the moon landing?"

Roberta bit off a retort.

"This is Special Agent Dawkins," an austere voice announced in Jackson's ear.

"Special Agent Dawkins, I need to authenticate a Roberta Pierce. She claims she's from the Denver office."

"Certainly." He cleared his throat. "Agent Pierce is a white female, approximately five-foot-eight, one-hundred-forty pounds. Strawberry blond hair hangs a few inches below her shoulders. Blue-green eyes, freckles at the top of her nose, and she speaks with a Midwestern accent."

"Thank you."

"Is there anything else I can do for you?" Dawkins asked.

"Yeah. Can you tell me if she's currently in Los Angeles?"

"I'm sorry, sir, but that information is confidential."

"I understand. Thank you."

"Convinced?" Roberta asked as Jackson closed his phone.

"No. You're still only one out of two."

Her shoulders slumped, and she opened her mouth to speak. He cut her off.

"Frankly, I don't care anymore. FBI, CIA, Mossad—it doesn't matter. All I care about is finding the Bible so I can get Abby back. And I've wasted enough time sorting out the program for this little performance."

Roberta blocked his path to the door. "I can help. You get Abby back, I mean."

"How?"

"Well, I'm assuming you don't have any other leads, or you wouldn't have called me, right?"

Jackson reluctantly nodded.

"Okay. Then I say we go after my attackers. I think they'll turn out to be the alleged Agents Andrews and Newton, but whoever they are, they have the Bible, right?"

Jackson sighed. She had a point. He could sort out who was who later. Right now, the priority was Abby.

"Okay, Alleged Agent Pierce, you—"

"Call me Robbie."

"Robbie. How unofficial. You got any way we can track these attackers of yours?"

She nodded. "They caught me off guard, as soon as I opened the door, so I didn't get a great look at them—not enough for a sketch artist or anything."

"Just enough to confirm they're the agents I wantingly described."

She let the remark pass. "But when I came to, I did see them get into a car and race out of here."

"Any chance you caught a plate?"

With a slight grin, Robbie nodded.

"Do you have a way to trace it?"

"Of course," she said, the grin widening. "After all, I do work for the FBI."

Chapter Nine

4:31 p.m.

AS SOON AS Robbie and Jackson merged onto the freeway, traffic bogged them down. Robbie, head rested on her hand, sighed for the fifth time. Then she looked over at Jackson. "How do you know Abby anyhow?"

"She hired me."

"Hired you. What, you're some sort of private investigator or something?"

Jackson nodded.

"And she hired you to steal the Bible from her brother, is that it?"

"I really can't say."

"I'm not going to bust you or anything. I'm just here to get the Bible too."

"Which brings up an interesting question," Jackson said. "Suppose we find it. You say it's a matter of national security that you possess it. So how do I give it back to Desmond in exchange for Abby?"

"We'll figure something out," Robbie answered. She spotted an opening and gunned her Ford Focus into the left lane. Jackson had offered to drive, but when she saw his car, Robbie had laughed and said she doubted it would make it all the way downtown. Besides, she got a mileage reimbursement.

For the next ten minutes, Robbie switched lanes, tailgated, grumbled under her breath, and honked her horn a couple of times. When northbound traffic on the 110 didn't improve, she cut across two lanes to exit on the Gardena Freeway. After a few blocks, she exited the freeway and announced, from there on, they would take their chances on city streets instead of the freeways.

"Answer me this," Jackson said. "Why would FBI agents take the Bible and hole up in a downtown hotel?"

Back at her hotel, as soon as Jackson had agreed to work with her, Robbie had explained that she had already put out a BOLO using the license plate of her attackers' car. Five minutes later, she'd received a phone call. The car had been spotted entering the parking garage of The Exquisite Hotel downtown. The timing had seemed a little convenient to Jackson, but Robbie and her "sources" were the only clue he had to go on. So here he was, riding with a potentially bogus FBI agent to one of L.A.'s swankier hotels to steal a four-century-old Bible from other potentially bogus FBI agents.

"They're not FBI agents," Robbie said in answer to his question. "And what would you expect an agent to do with the Bible?"

"I'm not sure," Jackson said, "but I would think they would take it to their office. Which brings up another question of why you were crashing at the beach eating a Mediterranean wrap and waffle fries."

"What are you, a psychic P.I.?" She stopped herself from cursing as the light at Rosecrans Avenue turned yellow, and she was forced to stop.

"I peeked in your trash while you were on the phone. Don't dodge the question. The jury's still out on you."

"I've been in L.A. for almost a week, running background on Desmond Vanderbilt, scouting, and prepping. Once I had the Bible, I went back to the hotel to figure out my next step."

"Why isn't that to take the Bible in?"

"Because I work out of the Denver office, remember?"

"So take it to L.A. Aren't you all on the same side?"

"Officially, yes. But I was working quasi-undercover, and except for pulling rank on you two, my objective was to stay undercover. Waltzing into the L.A. office with the Bible was never on the table."

"I see."

Robbie nodded, then floored the accelerator as the light changed.

"So how did you find out about the Bible?" Jackson asked.

"What do you mean?"

"I mean, Desmond always claimed the Bible was lost. How'd you know a week ago to come out to L.A. to scout and prep?"

"Working sources," she answered.

Jackson nodded with a smile. "Whatever you say."

She looked his way but didn't say anything.

Getting off the freeways hadn't done much to improve speed, and they continued to start and stop through South Los Angeles. Robbie took the opportunity to reach for her cell.

"Who you calling?" Jackson asked.

"Just making a reservation," she said. She raised the phone to her mouth. "This is Special Agent Donna Humphries with the FBI," she said in a voice that was deeper, a trace husky, and very authoritative. "We have reason to believe federal fugitives are staying in your hotel. Special Agent Roberta Pierce is almost on the scene. You're to give her full cooperation when she arrives."

Jackson watched with a grin.

"For now, do nothing," Robbie said. "Agent Pierce will handle things once she's on site. . . . Thank you."

"Federal fugitives?" Jackson asked.

"It helps to play it up a little," she said. "I didn't think Bible nabbers would spur them to action."

"Or allegedly fake FBI agents?"

She gave a snide smile. "Or that."

"So do you usually have to fake your authentication calls? I thought real FBI agents had somebody to actually make those calls."

"I told you, I'm outside my jurisdiction and undercover. I'm sort of winging this."

He nodded. They rode for a few minutes. "How'd you find us at the diner?" he asked when they hit another red light.

"Easy."

"I mean, why didn't you show up at my place or Abby's? Why the diner?"

Robbie paused just a beat. Maybe it was nothing. "I caught Abby as she was leaving. I figured she might have the Bible or might be meeting her partner." She shrugged. "Seemed like a wise choice to tail her and see what happened."

"You get lost?"

"Huh?"

"We were at the diner for close to half an hour before you showed up."

"I was doing recon."

He nodded.

"What?" she asked.

"What what?"

"That smirk."

"Nothing."

Robbie shook her head and gunned the engine as the light turned green, then immediately had to slow down as the car in front of her puttered along. She mumbled something that had started as a curse and morphed into nonsense. Jackson turned and looked out the window as means of diffusing the moment. It worked.

Traffic finally thinned, oddly enough, as they reached the Fashion District. Robbie began to hit all green lights and, with nothing to slow her down, drove like her rear bumper was on fire.

"You know your way around L.A. pretty well," Jackson said as she made a second sharp turn, onto Olive Street.

"I'm good with directions," she replied, cutting into the left lane. "And I did my homework."

He nodded.

"What? There it is again, that smirk."

"It's nothing. I'm just trying to figure out if I can believe anything you say."

"I thought we joined teams back at the hotel."

"We did. But I still like to know who's catching my passes."

Robbie smirked as she turned left onto 8th Street. "Who says you're the quarterback?"

"I do. Because you just threw a pick."

She glanced at him quizzically.

"The Exquisite is on the 700 block of Grand."

"Which is a one-way street south, I know," she said. "But 8th goes west, which means 7th goes east, which means I'd have to go all the way to 6th to go west again. This is quicker and gets us just as close."

Jackson nodded and hid a smirk. "If the entrance wasn't on Grand. And if 7th didn't run both ways," he said as Robbie pulled to the curb. He opened the door and got out. "It was zone out of a man look," he said across the top of the car, "but you still threw a pick."

Robbie shook her head and slammed her door. "Come on. And remember, my lead."

"Of course. I always defer to the FBI."

The Exquisite was a twenty-five-story, all glass exterior hotel that dominated downtown L.A.'s eastern skyline. Built just years earlier by a southwestern real estate magnate, it had made headlines for its price tag. Rooms went for a grand a night, suites for twice that. It made Jackson wonder why Andrews and Newton—FBI agents or not—were hanging out there.

The sun was setting in the southwestern sky, casting long shadows across the city streets and nearly blinding Jackson as it reflected off the gold plating around the hotel's front entrance. He followed a pace behind Robbie as she strutted across the marble floor of the atrium, ignoring the opulence of a flower garden and not-so-small waterfall in the center of the enormous space.

"Special Agent Roberta Pierce," she announced as she whipped out her badge and set it on the check-in counter.

A manager appeared out of nowhere and slid in front of the clerk. Jackson had never seen a hotel manager so elegantly dressed. His nameplate identified him as Jamison.

"Agent Pierce, we've been expecting you," the manager said, casting a cursory glance at her badge. "How may we assist you?"

Jackson nearly suggested he call the FBI to authenticate her credentials, but he didn't want the kick in the shins—or elsewhere—he was sure would follow.

"You have a car in your garage with a California plate," Robbie said. "Niner-Kilo-Romeo-Foxtrot-seven-seven-four. I need to know if that vehicle is indeed still here, who it's registered to, and which room they're staying in."

"Of course. One moment, please."

Robbie turned to Jackson with a very stern—professionally so—look as Jamison clicked away on a hidden computer.

"That car is registered to a Mr. and Mrs. Bryant. They're in a suite on the eighteenth floor."

"I assume you have a security camera on your parking garage exit."

"We do."

"Can you verify if the car is still here?"

"According to our records, Mr. and Mrs. Bryant checked in at 3:41 p.m. I'll run the footage back for the last two hours."

"I'd also like to see any images you have of them checking in. From that camera, perhaps," Robbie said, pointing up to a dark glass semicircle in the ceiling behind the counter.

"Of course," Jamison replied. "Please follow me."

They followed him behind the counter, through a door and down a narrow hallway, and into a room with TV screens lining the far wall and a bank of computers built into a dashboard in front of the TVs. Two men in mauve polo shirts sat in front of the computers as the TV screens flicked from image to image. There had to be a hundred different cameras around the hotel showing everything but the master bath of the penthouse suite.

"Hugo, please pull up camera G and roll the footage back to three-thirty," Jamison said.

A muscular Latino man in the leftmost of three chairs nodded and immediately attacked one of the computer keyboards. "On screen three," he said, directing everyone's attention to another bank of TV screens Jackson hadn't even noticed before, built into the dashboard with all three computers.

"Anything we're looking for in particular, Mr. Hampton?" Hugo asked as the footage began to roll.

"A California vehicle with a license plate of . . ." Jamison looked to Robbie.

"Niner-Kilo-Romeo-Foxtrot-seven-seven-four."

A moment later, Hugo stopped the footage. "There you are. Looks like a new-model Lexus."

"Is it still in the garage?"

Hugo turned back to his computer, and the footage resumed. For several minutes, they watched cars come and go in fast motion, none of them a Lexus with matching plates. When the footage hit real-time, Hugo announced the car must still be in the garage.

"Now can you bring up camera four, starting at the same time?" Jamison asked.

Hugo obliged, switching the feed to a camera showing the front desk. He paused the footage when Robbie flatly announced, "That's them."

Jackson acknowledged Robbie's stern look in his direction with a nod. It was them. "Agents" Ellen Andrews and Stanley Newton.

"Is there anything else you need to see?" Jamison asked.

"No. You said they're on the eighteenth floor?"

"That is correct."

"I'm going to need a key to their suite."

"Of course. Please follow me. Thank you, Hugo." Jamison led them back to the front counter where he quickly activated a keycard. "Room 1843. Any of the elevators on either side of the conservatory will take you there."

Robbie pocketed the key. "Thank you very much for your help."

"If there's anything else we can do, please do not hesitate to ask."

She nodded and started across the lobby, past the fountain that was made to appear to water the garden. About to turn to the rear bank of elevators, she stopped, grabbed Jackson's arm, and pulled him to the left.

"What?"

"Did you see that guy, over there on the bench?"

Jackson sneaked a quick peek over his shoulder. "What about him?"

"He was at the ball last night."

"You sure?"

"He was the Joker," she replied. "From *Batman*."

Jackson remembered Batman—in fact, he'd spotted him with Bianca the vampire, also known as Robbie. But Jackson hadn't seen the Joker.

"A friend of yours?" he asked.

"No."

"Let me guess . . . Houston FBI?"

"Very funny. Come on."

She punched the up arrow, and instantly one of the elevators dinged. She herded Jackson into it and closed the door before anyone else could join them.

"What's the plan?" he asked as they whooshed up to the eighteenth floor.

"Simple. We get them out of the room, then search it. There are only so many places to hide something in a hotel room."

"Yeah, such as a safe."

"Hotel safes are easy."

"You got a plan for getting them out of the room?"

"Of course."

"Well then, I'll just recline my seat and enjoy the show," Jackson said.

"You don't like the idea?"

"Did I say that?"

"No, but your sarcasm speaks volumes."

"So I've been told."

"I'm open to better ideas."

"You're the real, true, legitimate FBI agent, right? So why not knock on the door, show them your badge, and confiscate the Bible? It worked once before."

"Because people who would fake being FBI agents wouldn't comply with a real FBI agent. Especially if they're CIA."

"I guess you would know."

She lowered her eyes at him.

"Like I said, I'll enjoy the ride."

The elevator dinged and the doors opened on the eighteenth floor. Jackson allowed Robbie to go first and followed her into a hallway that was warmer and more inviting than his living room.

"First thing, we find the room," Robbie said. "Then we find a vantage point from which we can see them leave."

He nodded and followed her to the far end of the hallway. Room 1843 was the last door on the right before the hallway turned ninety degrees to the left. Robbie and Jackson followed the hallway and ducked into a small alcove housing a door to a maintenance room. It provided them a sheltered place from which to observe the door to room 1843.

"Now what?" Jackson asked. "Pull a fire alarm?"

"In a manner of speaking," Robbie said, reaching for her phone. She was about to dial when Jackson kicked her shoe with his. She looked up with a frown, but then followed his gaze down the hall, where the door to room 1843 had just opened.

Retreating as far as possible into the alcove, they watched as Andrews and Newton/Mr. and Mrs. Bryant hurried out of their hotel room and down the hallway. Wide-eyed, Robbie closed her phone. "What do you make of that?"

"I didn't hear a fire alarm. Let's go."

"No. Let's see where they go. If they have the Bible with them, we can't afford to lose it."

"What about searching the room?"

"You in shape?" she asked.

"Ish."

"You take the stairs. I'll watch the elevator and tell you where they get off. Then I'll search the room."

"And what if they go straight to the parking garage?"

"Then we'll forget the room, and I'll take the next elevator down and meet you at the car."

Jackson retrieved his phone, dialed Robbie's number, and took off for the stairwell. Truth be told, he was not real keen about chasing FBI agents, and even less enthused if they were fraudulent agents. But he had come this far, and Abby's life was potentially at stake.

Two floors down, he raised the phone to his ear. "Where they at?"

"Fourteen. You?"

"Fifteen and a half."

"You don't sound in shape."

He saved energy by not telling her to shut up. He doubted he could run down seventeen flights of stairs as fast as an elevator could drop the same distance, but that was okay, as he didn't want to burst out of the stairwell as Andrews and Newton stepped off the elevator. He just had to be close enough to spot them and tail them.

Jackson informed Robbie when he reached the tenth floor, and she told him the elevator had continued without stopping and was at five. He willed himself to run faster, and as a result, barely saw the figure climbing the stairs before he crashed into him.

They both tumbled sideways into the wall. Jackson bruised his shoulder but managed to avoid cracking his head. The other guy wasn't so lucky and fell to the stairwell floor with a curse.

"Hey, man, I'm sor—"

Jackson stopped as the man slowly turned, rising to his knees. It was the guy from the bench in the atrium, A.K.A. the Joker.

Chapter Ten

5:55 p.m.

FOR SEVERAL SECONDS, the man stared at Jackson, comprehension clearly showing in his dark green eyes. Then he lunged. Jackson sidestepped, and an attempt to grab his throat turned into an open-fisted punch to the shoulder. Jackson had no angle to throw a counterpunch but did have enough leverage to shove the man into the wall, knocking him off balance and to his knees again.

The guy was slow to get up, and it dawned on Jackson in that instant that he was likely tired from running up ten flights of stairs. Knowing that his opponent was more gassed than he was gave Jackson renewed energy. He sized the Joker up and, at the last second, went for a roundhouse kick instead of a punch to what looked like an iron jaw. It connected, and the guy slumped, not unconscious, but no longer a threat. After stooping to pick up his cell phone, Jackson continued down the stairs.

Heaving for air, he slowed at the landing between stories eight and seven and raised the phone. "Robbie."

"What's wrong with you? Are you in the lobby?"

"Slight delay," Jackson panted. "I just knocked the smile off the Joker."

"What? Never mind. Somebody else just broke into their room. Broke in."

"Where are Andrews and Newton?"

"They just hit the parking garage. I'm on my way down."

"Get the car," Jackson said, forcing himself to continue down the stairs. "I'll see if I can slow them."

Taking the stairs two at a time, he nearly sprained an ankle twice and was lightheaded when he reached the garage level. Andrews and Newton had at least a minute, maybe two on him. That meant they were very possibly already in their car and on the way to the exit. So he took off running.

Having never yet seen two parking garages laid out the same, Jackson had no idea how to navigate this one to most quickly get to the exit. But being on foot gave him an advantage in that he didn't have to follow the lanes. He was also aided by the fact that it was an underground garage, and he had entered it on the same level as the exit.

Jackson only had to jump across one barricade and jog up a short ramp to reach the gate. It was unmanned, requiring a scan of a claim check to exit. Still seeing no sign of Andrews and Newton's Lexus, Jackson reached for his wallet. He dug into a back pocket, behind the cash, where he kept various membership cards. At present, his library card struck him as least valuable, so he jammed it into the opening where the claim check was to go, hoping a foreign object in the slot would slow Andrews and Newton's exit.

The machine hummed strangely, then kicked the card out. Jackson dug around and found a Blockbuster card he had neglected to throw away, and stuffed both cards in at the same time. Two cards did the trick, as neither was spit back out, and he could see them wedged in the opening. Hearing a car approaching, Jackson ducked under the gate and out onto the sidewalk.

The sun had set, leaving a faint glow in the western sky. All around him, the lights of downtown Los Angeles were coming to life. Jackson felt as if he'd come out of a wormhole and was suddenly thrust into normalcy again.

The yelling emanating from his hand drew him back in. He lifted the phone to his ear.

"Jackson, what—Where are you?" Robbie asked.

"Outside the garage."

"Where are they?"

"I don't know." It dawned on him that Andrews and Newton could have used valet parking. The footage of the Lexus entering the garage hadn't shown clearly how many occupants had been inside the car, and Jackson guessed the valets parked in the garage as well. That meant Andrews and Newton could have called the concierge or the valet as they were leaving their room and picked up their car as soon as they made it down. But in that case, they would have taken the elevator to the lobby instead of the garage.

Robbie pulled Jackson back to the present. "I'm almost to the car," she said. "I'll pick you up out front."

Jackson heard a whirring sound, then a vroom as a silver car burst out of the garage opening. A Lexus.

Jackson quickly raised the phone to his ear to block as much of his face as possible. "Hurry. They just came out," he said, peeking at the car in an effort to identify the driver or passenger. All he could tell through tinted windows was that there were two occupants. "I'll meet you at the corner," he added and took off running.

Traffic was heavy on Grand Avenue, and the Lexus didn't get very far. It looked to Jackson as if the driver tried to cross three lanes of traffic onto 8th Street, but couldn't make it and had to continue south. Trying to keep an eye on the Lexus, Jackson flagged down Robbie and jumped into the car as she slowed almost to a stop.

"Where?" she barked.

"Go straight a block," he said, glancing over his shoulder at traffic on 8th, which wouldn't let her get over anyhow. The light had changed, and they barreled through the intersection. "South here," he said, pointing to the next street, and Robbie induced several horn blares as she cut over and squealed tires turning onto Hope Street.

"They wanted to go west," Jackson said.

"Which means—"

"Olympic."

Two blocks south, Robbie turned right onto Olympic. Jackson leaned forward, trying to pick out a silver Lexus in the midst of city traffic. Robbie drove like a maniac, which brought plenty of cars into view, but few into focus.

"There!" Jackson shouted as the light at Figueroa Street turned from yellow to red. He pointed around the corner, where a silver Lexus had just made the turn north. Ignoring the light—and northbound traffic—Robbie cranked the wheel of her Focus. Jackson, still not buckled in, nearly fell into her lap as she slid into the center lane. She floored the accelerator again, and they took off, less than half a block behind the Lexus.

"All right, Danica, slow down," Jackson said. "We got 'em."

"What did you mean about the Joker?" she asked as she merged into the left lane, mirroring the Lexus.

"I ran into him in the stairwell. He was going up."

"That doesn't make any sense."

"Why not?"

"What would he be doing in the stairwell?"

"Going upstairs."

Robbie sighed. "I mean, if he was with the guy breaking into their room, why wasn't he with him?"

"Did you recognize him?"

"I didn't get a good look. Could have even been a woman." They coasted to a stop one car behind the Lexus at the corner of Figueroa and 8th, in the shadow of 777 Tower. Figuratively. In reality, there were no more shadows and only the faintest of glows in the western sky. Somehow, the onset of evening reminded Jackson why he was part of this absurd palaver instead of at home on his deck—Abby.

"If he was the lookout," Robbie continued, "he would have stayed in the lobby."

"The Joker?"

"Right. And if he was with the guy who broke in, why was he late to the party?"

"Maybe there are two other groups after the Bible?"

"Can't be."

He shrugged.

The light turned, and the Lexus, and thus Robbie, turned west onto 8th Street. Less than two blocks later, she followed the Lexus onto the onramp to State Route 110.

"Another question," she said. "What spooked them?"

"Andrews and Newton?"

"Uh-huh."

"Not us?"

"How could we have?"

"Maybe the Joker was working for them and spotted us."

"Then why'd they wait so long to bolt?"

"Grabbing pilfered valuables?"

"More likely he made the guy who actually hit their room," she said. "But it still doesn't explain why he was climbing the stairs."

"Or who he is."

"I tell you who I'm betting he's not."

"FBI?"

Robbie turned and grinned without saying a word.

They cruised past downtown at a pretty good pace, slowing as they reached the Bill Keane Memorial Interchange, A.K.A. "The Stacks." It connected the 110 to the 101 and brought even more traffic into play. Even so, Robbie kept close behind Andrews and Newton in the Lexus.

They passed Chavez Ravine, home of Dodger Stadium. Still close behind the Lexus, they entered the southernmost of the Figueroa Street Tunnels. Measuring from 130 to 755 feet in length, the tunnels enclosed only the northbound lanes of the 110 and, for whatever reason, always seemed busier than the rest of the freeway.

Accordingly, Jackson and Robbie's entrance into the tunnel was accompanied by a barrage of brake lights. Robbie sighed as they coasted forward, releasing her white-knuckle grip on the steering wheel. Jackson took the opportunity to finally buckle his seatbelt, for when the chaos resumed.

"So what do you think," he asked, "where are they—"

A tremendous whoomp shook the ground in front of them. For a moment, Jackson thought he was experiencing an earthquake. But as the concussion shook the car, his eyes were drawn to a fireball just in front of them as the Lexus flipped onto its side and flew into the sidewall of the tunnel.

Robbie, like everyone else in the tunnel, slammed on her brakes. Some were faster at it than others, and the crunches of bumpers smashing echoed through the tunnel. Blaring car alarms accompanied the screech of scraping metal as the Lexus slid on its side and then on its top toward the north end of the tunnel. It finally stopped, facing at an angle, blocking the left two lanes of traffic. Beside it, a black van had spun during the explosion and blocked off the right two lanes. Combined, they left nowhere for traffic to go and created a very long fuse if the fire licking at the Lexus somehow spread.

"What was that?" Robbie asked.

"I don't know. I didn't see a trail. Then again, I wasn't looking."

"Bomb?"

"Timing seems convenient," Jackson said. He pushed open his door and got out. Naturally, some idiot too far back to see what had happened was honking. Car alarms were still resounding through the cavern, and the crackling of fire distracted Jackson from his scan of the tunnel. He had been looking to see if anyone appeared to be watching the accident with anything akin to appreciation, but quickly realized two people had been in the car. FBI agents or frauds, their lives were in danger.

And so, theoretically, was the Bible that could save Abby's life.

Robbie apparently had the same idea. After wedging her way out her door, she joined Jackson at the front of the car. But neither of them went any farther.

Two figures dressed head to toe in black had appeared from around the front of the van that blocked the two right lanes of the freeway. They hurried to the overturned Lexus and, oblivious to the flames, began rummaging through it. They jerked open doors, pulled a body from the vehicle, and even got the trunk open, albeit upside down.

Jackson stood frozen in place, stunned at what he was seeing until he saw a flash to his left. It was Robbie, dodging the vehicle in front of them and charging toward the Lexus. He followed, but before they were halfway to the car, the two figures found what they were looking for.

A woman's purse.

They turned and took off running, exiting the tunnel and heading north on foot on the empty freeway. Jackson again followed Robbie, who had changed course to chase down the duo. She hurdled the front fender of the van, he skirted it, and together they tried to close the gap. They were gaining a little when one of the two figures stopped and turned around.

Jackson realized the figure was leveling a gun at them, and gave Robbie a shove to the side, behind a small pickup that had pulled over after the explosion. He took one last step to push off and leaped after her, just as a trio of gunshots sounded. He landed hard on the same shoulder that had crashed into the stairwell wall back at The Exquisite, but aside from some skin off his elbow, he was none the worse for wear. Robbie appeared in similar shape, and Jackson quickly clambered to his knees and peeked around the rear of the truck.

The duo was making tracks again. What with having to dive behind vehicles to avoid bullets, Jackson knew he had no chance of catching them. So he helped Robbie to her feet, made sure she was okay, and jogged back toward the tunnel.

Emergency sirens were already beginning to wail in the distance. Jackson had no idea how EMTs or firefighters planned to get to the north end of the tunnel. They certainly weren't going to find a path through the tunnel—not anytime soon. Everyone had left their vehicles and rushed forward on foot to see what was going on, and a scene that a minute ago was bizarre and surreal was now just chaotic.

Several people were beating at the flames on the Lexus with jackets or sweatshirts. Another tried to douse them with his water bottle. Good

Samaritans had pulled a second body from the car and helped the man pulled out by the figures in black get away from the car. Despite rumpled and torn clothes and bruised and blood-streaked bodies, Jackson had no trouble identifying the two victims.

Alleged FBI Agents Andrews and Newton.

Everybody was talking at once. What happened? Is everyone okay? Was it terrorism? One voice stood out among the rest. Andrews, while dabbing blood from a cut on her forehead, announced to Newton that they had taken her purse. "They have it," she said to her dazed and sullen partner. Jackson did not think "it" referred to her new tube of lipstick or her Kohl's card.

The sirens were so loud they threatened to shatter eardrums, and when Jackson glanced over his shoulder, he realized why. Emergency crews were coming from the north, having entered the freeway at the next exit. Two fire trucks and an ambulance, with the sound of more in the distance.

With the arrival of the emergency crews, the chaos only increased. The same questions were posed by the frenzied onlookers, but now to the paramedics and firefighters attempting to control the situation. Are we under attack? What happened? Somebody threw out the word "terrorist," another the phrase "chemical agent." The panic level rose.

Another fire truck arrived, and several firefighters shoved the black van aside to make room for half a dozen more firefighters to get into the tunnel and surround the Lexus. As Jackson and dozens of others stood and watched, they doused the Lexus, and a pair of cops fresh to the scene began herding people back to their vehicles and trying to open at least one lane of traffic.

Andrews and Newton had been mobbed by the paramedics and shuttled to an ambulance, and the firefighters had the Lexus surrounded. With nowhere else to go, Jackson headed back to Robbie's Focus. Somehow, amid all the chaos and noise and the residual confusion, he heard his cell phone ringing.

Plugging his other ear with his finger, Jackson shouted his hello into the phone.

"Jackson Douglas?" an unfamiliar voice asked.

"Yeah. Who's this?"

"Mr. Douglas, this is Special Agent Bradley Steele. I'm with the Albany office of the FBI. You left a message for Agent Joseph, but he's in Belize through the weekend getting some much needed R&R, and I'm covering for him. Sorry, I just got your message. You had a question about another agent?"

"That's right."

"Robyn Pearson?"

"Actually, I've learned that's an alias. Her real name is Roberta Pierce. A.K.A. Robbie."

"Say that again."

"Pierce. Papa-India-Echo-Romeo-Charlie-Echo."

"Copy that. One second."

Jackson looked around as he waited. Where was Robbie anyhow?

"Mr. Douglas?"

"Yeah."

"There is no Roberta Pierce with the FBI."

"She says she works out of Denver."

"No, sir. No Roberta Pierce—or Robyn Pearson, for that matter, with the FBI."

"Thank you, Agent Steele. Wait. Agent Steele?"

"Still here."

"Can you check an Agent Ellen Andrews and Agent Stanley Newton too?"

"One minute."

Jackson took another look around but didn't spot Robbie. Or whoever she was.

"Okay, there's no Stanley Newton, but there is an Ellen Andrews. You want a description?"

"Please."

"Age forty, five-five, a buck twenty, long brown—"

"That's good enough," Jackson said. It clearly wasn't her. "Thanks, Agent Steele."

Jackson closed the phone on Steele's response and headed for Robbie's car.

Only it wasn't there.

Bottling the rage that wanted to come out in a scream, Jackson turned back toward the north end of the tunnel. He pushed his way past several rubberneckers and a police officer telling him to go the other way.

He was just in time to see the back end of a Ford Focus squeeze past the black van and a fire engine and accelerate away from the chaos.

Chapter Eleven

7:14 p.m.

SOMEHOW—JACKSON WASN'T quite sure—the authorities got the idea that he knew more about what was going on than the average Joe stuck in the southern Figueroa Street Tunnel. They were right, of course, but Jackson didn't know how they'd come to suspect his involvement.

They'd started by asking him the usual array of questions—Where were you in the tunnel? Could you see exactly what happened? Were you able to identify the black-clad figures who ransacked the Lexus? It actually took them twenty questions to get such basic information from Jackson, by which time the two right lanes of traffic had opened again. Meanwhile, crime scene investigators were going over the burned-out Lexus with a fine-toothed comb. They should have no trouble determining how the explosion started, Jackson reasoned, whether it was internal or external, a bomb or a missile or a well-aimed bullet. They certainly weren't getting anything by asking the observers they could detain the same questions they were asking Jackson, and his frustration began to mount. Every minute was a minute that "Robbie" and the Bible got farther away.

"Where's the van?" Jackson asked.

"I beg your pardon," a Detective Velasquez asked. His name and his accent indicated he was Hispanic, but his skin was lighter than Jackson's.

"There was a black van that turned sideways after the explosion. It blocked the right two lanes. And . . ." He closed his eyes to be sure. "I don't think it had a license plate, now that I think about it."

"There's no black van here," Velasquez replied, looking around him.

"I see that. Hence my questions."

Velasquez shot him a quick glare.

"Look, Detective, I've told you everything I know, all right? I'd really like to get out of here."

"Hold on a minute. Tell me more about this van. Was it a full-size, a minivan, what make and model? Anything."

"Uh, it was more like one of those delivery vans."

"So more of a truck?"

"No, it was a van. European style, low in the front, high in the back."

"Any markings? A delivery company, maybe?"

"Plain black."

"You see the driver?"

"No. I didn't even notice it until after the explosion. It was turned sideways, blocking traffic."

"Do you have any reason to believe it was involved in the explosion?" Velasquez asked.

Jackson shrugged. "Not really. I just know those two guys in black came from somewhere. The van blocked traffic, enabled them to get away on foot. It's a theory."

Velasquez nodded. "You gave the officer your contact info, right?"

"Yeah. Can I go?"

"Not quite," he answered. "Somebody else wants to talk to you."

"Who?"

"Well, that's where it gets interesting. You know who was driving that overturned Lexus?"

Jackson paused a beat. He had hedged around the question before and now shook his head. "I honestly have no idea, Detective."

Velasquez nodded. "They're a couple of federal agents. And they want to talk to you."

"Me?"

He nodded again.

"Why's that?"

"You'll have to ask them," Velasquez replied. "They're over in the far ambulance."

Jackson thought about trying to slip away without talking to Andrews and Newton, but the last thing he needed was to go from a person of interest to a suspect on the lam. If he wasn't already a suspect.

A hundred feet out of the tunnel, parked off the side of the road against a rock- and moss-covered retaining wall, was a second ambulance. The rear doors were open, and Andrews sat on the floor, legs dangling out, while a technician monitored her heart rate and blood pressure. Newton leaned against the rear door, the cockeyed grin back on his face.

"You wanted to see me?" Jackson asked.

Newton straightened a little. Andrews outright bristled. "Did you do this?" she asked.

"Blow up your car? Uh, no."

"What were you doing in the tunnel?"

"Driving."

"Bull."

"Ma'am," the technician said, "I need you—"

"I am fine, all right? You have taken my blood pressure four times. I am fine."

"Clearly," Jackson said.

"I wouldn't press her," Newton said with a glance at the technician. Reluctantly, he removed the blood pressure cuff from her arm.

"Can you give us a minute?" Andrews asked. When the tech was gone, she said, "All right, the truth."

"You first," Jackson said. "You told me you were FBI."

"We are."

"You called and confirmed, remember?" Newton said.

"Yeah, I remember. But I've been running into a lot of FBI agents today who aren't really FBI agents, and they all can prove the other guy isn't too."

"You're talking about Robyn Pearson?" Andrews asked.

"What's in a name?"

"Look, we don't know who this woman is," Andrews said. "But we are with the FBI."

"We're done here," Jackson said as he turned to leave.

"Wait."

He didn't wait. He instead forced Newton to catch up with him and take him by the arm.

"Let go of me," Jackson said, wrenching his arm free.

"Do not force us to arrest you," Andrews called out.

"You can't arrest me," Jackson said, his voice rising. Frankly, he didn't mind if Detective Velasquez or one of the other cops overheard. "You're not FBI. I know a guy, an agent in Albany. A legit agent. And he says you don't exist, unless you've had a recent growth spurt and some miracle salve to fight off aging. So either you level with me, or I'm walking."

Andrews exhaled and tried to kill Jackson with her eyes. But then she nodded.

Reluctantly, he walked back to the ambulance.

"Understand, this goes nowhere," Andrews said.

"Much like the rest of my day."

She glared at him again. "We're with the CIA."

"I don't suppose you can prove that anyway."

"No. We're undercover."

"And why are you posing as FBI?"

"Because the CIA scares people. And, technically, the Agency isn't allowed to operate on U.S. soil."

"And yet here you are."

"I told you, this is a matter of—"

"National security. Just what is in that Bible?"

"We're not allowed to say," Newton said.

"Of course you're not."

"We need to find the Bible," Andrews said. "Do you have any idea who stole it?"

"So far, Robbie and then you guys. I'm foggy after that."

"What were you doing in the tunnel?"

"I already told you."

"Okay, wise guy, why were you driving in the tunnel? And spare me your humor. Why were you following us?"

"What do you think?"

"I think you had better stay out of this. This is a matter of national security—an urgent matter. And we do not need you interfering and getting in the way. Is that clear?"

"Oh, perfectly."

"Good. Now Agent Newton will take your statement."

"My statement? I've already given my statement to the local LEOs. Get it from them."

"We have questions they may not have asked."

"Let me ask a question first. What does the CIA do if an uncooperative witness decides to walk away?"

"Try it and find out."

Jackson sighed, his eyes matching the hostility in Andrews'. But he went with Newton to a black SUV parked another hundred feet up ahead, closer to the second tunnel than the first. On the other side of the highway, a side road entered traffic. To Jackson's left, a guardrail and an iron fence blocked the way to another road that started under the bridge holding southbound traffic on the 110 before it continued west.

The figures in black had left on foot. If they'd had a vehicle stashed just beyond the iron fence, it would have made for a perfect getaway, with no way for any vehicle to follow them.

But Andrews and Newton had only left The Exquisite fifteen to twenty minutes before the attack. This hadn't been a drive-by shooting; it had been a well-planned and well-timed assault. And it had started with something that spooked Andrews and Newton from the hotel followed by an unsuccessful search of their room.

Jackson tried to interject some questions of his own in Newton's barrage, but the cocksure agent was having none of it. At most, he smirked at Jackson's questions; most often, though, he just proceeded with his next query. Jackson gave him little, and after twenty minutes, Newton finally gave up.

"Am I free to go?"

"Yeah."

"Do I need to not leave town or anything?"

"Were you planning to?"

"Right now, I've got half a mind to leave and never come back."

"Maybe that's a good idea," Newton said. "Just stay out of our way."

Before Andrews and Newton changed their minds, Jackson nodded and started walking. He hopped the guardrail and fence and headed west under the southbound bridge. He didn't expect to find any evidence of a getaway, but he never knew. And he had to find a cab anyhow since his ride had taken off in futile pursuit. Or to find a phone booth to change into her alter ego.

Jackson had no idea what to make of Robyn/Robbie anymore. She'd lied to him twice. And despite his wisecracks, he'd gone along with her both times. If once bit made twice shy, what did twice bit make? Stupid? In any case, Jackson was done with her. She had no better clue to find the Bible than he did now.

As he walked, Jackson kept his eyes out for a Caltrans traffic camera. Mouse had hacked into the system once, and could maybe do it again. But Jackson didn't see any traffic cameras, or any other cameras—nothing to tell him where the black figures had gone. If they'd even taken this route.

The neighborhood was sleepy, and Jackson realized he would have to call for a cab instead of finding one idling by the curb. And then another idea hit him. He dug out his phone and dialed a familiar number.

"What's up?" Reggie Cameron's baritone voice resounded through Jackson's earpiece.

"Hey, Hoss. You busy?"

"No more than ever. What's up?"

"Oh, not much. Just chilling in Chavez Ravine and could use a lift."

"Chavez Ravine? What are you doing out there, camping out for season tickets?"

"Very long story, but the short version is a bipolar fake FBI agent stranded me. You up to picking me up? If not, I'll call a cab."

"Yeah, I can swing it. You need anything?"

"Couple Quarter Pounders wouldn't hurt."

"You know, it kind of insults a restaurant owner when you ask him to pick up grub from another place."

"I'm fighting the clock too."

"On my way, J. Where exactly do I find you?"

Jackson told him to call when he turned off I-10, as he had to figure out where exactly he was. He clapped his phone shut and wandered west, trying to find a good intersection to which to direct Reggie. He also mulled some more.

Not counting himself, there were at least three other groups after the Bible. Agent Andrews and Newton, CIA or otherwise. Robbie, whatever her name was and whoever she was. And the guys in black. Then there were the guys who had broken into Andrews and Newton's room after they left. And the Joker. Were those latter three all working together? Did Robbie have a partner who was cluing her in? She certainly had someone who could mimic the resources of the FBI.

Jackson arrived at the corner of Academy Road and Solano Canyon Drive, just north of one of five Dodger Stadium gates. Concluding it was as good of a place as any, he sat down on the curb and asked himself what

Magnum or Rockford or Gibbs would do? This was the place all TV detectives always found themselves, with no available clues. So they had to backtrack, find their last hint of a clue, and follow it. Somehow, it always led them back to the scent of their prey, and by the end of the hour.

There was just too much that didn't add up. How did all these people know about the Bible? Just from Desmond's almost announcement last night? If so, why had all of them been there? Abby said Desmond invited who he wanted. So unless these people were all potential buyers in his planned auction, how could they have gotten in?

Unless they had started in. Maybe Desmond wasn't relying on Jackson's desire to save Abby to get the Bible. Maybe he'd sent his own group of thugs after it. The Joker had been at the party, not as an invite, but as one of Desmond's people undercover, and was hunting the Bible as a contingency in case Jackson didn't procure it. It was plausible. Abby said Desmond wouldn't get his hands dirty, that he would let his lawyers and accountants fight his battles. Thugs too, maybe?

It was all theory, conjecture, something short of a hunch. The bottom line was that Jackson didn't know anything. Anything except the fact that Abby's life was in the balance, and he had to find some way to find the Bible.

Reggie arrived at eight-thirty. It had now been two hours since the explosion and Robbie's disappearance. Needing to get to his own vehicle, Jackson directed Reggie to take him back to Robbie's hotel in Hermosa Beach. Maybe he'd get lucky, and she'd be there, and he could let out some frustration by wringing her neck.

Reggie had come through with burgers, fries, and—knowing Jackson—a chocolate shake. While he ate and slurped, Jackson caught up his best friend, sometimes advisor, and occasional wingman on events of the last twenty-four hours. Reggie drove in an almost reclined state, one hand on the wheel, the other reaching for his own burger on his lap and fries in the center console of his black Hummer H3. The vehicle fit the man, who stood six-three and weighed almost two-fifty. The tats up his arms and on his neck combined with his hulking presence to give him a scary appearance that couldn't be farther from the truth—unless you got between him and someone he cared about.

"So she's not FBI?" Reggie asked when Jackson was done.

"No."

"And they're CIA?"

"I doubt it."

"No?"

"No. She called it the Agency. Everybody inside calls it the Company."

Reggie raised an eyebrow at him.

"And something else about them just feels wrong. For all I know they're Russian agents—KGB or SVU or cosmonauts."

"Cosmonauts went into space, J."

"Whatever. At this point, I don't know who anybody is."

"So what you gonna do, man?" Reggie asked.

"Depends if you feel like raiding Desmond's place to see if Abby's there."

Reggie looked his way, his eyes admitting he was willing if Jackson was.

"It's a last resort," Jackson said.

"Just say the word."

The Hermosa Beach Pier wasn't the party scene that the more famous Santa Monica Pier was, especially in winter, but there still was a hubbub of activity around the beach and Pier Avenue. Jackson had Reggie drop him off by the pier, promising to call if he needed anything else. Reggie said he'd send him an expense bill for the burgers and gas money. Jackson laughed, knowing Reggie never would.

Jackson used the four-block walk to The Breakers Hotel to clear his mind. He realized that maybe Robbie could still provide him a lead. If she wasn't FBI—and it would take J. Edgar Hoover to convince him she was—then she had to be somebody. Was she CIA too? Or one of the dozen other agencies that were out there? A private investigator? A treasure hunter/art collector? While Jackson was sick of trying to figure out identities, hers might establish how she actually knew what she knew. If she was with some governmental agency, Jackson could buy that sources and chatter or whatever the current buzzword was for intelligence explained her knowledge. For all he knew, the CIA or the FBI or the NSA had bugged Desmond's phone.

But if she wasn't legit, and he doubted she was, how did she know? If Jackson could find her source of intel, it might give him another lead to pursue—someone higher up the food chain who could point him toward the Bible or toward another way to rescue Abby. It was a long shot, but short of he and Reggie launching an invasion, the only one he had. And long shots always worked out for the guys on TV.

All seemed quiet as Jackson climbed the steps to the second-floor corridor of The Breakers. No light peeked out from cracks around the windows to indicate anyone was in room 204. He knocked and waited, then knocked again. When Robbie didn't answer after a third knock, Jackson glanced around. He could see the lights of the pier from the veranda, almost hear the shouts and laughs and the music. But here all was quiet.

So he picked the lock. Fortunately, The Breakers still used actual keys, and fortunately, Jackson had thought to retrieve his picks from his car before leaving with Robbie earlier. It took him about a minute to pick the lock, and he slipped into Robbie's empty room without spotting another soul.

First thing, he turned the deadbolt. If Robbie came back, he wanted a barrier. Then he flipped on the light and made sure the drapes were completely drawn. Satisfied, he began snooping.

Two small duffel bags were full of clothes and basic personal belongings. There were no secret compartments with alternate IDs or techno spy gadgets. He moved to the closet, where he found one pantsuit, for posing as a serious FBI agent, not the undercover kind. The bathroom contained the usual female products. Nothing out of the usual.

Robbie's laptop was on the dresser, and Jackson lifted the screen. It was locked and needed a password. Jackson exhaled and tried to think. From what he knew about Robbie, what would she use as a password? Alias? Fraud? Gotcha?

He'd seen an Iowa Hawkeyes sweatshirt in Robbie's duffel, and tried both "Iowa" and "Hawkeyes." Neither worked. He tried them all lowercase, still with no luck. He tried adding a 1 at the end. He sighed. Just because his password was "fighton," it didn't mean everybody used some derivative of their school nickname, fight song, or mascot.

Mascot.

USC had defeated Iowa in the Rose Bowl just a few weeks ago, and Jackson had heard something about a Herkey Hawkeye. He gave it a whirl. Nothing. Was Herky spelled without the E?

Bingo.

The computer loaded, showing a single farmhouse and windmill atop a rolling hill, bathed in late afternoon sunlight under a perfect blue sky. Iowa countryside?

There were no icons on her desktop, save for the Recycle Bin. It was empty. Jackson searched through her programs, found nothing unusual, and then noticed a Firefox window open in the system tray. He clicked to open the window and saw it was a mapping site, showing an address in Pico Rivera. He committed the address to memory, then clicked the back button a few times. It led him to a Google search screen, with the name Luis Cortez typed in the search bar.

Jackson scanned the links the search engine had pulled, but none of them jumped out at him, and none of them appeared to have been clicked. Jackson mulled the name for a few minutes. Other than sounding vaguely familiar, it didn't mean anything to him.

He tried some of his own searches: "Luis Cortez Bible." "Luis Cortez Vanderbilt." "Luis Cortez FBI." They all generated some links, but nothing that looked pertinent.

As a last resort, Jackson checked out Robbie's history. There wasn't much there; a paranoid fake federal agent would likely delete her browsing history frequently.

Jackson was left with nothing but a name and address. Maybe they went together; maybe they didn't. He tried Mouse's phone again, still with no answer. Surely he wasn't working all day, was he? More likely lost in a virtual world.

Next Jackson called Maggie. A reporter with the *Los Angeles Times*, she could often dig up information for him. And finally, somebody answered one of his calls.

"Jack, what's up?"

"I need a favor, Maggie."

"How unusual."

"Would it be crass for me to mention saving your life a few months ago? Or that little loan?"

"I told you, I'm paying you back."

"Consider this the interest."

Jackson could picture the look she was giving him through the phone, and it very much made him wish he wasn't busy chasing Bibles and rescuing kidnapping victims so he could spend his Saturday night with her. He'd have to settle for a few minutes on the phone.

"Does the name Luis Cortez mean anything to you?" he asked.

"Luis Cortez? Nothing rings a bell. Want me to check the archives?"

"Would you?"

"Sure." Jackson heard a TV in the background, some rustling, then Maggie asked, "So what you been up to all day?"

"Chasing the wind."

"Huh?"

"Sorry, it's an Old Testament reference."

"I know, from Ecclesiastes. I wasn't dropped onto earth last night. I meant, huh as in how so? Work?"

"Yeah?"

Her tone changed. "With Abby?"

"Until she was kidnapped."

"What?"

"I know—my life consists of rescuing kidnapped women."

"I'm sorry, Jack. I didn't know."

"It's fine."

Neither of them spoke for a while.

"Okay, I'm in," she said. "Luis Cortez. E-Z?"

"Yeah."

"Um . . . a Luis Cortez, a Venezuelan-born baseball player for the Tigers. Oh, wait, that's minor leagues. Let me see . . . Here we go. Luis Cortez, a member of the North Coast Cartel in Cartagena, Colombia. I'm scanning the article here . . . He worked for them in L.A., and it looks like he might have turned . . . Yeah, there were rumors at least he was an informant for the CIA."

"That could be something. When?"

"Um . . . looks like the CIA busted the cartel in 2000."

"What's Cortez been doing since then?"

"I don't know. Let me run him through our database."

That took a few more minutes, and Maggie announced that Cortez ran a chop shop in Whittier. "Looks like he's been a taxpaying, law-abiding citizen for the last decade or so."

"We gave him citizenship?"

"Maybe. No, he was born in La Palma."

"I thought you said he was with the cartel in Colombia."

"The cartel's in Colombia. He worked this end of the pipeline."

"I see. You happen to have an address?"

"Uh, Jack, what are you thinking?"

"An address, Maggie? Please?"

She sighed, searched some more, and then read him an address. In Pico Rivera. The same address from the mapping site on Robbie's computer.

"Thanks, Maggie."

"You're not going to see this guy, are you?"

"You just said he's been legit for the last decade."

"Looks legit. But trust me, if he worked for a Colombian cartel, I don't care if he did become a CIA informant and has been clean for the last dozen years, you don't want to mess with this guy."

"Noted, Maggie. And thanks."

She sighed—more like growled, really—as Jackson closed his phone. It was thin, but he had a potential lead. Just like the TV P.I.s. Cue the synthesized theme music and star's voiceover as he careened onto the highway in his sports car.

Chapter Twelve

10:47 p.m.

JACKSON DIDN'T MAKE it out to Pico Rivera as often as he'd like, so it took him a while to find Cortez's place on Underwood Street. Fortunately, the flashing police lights guided him to the house.

A trio of squad cars was accompanied by a pair of ambulances. They blocked most of the street, and Jackson parked several houses down and joined the throng of people forming behind police tape that was still being strung.

Jackson had dreamt when he started as a private investigator that he could use his brother's position as an LAPD officer to get him in the good graces of cops at crime scenes. With Grant dead, that plan didn't really work. Besides, these guys were LASD—Los Angeles Sheriff's Department.

He mixed with the neighbors for a while, trying to glean some info. He gathered that there had been gunfire, anywhere from a single shot to an *Open Range*-style shootout, depending on whom he asked. But nobody knew anything more or even remotely substantial.

Jackson trusted his eyes more than the locals anyhow, and watched as paramedics brought out a stretcher and a body bag. A man on a second gurney was bleeding and sucking oxygen as he was carried out, but didn't appear critical.

"Luis! Luis!" A female voice pierced the night as a heavyset Hispanic woman burst through the crowd and the police tape, charging toward the injured man on the gurney. The police restrained her before she could get to him, but she kept shouting Luis's name.

As they ushered her away from the gurney and toward one of the squad cars, Jackson shouldered his way through the crowd, back to where an LASD officer was restringing the police tape. "Officer, what went down here?"

"Looks like a gang shooting."

"Cortez dead?"

The officer looked up. Gallardo, if Jackson was reading his name tape right in the flickering red and blue light. "You know him?"

"Know of him is all."

Officer Gallardo nodded. "I really can't divulge any info."

Jackson nodded. "There a detective on the scene?"

Gallardo pointed his thumb over his shoulder. "Detective Kowalski. Good luck."

Jackson thanked him and circled the ambulance. Detective Kowalski was easy to recognize. Off-white shirt, loose tie, old worn jacket, and a look on his face that said he wanted to be in bed. His brown hair was thinning, matched in color—if not thickness—by a huge mustache. He was straight out of the 1970s and '80s detective shows Jackson loved so much. As Jackson approached, Kowalski broke away from the hysterical Hispanic woman and had a conference with another officer.

"Detective Kowalski?"

He turned. "Yeah, who are you?"

"Jackson Douglas. I was on my way to see Cortez. He the vic?"

Kowalski scrunched his face. "What business did you have with Cortez?"

"I'm looking for somebody. I thought he might know where I could find her."

"What'd you say your name was?"

"Jackson Douglas."

"Douglas. Should I know you?"

"I doubt it."

Kowalski nodded. "Cortez took a round in the shoulder and another in the leg."

"He's alive?"

Another nod.

"What about the other guy?"

Kowalski scrunched his face again. "You know him too?"

"No. Just curious."

A frown intensified in the detective's forehead. "What's the name of this woman you were hoping Cortez could help you find?"

Jackson smiled sheepishly. "Well, Detective, that's the thing. I'm not quite sure."

"Douglas, I don't have time for curiosity. Why don't you go see Officer Mertz?" He nodded to a beanpole writing in a notebook by one of the squad cars. "He can take your statement."

Jackson tried to reply, but Kowalski raised a hand and hollered. "Brett, take this kid's statement."

With no choice, Jackson ambled over to Officer Mertz, answered a bunch of meaningless questions, and managed to pry out of him that Cortez and the other guy were the only two involved in the shooting, and the other guy was indeed dead. No name, no condition of Cortez, and by the time he was finished answering Mertz's questions, no ambulance remained at the scene.

"Hey, Detective," Jackson called as Kowalski emerged from the house.

"Yeah," he replied with a heavy sigh.

"Look, I know this never works, but I'm a private eye. Any chance I could have a look around inside?"

"No. You talk to Mertz?"

"I did."

He nodded. "Why are you so interested in this guy Cortez?"

"He might be a link to a missing client."

"Yeah, well, I suggest you call Missing Persons. If our homicide has anything to do with your client, they'll link it up."

Deeming further resistance futile, Jackson blended back into the crowd and returned to his Granada. The night had grown cool, and Jackson sat with the windows up, watching the scene from half a block away.

If he left, he was back at square one. His only remaining play to get Abby back would be to go after Desmond, and—Reggie's help notwithstanding—that could get messy. So he decided to wait. Sure, Robbie could have been researching Cortez for some other reason. She might even have conducted a decoy search on the off chance Jackson showed up at her hotel, broke in, and hacked her computer. But he doubted it. And the fact that Cortez had been shot confirmed his hunch that he was connected to the Bible. But how?

While waiting for the cops to leave, Jackson made a few phone calls. The first was to Robbie. He had tried her on the way to her hotel and again on his drive to Pico Rivera, getting her voicemail both times. He got it a third time, passed on leaving a third message, and dialed Sam.

"This is Sam."

"Hey, Sam. It's Jackson. Did I wake you?"

"No, I've got late shifts the next few days, so I'm getting my body clock set. Say, how was the ball? I thought for sure you'd call and give me the scoop today."

"Sorry, but it's been hectic."

"What's going on?"

"I need a favor."

"Okay."

"Any chance you can find out the status of a gunshot victim in Pico Rivera?"

"Jackson." She was quiet for a moment. "The last time I looked up a gunshot victim for you, you ended up chasing down gangsters."

"I know, Sam. But a woman's life is in danger."

"Who?"

"Abby."

"Your date last night?"

"It wasn't—Yeah. She's been kidnapped."

Sam paused for another few seconds. "Let me make a call, okay?"

"Thanks, Sam. Name's Luis Cortez. He and another man got into a shootout, and the other guy was killed."

"In Pico Rivera?"

Jackson confirmed and gave her the address. "I need the other guy's name, if you can get it, and where they took Cortez."

"I'll call you back," she said.

Jackson thanked her and called Maggie.

"Favor number two?" she asked.

"Yeah. Cortez got shot."

"By you?"

"No. And I couldn't get anything out of the local LEOs. Can you scan the wire, see if anybody knows anything, particularly the name of the other victim. He's dead."

"Are you okay?"

"Peachy."

"I'll call you back."

"Thanks."

Jackson closed his phone and waited. The crowd was dissipating, and only one squad car and an unmarked vehicle remained in front of Cortez's place. Jackson waited some more, mulling as he did. He had nothing to link Cortez to Robbie other than her internet search, nothing to connect him to Abby or Desmond, to the Bible, or to anyone else hunting it. Maybe, if any of them were really CIA agents, it was a link since he'd been a CIA mole or snitch or whatever. But that was pretty thin. And yet his gut told him this wasn't a coincidence.

Sam called back first. She'd crapped out. Jackson thanked her anyhow.

A few minutes later, as the last unmarked car was leaving the scene, CCR's "Bad Moon Rising" sounded from Jackson's phone. Ducking down to avoid the headlights of the oncoming car, Jackson opened his phone. "Maggie?"

"All I could find was a double-shooting in Pico. One dead, one injured. No names. Oh, and they mentioned a potential suspect was in custody."

"Man, woman?"

"Doesn't say."

"Any mention of which hospital?"

"No. Sorry."

"Yeah. Thanks."

"I'm planning on turning in. Any more favors?"

"No. Thanks again."

"Be careful, Jack."

He closed his phone and heeded her advice. He waited ten minutes to make sure everyone was gone from the house. Then he drove past it, made a lap around the next block, and parked on the side of the street, several houses down, in the shadow of an old oak tree.

Cortez's house was a ranch with a small porch, carport, and a hedgerow on the northwest side. Jackson used it for cover and snuck around to the back, where he again took his time to make sure nobody was watching him. Then he picked the lock on a sliding glass door leading to the patio and let himself in. No audible alarm, no dogs, no police guard sitting at the table, smirking in the dark.

Jackson spent an hour looking around Cortez's place. He rifled through papers, peeked in desk drawers, even checked under mattresses and rugs. The Bible wasn't there, and there was nothing to link him to it or the pursuit of it. If Cortez had a computer, the cops had taken it.

Next, he surveyed the crime scene. The front door showed no signs of having been jimmied or broken, same as the sliding glass door leading to the patio. There was a smeared bloodstain on one wall, drops of blood by the front door, and a small smudge of blood across the carpet by the door. There was also splatter on the baseboard behind the door. And of course, a pool of it by the couch. Plus a bullet hole in the wall behind it. He tried to put the pieces together, but nothing came to him. Then again, he wasn't Abby Sciuto, and blood spray patterns weren't his thing.

It didn't matter. It didn't give him any clue as to how Cortez and the mystery shooter were connected to the Bible or where it was now. Maybe news would break by morning, but Jackson had no idea how long Desmond would wait before harming Abby. Or if he ever would harm her, for that matter. After all, she was his stepsister, and Abby had told Jackson that the family had been fairly close. Then again, if everything else she'd said about Desmond was true, he didn't seem like the type of guy who valued stepfamily. And Jackson couldn't afford to call his bluff.

So he did what any good poker player would do. He bluffed as well.

Returning to his car, Jackson got out of the neighborhood before some insomniac got suspicious of his Granada. Safely on the freeway and headed toward home, Jackson called Desmond.

"Mr. Douglas."

"I have the Bible."

Desmond didn't react for a moment, and Jackson wondered if he could somehow know Jackson didn't have it.

"How do I know you're not bluffing?" Desmond asked.

"Simple. Put your cards on the table."

"You're suggesting a swap?"

"Abby for the Bible."

"Okay," Desmond answered warily. "That can be arranged. But know if you're bluffing, you'll be sorry."

"Works both ways, Des. Abby had better be returned without a scratch and in a good mood, or we'll reenact an Old Testament scene of my choosing."

"Save the dramatics, Mr. Douglas."

Jackson forced himself to breathe. "How about the beach, say arou—"

"I'll pick the time and place," Desmond interjected.

"That doesn't sound too fair."

"I don't care." Desmond paused. "Hansen Dam. You know it?"

Inhale. Exhale. "I do."

"Take the east road in, down to the river. I'll find you."

Jackson gritted his teeth. "When?"

"Five a.m. Alone. And don't be late."

"I never am."

Chapter Thirteen

Sunday, January 20
3:32 a.m.

JACKSON SPENT ALL of an hour at home, during which time he changed clothes, ate, and did research. He didn't get a wink of sleep. Nor did he call Reggie. Desmond had said to come alone, and Jackson didn't know what Reggie could do, other than play the sniper. But he hoped it didn't come to that.

He also picked up an old study Bible, one that was approximately the same size as the Vanderbilt Bible. It was brown, like the Vanderbilt Bible, and had a zip-up case to go with it, from the days when zip-up cases were in style. He figured it would provide him with a little extra time, which could be critical if his still-forming plan was to work.

Armed and fed, he journeyed east and north to Hansen Dam Recreation Area. Situated at the north end of the San Fernando Valley, the park was located just off Interstate 210. The dam had been constructed in 1940 as means of flood control. When the Tujunga Wash wasn't flooded—and it certainly wasn't now—the dam was little more than a dike around which a golf course, baseball diamonds and soccer fields, and the Hansen Dam Aquatic Center had been built. There was also plenty of open wilderness "behind" the dam, including Hansen Lake and the serpentine creek known as Tujunga Wash.

Jackson had scouted the area from satellite photos and memorized all the entrances into and out of the park. Unfortunately, the satellite photos were several years old and subject to change. There hadn't been any floods lately, but Jackson had no idea what landscapers or developers had done to the park. He'd be operating blindly until he got there, and even then, he'd be working in pitch black conditions.

This was so Jack Bauer, he thought as he approached the turnoff to the dam. Bauer was always meeting people in strange locations at odd hours to save some woman while combatting terrorists. And Bauer would be able to sympathize with Jackson. Nobody was ever who they said they were in his world either.

Jackson intended to be early and hoped Desmond didn't. He also hoped he only brought Abby and no re-enforcements, but doubted it. Desmond was a major-league twerp.

Vehicular access wasn't exactly permitted where Desmond had arranged the exchange. But Jackson managed, driving on a bike path for a little while, and ultimately off-roading it on little more than a horse path. He arrived down by the river, turned the car around, and waited.

He didn't like exchanges. Too much could go wrong, and it was almost impossible to pull off so that both groups left happy. Especially when one party didn't have the item it was supposed to exchange. And this wasn't an even trade. A Bible, even one worth hundreds of thousands of dollars, didn't compare to a person's life. Jackson had far more to lose than Desmond did, and less to gain. Desmond was playing for big money. Jackson was only trying to return to the status quo ante.

Having over an hour before Desmond was due, Jackson used the time to plot and strategize for all contingencies. These things always went sideways— just ask Bauer—and the key was having a plan B and C and D. That, and ability to improvise.

To that end, Jackson prayed for wisdom and guidance and maybe some divine intervention if the need arose. Ultimately, he prayed for Abby's safety. Beyond that, he didn't care about much.

Then he thought and plotted some more. He believed God could pull one's bacon out of the fire, but he also believed God gave people wisdom and common sense to think ahead of time so as to keep their bacon out of the fire in the first place. Jackson just hoped his bacon wasn't already in the fire. It was a shame to burn good bacon.

From his position in the valley, Jackson could see traffic up on the interstate, and the glow of greater L.A.'s millions of lights reflecting off a clear sky. And yet, it was all forever away. Around him, he could just make out the scrub and bushes and a few trees that separated the dirt paths that converged on his location. In a pinch, he could get the Granada through two of the paths, he calculated.

His phone told him it was 4:37. He did yet more thinking. Several years back, he had first started to think that maybe he'd discovered God's purpose for his life. By becoming a P.I., he could help the little people, do good where the cops and other authorities couldn't or wouldn't. Twenty-five killings later, he now regarded himself, as Dr. Zachary had put it, as *The Dark Knight*, bearing the responsibility for doing society's dirty work. It had to be done— some of it, at least. But it was hard to reconcile with being a Christian, where values of meekness, peace, gentleness, and love were lauded. However, there were plenty of Christians in the military. God-fearing men, like his father, had served. Sometimes pulling a gun wasn't contrary to Christian values— sometimes, it was actually in line with them. It just seemed that the line could very easily become blurred.

Twice Jackson saw headlights and thought Desmond had arrived. Then he caught a reflection of light from somewhere and saw a dark sedan two hundred feet ahead on the path he had driven in on. It stopped a hundred feet away, slightly uphill.

Jackson flicked on his lights, illuminating the car. It was a black Cadillac with tinted glass that kept him from seeing the number of occupants. The driver flipped his lights on in return, and they sat there for a moment. Then Jackson opened his door with his left hand, tucking his Glock into the back of his jeans with his right. He leaned on the door, showing both hands.

The driver of the Cadillac also got out and stood beside the car. It was Desmond.

"We going to do this?" Jackson asked.

"Bring me the Bible."

"Not until I see Abby."

Desmond shook his head. "I want to see it first, confirm that it's the real thing. I'm not falling for any parlor tricks."

"Maybe you didn't hear me," Jackson said, closing his door. "Not until I see Abby."

"You don't get to control the terms, Mr. Douglas."

He waited five seconds before speaking a single word: "Abby."

Desmond breathed a few times. "She isn't here."

"What?"

"You're going to have to trust me. The Bible, then Abby."

Jackson wasn't exactly Wild Bill Hickok, but he had a decent draw, and in one fluid motion had his Glock—safety off—aimed at Desmond's chest. "How's that for a parlor trick? Now it's your turn to play David Copperfield. You produce Abby, or I do something very unbiblical."

"You shoot me, and you'll never see Abby again."

"She's your sister."

"And your girlfriend."

"Newsflash, Des, she's not my girlfriend. In fact, I just met her, so her life's a lot smaller loss to me than yours is to you," Jackson said, hoping his voice didn't crack. He was glad Desmond was as far away as he was, because he was pretty sure the insides of his kneecaps were clattering.

"Fine," Desmond finally spat. He very slowly reached into his shirt pocket with his thumb and forefinger and pulled out a phone. Jackson didn't blink while Desmond dialed and had a very quick conversation. Less than a minute later, a second car appeared beside Desmond's Cadillac. "She's inside," he called.

"Let me see her."

"Not until you put the gun down."

"Which kneecap is your favorite?" Jackson asked.

"You're bluffing."

"So call."

Desmond took another couple of breaths. Then he waved his finger in a circle. The rear door of the second car opened and a man stepped out. He was followed by a blond woman with a gun to her head.

Abby.

The driver's door opened next and a second man got out. His gun was aimed at Jackson.

"Consider that my raise, Mr. Douglas."

Jackson swallowed. He smelled burning bacon.

"Now show me the Bible."

"Better idea," Jackson said, trying to stall. "You send Abby over to get it."

"No way."

"Keep your gun on her. When she gets here, I walk the Bible to you. No gun, and you keep yours on me."

Desmond thought for a moment. Then he nodded. "If you're bluffing, you're both dead."

"We have a deal?"

"Deal."

Desmond nodded at his thug, who gave Abby a shove down the path. She walked slowly, uncertainly. Jackson kept one eye on her and the other on Desmond, who was still in his sights.

"It's okay, Abby," Jackson said when she was halfway there. "Keep walking, easy does it." He moved behind the open car door. Switching his gun to his left hand, he opened the back door as Abby approached. There was just enough light for him to see that her eyes were wide with fear.

"Do exactly what I tell you," he whispered.

She nodded.

"The Bible's on the backseat," he announced for Desmond to hear.

She came around behind him.

"Wait!" Desmond yelled, and they both froze. "I want her to bring it back to me."

"That wasn't the deal."

"It is now. She brings it to me."

Jackson turned an eye to Abby. "Trust me." Back to Desmond. "Deal. But your guys drop their guns first."

"When she gets here with the Bible."

"Agreed." He nodded at Abby and dropped his voice. "When I nod, act like you're reaching in for the Bible but dive on the floor."

"What?"

"Just trust me."

She nodded.

"What are you waiting for?" Desmond asked.

"She's scared, you moron. Give her a minute."

"Bring the Bible here now!"

Jackson turned to Abby. He nodded.

She dove into the backseat, and he dove in after her, driving her onto the floor and covering her with his body. It took only a few seconds, but then bullets began flying. Abby screamed. A window exploded. The shots were deafening.

And then they were drowned out.

By the honking of a car horn.

The shooting stopped, replaced by shouting as a flashing red light bathed the back of the Granada in a dim glow.

"Stay down," Jackson said, peeking his head up. Glass fell onto the floor. He stood all the way, shaking the crumbles of glass off him. He surveyed the scene for a moment, then tossed his Glock on the front seat and reached to help Abby up.

"What . . . What's going on?"

"The cavalry's here. Careful, there's glass everywhere."

"What? The cavalry?"

Jackson looked up at Desmond's two vehicles, which had been joined by a third, a black SUV with high beams on and a flashing red light on top of the roof.

"Are you okay?" Jackson asked, returning his focus to Abby.

"I'm . . . I'm fine—What's going on?"

"Just sit down, okay?" he said, first brushing a few pieces of glass from the backseat, then helping her sit down. "I'll be back."

"Jackson?"

"I just have to check in with our friends from the Bureau. I'll be right back."

She nodded.

"You're safe now. It's over."

She nodded again, and he jogged up the hill to where Andrews and Newton were handcuffing Desmond and two other men.

"Mr. Douglas," Andrews said.

"I thought you weren't going to make it."

"We've been here all along," she replied.

"Who are you?" Desmond asked. "Cops?"

"FBI," Newton answered. "Same result for you, though."

They marched Desmond and his pals back to the SUV, then rejoined Jackson.

"The girl okay?" Newton asked.

"A little shook," Jackson said, glancing over his shoulder, "but yeah, I think so."

"Good."

"Well," Andrews said.

"Yeah?"

"Do not play cute, Douglas. On the phone, you said if we showed up we could bust a kidnapper and recover the Bible."

"I did," he said.

"So where is it?"

"I don't have it."

"What?"

"I've heard rumors about the CIA," he said. "You guys are kind of mission-driven. I thought if I didn't put a carrot at the end of the stick, you might not show up."

"You're saying you don't have the Bible?" Newton asked.

"Afraid not. Last I knew, you guys had it, then you got blown up on the freeway. Your guess is as good as mine."

Andrews blew out an angry breath. "You are obstructing justice, Douglas."

"Justice is debatable. And if anything, I helped you bring these three to justice."

"Arresting kidnappers is a little below CIA pay grade," Newton replied.

"Yes, but doesn't it make you feel warm inside?"

Andrews shook her head. "We ought to take you in too."

"You do that, and I don't give you my lead."

"Your lead?"

Jackson nodded. "A genuine one, too."

"Go on."

"A guy by the name of Luis Cortez. Robbie—or whatever her name is— did some research on him. I went to his place just in time to find out he'd been involved in a gunfight with some guy. The cops wouldn't tell me anything, but maybe you can persuade them to confide in you."

"What is Cortez's connection to all this?"

"I don't know. But it's all too coincidental to me. And there are rumors he had ties to the CIA back in the day, so if there are goods on him, you two should be able to find them."

"Is that all?" Andrews asked.

"Yeah. Scout's honor."

"Just for the record," Newton said, "if you don't have the Bible, what was your plan if we didn't show?"

"I was just trying to figure that out when you moved in."

Chapter Fourteen

5:31 a.m.

ANDREWS AND NEWTON had some questions for Abby, and she had some for them. Neither got the answers they were looking for, such as where the Bible was, what would happen to Desmond, and so forth. When the alleged CIA agents were finally finished, Jackson helped Abby back down the hill to the Granada.

"Are you sure you're all right?" he asked as he opened her car door.

"I'm fine, Jackson. He didn't hurt me."

"Okay. Let's get you home." Jackson closed her door and circled around to his side. The SUV was gone, leaving Desmond's two vehicles atop the hill. It felt like a modern-day ghost town, and Jackson would be glad to get out of the basin and back to civilization.

"Actually, Jackson," Abby said as he got in, "could we go somewhere to get something to eat? I'm starved."

"You don't want to go home first?"

Abby shook her head. She was wearing the same clothes she had worn the day before, but other than appearing tired, didn't seem to be much the worse for wear. "I just want something to eat, and then I want to find the Bible."

"Okay. What sounds good?"

"Anything."

As they got out of the park and onto the interstate, the sun was still close to an hour from rising, but the eastern sky was already starting to lighten. It served as a reminder that Jackson hadn't slept in almost twenty-four hours.

"What aren't you telling me, Jackson?"

"A lot."

"Do you know where the Bible is?"

"No."

"Any clues?"

"Not really."

"None at all?"

"It's a long story. Let's get something to eat, and I'll fill you in."

They found a Denny's in Burbank that was just starting to wake. They quickly ordered and then took turns reporting on events of the last dozen hours.

"Desmond came back just after you left," Abby said. "He was all nice and charming, fake Desmond. He offered to take me out to get a coffee, as a peace offering." She shook her head. "I should have seen through it."

Jackson gulped his coffee.

"I thought maybe I could talk to him, get some more information, something that would help us find the Bible again. But we just drove into some alley where he picked up a friend of his with a gun. They took me back to his place and locked me in one of the spare bedrooms."

"They didn't search your place?"

"No."

"Hmm."

"Why?"

"Someone did. Tossed it pretty good."

She shrugged. "I suppose he could have had somebody else go in after getting me out."

Jackson raised an eyebrow.

"What?"

"We keep finding more and more people involved in all this. It could have been a third party."

"More people. Like who?"

"I'll get to that. What happened then?"

"Nothing. I just sat in the bedroom all day and night. They brought me a sandwich once, but that was it. I didn't even see Desmond again until we got to the dam. Even now, I still can't believe he did it."

Andrews and Newton had already asked most of the questions Jackson would, and Abby had identified the man who'd held the gun to her head at the dam as one of her captors. Andrews and Newton said that LAPD would likely be in contact about pressing charges, and in the meantime, Jackson saw no point in rehashing things any further.

So he recounted his afternoon, evening, and night for her. He lost her when it came to finding Luis Cortez's name on Robbie's computer and then finding Cortez had been wounded in a gunfight at his Pico Rivera home. It was okay, he assured her, he got lost there too.

"So Robyn isn't Robyn?" Abby asked with a bite of waffle on her fork.

"Nor Robbie."

"And she isn't FBI?"

"No."

"And Andrews and Newton are really CIA posing as FBI?"

"I have my doubts about that too."

"So who are they?"

"Beats me."

She shook her head. "And we have no clue who has the Bible?"

"No."

"So what's our next step?"

"Sleep."

"I mean to find the Bible."

"I'm not sure there is a next step, Abby. I've pretty much played out the string. And besides, I think we're getting in over our heads. You've been kidnapped. Cortez was shot, another guy killed. Andrews and Newton were almost blown up."

"Come on, Jackson," Abby said, leaning across the table. "You've never run when things got hard before."

"You don't know me too well," Jackson said. "I try to run long before they get too hard."

She sat back. "That's not what I've read. Not when you stared down the leader of the Grays. Or saved that girl in Nevada."

"No. And I didn't quit when your life was in danger, either. Now that it's not, I say we get out before that changes again."

"So you are quitting?"

He drained his fourth cup of coffee. Pancakes made him thirsty. "At this point, paying me is just a waste of your money. I have nothing else to pursue."

Abby pushed a bite of waffle around her plate.

Jackson refilled his coffee. "I'm sorry, Abby. Really." He shrugged. "Maybe we'll hear something about Cortez or his victim, and we'll have a thin lead to pursue, but right now . . ."

"I get it," she said. "I just . . . To have it and then lose it."

Jackson's cell rang, an unfamiliar number. Not Maggie, unless she was at work. Surely not this early on a Sunday morning. Not Sam, either, and he knew she didn't work until later unless she had been called in. "Excuse me," he said to Abby before taking the call. "Hello?"

"Jackson?"

"Yeah. Who's this?"

"Robbie."

He very nearly clapped the phone shut. Instead, he switched it over to the other ear. "We're playing this hand to the finish, I see."

Abby raised her eyebrows, and he nodded to confirm.

"I deserve that," Robbie said.

"And then some. What do you want?"

"I need your help."

"Good luck with that."

"The Sheriff's Department is holding me, Jackson. They think I was involved in a shooting."

"Let me guess, Pico Rivera."

"Wow. You're sure you're not psychic?"

"Never would have answered the phone if I was."

"They think I killed a guy, Jackson. Or at least shot a guy. They don't know what to think. But I'm in trouble."

"Perhaps you should contact ol' Agent Dawkins at the Denver office," Jackson said. "Have him pull a few strings."

Abby had set down her fork, straining to interpret half of a conversation.

"Look, I'll explain everything," Robbie said. "I just need you to get me out of here."

"And how am I supposed to do that? I don't think the cops will let you go on my word."

"I meant bail me out."

"I like that in a woman," Jackson said. "The chips are down, and she can still make jokes."

"I'm serious. I'll pay you back."

"For all I know, you were involved in the shooting. Why would I help you get free?"

"Because I can help you find the Bible," she answered.

"I'm sorry, could you repeat that? I couldn't hear you because there was a little boy over here crying wolf."

"Jackson, I know how to get the Bible back."

"Good. Then barter with the cops."

He clapped the phone shut before she could get out another word.

"Robyn?" Abby said.

He nodded and summarized the conversation.

"She has a link to the Bible?"

"So she claims."

"That's our lead. Dropped right into your lap."

"You forget who we're talking about," he said, picking up his coffee mug.

"I know she might be lying, but if it could be a clue . . ."

"Abby, she's in jail right now. The cops think she's involved in the shooting at Cortez's place. She's just saying what she needs to say to get out of there."

"Maybe. But maybe she actually has something. You said she chased after the men in black after the explosion in the tunnel. Something led her to Cortez. Maybe she tracked them to him, or . . . I don't know. But what do we have to lose?"

Jackson set down his mug without drinking. "Besides our sanity?"

"Come on, Jackson, please? It gets you another day's pay to go hear her out."

He sighed and reminded himself never again to judge those stupid townsfolk who kept listening to the wolf boy.

*   *   *

7:41 a.m.

TRAFFIC WAS heavier than it should have been early on a Sunday morning, and it took Jackson and Abby longer than expected to get to the Los Angeles Sheriff's Department's Pico Rivera station. Robbie was sitting in the waiting room when they arrived. She wore jeans and a brown pullover, her hair in a ponytail so loose it really couldn't be classified as a ponytail. There were bags under her eyes and a vacant gaze in them. She looked as if she had been pulled through the wringer, and Jackson said as much as she signed for her personal items.

"You should try being questioned for six hours some Saturday night."

He huffed, remembering Vegas. "Been there, done that. Why aren't you in jail?"

"They're letting me go," she replied.

"Letting you go?"

"Their brilliant forensics department finally concluded my gun wasn't fired, and both of the vics were shot with nines anyhow."

"Nines?" Abby asked.

"Nine-millimeter rounds."

"Oh. So you're free to go?"

Robbie nodded and stood. "I was just waiting for a ride."

Jackson sighed and led the way out into the parking lot. The sun was out in full force, and the day was warming quickly. He stopped. "Okay, so who are you?"

"I'll tell you everything," Robbie said. "I owe you that much."

"That's not all you owe," Jackson said, leaning against the rear door of the Granada.

"Ooh, what happened to your window?"

"It got shot."

"By who?"

"Guys with bad aim." Other than a shattered left rear window and a hole in the front bumper, the car was unscathed. And Abby had already assured him she would pay for the damages. He hadn't argued. "Now spill."

"I will, okay, I promise. But first, can we get something to eat. I'm starved."

"You missed breakfast."

"Jackson," Abby called from across the car. She had made him promise to be nice, in hopes that a little kindness would persuade Robbie to be sincerely helpful. He'd had his doubts, but had given his word.

"Okay, breakfast. But I want a full explanation."

"You'll get it."

He nodded and slowly stepped aside. "Watch out for glass on the floor."

They all got in, and as he backed out of the parking lot, he asked, "You got a dining preference?"

"No," Robbie replied, fixing her ponytail. "Just someplace with hot food."

He drove in silence while Robbie pried details of Abby's capture and rescue from her. The wrap-up finished as they arrived at an IHOP. Once they got a table, Jackson waited anxiously for Robbie to scour the menu and order. Then he leaned into her line of sight. "Okay. Now, the truth."

She nodded. "My name is Whitney Raines. I'm with the Canadian Security Intelligence Service."

"The what?"

"Canadian Security Intelligence Service, or CSIS. It's sort of our version of your CIA."

"So you're Canadian now?"

"All my life, actually."

"Where were you born?"

"Calgary."

"Don't you mean Cal-ga'-ry?" Jackson said. "That's how Barry Melrose pronounces it."

"Who?" Whitney and Abby both asked.

"Never mind. You don't sound Canadian, eh?"

"I've worked hard to speak without an accent. Helps in my line of work."

"Which is what exactly?"

"I can't go into specifics."

"I suppose you can't prove you're with the CSIS either."

"How? Show you an ID? You'll think it's fake. Tell you to call my headquarters in Ottawa? You'll think it's a rigged line."

"How about you tell us what the CSIS wants with Alec Vanderbilt's Bible?"

"I can't do that."

He nodded and slid to the edge of the booth. "I take it you have enough money to cover your breakfast?"

"Wait."

"What? You can break CSIS confidence over the cost of ham and eggs?"

"I can help you find the Bible."

"How?"

"I need to know we have a deal."

"And I need to have some reason to believe you're Whitney Whoever."

"Whitney Raines."

"Wasn't that some superhero's alias, by the way?"

Whitney huffed.

"You want a deal?" Jackson said. "You tell me why you're after the Bible, and then we'll talk. Otherwise, enjoy your breakfast."

"What makes you think I won't just make something up?"

"Try me."

Whitney locked eyes with Jackson. "Okay. But I can't tell you everything."

"Of course not."

"And what I tell you stays right here."

He nodded.

Whitney looked to Abby, who nodded too.

After a drink of orange juice, Whitney said, "Alec Vanderbilt spent six months in Montreal in the winter of '75 and spring of '76. The cover story was that he was there trying to acquire several Group of Seven landscapes and scouting the market for a Morriseau."

"Wasn't he?"

"Maybe. But his contact at the Montreal Museum of Fine Arts was a woman named Amélie Fournier. Fournier was on the RCMP Security Service's watch list because her father, Felix Fournier, had been a predominant member of the FLQ."

"Hold on," Jackson said. "The RCMP. What do the Mounties have to do with this?"

"The CSIS wasn't formed until 1984. Prior to that, the RCMP Security Service handled domestic intelligence and security."

"And who is this FQL you mentioned?" Abby asked.

"FLQ," Whitney replied. "It's the *Front de libération du Québec*—that is, the Quebec Liberation Front. They were a terrorist group in the late '60s, focused on a free and sovereign nation of Quebec."

"And Fournier's father was part of this FLQ?"

Whitney nodded. "When she was linked to Alec, a suspected CIA agent, it piqued interest."

"So what does that have to do with the Bible?" Jackson asked.

"Amélie Fournier disappeared in the spring of 1977, without a trace. Left a high-paying job, a society boyfriend, and just disappeared." She paused as the waitress delivered her breakfast plate. She spent a minute doctoring her chicken, biscuit, and eggs with salt and Tabasco sauce, then began digging in.

"You were saying?" Jackson said.

Whitney swallowed. "Right. When Fournier disappeared in '77, the Canadian authorities were baffled. She was something of a celebrity, at least in Montreal and in the art world."

"A museum curator was a celebrity?"

"She was beautiful, an aristocrat, wealthy, and her father was linked to terrorism. Anyhow, her disappearance raised all sorts of theories and became a favorite talking point at cafés or a hobby for would-be detectives. Who wouldn't want to be the one to find a rich, beautiful missing woman?" Whitney shrugged. "The theories grew wilder and stranger as time went by, and Fournier became a part of Canadian folklore."

"I'm going to order lunch if this takes much longer."

"You're not big on patience, are you?" Whitney asked.

"I sort of lost my patience when I spent yesterday being jerked around."

She sighed and then took a deliberate bite of eggs. "In 1986, the Vancouver Art Gallery was robbed, almost a million dollars' worth of paintings. A year later, a museum in Red Deer, Alberta, was hit. The authorities didn't have much in the way of leads, but Fournier became a suspect."

"Felix or Amélie?"

"Amélie."

"Why?"

"Both the Vancouver Art Gallery and the museum in Red Deer had employees who later admitted to having a liaison with a woman matching Amélie's general description around the time of the robberies. Several of the pieces that were stolen had long been on her list at the Montreal Museum. There were a number of other leads—nothing substantial, but—"

Jackson rolled his fingers, telling her to get on with it.

Whitney huffed. "Into the early '90s, Amélie Fournier became a legend, suspected in almost a dozen robberies of museums, galleries, and high-end estates across the country. There was never nearly enough evidence to indict her, but somehow always enough to feed the legend . . . almost as if she was playing with the authorities."

Whitney took a quick bite of her biscuit. "Trust me, I'm tying this together. It all came to the attention of the CSIS in December of 1994 when our headquarters was hit."

"Hit?"

"A high-tech break-in, computers hacked, files ransacked. Imagine if the CIA headquarters in Langley was breached and over five hundred top-secret files were either missing or compromised. That's what happened."

"And you all suspected Fournier?"

Whitney nodded. "The style matched hers, very high-tech, very sophisticated. And she was in Ottawa at the time, which of course put all the museums and galleries on high alert. But no one thought she'd break into CSIS headquarters—or that she could."

"You have anything else to tie her to it?" Jackson asked.

"Nothing ironclad, but lots of odds and ends. Most of it I can't share with you."

"What does all this have to do with my father?" Abby asked.

"I mentioned Fournier was spotted in Ottawa around the time of the break-in," Whitney answered. "Two nights before it, in fact, she was seen having dinner with an old associate. Care to guess who?"

"Alec," Jackson said.

Whitney nodded. "Alec."

Chapter Fifteen

8:21 a.m.

"ALEC?" ABBY ASKED. "Was in Ottawa in 1994?"

Whitney nodded again and scooped some eggs onto her fork with the last piece of her biscuit. She swallowed the bite and had some juice. "In December. Just before he 'retired' from the CIA on the 31st."

"He retired in 1977," Abby said.

"That's one version of the story."

"And another version says he was still working for them till he died," Jackson said. He looked at Whitney. "That's a very entertaining story, but it still doesn't explain why you're after the Bible."

"Think about it. Fournier took classified files, some of which have become antiquated, but some of which are still vital to Canadian national security. I wasn't lying about that. This has always been a matter of national security. I just didn't say which nation."

"Fine, you get points for cleverness."

Whitney sighed. "Fournier had ties to Alec Vanderbilt back in the '70s and was seen with him just before the break-in at CSIS headquarters in '94. Alec was a CIA operative and, according to our records, he retired shortly thereafter. And his Bible is considered by everyone to hold his CIA secrets, which, as I do math, are very likely CSIS secrets."

Jackson sat back. "Is any of this verifiable?"

"Some of it you could find online. But most of the details are probably classified."

"How convenient."

Whitney shrugged and wiped her mouth. "Am I allowed to go to the bathroom?"

"And slip out the window if you want."

She sighed as she edged out of the booth. Jackson turned to Abby. "What do you think?"

"I can't believe it," she said. "Alec wouldn't be part of a break-in like that."

"Even if he was still working for the CIA?"

"I don't know . . . I mean, isn't Canada one of our allies?"

"I think the theory is that Alec and Amélie were both rogue agents."

Abby shook her head. "No. Not Alec. He had his faults, I know. But he wasn't a double agent. He didn't betray his country. There's no way."

Jackson nodded. "Okay. So do we stay or go?"

"She said she has a link to the Bible, Jackson."

"And you trust her?"

"I don't know. But we have nothing now. If she's lying, we still have nothing. But just maybe her lead will pan out."

"Okay," he said. "It's your call. And your money."

Abby nodded. "You really think she's a quack?"

"Honestly, I have no idea. That's quite a story to have rehearsed or made up on the spot. But nothing with her would surprise me."

"I've been trying to remember December of 1994 if Alec might have been in Ottawa. I just can't remember. It was a few months after Mom died, but . . . I can't remember. Life was pretty hectic for a while."

"I understand," Jackson said.

Whitney returned, looking a little more vibrant. She had shaken out her ponytail, and there was a touch of a spark in her blue-green eyes.

"Answer me one more question," Jackson said.

Whitney nodded.

"If you're really a CSIS agent and you're trying to find the Bible so you can take it back to Ottawa and protect government secrets, and if the CIA is after it for the same reasons, if we help you find it, aren't we committing treason?"

She shrugged. "I don't know. And I don't care. You helped me out, so I'm helping you out. But if you don't want to be a part of it, fine. I'm going after the Bible."

"Okay, so that's the next question. What do we get out of helping you?"

"First dibs after the CSIS has a chance to look the Bible over. If we're wrong and there isn't anything pertaining to Canadian national security or if we can remove the classified information, you can have the Bible," she said while looking at Abby. Her eyes cut back to Jackson. "Will the CIA make you the same deal?"

Jackson looked to Abby, who nodded slightly.

"Okay," he said to Whitney. "Where is it?"

She took a swig of juice before answering, apparently enjoying torturing Jackson. "I don't know."

"What?"

"I said I could help you find it. I didn't say I knew where it was."

They were in a public place, so Jackson didn't leap across the table to strangle her. Instead, he sighed and spoke through gritted teeth. "How can you help find it?"

Whitney took another drink before answering. "Now be patient." She paused for effect. "Something about that explosion in the tunnel bugged me," she said.

"The way you ran out and left me without a ride?"

"Sorry about that. But it hit me. In the late '90s, the CIA took down the North Coast Cartel in Colombia. One of their big raids involved taking a convoy on a highway outside Cartagena. It was a bridge instead of a tunnel, but they flipped a car, blocked off the other lanes, and used the backup of traffic to catch the other members of the cartel. They busted nine or ten guys," she said.

"The North Coast Cartel," Jackson said. "Luis Cortez."

"Right. The CSIS was a partner—admittedly a minor one—with the CIA in the drug war in Colombia, and we knew that they had a couple of guys in the cartel—one in Cartagena and one in L.A. working the U.S. side. After this explosion jogged my memory, I did some digging and found Cortez's name. I also ran the plates on the van that blocked the other two lanes of traffic. It belonged to a delivery company—"

"Hold on," Jackson said. "There weren't plates on the van."

"There were until I removed them. I didn't want Andrews and Newton or whoever they are on the same trail I was on."

"You removed them? When?"

"While you were checking on Andrews and Newton. I saw an opening, and I took it. You were on the phone, and . . . I'm sorry."

Jackson just shook his head.

Whitney added more Tabasco to her final few bites of eggs. "As I was saying, the plates belonged to a delivery van from a company in Downey that is owned by a man named Javier Cota. Cota is married to Cortez's sister Maria."

"The Bible . . ." Abby said.

"I'm getting to that. I went back to my hotel and did a little more research on Cortez, trying to see what he was up to these days, to see if he could be involved in all this. The CSIS had nothing on him since the cartel fell, and . . . Anyhow, I didn't find much. But I figured I had enough to pay him a visit. I showed up and found him on the floor by the door and another guy dead by the couch. I only had a few minutes to look around before the cops showed up and I miscalculated my exit timing. They caught me coming out the back door, made me for the shootings, and the rest is history."

"Except for the link to the Bible," Jackson said.

Whitney smiled as she pushed in her plate. "The dead guy didn't have any identification in his wallet, but I recognized him anyhow. His name is Amir Assar, an international thief for hire. He's a favorite in the art world. You want a painting, call Assar."

"So what was he doing at Luis Cortez's place?"

"I don't know, but I have a theory. Cortez had a business card in his wallet for Regina Archambeau."

"Archambeau," Jackson said. He looked to Abby, then back to Whitney. "The Regina Archambeau who had a child with Alec Vanderbilt?"

Whitney nodded. "Now suppose she was after the Bible. She hires Assar to procure it for her. If Cortez was behind the explosion in the tunnel and his people took the Bible from Andrews and Newton, then Assar showed up to take it from him, they got in a shootout . . ."

"Why would Cortez want the Bible?" Abby asked.

"And how would Archambeau or Assar know that?" Jackson asked.

"And who has it now?" Abby asked again. "The police didn't find it at the house, did they?"

Whitney leaned forward. "I have a theory, I don't know, and I'm still getting to that," she said. "But what do you say we get out of here?"

"And go where?"

She shrugged. "Somewhere a little more private. The breakfast crowd is starting to make me nervous. You never know who's listening."

Jackson looked around. The restaurant had filled in, but he hadn't paid much attention to anyone else in the place. A rare oversight. He agreed, and after Whitney paid for her breakfast, the trio got into the Granada and headed west. Whitney sat in the middle of the backseat, leaning forward so she could communicate despite Jackson's blown out window.

"I said that Alec retired from the CIA in '94, and, Abby, you said it was in '77. There were also rumors that he was still involved as a non-official cover—or NOC—operative doing part-time work, mostly in the States, for the Company up until he died, like you said, Jackson. If that's true, maybe Cortez fears his name is in the Bible, something that would incriminate him as a CIA informant."

"Isn't the North Coast Cartel long gone?" Jackson asked over his shoulder.

"As an organization, yes. Most of the members are dead, in prison, or involved in other criminal organizations. But there are still plenty of people who wouldn't hesitate to extract some retribution on anyone who helped bring down the cartel—especially if he was an informant."

"Okay, so that's a possible motive for Cortez," Jackson said. "Or maybe he was hired by somebody else to get it."

"He's been clean for a while now," Whitney said, "and he's not the type you would typically hire for this sort of thing, but I suppose we can't rule it out. As for how Archambeau or Assar knew he had the Bible, I don't know. But they've just entered this thing as far as we know. Who knows how long they've been hanging on the outside, monitoring, putting pieces together. And who knows what kind of intel they have."

"So where does that leave us?" Abby asked. "We still don't know where the Bible is."

"No, I think we do," Jackson said before Whitney could reply. "Assar shows up at Cortez's place, and, judging by the scene, was admitted by Cortez. If he had broken in, the shooting wouldn't have left Cortez by the door and Assar by the couch, like you said."

Whitney nodded.

"If anything," Jackson continued, "it would have been the other way around, but more than likely there would have been broken down doors or some signs of a struggle. There wasn't even any indication that someone had picked the lock."

"Unless he broke in without actually breaking anything," Abby said. "Isn't he an acclaimed art thief?"

Whitney nodded. "But then why would Cortez have been by the front door and Assar by the couch?"

"Maybe Cortez just got home."

"There were no keys in his pocket, in the door, or anywhere around him. So unless he doesn't lock his doors—unlikely in that neighborhood—I agree with Jackson. He knew Assar was coming. He opened the door for him, closed it without locking it, and before he sat down, the two got into it and shot each other."

"That's how I'd see it," Jackson said.

"Okay, so what does that mean?" Abby asked. "You said you thought you knew where the Bible was."

He nodded. "Since the Bible wasn't there, it means—"

"There was a third person at the house," Whitney interrupted.

"Who now has the Bible," Abby said.

"Right."

Abby's smile quickly turned to a frown. "Unless the Bible was never at Cortez's place and this Assar person had bad information."

"That's possible," Jackson said. "But Assar—"

"Assar isn't the kind to have bad intel," Whitney said. "Nor is his employer."

"His employer?" Abby frowned. "Who—"

"Regina Archambeau," Jackson said.

"Regina? You think Regina hired him?"

He nodded. "And if Assar was working for her, maybe Cortez was too."

"I'm not following."

"Andrews and Newton took the Bible from Whitney and retreated to The Exquisite Hotel," Jackson said quickly, again speaking before Whitney had a chance. "As we showed up to take it back, somebody else broke into their room just after they left."

"Assar?"

"Then Cortez hijacks them on the freeway," Whitney continued. "We assumed it was two different groups, but maybe it was just a two-pronged attack. Somebody gets them to leave the room, Assar goes in just in case they left the Bible behind, and Cortez and his crew are ready with the ambush in case they took it with them."

"And you think Regina is the mastermind behind it?" Abby asked, the skepticism apparent on her face.

"Cortez had her card, indicating they were acquaintances of some kind," Whitney said.

"So if they were working together, why the shootout?"

Jackson shrugged.

"They had a falling out," Whitney said. "Or a disagreement over what to do with the Bible."

"Or Regina had one of them take the other out, and it went sideways," Jackson said.

"Regina," Abby said. "Oh my gosh. I can't believe it."

"How well do you know her?" Jackson asked.

"Not that well. I saw her a few times, and she was always amicable. Mostly, I know her from our mutual activity in the local art community. And I have to say, if she were going to steal the Bible, this Assar guy seems more like her style than Cortez."

"Yeah, the Regina-Cortez connection seems a little far-fetched to me too," Whitney said. "But he had her business card. I can't think of any other reason a former cartel member who runs a chop shop would have her business card."

"There are a lot of questions," Jackson said. "How did they ever become partners? Why the contrasting styles of Cortez and Assar? How did Team Regina keep track of the Bible? Who is the Joker?"

"The Joker?" Abby asked.

"Guy we saw at the hotel, who was the Joker from Batman last night—no, two nights ago—at the ball." He shrugged. "Either way, I think Regina's our best lead. Our only lead."

"I agree," Whitney said.

"So what do we do?" Abby asked.

"Research," Jackson and Whitney said simultaneously. "The boring side of being a P.I.," he added. "Or a Canadian spy."

Chapter Sixteen

8:55 a.m.

"SO WHERE ARE we headed anyhow?" Whitney asked, again leaning forward against Jackson and Abby's seatbacks.

"Her place," Jackson said. "You said you wanted someplace private, and she could probably use a change of clothes."

"And a warm shower," Abby said as Jackson's phone rang. He dug it out of his pocket.

"Hello?"

"Douglas," a Hispanic voice drawled. "How are you, man?"

"Diaz?"

"Who else, man?"

Whitney leaned forward. "Who's Diaz?"

"To what do I owe the pleasure, Pablo?" Jackson asked.

"I hear you got shot, man. It's becoming a dangerous business, no?"

"Is this your version of a fruit basket?"

"Hey, man, I'm just calling to say hello."

"I'd be a lousy P.I. if I believed that, Pablo."

Whitney leaned forward and turned to Abby. "You know who he's talking to?"

Abby shook her head.

"What's going on?" Jackson asked.

Pablo clicked with his tongue, an annoying sound he often made, as if there was an invisible sucker in his mouth. "All right, all right. I hear you got a case."

"Where do you hear that?"

"I've got ears, man. And I might have something of interest to you."

"What's that?"

"On the phone? Really, bro, you know better than that."

"I'm busy, Pablo. You'd better not be jerking my chain."

"Never, man. You know me, I'm deeply religious. I'd never joke about the Bible, man."

"The Bible?"

Pablo paused, and Jackson could imagine the twinkle in his eye. He hated that twinkle.

"You got ears too. So what do you say?"

Jackson sighed. "Okay. When and where?"

"I need my morning java, man," Pablo said. "How 'bout Starbucks at 26th and Wilshire? Can you be there by nine-thirty?"

"Won't you be at church, being deeply religious and all?"

"Come on, Douglas."

Jackson lowered the phone and looked at the time. "Nine-thirty."

"You won't regret it, man."

"We'll see about that."

Whitney pulled herself forward so that she was almost in the front seat. "Who's Pablo?" she asked before Jackson closed his phone.

"A P.I. I know. He's a hack."

"What's he want?"

"He says he knows something about the Bible."

"Do you believe him?"

"As much as I believe anybody else," Jackson said. "Change of plans. We're meeting him."

"Why not drop us off?" Whitney asked. "We're close to her apartment."

"Because I'm not letting you out of my sight. You have to pee, you're going to do it whistling with the door open."

"You have trust issues."

"I wonder why."

Traffic had improved, and they cruised along Interstate 10 at the speed limit. As they neared Starbucks, Jackson made Abby and Whitney promise to let him do the talking. He knew Pablo; they didn't. Let him handle things. They both agreed. Whitney twice.

Mouse, a "barista" at Starbucks, was not working, but that wasn't unusual; it was the a.m. Pablo was already seated in the corner with a Trenta cup in front of him. Jackson ignored the lines and led the way to Pablo's table.

"Man, you're living large," Pablo said, looking from Abby to Whitney and grinning. Pablo was always grinning, usually lopsidedly, his blue eyes spinning. He wore clothes even baggier than was necessary for his husky frame, and his dark black hair was gelled into a fauxhawk. Pablo hadn't changed a bit.

"These are my Mormon cousins," Jackson said as he straddled a chair. "What do you got, Pablo?"

"What, no pleasantries, no introductions?"

"Lily and Catherine," Jackson said with a pair of nods. "Now what do you want?"

"Okay, okay, man. You sure you don't want some caffeine, bro? You're a little temperamental."

"Just the facts, Pablo."

Pablo took a long drink of his brew and nodded. "Okay, man. Word on the street is you're looking for an old Bible, man. A *muy caro* Bible."

"What else does the word say?"

"That you don't know where it is."

"Kind of redundant, or I wouldn't be looking for it."

"So it's true?"

"Didn't say that. Just clarifying your word."

Pablo looked at him.

"I thought you said you had something of interest."

"I do, man, I do. I hear the Bible was in the hands of an *ese* named Cortez."

Jackson didn't say anything.

"That name mean anything to you, man?"

"Cortez? What are there, about five thousand Cortezes in L.A.?"

"His Christian name's Luis. Word is, he used to run with one of the Colombian cartels."

"The word say anything else?"

"That's not enough, man?"

Jackson shook his head as if confused. "Luis Cortez? That narrows it to a hundred maybe. Am I supposed to cold-call them all and ask if they know anything about this Bible the word says I'm looking for?"

"That name don't mean nothing to you?" Pablo asked. He looked to Abby and Whitney, who, to their credit, remained stone-faced. Pablo's shoulders slumped. "Okay, man, okay. This Cortez lives on Underwood Street over in Pico. He runs a chop shop by day."

"I thought you said he was with a cartel."

"Used to be, man, used to be." Pablo leaned forward. "And I hear he was shot last night."

"Sounds like trouble from his old life," Jackson said. He shook his head again. "What does that have to do with the Bible?"

"I gotta do your work for you, man?"

Jackson nodded and stood. "You hear something real, give me a call."

"You for reals, man? That's all I get?"

"I was thinking the same thing, Pablo. Stay out of trouble."

Jackson headed for the exit, with Abby and Whitney right behind him.

"Apparently word on his street's a little slow," Whitney said.

"He's just fishing. The real question is why."

"And for who?"

"Just how many people are after the Bible?" Abby asked.

Jackson shrugged as he opened her door.

"Thank you."

"Where'd you meet that guy anyhow?" Whitney asked.

"Shared case," Jackson said as he circled the vehicle. "Get in."

It had been a cheating boyfriend case, the only such case Jackson had ever taken. He'd been suckered by a pretty face and puppy eyes and gotten involved in a mess. Pablo had been reasonably helpful, despite his intentions. Jackson had known then the guy was a B-lister, but he never knew when a stooge like Pablo could come in handy. Just not today.

"Not going to get my door for me?"

"Hop through the window, Daisy."

Whitney huffed.

They drove back to Abby's apartment, where, after getting over the shellshock of seeing it tossed (and resignedly putting off straightening it up until later), Abby took a shower while Jackson and Whitney got busy researching Regina Archambeau, beyond what Abby knew of her. Jackson used Abby's computer and also placed a call to Mouse, who was still not answering. Whitney made hushed phone calls while she paced around the kitchen, sweeping cans and boxes out of her way with her foot to create a path. She started to report out to Jackson just as Mouse finally called back.

"Hey, dude. You rang?"

"Yeah," Jackson said. "I need a favor."

"Shoot."

"I need anything you can dig up on a woman named Regina Archambeau."

"Like what, you want me to Google her?"

"I was thinking something a little more . . . involved."

"You got something specific in mind? I can't just hack the world."

"Any chance you can tap into her phone, see who she's called, maybe track her movements?"

"Maybe. You know her number?"

"Thought maybe you could find that too."

"Regina Archambeau?"

"Yep."

"Can you spell it?"

Jackson did. "She's a major player in the L.A. art community, in case you run into multiple Regina Archambeaus."

"Wow, you've hardly left me any work at all," Mouse said.

"Just give me a call when you have something, will you?"

"Sure."

"Thanks, man."

Jackson closed his phone.

"Is this how you operate?" Whitney asked. "Have somebody else do all the work?"

"A wise man asks for help," he answered. "What'd you find?"

"Interesting stuff. For example, she was married to a Watson Woods for six years from 1979-85. He was a low-level paper pusher for the CIA until he had a heart attack in '83. He died fourteen months later, and Regina never remarried.

"CIA," Jackson said.

Whitney nodded. "Apparently she was drawn to G-men, because she had a not-so-secret on-and-off affair with Alec Vanderbilt for the latter half of the '70s. Regina, Amélie, not to mention his wives. The guy got around."

Abby stood in the doorway, still fluffing her hair dry with a towel. She looked at Whitney for a moment, then turned to Jackson. "What do we know?"

"Depends if our Canadian friend found anything but the *Entertainment Tonight* scoop."

Whitney huffed. "Nothing biographical, but I do know where we can find her."

"Where?"

"She lives on Santa Catalina Island," Whitney answered. "She's also got a summer place at Lake Tahoe, but I think we can rule that out. I have DMV records, tax records, auction history—pretty much everything your friend could find," she said to Jackson. "Nothing that will help us much."

Abby sat down beside Jackson and peeked at the computer screen. "What have you found?"

"Basic biographical info, what you'd expect to find online. But there's one especially interesting tidbit."

Whitney leaned on the arm of the couch.

"I found some artsy-fartsy blog that said Regina's hosting a gala tonight at the Catalina Casino," Jackson said. "Some highfalutin celebration of local artists and a fundraiser for saving the whales or something. I skimmed on the details."

"How thorough," Whitney said.

"Tonight?" Abby said. "I never heard anything about it."

"I think it's pretty upscale."

"Ouch," Whitney said.

"I meant—"

"I know what you meant," Abby said. "Regina and I don't run in the same circles. Still, I'd think I'd have heard something. But maybe she purposefully kept it secretive."

"So we hit her place tonight while she's at the gala," Whitney said.

"Abby," Jackson said, "if you're Regina, where do you keep the Bible? At home or in a safe deposit box somewhere?"

"At home, for sure. A few collectors just want to possess works, but most want to be able to see them, or have others see them."

Jackson nodded. "Then yeah, we hit her place tonight."

Whitney stood.

"Wait a second," Abby said. "You're going to break into her house? She'll have a security system, maybe guards. And if she does already have it in a display case instead of a safe, the case might be locked, laser protected, patched into the alarm system. And what if we get caught? This isn't taking the Bible from my brother who allegedly never had it to begin with."

"Are you saying you want to back out?" Jackson asked.

"No. I'm just saying . . . can we really pull this off by tonight?"

"I don't know," Jackson said. "Whitney, can you get blueprints or security specs from the CSIS, or do they have a satellite with thermal imaging or something we can tap into?"

"I doubt it, I really doubt it, and no."

"No wonder Canada never won a war," he muttered.

Whitney crossed her arms. "Maybe your little phone-a-friend can just hack us in."

"Else we'll wait a few hours. By then maybe you'll be with a better agency."

"Or you'll be more competent and won't have to ride my coattails everywhere."

"Guys," Abby said, "we need to focus. We're talking about breaking into the house of one of Southern California's most highly-respected art collectors."

For some reason, the gravity of what they were discussing hit Jackson when Abby spoke up. A look into Whitney's eyes indicated it had registered with her too.

Abby exhaled. "Now, tell me one of you has a plan."

Chapter Seventeen

1:11 p.m.

COMPOSED OF ALMOST seventy-five square miles of wilderness, Santa Catalina Island sat twenty-two miles southwest of the California mainland. Its rugged wilderness was home to bison, bald eagles, rattlesnakes, and—just off the western coast—great white sharks. Six indigenous species of plants grew on the island, which enjoyed a cooler climate than L.A. in the summer, but winters that were just as warm and balmy. Tourism drove the small island. Some flocked to the shops, boutiques, and bed and breakfasts in Avalon, the island's main population center. Others preferred the seclusion of unincorporated Two Harbors on the opposite end of the island. And many just wanted to rough it, camping and exploring the island at their own pace. Hiking, horseback riding, scuba diving, snorkeling, golfing, and parasailing all drew people to Santa Catalina.

Jackson had never been, despite the close proximity. But that was about to change.

He, Abby, and Whitney had done some more research, with an assist from Mouse, and then had swung by Jackson's place and Whitney's hotel, respectively, so they could each shower and change and pick up a few things they might need that evening. He had half expected Whitney to run off while he had been in the shower, but she had stayed and bonded with Abby. The trio had made a few more stops to buy additional gear and then had taken the Granada—with a sheet of plastic held by duct tape covering the vacant rear window—to Marina del Rey, where they had boarded the ferry to Catalina Island.

Forty-eight hours ago, Jackson had been putting finishing touches on his costume for the masquerade ball. If only he'd had the good sense to walk away then.

At least it was a beautiful day, the warmest of the year, with bright sunshine sparkling on the water. The sky and the ocean were complementary shades of blue, and the breeze on his face felt good as the two-tiered ferry churned south along the coastline past the airport, Hermosa Beach, and Palos Verdes Point.

Whitney joined Jackson on the top deck of the ferry. Abby was down below, making phone calls, trying to get more information on Regina's gala. She and Jackson had scoured several websites but found very few details. It was obviously A-list only. If you didn't know, you weren't invited.

"Tell me about yourself, Jackson," Whitney said. She had changed into a gray T-shirt and different jeans, her hair back in a trademark ponytail. If she wasn't so vexing, Jackson might have enjoyed a chat with her while cruising toward a resort island. Instead, he felt catty.

"I'm a Pisces still searching for someone who will help me unleash my inner child, and I like cats and long walks on the beach."

Whitney glanced over at him. "You are definitely not a Pisces."

"What's your angle?"

"My angle?"

"The 'tell me about yourself' bit. Unless this is the most elaborate blind date setup in history, you're working an angle. What is it?"

Whitney shrugged. "I just like to know who I'm working with, that's all. I want to know I can trust you."

He laughed. "That's rich."

"I mean that you're not going to lose focus on me. I've seen you checking out that blonde over there."

"What blonde?"

"That's rich."

"No, seriously, what blonde? The first mate in a striped tank and skinny jeans, the tomboy tourist with a Twins cap, or the runway model cuddling with her heartthrob?" He smirked. "Or were you referring to the teeny-bopping melanoma behind you?"

Whitney closed her eyes. "The first mate is a brunette with blond highlights, the tomboy isn't in your line of sight, and no one has checked out the melanoma since the Clinton administration."

"Very good," Jackson said. "You get the Shawn Spencer award for the day."

"You still haven't answered my question."

"I can focus. And I don't check out other guys' girls."

"Really? What kind of P.I. are you?"

Jackson's phone rang before he could retort. It was Mouse, who had been working on finding specs of Regina's Catalina Island home.

"Yeah, Mouse," Jackson said, turning and leaning against the railing.

"Okay, it's not exactly Fort Knox, but it's not Grandma's cookie jar, either."

"Lay it out for me."

"I've got building blueprints from an architect's website. Looks like this house is as much a piece of art as it is a house. Anyhow, it doesn't show any security panel wiring, but it's gotta be there. I also hacked into her e-mails and found an order for a Browning G Series display case. State of the art glass enclosed. Comes with its own alarm or can be wired into the home security system too."

"Super. Anything else?"

"No. I tried getting to her phone, but it must be encrypted. If I had more time . . ."

"No worries. Can you get me the blueprints?"

"I'll send them to your e-mail."

"No, send them to Abby's instead," Jackson said, and gave him her address. He thanked his pal, wished him a happy afternoon of macchiato mixing, and closed his phone.

"The Geek Squad come through?" Whitney asked.

"Tell me about yourself," Jackson said. "Are you always this condescending toward people you work with?"

She faked a smile.

"We should find Abby," Jackson said. "Mouse sent some blueprints."

They headed downstairs, with Jackson flitting his eyes at the runway model and heartthrob as they passed. Codes of ethics what they were, he was only human.

Abby had just gotten off the phone, and her dejected face told the story of her research. She had learned the gala started at six, but that was about it. Jackson told her about the e-mail from Mouse, and she pulled it up on her phone. The blueprints were hard to read on such a tiny screen, and without knowledge of what kind of alarm system Regina had, they could only help so much.

"What are we up against legally?" Abby asked.

"Two to three years," Whitney said. "Grand theft."

"But the Bible isn't hers," Abby said.

"Possession is nine-tenths . . ."

"It's the same as it was with Desmond," Jackson said. "The only way we can get in trouble for stealing the Bible is if we're caught red-handed or if she could convince the cops it was hers to begin with. Bigger problem is getting pinched on a B&E."

"Or getting caught by someone other than the cops," Whitney said.

"What's a B&E?" Abby asked.

"It's a wobbler. Could go up to six years."

"Six years?"

"B&E's technically burglary. After dark, with intent to steal valuables . . . Yeah."

"Maybe this isn't such a great idea."

"We won't get caught," Whitney said.

"Jackson?"

"It's up to you," he said. "I'm not wild about breaking into her place, but the way I see it, I'm not stealing, I'm reclaiming personal property."

Abby didn't appear convinced.

"Okay," Whitney said. "I need to know if I can count on you guys, because if not, I'm running my own deal."

"No, I'm in," Abby said.

"You sure?"

"I'm sure."

"Because you don't look sure."

"I'm exhausted, stressed, frustrated, and this is all happening kind of fast. But I am sure. I want the Bible."

Whitney nodded. "And you?"

Jackson nodded his head in Abby's direction. "Her wish is my command."

"Okay."

"Same deal as before?" Abby asked. "If there isn't anything critical to Canadian national security, it's mine?"

"Yes, but I get the first look at it," Whitney said.

"As long as I get to see it before it's taken away," Abby said.

"I can't let you see classified government secrets."

"A redacted version."

"Agreed," Whitney said.

Jackson shook his head. "This is officially my last case."

Abby sat back. "So what's first when we arrive?"

"The gala's at six," he said with a sigh. "So that doesn't give us a lot of time to scout and plan based on real-time intel."

"We should also check into a hotel as a safe house or rally location, in case we can't get off the island right away," Whitney said. "And run a test on our comms."

"We don't have comms," Jackson said.

"I thought you had earwigs."

"I may or may not have forgotten them."

"What?"

"Forgive me, I didn't get much sleep the last two nights."

Whitney growled.

"Speaking of," Abby said, "I'm thinking of dozing here. We have almost another hour, don't we?"

"Yeah," Jackson said. He looked at Whitney. "I'm going back up top and ogle that blonde. Want to come along?"

Whitney rolled her eyes but followed. "Tell me," she said as they climbed the stairs, "does this smart-aleck routine normally get you women?"

Jackson turned back to answer her. "Who says anything about trying to get w—"

He started to turn back around, but was too late and couldn't avoid running into a woman who had just started down the stairs. She fell backward, and Jackson lost his balance and had to cling to the railing to avoid falling on top of her.

"Katie!" a man hollered. Jackson turned and saw the heartthrob running across the deck, and it hit him that the woman on the ground with hair in her face and her purse sliding across the deck was the runway model blonde.

He reached a hand to help her. "I'm so sorry," he said. "I didn't—"

"Realize he was such a klutz," Whitney said, also helping Katie to her feet.

"Are you all right?" Jackson asked as she stood.

"I think so. Just startled."

"I really am sorry."

"It's fine."

The heartthrob arrived, an anxious look on his face. "Are you okay?" he asked, putting his hand on Katie's back.

She nodded.

"Are you sure?"

"I'm fine, Fred."

He nodded and stepped around her to pick up her purse.

"I'll get out of your way," Jackson said with a grin. "I'm sorry again."

"Don't be," she said. "Accidents happen."

"It's how we met, after all," Fred said, putting his arm around her waist and squeezing. "I spilled my beer on her at an Angels game."

Katie grinned. "And now we're on our honeymoon."

"In that case, we'll really get out of your way," Jackson said. He offered a "Congratulations" and another smile as he pushed past Fred and Katie.

"That was smooth," Whitney said.

"Yeah, well."

"Wanna try that 'I'm focused and don't check out hotties' reassurance speech again?"

"I wasn't checking her out. I was answering your stupid question."

"Well wipe that dumb look off your face, Douglas. She's married."

"He is too, Raines. I saw the way . . ." He frowned.

"What?"

"Raines. I think Jeff Goldblum was in a short-lived TV show called *Raines*. I always liked him. The way he s-stu-stutters and st-stammers and . . . pauses while looking off to the side."

Whitney shook her head, perhaps mumbling, "Unbelievable," under her breath as they approached the railing. For several minutes, they silently watched the bow break through the waves.

"So you ever done something like this before?" Whitney asked.

"Yeah, back when I was in college. I dated this girl, a would-be marine biologist. She had a thing for dolphins, so I took her on an afternoon cruise."

Whitney rolled her eyes. "I mean breach an estate on a retrieval mission."

"Yeah. Two nights ago. Big success."

"Forget I asked."

"The answer is no," Jackson said. "Not exactly like this." He looked around to make sure they weren't being listened to. "But if your CSIS files hold a candle to the CIA's or FBI's, you can find out all about me. I've taken down L.A. gangbangers, hit a Vegas penthouse, and took a U.S. senator hostage in his own home, not to mention stormed a militia-operated Air Force base. All in the name of justice."

Whitney stared at him. "You're *that* Jackson Douglas?"

He nodded.

"I heard about you. They said you were a terrorist."

"That was the original story, before the directors of several agencies and half the Joint Chiefs cleared me."

Whitney looked out at the rising coastline of Catalina Island and shook her head. "I guess you're not some wet-behind-the-ears P.I. after all."

"Not anymore."

She turned back to him. "I just want to make sure I know who I'm dealing with. I've been burned by rookies before."

"And I've been burned by people who have lied to me."

"No more lies. Until we have the Bible, we're a team." She extended her hand, and Jackson shook it. Then Whitney leaned back on the railing. "I have a bad feeling about this, though," she said.

"Why's that?"

"I somehow doubt we'll be the only ones making a play for the Bible."

*　　　　　　*　　　　　　*

2:34 p.m.

THE CITY of Avalon was built in and on the slopes of a canyon on the southeastern end of Catalina Island. The terrain formed a natural C around Avalon Bay, and the ferry dock at the bottom and a man-made jetty at the top closed the C even farther. Sailboats, yachts, pleasure craft, and inflatable boats were docked at one of several piers or else at moorings in the bay. Even a Carnival cruise ship lay anchored a quarter mile out to sea.

Despite all the other brilliant scenery—cerulean seas, rocky terrain, abundant foliage, and colorful structures in the valley and perched on the hillsides—the Catalina Casino was the preeminent visual draw on the island. Situated at the northern tip of the C, the twelve-story cylindrical structure was not a gambling casino as Jackson had always assumed. Rather, it housed a museum, a movie theater, and the world's largest circular ballroom, with space for over a thousand dancers. Surrounded on three sides by water and outlined against a cloud-dotted sky, the brilliant white exterior and orange-red clay tile shingles gave the magnificent structure a Mediterranean feel. Late in the afternoon and into the evening, with a setting sun casting long shadows to contrast with the bright colors of the casino and surrounding terrain, it would provide an elegant locale for Regina Archambeau's gala.

Jackson, Abby, and Whitney disembarked from the ferry and made their way on foot to the heart of Avalon. Vehicles were carefully restricted on the island, and a majority of residents used golf carts instead. Or walked. The carts were also available for rent, and as the trio walked, they considered renting one. But first, they headed for the Crystal Hotel on Metropolis Avenue. It was centrally located in Avalon, equidistant from the ferry dock, the Casino, and Regina's place on the hillside.

Abby booked a single room while Jackson and Whitney discussed how precisely to survey Regina's house. It was on the edge of town, but still close enough to a handful of other buildings that they couldn't be too overt about it. They discussed some sort of undercover endeavor to get them on the grounds and inside the house, but they didn't have a lot of time to set something up. Besides, the less they showed their faces, the better.

"Oh great, now she's got wandering eyes," Whitney said. Abby was smiling and talking to a good-looking stiff by the check-in counter. "What if we stick to the same M.O.?" she asked Jackson. "Go in as FBI?"

"How many times do you think you can get away with impersonating a federal agent before getting busted?"

"I have the badges for a reason. And with the CSIS, I sort of have immunity."

"Immunity?"

"As good as."

"What about me?" Jackson asked. "I just play the sidekick?"

"Yes. Or my consultant. Or something."

"No, too risky. Regina's no dope."

"Are you saying you are since you fell for it?"

Abby interrupted them. "Uh, guys, we have a problem."

"What's that?" Whitney asked.

"That guy headed for the stairs," she said, pointing at the good-looking stiff. "We dated a few times an eternity ago, and we've stayed friends."

"Very touching."

"He co-owns a gallery in Hollywood," Abby continued. "He's here to attend the gala tonight, and he said Regina plans to unveil a new discovery."

"Where have I heard that before?" Jackson said.

"I asked if he knew what it was, but he wasn't sure. Said she just sent out an update this morning and promised it was something out of the box, not your traditional sculpture or painting."

"The Bible," Whitney said through clenched teeth.

Abby nodded.

"Well, so much for an estate breach," Jackson said.

"Did you get a room?" Whitney asked.

Abby held up a keycard. "Second floor, like you asked."

"Let's go get a little privacy. Who knows who else might be around."

"I don't get it," Abby said when the door to their small room was closed behind them. "How can she get away with suddenly announcing she has the Bible? Two nights ago, Desmond was going to make the same announcement."

"But he didn't," Jackson said. "He never actually said he had the Bible."

"And it's not like she and Alec were strangers," Whitney said. "She can claim it was a long-lost gift from him to her."

"But why would she do it?" Abby asked. "Why now? I mean, she steals it from Cortez, who stole it from Andrews and Newton, who stole it from . . ."

"Me," Whitney said.

"Who stole it from us, who stole it from Desmond, who stole it from Abby in the first place," Jackson said. "I see what you're saying. Why not stash it away and wait six months until the heat dies down?"

"Yeah, but now she can have who knows how many witnesses," Whitney said. "All of her high-society friends see that she has the Bible and see her claim it's hers. It establishes ownership, at least in the mind of public opinion."

"Which gives her a claim to make to the authorities in the event it gets nabbed," Jackson said. "Something none of the rest of us—including Desmond or her yet—have had."

"But how will she explain it?" Abby asked. "She wasn't in the will; Tate wasn't in the will."

"Oh, she'll come up with something," Whitney said.

"Says the master storyteller," Jackson chimed.

"So what do we do?" Abby asked.

Whitney exhaled. "We have to stop her from revealing she has the Bible."

"Great," Jackson said. "Instead of crashing Regina's estate, we crash her party instead."

"That or try to hit her in transit. Or go after it at the estate now."

Jackson and Abby both shook their heads. "No way," Jackson said.

"Well, either of you have a way to suddenly score an invite?" Whitney asked. "Your friend from the lobby, maybe?"

Abby shook her head. "I doubt it. He implied he was with somebody."

"What about you?" Whitney asked Jackson. "You don't happen to know any art critics or local artists, do you?"

Suddenly Cate Blanchett flooded his mind, followed by the lady he'd seen dressed in white at the masquerade ball—Tolkien's Lady of the Wood, Galadriel. He finally identified the face behind the mask, and it caused his throat to run dry.

"Yeah," he said with a sigh. "I actually think I might."

Chapter Eighteen

Three and a half years ago . . .
Saturday, October 10
5:47 p.m.

"YOU NOT ENJOYING yourself?" Grant asked.

"I'd enjoy myself a lot more if you'd keep your eyes on your urinal."

"What, you got urinal phobia?"

"They are a little strange, yeah."

Grant chuckled under his breath. "Is this the spot where I ask to pull your man card?"

Jackson zipped his jeans. "Just to get this straight, you're defending manliness, and your platform is 'it's cool to pee side by side'?" He headed for the sink.

"Seriously, what's eating you, Jack?"

He hit the faucet on. "I don't know."

"Come on, bro. It's a beautiful day, you're in the company of three beautiful girls."

"Aren't you the guy who always complains when I 'admire the scenery' and who warned me to be on my best behavior today?"

Grant shrugged. "I know you weren't wild about coming, but I thought you'd at least enjoy the 'eye candy.'"

Jackson shook out his hands, bypassing the jet engine disguised as a hand dryer. Would it really destroy the planet to have paper towels in public bathrooms?

"Candy's great," he said. "Unless it's so cold it gives you a toothache." He left Grant to finish up and pushed through the door and out into the brilliant California sunshine. Grant was right about one thing, it was a beautiful day.

A door opened behind Jackson, and the brook of female conversation gushed out. He ignored it, keeping his eyes out on the perfectly blue ocean.

He'd lived within spitting distance of the Pacific all his life, yet it never got dull.

"Quite a view, isn't it?"

The voice was a little deeper, meaning it was Heather McKenzie's. Jackson glanced her way. She was the least glamorous piece of candy, but still a head-turner. Trademark blue eyes, wavy blond hair, perfect features, and model figure. The only possible imperfection was a slight upturn at the point of the nose, but Jackson hadn't settled for sure if that was anatomy or attitude. Which is why he was a little surprised at this gesture of civility.

"Yeah," he answered, and returned to the ocean view. He remembered his talk with Grant and how much this day meant to him, so he decided to return the civility with a little conversation. "Grant said something about you working with models?" he said, draping his arms over the railing.

Heather laughed. "Not fashion models. I work part-time for a company that makes scale 3-D models, and I do the fine detailing. And I do some of my own work, just for fun." She laughed again. "I could see the excitement in your eyes."

Jackson shook his head and started to justify himself, but was distracted by the clanking of bangles as two manicured hands appeared on the railing to his right. They were connected to slender arms that belonged to the youngest piece of candy, Holly McKenzie. Higher voice, shorter stature, same eyes and hair, both a shade lighter. Whereas Heather wore a sickening powder blue (UCLA's primary color) blouse and a white skirt, Holly was decked in a pink baby doll top and designer denim shorts. Plenty of shiny jewelry and a slightly more extroverted personality to go with it. Maybe even a flirtatious personality. Certainly lively. It was like a second coating of dark chocolate.

"Go easy on him, Heather," Holly said. "He probably had his hopes up that you could introduce him."

"Aha, so that's why you agreed to come today, huh?"

"No, I came for the conversation and camaraderie."

"It's worse than that," said a silky voice from behind them. "He probably expected to get a date with one of you."

The third piece of candy. A king-sized Snickers that reduced Heather and Holly to stale chocolate-covered peanuts by comparison.

"Is that it?" Heather asked.

"So which one of us?" Holly teased.

Jackson sighed. He spotted a sailboat way out on the horizon, tacking toward the setting sun, and envied its passengers. Especially if it happened to be a passenger, singular.

"Knowing Jackson, he was probably hoping for both," the Snickers said.

He turned around to retort but stopped with his mouth half open. How did he insult someone who looked like that?

Wavy blond hair that tumbled over her shoulders. Ice blue eyes like sapphires inlaid in creamy, flawless skin. Perfect ears, nose, mouth, and a neck that would have made Solomon swoon. Her figure was athletic, graceful, with just the right amount of curves. A red cap-sleeved sundress flitted about her in the breeze, one second accentuating her figure, the next teasing at it, reminiscent of the ebbing and flowing waves on the beach. She stood with a posture and confidence that could command any room, yet with a natural ease that would draw the eye of every red-blooded male. Jackson couldn't help but marvel at six-feet-nothing of God's perfect handiwork.

On the outside, at least.

"Well said," Hillary McKenzie taunted, forcing Jackson to close his mouth.

"Everybody hungry?" Grant asked, finally emerging from the bathroom.

"Fly get stuck?" Jackson asked.

Hillary smirked at him out of the corner of her mouth before turning and taking Grant's hand. They led the way, hand-in-hand, down a boardwalk that connected several shops and restaurants while providing views of the Malibu hillside and the ocean. Jackson trudged along a few paces behind Heather and Holly, his stride matching his demeanor. This little outing had been Grant's idea, siblings of a semi-serious couple getting to know each other or some such nonsense. It was bad enough that he was missing USC's game, but now he had to duel with Hillary and her seconds. Jackson wanted to give in and just be a grouch the rest of the night, confirm what they thought about him. But he was lulled into a sense of acquiescence by blond hair that bounced with every step in front of him. When they weren't talking, they really were quite cute.

Holly lagged back and matched her pace with Jackson's. "You mad?" she asked.

"Not mad."

"We were just teasing, you know."

Great, now he was the guy who had to have teasing explained to him.

"Too bad," he replied. "I was going to pick you."

She winked and grinned and took his hand to pull him even with Heather. She let go, but the act had buoyed Jackson's spirit. He may be a sucker, but at least he knew it.

Holly grinned again as they arrived at Jillian's, an upscale surf and turf bistro. They were seated on an outdoor terrace with views of Malibu Beach and the Santa Monica Mountains. The air was still warm and pleasant and did wonders with multiple strands of blond hair. The group spent ten minutes scanning their menus, chatting about the matinee they had seen, critiquing the lack of organic offerings and the value of them in the first place, and considering how they were going to split the check.

"It's on me," Jackson said.

"Really?" Holly asked.

"You don't have to pay," Heather said.

Jackson shrugged. "Grant paid for the movie; I'll pick up dinner."

Hillary shot him a look.

"What?" he asked.

"What are you trying to prove?"

"Nothing."

She huffed.

"Hillary," Holly said. "I think it's sweet."

Hillary raised her eyebrows but said nothing more, and the conversation turned to the menus and who was getting or recommended what.

After they had ordered, the three McKenzie sisters excused themselves to the restroom. It had only been a half hour since their last pit stop, but that was women, right? Besides, what did Jackson care? Holly had left her smartphone on the table, and as soon as they had disappeared inside, he reached for it.

"What are you doing?" Grant asked.

"Checking the score."

"I figured that. I meant paying for dinner."

"Oh, that. I'm smitten, and I'm trying to impress Hillary's sisters."

"Are you?"

"I'm trying to be a dude, all right?"

"A dude?"

Jackson nodded. "I figured it's the swell thing to do."

"Would you be acting so swell if they weren't both tens?"

"Did Mr. Politically Correct just refer to women by a number used to classify their physical appearance?"

"I'm just trying to read you, Jack."

"Why? Just enjoy a free meal. Let me handle my motives." He looked back at the phone. "Any idea how the heck these things work?"

Just before the girls returned, Jackson found his way onto the internet and saw that USC was leading Arizona 14-3. That was comfortable, given the Trojan's defense, so he relaxed and enjoyed the evening breeze as he sipped iced tea.

"So, Jackson," Heather said when the three girls were back, "Hillary tells me you're a claims adjustor."

He looked at her and took a drink.

"And I thought it was just your attempts at wit that left you speechless," Hillary said.

"Sorry, I was just being careful not to trip over the punch line."

"No, I'm asking for real," Heather said, squeezing her lemon into her tea.

"Yeah," Jackson answered.

"So you investigate claims to make sure there isn't fraud or deception?"

"Among other things. I'm still pretty low on the totem pole. Save it," he added at Hillary, stopping her before she could get anything out.

"Have you ever uncovered any deception by clients?" Heather continued.

"A little embellishment, maybe."

"But no deception?"

"No."

"What would you do if you found it?"

"Probably ask for a cut," Hillary said.

"Anyone else find it odd that this talk of ethics comes from a defense attorney?" Jackson asked.

"I'm serious," Heather said again. "If you did find something, would you report it?"

Jackson nodded. "Yeah."

"What if you thought they were right?"

"Huh?"

"I mean, what if you found somebody who was putting in a quote-unquote fraudulent claim, but you thought they deserved it?"

"You mean where the insurance company was being negligent?" Grant asked.

Heather shrugged. "Something like that."

Jackson reached for his tea. "I don't know. Depends on the situation, I guess."

"So you would help somebody scam your own company?" Hillary asked.

"I didn't say that."

"You didn't not say it either," Grant said.

"Okay, what if it's Great Benefit Life not paying for Donny Ray's nosebleeds and Claire Danes is clinging to you in movie theaters?"

"What?" Holly asked.

"*Rainmaker*," Jackson said. "Before your time. The point is, what if my insurance company's ripping these people off? I'm just supposed to sit back and let it happen?"

"That's what I'm wondering," Heather said.

"No, that's when you follow legal recourse instead of taking matters into your own hands," Grant said, his eyes honed in on Jackson.

"Yeah, but the legal recourse meets a dead end in Jon Voight or Hillary Reagan McKenzie over here. Then what?"

Holly leaned forward. "Where's this coming from, Heather?"

"The topic's been on my mind lately," she said. "When is it okay to break the rules?"

"It's not," Grant said.

"Never?" Heather asked. "You'd never break the rules?"

Grant shook his head.

"What if breaking the rules was the only way to . . . I don't know, catch a criminal?" Holly asked.

"That's a slippery slope," Hillary said.

"Maybe," Jackson said, "but life isn't lived on a grassy flatland. What if Magnum doesn't shoot Ivan, and he gets back on a plane to Russia and never pays for his crimes?"

Grant rolled his eyes.

"Or the founding fathers decide to put up with 'a long train of abuses and usurpations' instead of declaring independence, and we're all sitting around drinking tea right now," he closed with a British accent.

"We are drinking tea," Holly said, nodding at their glasses of iced tea. She then winked at him.

"She's cute. Is she house-trained?"

Holly whapped him. Then turned to Heather. "I still want to know why you're asking."

Heather took a drink of her tea. "A friend of mine worked at an art gallery, and just got fired because they found out he fudged the provenance records for a painting. But he did it so that the original and rightful owner would be able to retain it instead of having it go to auction. It's a long story. Anyhow, I know the Bible says we shouldn't lie or deceive, but are there ever cases where it is acceptable to break the rules for a good purpose?"

"Yes," Jackson said at the same time that Grant said, "No."

"This should be good," Holly said.

Their waitress—a brunette for a change—brought dinner at that moment, and they waited until she was gone to resume their conversation.

"There's never a right time to do the wrong thing," Grant said.

"Ben Franklin?" Jackson asked.

"Dad."

"Burn," Holly muttered, reaching for a crouton from her grilled chicken salad.

"So if Dad had been captured by the Russians and asked the location of a top-secret Navy installation, he should have told them instead of lie?"

"That's different. That's war."

"All's fair in love and war," Holly said.

"The Bible says *'thou shalt not kill,'*" Jackson said. "You going to shoot a convenience store robber if it saves a pregnant hostage?"

"It doesn't say 'kill,'" Hillary replied evenly as she reached for her water. "It says *'you shall not murder.'* There is *'a time to kill,'* there is never a time to murder."

"It's a very faint gray line," Jackson said.

"For some people, maybe."

"What about sneaking snacks into a movie theater?" Holly asked with a sideways wink at Jackson.

"Who helped herself to half of my contraband Skittles?"

She shrugged her shoulders in a quiet giggle.

"Don't look to Jackson for ethics," Hillary said.

"Why? Because I didn't study them for eight years at Volleyball U?"

"Jack," Grant said, warning with his eyes.

"I didn't mean to start a fight," Heather said. "I'm just sorting through this issue right now."

"I think it's somewhere . . ." Holly's voice trailed off as the Black Eyed Peas' "Let's Get it Started" came over the restaurant sound system. She began to bounce and sway to the music, silently mouthing the words.

"You were saying, Fergie?" Jackson asked.

"Um, it's somewhere in the middle. There are some hard-and-fasts and some rules that can be broken if the situation calls for it."

"So who determines if the situation calls for it?" Grant asked.

"You two," Jackson muttered as he picked up his burger. "Cops and lawyers."

The argument died there, in part because neither side seemed coercible and in part because the food at Jillian's was delicious. And in small part, because Holly was busy grooving to the Top 20. Jackson glanced her way, but instead of shying away, she raised her arms as if she was on the dance floor and dramatically mouthed a few lines along with the Peas.

Talk turned to work. Grant was nearing two years with LAPD; Hillary had been with Conway, Davenport & Rankin for more than a year; Heather worked part-time at a gallery, part-time "with models," and part-time on her own; and Holly was in her final year at UC-Santa Barbara and didn't work. Then there was Jackson, twice a college "dropout," a washout with the U.S. Army, and holder of every dead-end job from Tijuana to Malibu. At least to hear Hillary tell it. So he took some more ribbing and debated excusing himself to the restroom and sticking them with the check. Maybe he could find a sailboat . . .

Instead, he drifted to the background and let them talk. He'd made up his mind about Hillary long ago; he would never be friends with the Ice Princess. But he had to admit Heather and Holly weren't too bad, despite their teasing and the obvious similarities (beyond the aesthetic) to Hillary. If his premonitions proved correct and Grant and Hillary ended up tying the knot, family gatherings might not be altogether dreadful. At least the scenery would be okay.

After dinner, the group took a sunset walk on the Malibu Pier. Grant and Hillary were locked arm-in-arm, and although they didn't wander off alone, they might as well have. That left Jackson alone between Heather and Holly, who was busy on her phone. Texting college guys, no doubt.

He turned to Heather. "You get your answer?"

"Hmm?"

"About ethics and when rule-breaking is allowed?"

"No."

"Maybe there is no answer. I don't mean to propose moral ambiguity or relegate the Scriptures to some impractical book of trite ideas."

"No, of course not," Heather said.

"But, there are lauded rule-breakers in the Bible, people who acted on faith and conscience instead of the law. So maybe it is like *The Dutchess* here said, that it depends on the situation."

Heather nodded and thought for a moment. "So how do you know in the situation? If you don't have a hard-and-fast rule to live by, how do you know what to do in the heat of battle?"

"That," Jackson said, "is a very good question."

Chapter Nineteen

Sunday, January 20
3:14 p.m.

BALMY BREEZES SWIRLED through the canyons and out to the beaches of Avalon as Jackson stepped onto the trio's small balcony for some privacy. Sighing heavily, he dialed a number he'd never expected to have in his phone's memory.

"Hello?"

It was a male's voice.

It should not have been a male's voice.

"Yeah . . . is Hillary there?"

"Can I tell her who's calling?"

"It's probably better if you don't."

"Okay, have it your way."

"No, hold on," Jackson said. "Tell her it's Jackson."

"Sure, just a minute."

Cell phones being what they were, voice identification wasn't easy, but Jackson had this guy pegged. Abercrombie polo, board shorts, flip-flops. You could just tell in the voice, the tone.

"Hello?"

That was the silky soft voice of Hillary, a purr that could melt granite one moment and harden lava the next. Jackson forced his mind elsewhere.

"That Brian?" he asked.

"What do you want, Jackson?"

"I hate to say this, Hill, but I need a favor."

She paused. Bristling at the use of his nickname for her, probably. "Okay," came her measured reply. "But no *quid pro quo* this time."

"Trust me, I have no intention of offering to repay you in any way."

"What do you need?" If he wasn't mistaken, he almost heard a smile in her voice.

"You happen to know if Heather has plans tonight?"

"Excuse me?"

"Heather. Is she by any chance invited to an art gala on Catalina tonight?"

Another pause. "Jackson, are you calling me to ask my sister out on a date?"

"No. Wow, no. I've got the date. I just need an invite to the gala."

"And what does that have to do with Heather?"

"I don't know. I was hoping she could pull a few strings or something."

She answered with silence.

"Hillary?"

"Heather works at an art gallery," she answered. "I don't think she has any strings to pull."

"Well, she was at Desmond Vanderbilt's masquerade ball Friday night, and that was high-society elbow rubbing. And I'm out of options."

"You really like this girl?"

"It's technically not a date, Hill. It's a case."

"You're working again?"

"I am."

"And you need to go to an art gala on Catalina for a case?"

"I do."

Yet another pause. "I still don't know why you're calling me, Jackson. Surely a good private investigator could find Heather's number."

He wasn't sure if she was paying him a compliment by calling him good or if she was insinuating that he wasn't good. With Hillary, he kind of guessed the latter.

"I'm in a time crunch," he said. "And I was kind of thinking the request might carry a little more weight if it came from you."

"You mean if I remind her that you saved my life, so she owes you?"

"You may want to word it a little softer than that . . ."

"I'll give her a call."

"Thanks, Hill. Ary."

"Nice catch. I'll call you either way."

"Say hi to Brian for me."

"Bye, Jackson."

He closed the phone. There, that hadn't been so terrible. A kidnapping, a couple dozen deaths, and a daring rescue could sure build a reasonable bridge.

Abby and Whitney were both waiting anxiously when he returned inside. "Well?" Whitney asked.

"She's going to make a call. It doesn't sound too promising."

"I know a couple of people," Abby said. "I'll make a few calls too."

"What about you?" Jackson asked Whitney. "Can't the CSIS get us in?"

"How?"

"I don't know. The feds are always getting people into parties as ambassadors and diplomats and their arm candy. At least on TV."

"I can place a call," she said. "But we need to consider Plan B."

"What's that?" Abby asked.

"I don't know. Would Desmond have been invited tonight?"

"He's in jail."

"Meaning his invite would go to waste."

Abby shook her head. "I don't think so, anyhow."

"Then I guess we only have one other option," Jackson said. "Crash the party."

For the next half hour, Abby and Whitney made phone calls and waited for responses while Jackson watched the end of a very exciting Eagles-Packers playoff game. He should have been with Reggie right now, downing a pizza or some burgers instead of holed up with two women trying to get an invitation to an art gala.

Green Bay won on a last-second field goal, and while the Cheeseheads were losing their minds, Jackson's phone rang. It was Hillary.

"I gave Heather your number," she said. "She's got a line on an invitation."

"That's great."

"But you should know, she's still mad at you."

"For what?"

"The shower."

"The shower? That stupid couples' shower she wanted to throw you and Grant?"

"That's the one."

Jackson shook his head. "But she's calling?"

"Any minute."

"Thanks, Hill. I o—"

"Owe me one?"

"Sorry, force of habit."

"You being in debt a habit? I believe it."

He thanked her again and updated Abby and Whitney, neither of whom had received any favorable replies to their inquiries. Within five minutes, his phone rang again.

"Hello?"

"Jackson?"

"Heather?"

"I talked to Hillary," she said. "She said you're working a case and need an invitation to the Archambeau Gala tonight."

"That's right. Any way you can make that happen?"

"She also said you saw me at the Vanderbilt Ball on Friday?"

"I did."

"And you didn't say hello?"

"I didn't recognize you until today. Honest. That whole mask thing."

"Let me guess . . . the coarse pirate who was hitting on everyone?"

"I only hit on like two people, and that was for cover."

Heather sighed. "Tim knows a guy at Cirrus who is on the who's who list of L.A. art dealers and collectors. His sister, also an A-lister, knows Regina and, if the price is right, could put your name on the list, even at this hour."

"This is sounding like that episode of *M*A*S*H* where Hawkeye needed new boots," Jackson said. "But I'm in. What's the price?"

"Nothing. Consider it a favor for the man who saved my sister's life."

"Did she tell you to say that?"

"No."

"Okay. Thanks, Heather."

"What's your date's name?"

"Uh, just put it under Jack Goldman and guest."

"Jack Goldman?"

"I'm sort of undercover."

"Whatever you say. You'll be on the list," she said.

Jackson stopped himself just before telling Heather that he owed her one. Instead, he thanked her again, then closed his phone and turned to Abby and Whitney. "We're in."

*   *   *

5:58 p.m.

"NOT BAD for two hours, huh?" Whitney asked, spinning in front of the bathroom door.

"I was going to say for a Canadian, but sure."

She gave him the evil eye, and duly so. After Heather had come through by getting them into the gala, the trio had blitzed Avalon's shopping centers for clothes and accessories to wear to it. Jackson had been able to rent a tux that, without time for alterations, was a little long in the sleeves and pants. But it was doable and better than the other way around. Whitney had purchased a mauve floor-length evening gown, and shoes and a purse to accompany it. Abby had helped her with her hair and makeup while Jackson watched the AFC Championship Game, and he had to admit, Whitney looked pretty good. For a hurried Canadian.

"You two should get going," Abby said. Since Regina would recognize her, she wouldn't be able to attend, and Whitney probably wouldn't have gone for being the one left behind anyhow. Plus, Abby had work to do, like booking return passage on the seven-thirty ferry—the last to leave the island for the night. Jackson and Whitney's strategy was to time their exit—with the Bible—so as to have just enough time to stop at the hotel, change into something less conspicuous, and join Abby on the ferry back to the mainland.

"You ready?" Whitney asked Jackson.

He nodded. "Let's roll."

It was a five-minute walk from their hotel to the casino. The sun had set, and the air was cool in the added shadow cast by the cliffs on their left. To their right, palm trees lined the edge of the harbor, the water pristine at dusk. Sailboats and yachts were moored in row upon row, many dark, but many with lights twinkling against the evening sky. And ahead of them, the majestic Catalina Casino towered over the surrounding sea like a giant turret guarding the island.

"I hope you're good at winging things," Whitney said.

"I thought we strategized quite well through the bathroom door."

She shook her head. "You men have no idea what goes into a night like this for a woman. You just run some gel through your hair and throw on a pair of pants and a jacket, and if you can figure out the cufflinks, it's all good."

"Yes, but we don't look as resplendent as you do."

Whitney looked up at him. "Don't mess with me."

"Hey, how fast do you think you can run in that dress?"

"Not very. Why?"

"I'm just thinking, if I get my hands on the Bible and take off, you won't be able to catch me."

"No, but the bullets from the Walther PPK strapped to my thigh will."

Jackson grinned. "Fair enough."

The gala officially commenced at six, and already a good number of people were milling around outside the casino or making their way inside. Jackson and Whitney joined a small line filing past a maître d' checking invites.

"You sure this former girlfriend of yours came through?"

Jackson sighed. "Sister of my brother's former fiancée, and yes."

Whitney nodded.

"Name, sir?"

"Jack Goldman."

The maître d' nodded and scanned the list. "Here we are. Mr. Jack Goldman and guest. Enjoy your evening. Ma'am."

"Thank you."

Up close, the casino was even more impressive. Giant pillars supported a covered colonnade that encircled the structure. Jackson and Whitney entered through a doorway beneath a beautiful mural of California marine life. Ramped walkways that reminded Jackson of those at a football or baseball stadium carried them to the top level and the casino's spacious ballroom. Already, the party was in full swing.

A small symphony in the midst of a vaguely familiar classical piece occupied the stage at the far end of the room. On the spacious dance floor, various works of art were on display. Paintings, sculptures, figurines, more stuff Jackson couldn't identify. Waiters and waitresses dressed to put Jackson to shame circulated among the finest of Southern California's finest, serving champagne and ritzy hors d'oeuvres. Jackson wanted nothing more than a couple of slices and a cream soda.

"Think it's out yet?" Whitney asked, her eyes scanning the room.

Jackson drew his eyes down from the arched fifty-foot ceiling and the golden chandeliers in the middle of the room to the works of art on display. "I don't know. Let's make the rounds."

For ten minutes, Jackson and Whitney mingled with complete strangers as the crowd continued to grow. They also circled the room, looking for the Bible. Jackson didn't spot it and assumed Regina was saving it for a grand reveal, à la Desmond a few nights prior. But then he saw Whitney on the fringe of one of the largest assemblages of people, and he drifted her way. A dozen men and women formed a semi-circle around a display case, their fingers caressing champagne flutes. Jackson joined Whitney in peering over the shoulder of an elderly couple. In front of them was the Vanderbilt Bible.

It was inside a glass case that gave every indication of being attached to the pedestal supporting it. No doubt locked, maybe even wired with an alarm. Jackson nudged Whitney, and as the orchestra paused to light applause and then began another piece, they moved off to the periphery.

"Like we figured," she said.

"Yeah. How long you need with the glass cutter?" he asked, looking down at her purse.

"Mere seconds. But not getting seen and not triggering the alarm . . ."

"Yeah."

"What's the time?"

"Twenty-four," he said, consulting a cheap watch that hid under his long jacket sleeves.

"Okay, MacGyver. Should we see what we can find around here?"

They split up, Whitney heading to the bathroom to "powder her nose" and Jackson grabbing a drink from the open bar and going for a stroll on the 360-degree veranda. He sauntered along, nodding at other partygoers, faking sips of Scotch, and looking for anything that could be helpful in their ad hoc plan. They'd left the mainland planning for a home invasion in the dark, not a smash and grab in front of hundreds of people, and despite their conversation through the bathroom door, they'd come to the casino with little more than determination.

Fifteen minutes later, he met up with Whitney in a now more crowded ballroom. "Find anything?" he asked.

"There's a janitor's closet by the stairs," she said. "It's locked, but we can pick it. It's bound to have aerosol cans, cleaning supplies, who knows. You?" she asked, looking around.

"Fire extinguisher. It'll create a boom if we can get it to explode."

"You see any fire alarms?"

"Wasn't looking. I'm hoping to stay out of federal crime territory."

"We need more than just booms," Whitney said. "We need a visual too."

"Maybe the janitor's closet," Jackson said. "Surely a CSIS agent knows how to make fake smoke."

"You got the matches from the hotel?"

He nodded.

She took a deep breath. "Okay. How are we for time?"

"Early. Quarter to seven."

"I say we go now."

"I say we don't want to be sitting on a ferry for ten minutes while the police are looking for terrorists. It's five minutes to the hotel, five to change, five to the ferry. Add five to get out of here, and we don't want to start anything before seven."

"So what, you want to peruse the art some more?"

"No, I think—"

"What is it?"

Jackson turned his body slightly. "Your four o'clock," he said.

Whitney glanced over his shoulder, and her eyes went wide.

A man and a woman stood at the entrance to the ballroom. His muscular frame was threatening to burst through his tuxedo while a debonair grin hinted at a highbrow brain to accompany the brawn. Her purple gown was almost as eye-catching as the figure it concealed, and she stood tall and scanned the room like a prey animal in the open prairie. Jackson had only seen their faces for a second, but it was enough to recognize them as the honeymooners from the ferry: Fred and Katie.

"What are they doing here?" Whitney asked, turning so they couldn't see her face.

"Maybe they're big art fans."

"You believe that?"

"Not really, no."

"They could be," Whitney said, sneaking another look. "I mean, people do plan honeymoons around events."

"Speaking from experience?"

"No."

He nodded. "Maybe we should feel them out," he said.

"Which one?" Whitney asked.

"I'm serious. We've got a few minutes. Strike up a casual, 'Hey, didn't I see you on the ferry,' conversation. Are you good at reading people?"

"We don't have time."

He checked his watch. "We have five minutes."

"I don't think we do," Whitney said, nodding past Jackson. He turned and saw Fred striking out for the bar. On the other side of the room, Katie had blended into the crowd.

"You got eyes on him?" Jackson asked.

Whitney nodded.

"Give me five minutes with her. I'll see what I can find out."

"How?"

He grinned. "Charm."

"You better have a lot of it, because you and him . . ." She shook her head. "On her honeymoon?"

"Five minutes."

Jackson slipped into the crowd, juking around shoulders like a USC tailback. Katie was admiring a sculpture of some unidentified mass when Jackson leaned in to get a closer look. He casually lifted his head and waited a few seconds until her eyes rose.

"Katie the honeymooner, right?" he said with a wide grin.

Her face blankly studied his for a second before she offered a very brief, very cursory smile. "That's right."

"I trust the rest of your ride over was uneventful."

"It was," she said coolly.

"I'm afraid I'm not much for the abstracts," Jackson continued. "Are we looking at a game of Jenga gone awry or a wreck in turn three at Talladega?"

There was a flicker for just a second. Too short to be considered a smile, more a flash in the eyes. Then utter disinterest clouded her face. "I'm not sure," she said.

He nodded. "You're not here alone, are you?"

"No."

He nodded again. "Well, I don't want to look like a poacher." He smiled. "Enjoy your evening."

"You too," she said as he drifted back toward Whitney.

"You want me to call an ambulance?" Whitney asked. "That was a pretty bad crash and burn."

"You were supposed to be watching Fred."

"He's on the veranda. Learn anything?"

Jackson nodded. "She's not here for the art."

"How do you know?"

"I made a crack about abstracts, you know, the type of thing real art snobs would hate, while she was looking at an abstract sculpture."

"And?"

"And, she looked bored."

Whitney frowned.

"Bored, not angry or disdainful. And I thought I saw a flicker of amusement first. I think she was trying to get rid of me."

"That I'll agree with."

"It doesn't mean they're here for the Bible. Fred could be the art buff, and she's the lackey wife, but then . . ."

"Why is she looking at all the displays?"

"And headed toward the Bible," Jackson said. He looked around. "Any sign of Fred?"

"No. Still on the veranda."

"What about Regina?"

"I haven't seen her," Whitney said. "Why?"

"She'll be the hardest one to get away from the Bible. *A Scandal in Bohemia* sort of thing. It'll pay to know where she is."

"I don't see her, but there have to be five hundred people in here."

"Yeah. What do you say we thin it out a little?"

Whitney nodded, but before either of them could take a step, the lights went out. The orchestra's music trickled to silence and the buzz of conversation in the room hushed, then returned in the form of hundreds of anxious murmurs. Jackson blinked a few times, trying to get his eyes to adjust to the darkness, but he could barely make out Whitney in front of him.

She grabbed his arm, he first thought in fear. Then her lips nearly brushed his ear. "This is lucky. Let's make our move."

"Where?"

"How close is the nearest fire extinguisher?"

"As I walk or as the bat flies?"

"This is not the time for—"

The lights flickered, then came back on. Everyone looked around, their murmurs turning into relieved chuckles. Somebody said something that half the room heard and laughed even louder at. It seemed to reset the mood, and the orchestra began playing again, mid-piece.

Jackson took Whitney's hand and pulled her toward the center of the ballroom, toward the Bible display. A handful of people were congregated around it, all of them focused on a woman on the floor who appeared to have fainted. Jackson paid her no attention, instead scrutinizing the glass case that housed the Vanderbilt Bible.

"That's not it," he said.

"What?" Whitney asked.

"That's not the same Bible," Jackson said. He quickly scanned the room, not spotting Fred or Katie. "They took it."

Chapter Twenty

"ARE YOU SURE?" Whitney asked.

He continued to pan around the room, looking for Fred or Katie. Fred could blend in with all the other penguins, but there weren't many blond bombshells in purple dresses. In fact, Jackson didn't spot any.

"You see them?" he asked.

Whitney looked up from the display case. "Jackson, how do you know this isn't it?"

"Because it doesn't look quite right. And because of the hole in the back of the case."

Whitney looked back down. The Bible had been placed inside a square glass box, slightly elevated and tilted toward the front. It drew all the attention, rightly so, away from the back panel of the display case. The back panel where a foot diameter circle had been cut out, removed, and then replaced.

"So what is that?" Whitney asked

"An idol-sized bag of sand. A knockoff."

"What?"

"They did what we were going to do, only better."

"How do you know it was—"

"It was them."

She joined him in looking around the ballroom. With the orchestra at it again, and with the majority of the partiers unaware of the woman now sitting on the floor amid a circle of people, the party was back in full swing.

"I don't see them," Whitney said. "You got a plan?"

"Actually, yeah. You see Regina?"

"Your two o'clock, coming this way."

166

"Good," Jackson said. "We have to stop them from leaving the island." He struck out toward Regina. "Ms. Archambeau!"

She didn't see him at first.

"Ms. Archambeau," he said, taking her by the arm. She was too thin and overly tanned, with short choppy hair and beady eyes that bored a hole into him.

"Unhand me."

"Someone stole the Bible."

"What?"

"The Bible's been stolen," he said, pointing at the display case.

Regina's eyes widened as she wrenched free from his grasp and hurried to the display case. She spied the hole in the case and the replacement Bible and turned her eyes to Jackson. "Who are you?"

"That doesn't matter. But you're looking for a man and woman, both tall, blond, good-looking. He had a tux, she wore a purple dress, hair down. Twenties or thirties. Gave names as Fred and Katie."

"Are you a cop, some sort of federal agent?" Regina asked.

"No, but you might want to call them. If they get off the island with it, they're gone."

Regina's eyes came alive, and she turned into a flurry of motion, gesturing, calling out for someone named Stephen, and digging into her clutch for a cell phone. Jackson looked for Whitney but didn't see her anywhere. Lost in the crowd, or off on her own again?

A stiff arrived, and Regina briefed him in between snatches of a conversation on the phone. It sounded like she was calling the police, and until he got complete instructions, the stiff eyed Jackson like a fighter before the opening bell.

Regina snapped her phone shut. "The police are coming. Stephen, shut down the exits. No one leaves."

He vanished.

"What's your name?" Regina asked.

"Jack Goldman."

"I don't know you." It was sort of a question, sort of a statement.

"I doubt it. I was a last-minute invite. A friend of a friend."

She waved him off. "How do you know what you know?"

In a pinch, Jackson found the truth was often quite effective. As long as it wasn't set free to run around willy-nilly.

"We met them on the ferry, exchanged names. Just before the power went out, they were hovering around the Bible. Now it's gone, and so are they."

"That doesn't mean they stole it."

"No, but if I were you, I wouldn't want them getting on the next ferry out of here."

"The police have been—"

Her phone rang, and she was back in the middle of a one-sided conversation, barking orders. She was scary, and her eyes instructed Jackson not to leave. So he used his to look for Whitney. She had truly disappeared.

Regina suddenly thrust the phone at Jackson. "Detective O'Hern. Give him the description."

Three minutes and a detective had called her back? Not bad. Jackson took the phone and spent five minutes with a nasally detective who asked him the same questions Regina had, especially concerning Fred and Katie's descriptions. Detective O'Hern asked to speak with Regina again, so Jackson passed the phone back.

By now the crowd in the ballroom knew something was up, and some them had circled around the Bible display case. Jackson tried to inch away, but Regina snapped him back. "He said he wants you to wait here until he arrives."

Jackson sighed and seriously considered making a run for it. But there was no need to make himself a suspect. With a ten-minute head start and apparently a better plan for stealing the Bible, Fred and Katie were too far gone for him to catch them. Maybe not too far for Whitney, if she was on their trail. And still going by the name Whitney. If the Catalina cops were worth two cents, they should be able to keep the duo from boarding the 7:30 ferry. Then, it was a matter of time. So Jackson began running scenarios in his head, a cross of trying to figure out how to get the Bible from Regina once she got it from the cops once they retrieved it from Fred and Katie, mixed with trying to figure out how to tell Abby he was very sorry but he quit.

It was 7:19 before Detective O'Hern made his way to the Catalina Casino Ballroom. Jackson knew because he checked his watch every two minutes. It was another twenty minutes before O'Hern had taken Regina and Jackson's statements and given him permission to leave.

The balmy fresh air was a relief when Jackson finally stepped outside. Aside from a few police vehicles parked along the side of the road, there was nothing to suggest the turmoil up in the ballroom. A couple dozen people were coming or going, the party still in full swing despite a police investigation. Jackson looked for purple or mauve dresses, expecting to see neither.

The main road from Avalon curved around the cliffs and headed northwest. Jackson briefly considered that Fred and Katie might have fled that way, but he doubted it. Although it ran along the coast, the road ultimately led them farther inland, away from the ferry docks or the marina or any viable exit. Unless they had a chopper awaiting them at the airport, in which case the chase was moot anyhow.

So Jackson jogged back toward Avalon, keeping his eyes peeled. He watched several small boats headed out to sea, wondering if any of them contained Fred and Katie. He stopped, remembering that Whitney had her purse and thus her cell phone. He dialed but got no answer. She was quickly climbing to the top of his most likely to get strangled list.

"Jackson!"

He turned to see Abby running his way. "What are you doing here?" he asked.

"Jackson, what's going on? I just saw Agents Andrews and Newton chasing two people down the street."

"Andrews and Newton? What were they wearing—the other couple?"

"Uh, he had a white dress shirt and black pants. She had a white skirt and a dark cami top."

"Long blond hair?"

"Yeah. Why?"

"Where did you see them?"

"From the balcony. They were headed inland on the next street over."

"Any idea where they went?"

"Sort of. I had this feeling something was going on, so I grabbed Whitney's binoculars. There's a park with a lot of trees kind of south of the hotel, and I lost them for a minute. Then I realized the binoculars had night vision too. Once I figured out how that worked, I found the other couple still heading inland. I think Andrews and Newton must have lost them, though, because I didn't see them come out on the other side."

"Where'd the other couple end up?"

Abby bit her lip. "I don't know. I think I saw them jump a fence near the edge of town, but they were getting really far away, so it might not have even been them. It made sense based on where they had last been, but there were a lot of buildings and hills, and the night-vision was grainy . . ."

"That's still good," Jackson said. He turned her around, and they continued back toward the hotel. "Any further sign of Andrews and Newton?"

"No, but I did see a helicopter flying away from the pier," she said, looking skyward. "Just a little while ago. It must be gone now. Anyhow, it was past 7:30, so I decided to come looking for you. Where's Whitney?"

"I don't know," Jackson said, and summed up the events of the last hour and a half.

"And you think this Fred and Katie stole it?"

"Yeah. He sheds his jacket and tie, she rips off the dress, and suddenly they're a couple of tourists on the way home from dinner."

"With my Bible in their possession. Oh my gosh, I almost forgot. He had a backpack too. That was the other thing that made me suspicious. It seemed strange for a guy dressed like that to have a backpack."

"There's a lot strange going on," Jackson said.

They returned to the hotel and Jackson quickly changed out of his tuxedo. Then he joined Abby on the balcony. Using Whitney's night-vision binoculars and maps of Avalon, they pinpointed the route Fred and Katie—presumably—had taken through the city.

"It's all residential," Jackson said, ducking back inside the hotel.

"Maybe they know somebody," Abby said.

"Or maybe they were just running. But if it's me, I don't just run. I have a plan and run to something. And they had a plan all right."

"So where did they go? Where would you go?"

Jackson set the map in front of her. "Here," he said, pointing toward a hotel at the southern edge of Avalon, built into the steep, wooded hillside.

"You think they holed up in a hotel?"

"Or tried to. I'm guessing there aren't many vacant rooms on the island tonight." He shrugged. "But maybe they had reservations. Or maybe they were turned away. But we might be able to find someone who saw them and knows where they went."

"So let's go."

"Hold on. I want to try Whitney again. Use your phone?"

Abby frowned. "Okay."

"She might recognize my number and block it."

He dialed, getting a generic voicemail greeting.

"Robyn-Robbie-Whitney-Whoever, this is Jackson. Have you been arrested again? If so, I'm chuckling at the irony. If not, where are you? We have the Bible. Call me."

"Why'd you tell her that?" Abby asked when he ended the call.

"If she's got it, she's in the wind anyway, so no harm done. If not, it's the only thing I can think of that will get her to call back."

"How do we play this at the hotel?" Abby asked.

"Depends."

"On what?"

"Whether the clerk's a man or a woman." He looked her over and said, "Let's go."

Avalon was teeming with excitement. Late evening in a tourist town, that wasn't so unusual. But the police presence was—two motorcycles, a couple more officers on foot, and a chopper circling somewhere overhead. The civilians were asking questions and looking around anxiously, obviously aware that something unusual was going on.

As Jackson and Abby moved farther inland, the hubbub died down, and they walked through mostly quiet streets. The houses were a conglomeration of different styles, a mixture of Caribbean shanty and Hamptons chic. They were stacked side by side, with no yards or setbacks from the street. Which explained the kids playing in the streets.

Las Escaleras Hotel (The Stairs, in Spanish) was aptly named. With ground space at a premium, the hotel actually consisted of a series of bungalows built at intervals along the side of a hill, such that they appeared like stairs climbing the ridge. Internal staircases and ramps, ranging from just a few steps over a couple dozen feet to a two-story staircase with an elevator instead of a ramp near the top of the ridge, connected the bungalows, which were big enough to house four to six suites each. From above, the entire string looked like a Z, with the lobby at the lower of the two elbows of the Z.

A winding road—more like a cart path on a golf course—led up from Avalon through the trees to the entrance of Las Escaleras. Breathing deeply from the steep climb, Jackson and Abby paused before entering the lobby. Jackson peeked through the glass doors and stepped back. "It's a woman manning the desk. I'll go distract her. Be ready."

"To do what?"

"Come check the register or the computer and see if they're signed in. They gave us the names Fred and Katie, so I'm guessing those are their aliases on the island. If not . . ."

"And what are you going to be doing?"

"I don't know."

"You don't know?"

"I have to figure out how to distract her."

"You haven't figured that out yet?"

"I'm winging it. Wish me luck."

He gave a hopeful smile and entered the lobby. Directly ahead of him, a panel of windows looked out onto a patio in the crook of the Z, where guests could enjoy a beautiful brunch with views of Avalon and the Pacific. On either side of the windows, grand staircases and ramps led up and down to adjoining bungalows. Ferns and palm trees—fake, Jackson assumed—lined the walls. Everything appeared new, very sleek and modern, with a decided Spanish flair. That included the woman manning the desk. Girl, really, no more than twenty-one or twenty-two. Dark wavy hair, and one extra button undone on her white dress shirt. Jackson pasted on his charming grin and strolled up to the desk.

"Can I help you?" she asked with a slight accent.

"Well, that depends . . . Gabby," he said, bending slightly to read her nametag. "Are you a romantic?"

"I'm sorry, sir. What?"

He managed to grin while appearing on the verge of tears. "My fiancée—well, technically my ex-fiancée—is here, I think, visiting her cousin and her husband. It's a long story." He turned the grin into a puppy-dog face. "I'm hoping you can tell me which room they're in."

"I'm afraid it's against our policy to reveal guest information," Gabby replied.

"It is?"

She nodded.

So much for Plan A. Fortunately, he had a contingency.

"Hmm. In that case, could you give her a note for me?"

"I suppose," she said with a thin smile. "If they're here. What is your fiancée's cousin's name?"

Jackson smiled pathetically. "I don't know. Em says I'm never paying attention, and I'm afraid she's right."

"I'm sorry, but how—"

"When I checked in at the Crystal across town, they required a photo ID. I'm hoping you do the same, and could match a description." He pleaded with his eyes. "I'm desperate."

"I can try."

"Great!" He sighed with relief. "Her cousin is a redhead, tall, beautiful," he said, hoping that a tall redhead—and only one—was registered at Las Escaleras with another man in the room. It was admittedly a long shot, but such was the downside of winging it. And if he crapped out, Gabby still hadn't seen Abby, so they weren't out of options.

"I think I know who you mean," Gabby said, and Jackson hid his surprise. "She just checked in about an hour ago. Her husband's a big guy, cowboy hat."

"That's him! I know you can't tell me what room they're in. I get that. But if you could pass on a note, I'd really appreciate it."

Gabby's smile was wide now. "Sure."

"Do you have a pen and some paper?"

Gabby reached under the desk and provided Jackson with a pad of Las Escaleras stationery. He quickly jotted down a bunch of lovey-dovey mumbo-jumbo and folded the paper. He handed Gabby the note, thanked her again, and turned for the door. When he reached it, he took a quick glance back and saw that she was already headed for the stairs going down. Perhaps docked points for naiveté, she should be given high marks for expediency and customer satisfaction.

"Do I go in now?" Abby asked.

"Change of plans," Jackson said, peeking back through the glass. "I've got this."

"Okay."

When Gabby turned and disappeared from sight, Jackson hurried back inside. He hadn't seen any security cameras his first time in the lobby, but he assumed they were there. In case they were monitored in real-time, he hurried.

He stepped inside the circular desk and reached for the mouse at the nearest computer. It was locked. He moved to the next, and a black screen disappeared when he touched the mouse. The hotel's software was open, and it took him less than a minute to figure out how to see a list of all current guests. His eyes scanned the list hurriedly, knowing Gabby wouldn't be gone much longer and that hotel security could arrive at any minute.

Nothing, and he ran his eyes up the list a second time.

There.

Fred and Katie Johnson. Room 704. Paid with a credit card. It was all he needed, and he minimized the software application and hurried around the desk and outside to where Abby was waiting for him.

"Did you find it?" Abby asked.

He nodded. "They're here."

"Now what?"

"Now, we keep an eye out. Nobody else seems to have tracked them here, so my guess is they'll lay low, maybe stay a few nights. Their cover is honeymooners . . ."

"But don't the police have descriptions? How long until somebody who saw them talks?"

He shrugged. "Might only be one person besides us who knows they're here. But you're right, they could leave anytime."

"So what do we do?"

"Scout," Jackson said. He nodded at the backpack he had been carrying until they reached Las Escaleras, and which Abby was now holding. "I'm going to see what I can find on your computer. Floor plans, exits, courtyard layout, etcetera. You go find room 704."

"What?"

"Just walk in like you own the place, as if you're going to your room. Find out where room 704 is located—up, I assume. Find out which direction it faces, how many ways there are to get there from the lobby, available exits—as much as you can. Then come back. You'll look like a guest who ran back to the room to grab something if anyone happens to be watching you."

Abby nodded and took a deep breath.

"You'll do fine," Jackson said as he opened her laptop.

Abby took another deep breath to summon her courage and headed inside. Meanwhile, Jackson Googled Las Escaleras and pulled up a satellite view that enabled him to zoom in far enough to analyze the hotel's outdoor amenities: three connected swimming pools and three hot tubs in a somewhat level spot inside the upper crook of the Z; a flower garden with several winding pathways and two gazebos farther east, along the slope of the ridge; the patio café and a gently sloping grassy area west of the lobby.

He also tried Whitney again, using his phone, with no luck. He decided it was his last call. Why did he want her anyhow? She was thoroughly unreliable and untrustworthy. They were better off without her.

Abby returned in five minutes, and they compared notes. It ended with her again asking, "Now what?"

"Now," Jackson said as he looked out over Avalon, "we set up a choke point."

Chapter Twenty-One

10:07 p.m.

IT HAD TAKEN some doing.

But the gauntlet was set.

Surveillance had indicated that room 704 at Las Escaleras was on the south side of the first floor of the third to last bungalow up the ridge. There were only two exits from the bungalow—the stairs (or elevator) leading up to Bungalow 8 and the stairs and ramp leading down to a small atrium between Bungalows 7 and 6. The atrium, in addition to housing a small seating area, restrooms, and vending machines, provided access to the pool and garden area. A staircase and ramp also led down from the atrium to Bungalows 4-6 and ultimately the lobby. The only other egress to the outside was an emergency exit in Bungalow 9.

The goal of any good gauntlet was to control the direction of movement, and the design of Las Escaleras naturally would funnel guests in Bungalow 7 either up to Bungalow 9 or down to the atrium, and from there either out to the pool deck or down to the lobby.

If Fred and Katie exited via Bungalow 9, they could follow either a steep, rocky hiking path up along the top of the ridge, where it connected to several other hiking paths in the hills south of Avalon, or a similarly steep path down the side of the ridge to the garden, the pool, and ultimately the atrium. Given the lack of avenues upon exit, the steepness of those avenues, and the comparative difficulty (two long flights of stairs) to get to Bungalow 9, Jackson ruled it the least likely.

If Fred and Katie came all the way down to the lobby, they could exit onto the patio and lawn, which dead-ended unless they entered the woods, or they could exit the front door to the road leading back to town. It was the most logical exit.

And if they exited to the pool and garden, they could ultimately go through the garden and up the steep path to the Bungalow 9 exit, take a more level hiking trail along the side of the ridge and to parts unknown, or veer off that side-hill trail and take another path that would lead down to the lobby and eventually zigzag all the way down to Avalon.

It had taken some time to trace each of the paths from satellite photos, but Jackson had finally gotten a hold of Mouse, who had been able to provide some better images. Even so, the surveillance and planning had only been half the battle.

While Abby had kept watch on Las Escaleras, Jackson had returned to their hotel and packed up everything he could. He'd also changed into a green polo of Whitney's. It was incredibly tight, but with his khaki pants, was a match to several staffers Abby had seen in the hotel. He had returned to Las Escaleras and, while a different clerk was on duty at the front desk, he and Abby had hurried through the various bungalows up to the atrium and out onto the pool deck.

The pool deck was approximately the size of a basketball half court but split into three separate patios, each with a small pool. The patios, each at a different elevation, were connected by short staircases or ramps, and the upper pool flowed into the middle, which in turn flowed into the lower. The pools had been mostly empty, and the patios around them completely so. Jackson, acting as a pool manager or some such hotel staff, had directed Abby—ostensibly an intern—where to begin stacking chaise lounge chairs. Extended in a row, they now blocked immediate access from the atrium to the stairs leading to the lower pool. Several stacks also made a hard turn to the right impossible, further restricting Fred and Katie's evacuation options. The choke point was narrowed.

Still posing as a hotel employee, Jackson had told the two swimmers that the pools were closing. They hadn't questioned him, and five minutes later, he and Abby had been alone. Jackson had taken a hose off the end of the atrium and tied one end around the baluster of a wood footbridge spanning the waterfall from the middle pool to the lower pool. Then he had draped the hose across the bridge and hung it into the middle pool. Innocuous looking, if even noticeable.

Shortly after ten, he and Abby sat down on a couple of remaining chaise lounges and went over their plan once more. As near as he could tell, they had conducted their setup unobserved. They at least hadn't been interrupted by legitimate hotel staff.

"I'll flip you for the pool," Abby said.

"No, it's better this way," Jackson said. "In case you happen to run into them inside. They don't know you yet."

She nodded.

"Ready?"

Another nod.

"Okay, here goes nothing." He reached for his cell and made the first call.

"This is Newton."

"Agent Newton?" Jackson said in a faint Hispanic accent. "This is Officer Rivas. We think the duo you're looking for just entered Las Escaleras on the south side of town."

"Are you on the scene?"

"No, sir, we got a tip."

"Reliable?"

"Hard to say, sir. But I have no reason to suspect otherwise."

"Officer Rivas, hold your position. We will be right there."

Jackson closed his phone. "All right, the ball is in play."

He and Abby crossed the bridge with the hose draped over it and then made their way down one of the footpaths leading through the trees and, ultimately, to the road from Avalon. They stopped well short of the road, still in the trees, but with a view of any approaching vehicles or pedestrian traffic.

"What if they come by helicopter?" Abby asked.

"We won't miss them, at least."

They waited almost ten minutes before Jackson saw a police car heading up the path. He nodded, and Abby quickly called the hotel front desk. "Yes, can I speak to Fred or Katie Johnson, please? Room 704." She looked at Jackson while waiting.

"Woman?" he asked.

"Man."

"Good."

"Hello, Mr. Johnson," Abby said a moment later. "This is Diane at the front desk. We've just received word that your credit card has been flagged for suspicious activity. It's hotel policy that we put your room and any incidentals down under a different account. Would you be able to stop down so that we can rectify the situation? . . . Yes, and I'm terribly sorry to disturb you at this hour, but we literally just received the notification. . . . Yes, sir, I'm afraid it's hotel policy. . . . Thank you, sir."

She disconnected the call and smiled up at Jackson. "He's coming."

"You're a natural grifter, you know that."

"What?"

"A blond-haired, English-speaking Sophie Devereaux. I mean, American-English-speaking."

"What are you talking about?"

"Nothing. Let's get in position."

The next part of his plan was where things could fall apart. Jackson's brilliant intent was for Fred or Katie to come down to the lobby, see the police presence—or better yet, spot Andrews and Newton—and split, figuring their cover was blown. They would be forced to run back up away from the lobby and would choose the atrium as their point of exit, where Jackson and Abby would be waiting. But if the timing was off, or if Andrews and Newton actually spotted Fred and Katie or Jackson and Abby, or if Fred and Katie decided to burrow instead of rabbit, or if any other number of details didn't work out quite perfectly, the whole thing could come off the rails. That downside of winging it again.

Abby waited in the atrium, with a view of the exit to the pool and garden, her attention on her phone. Although he didn't own one, Jackson was coming to realize smartphones were a P.I.'s best friend, because you could camp out anywhere and look perfectly natural as long as your face was buried in a phone.

Meanwhile, Jackson retreated back up the path and was relieved to see the pools were still empty. Suddenly flashing back to a very scary childhood game of Three Billy Goats Gruff with the neighbor girl Tammy, Jackson waded into the pool and made his way under the bridge.

And waited.

The night was balmy, especially for January, but after a couple of minutes, the heated water of the pool felt cold. No wonder the pools were empty.

This was the down time when Jackson's mind always presented the dissenting opinion. What if Abby screwed things up? After all, she wasn't a professional. Or what if Fred and Katie belonged to some government agency—American or otherwise—not prone to being kind to civilians who got in their way? Or what if this half-baked, harebrained, ad hoc plan didn't work at all—say because Fred and Katie didn't take the precise evacuation route Jackson calculated they would?

He pondered for several minutes until the atrium door flew open and two figures emerged. Even though they had changed clothes, and even peering through slats in the bridge, Jackson recognized Fred and Katie.

She immediately turned right, scrambling over the chaise lounges to climb to the upper patio. Fred hesitated for a moment, and Jackson feared he would opt for the other bridge, the one spanning the falls between the upper and middle pools. But it led to the garden, same as the path Katie had taken, instead of to the trails leading away from the hotel. It had been a gamble on Jackson's part, betting that Fred and Katie would know the best means of egress, but it paid off a moment later when Fred came Jackson's way. He carried a small satchel in his arm, like a football. Jackson looped his arm around a support beam on the bridge and coiled the hose around his opposite hand.

Fred slowed for a moment, but then charged up the bridge. Jackson pulled on the support beam to hoist himself up, at the same time jerking the hose tight. At first, he thought he'd pulled it taut too early, but then he heard and felt the vibrations as Fred plunged headlong down the bridge.

Jackson dropped the hose and stroked to the edge of the pool. He climbed out as Fred stopped rolling at the bottom of the bridge, looking dazed but more stunned than hurt. The satchel was on the pavement beside him, and Jackson thought about scooping it and running. But Abby had followed Fred from the bungalow, per Jackson's hastily conceived instructions, and he didn't like the idea of the two of them running and hoping they were faster than an angry Fred.

So he improvised.

He pantsed Fred.

They were athletic pants, and came down without much hassle, especially since Fred wasn't quite up for a fight after his fall.

"What are you doing?" Abby asked as she crossed the bridge.

"Take it and go!" Jackson said. "I'll catch up to you."

Without a word, she scooped up the satchel and took off down the path into the woods.

Fred was still a little out of it and didn't resist as Jackson wound his pants as tightly as he could around his ankles, then rolled him into the pool. Before the splash, Jackson was off and running. Katie had made a dash through the garden and up toward the ridgeline, and apparently hadn't looked back, as she was nowhere to be seen. It made sense. She and Fred had thought they were being chased, so they had split up and forced their pursuers to do likewise. But they hadn't known they weren't being chased so much as lured. At any rate, she was out of the picture, and Jackson hoped Fred would flounder around in the pool for a while before getting out, getting his pants back on, and giving chase.

As he ran after Abby, Jackson slowed only long enough to extract a Ziploc from his pocket, and his cell phone from inside the Ziploc. He dialed as he ran, calling the hotel.

"Las Escaleras, how may I help you?"

It sounded like Gabby, but he figured his panting would disguise his voice. "Yeah, a couple of people just ran through the pool area. One fell in, and the other took off toward the garden. I think they were chasing each other."

He ended the call before getting a response and concentrated on following the path in the darkness. It wound through the trees, curving along the ridge and opening in several places to offer hikers dramatic panoramas of Avalon. A little while later, it split, with one path going down toward the road and lobby, another winding more slowly down to the bottom of the hill and Avalon, and a third rising toward the top of the ridge and, ultimately, Katie.

Jackson's plan called for him and Abby to return to their hotel, but as he ran after her, he questioned the wisdom of that plan. If he and Abby had found Fred and Katie, who was to say they couldn't find them right back? Or that Andrews and Newton wouldn't find them? Or the police? But until the ferries started running in the morning, it was their only option.

After a pair of switchbacks, the steepness of the slope lessened, and the path ran more directly down the hill. Jackson thought he heard Abby ahead of him, and a moment later, caught a flash of her yellow shirt in the faint moonlight. A few more strides and he caught her.

"How much further?" she asked, stopping, heaving for air.

"Around this curve, then fifty yards to the edge of town, max. Want me to carry everything?"

She nodded, and he took the satchel from her, as well as the backpack with all their belongings and her computer—in case they didn't make it back to the hotel as planned. It occurred to him to open the satchel and make sure the Bible was inside. He doubted Fred and Katie would have left it behind or bothered with a decoy in the heat of the moment, but stranger things happened on TV. (Or in Jackson's real world, apparently.) But this wasn't the time or place to check the satchel's contents, so he just urged Abby on.

A few paces later, she slowed again. "I need . . . a break."

"I know, but they're going to be behind us. If not them, the cops, Andrews and Newton, hotel security."

She blinked heavily.

"You've got the Bible, Abby. We just need to get back to the hotel. Dig deep."

She nodded, and he took her hand to help her along. But by the time they reached sea level and emerged from the woods, he was doing more pulling than helping. That was okay. A slower pace would help their cover. If they sprinted through the streets of Avalon, it would attract attention. And truth be told, he was gassed.

"Shouldn't—" Abby started.

"Shh." Jackson put up his hand. He heard distant shouts, and it slowly dawned on him that his and Abby's last stop had been in a spot visible from one of the panoramic viewpoints on the trail.

"Uh, we'd better move," he said. "They've made us."

Abby moaned but followed Jackson as they started west along the tree line, his plan being to get to cover as soon as possible so they couldn't be tracked. Especially since they were going to have to zig and zag back to their hotel. Unfortunately, that plan meant crossing the road leading up to Las Escaleras' lobby. A risk they had to take.

"Jackson . . ." Abby panted a minute later. "Jacksss . . ."

He turned to see that she had slumped to the ground. Kidnapped the day before, held overnight, rescued dramatically with bullets flying, then thrown right back into the chase. If she was like him, she hadn't eaten since the morning, except for a bag of animal crackers from a vending machine at the ferry dock in Marina del Rey. It was no wonder she had no energy, and he kicked himself for putting her in the situation as he turned to help her up.

"You want me to carry you?" he asked, not knowing if he had the energy for it. Seeing hers fail had sapped his as well.

"No, I'll—"

Clopping hooves interrupted her and Jackson turned to see three horses skidding to a stop in front of them. Two of them were riderless. The third carried a woman with a mid-length blond ponytail.

"Come on," Whitney said. "Mount up!"

Chapter Twenty-Two

10:36 p.m.

JACKSON STARED UP at Whitney in disbelief. Had it not been for Abby's recent collapse—and the sudden sausage-like feeling in his legs—Jackson would have told Whitney to go find a sunset to ride off into. Or punched her steed in the face like Mongo in *Blazing Saddles*. But he couldn't afford to look a literal gift horse in the mouth.

Jackson helped Abby onto the near horse and then circled the far one. He'd ridden a couple of times before, just enough to know what he was doing. The horse, full-grown, brown with a white blaze (he also knew enough to know the spot on the nose was called the blaze), seemed perfectly content and at ease with him. In his limited experience, the horse's attitude really made the difference.

"You have it?" Whitney asked.

Jackson nodded.

"Follow me," she said, turning her horse and spurring it on. It took off at a gallop, and Jackson nodded at Abby. With someone else ready to do the running, she appeared to have regained some strength, and urged her horse to follow Whitney. Jackson's steed was a little slow to match their pace, but a gentle kick to the flank changed that.

Whitney led them southwest, past the base of Las Escaleras, along a treed fence line beside the island's golf course, and then west past several condominium complexes and a resort. Within five minutes, they had left Avalon behind and were climbing along a narrow dirt path that hugged the edge of a ridge. Jackson had taken a few peeks over his shoulder and seen no pursuers, but he now concentrated on worrying about his horse's footing until they had topped the ridge.

The path followed the ridge for several hundred yards, and the three riders kept their horses to a steady trot. Jackson knew there was a bison herd on Catalina and some crazy species of turtle—or maybe that was the Galapagos Islands. Other than that, he had no idea what to expect as they moved farther and farther away from Avalon. The terrain was rugged and mostly barren. Where was Whitney leading them?

He took one more glance behind them. The lights of Avalon circled the bay below them to the right. Las Escaleras was almost directly behind them, and there had been no signs yet of pursuit. It would have to be on foot or horseback to follow them on this particular path. Or maybe a dirt bike. But there were tons of other paths that cut through the wilderness—that was the other thing Jackson knew from his brief reconnaissance of the island. Then he remembered the helicopter and, noting the relative lack of trees in the vicinity, determined they hadn't made such a great getaway after all.

The path left the ridgeline and went down into a ravine, and Jackson urged his horse past Abby and alongside Whitney's mount. "Can we talk?" he asked.

"Not yet," she said. "We need to cross that ridge first."

With Whitney leading the way, the horses picked their way up the side of the ridge she had indicated, then carefully descended the other side. It brought them to a small meadow, lined by two ridges left and right that merged a few hundred yards in front of them.

Jackson called his horse to a halt. Abby also slowed, forcing Whitney to stop as well.

"We should keep moving," she said.

"I want answers first."

"You'll get them. But we have a long ride ahead of us."

"To where?"

"Two Harbors."

"That's on the other side of the island," Jackson said.

"Yeah. Avalon is going to be crawling with cops, FBI, CIA, everybody," Whitney said, bringing her horse back to Jackson and Abby. "The only other way off this rock is the ferry at Two Harbors. Unless you want to charter a private plane or chopper to come get us. So we keep riding. You want answers, you get them as we ride."

She spun the horse around and took off at a fast trot. Jackson bristled for a moment and very nearly thought about letting her go. They had the Bible and didn't need her.

But she was right about getting off the island.

With a sigh, he started after her. Abby followed, and when they caught Whitney, the trio slowed their horses to a walk and rode three-wide through the valley.

"What do you want to know?" Whitney asked.

"What don't I? Start with where you went."

"I went after them," she answered. "They had the Bible; you seemed more concerned with Regina . . ."

"So link up chasing Fred and Katie with showing up on three horses."

"To make a long story short, I was surveying things and saw you were going to need an exit strategy. I found the horses and here we are."

"That is short, all right," Jackson muttered.

"Where'd you find the horses?" Abby asked.

"A local stable. I think they give rides."

"Great," Jackson said. "We're horse thieves. You know what they do to horse thieves?"

"String 'em up?" Whitney asked with a smirk.

"I see you've traded in your evening attire," Jackson said. "Where?"

"At the hotel."

"When?"

"About nine-thirty, quarter to ten, I think."

"When we were gone," Abby said.

Whitney turned from her to Jackson. "I see you're wearing my shirt."

"I like green," Jackson said, suddenly remembering that he was wet and cold. He thought about trying to get a spare shirt out of the backpack, but changing on a moving horse was beyond his abilities. So he focused on the questions he still had for Whitney. "Why didn't you answer your cell?"

"I was kind of . . . indisposed," she said.

"Indisposed how?"

"I can't get into that."

"Can't or won't?"

"Can't."

Jackson huffed.

"Have you forgotten I'm a government agent?" she asked.

"Not since you last remembered it."

"Look, when we got separated, I used my resources to try to recover the Bible. I can't go into all the details, okay, but I found you guys, saw you were in trouble, and I improvised. Like I said, unless you've got a line on a chopper, this is our best bet."

"Can't we sneak back into town in the morning?" Abby asked.

"Too risky."

"Jackson?"

"Yeah, she's right," he said. "Andrews and Newton will be hunting us down, and they'll probably have the cops at their disposal. Then there's Fred and Katie, who will either be working with them or against them, but definitely looking for us."

"Won't they look in Two Harbors as well?"

"Eventually," he said. "But unless they saw us ride off, they won't think that we could have made it that far."

"By the way," Whitney said. "It isn't Fred and Katie."

"No?"

"No," she replied. "I called HQ. Without a photograph, they can't be sure, but they're a perfect match for Mats Bjornstad and Annika Danielsson, a pair of Swedish art thieves."

"Swedish art thieves?" Jackson asked.

"And good ones. They're equally wanted and respected from Stockholm to Malmö. To all of Europe, actually."

"Of all the vodka joints," Jackson said. He shrugged. "It does explain their good looks."

"Oh? Are Swedish art thieves biologically better looking than American ones?" Whitney asked sarcastically.

"Swedish people in general," Jackson said. "Did you see their women's curling team last Olympics?"

Whitney shook her head. "Two Harbors is about ten miles as the crow flies. And these aren't crows."

"You got a compass, *bandita*, or are you reading the stars?"

"As a matter of fact, both. I even have a map. You have the flashlight in that bag?"

Jackson nodded and stopped his horse. "What, couldn't memorize the entire route?"

"I was crunched for time," Whitney said as she coaxed her horse beside him. She unzipped the backpack and began digging through it.

"Grab me a spare shirt, will you," Jackson said.

"You can keep that one, by the way," Whitney said as she handed him an extra T-shirt from the backpack. While he changed, she studied the map with the flashlight. "We need to climb this ridge," she said, gesturing with the flashlight to the slope on the left. "Then we catch a path that will lead us through the interior. It's longer, but it keeps us from hitting the main road to the airport."

Jackson wadded up Whitney's wet polo. "Lead the way, Calamity Jane."

*   *   *

Monday, January 21
1:43 a.m.

AFTER SEVERAL hours of riding a horse on hilly terrain while wearing wet pants, Jackson was craving some talcum powder. And a different tour guide.

Whitney had led them northwest until they had a glimpse of the dark Pacific to their left. Then they had followed a trail more northward, winding along the inside of a steep ridge. So far they had spotted one campfire on the western side of the island and a couple of low-flying aircraft. Not low enough to spot three horses without a searchlight, such as could be mounted on a CIA helicopter. Jackson had been expecting it at any moment since they left Las Escaleras, and still hadn't written it off. But a chafing backside was taking precedence at the moment.

When the path led them back into a valley, Jackson again prodded his horse up alongside Whitney's. Conversation had been minimal over the last few hours, with Whitney not filling in any more details about why she hadn't maintained contact with Jackson and Abby, how she had monitored them, or how she had known to show up with three horses at just the right time and place. But Jackson didn't care anymore. He had the Bible, and until he got an edict from the CSIS, he wasn't letting her touch it. If even then.

"Are you still mad at me?" Whitney asked.

"Let's just assume that's pretty much a permanent condition."

"Why? I saved your life."

"You can't push somebody into a lake and then claim to be a hero when you pull them out."

"What do you mean? I didn't push you."

"You sure weren't helping us. If we had a third person, we might not have needed an equine rescue."

Whitney looked away.

"And frankly," he continued, "I'm just plain sick of you running away every time things get hairy and switching identities twice a day."

She huffed.

"Which reminds me, you've been Whitney all day. Want us to look the other way while you change into someone else?"

"That's funny. Tell me, do your clients generally appreciate this sarcasm?"

Jackson turned around to where Abby was trailing them by a few horse lengths, and obviously listening in. "Abby, job approval rating?"

"Eight, eight-five. You did try to quit a few times."

He turned back to Whitney. "That's fair."

She shook her head and looked away. Jackson thought she might be crying. Women were so . . . fragile.

"Look," he said. "I haven't slept since Friday night, I've been lied to by just about everybody, I'm stealing and conning everybody, and I haven't had a meal since . . ." He turned back to Abby. "What time did we have breakfast?"

"Six, maybe?"

Whitney looked his way, and the moon revealed no tears. "You stink at apologies too."

He shrugged.

She reached into her pocket. "Here. It's not much." She flipped him an energy bar before tossing one back to Abby as well. "Better than nothing."

"Thanks."

They climbed another ridge, onto a plateau of sorts. It gradually descended into another valley. Catalina was nothing more than rows and rows of ridges and ravines. After lagging back to check on how Abby was doing, Jackson caught up to Whitney, who was studying the map by flashlight again.

"How much farther?"

"Couple of miles," she said. "Maybe less."

"What do you know about Two Harbors?"

"There isn't much to know. It's tiny."

"How tiny?"

"Three hundred, in the summer. Half that now, probably."

"We'll stick out," Abby said, having drawn alongside them.

"Three strangers riding into town on horseback in the middle of the night," Jackson said. "Nah."

"Would you rather be back running from the CIA, cops, and Swedish thieves?" Whitney asked.

Jackson held up his hand in surrender.

"I did some research. There's a bed and breakfast on the edge of town. If we can get a room there, we can stay out of sight until the ferry leaves."

"When's that?" Abby asked.

"Three p.m."

"Super," Jackson said.

"Did Mats or Annika get a make on either of you?" Whitney asked.

"Hard to say," Jackson said. "Mats, yes, for me. He was pretty dazed at the time, so I doubt he would recognize Abby. And they didn't see me with her on the ferry, either."

"What about hotel staff? Did they see her?"

"Yes, but they don't know she was involved in anything."

"Good. As far as Regina or the CIA know, it's just you and me. So if we send her in to get a room, her face shouldn't trigger any alarms."

"Unless they consider her a known associate."

Whitney tipped her head in concession.

They rode through the darkness for another hour, not pushing their horses. Jackson was not an animal lover, at least not in the sense of hugging and petting and cuddling them. But he appreciated horses. They never complained, even when forced to ride over hill and dale in the middle of the night. Then again, if they could sleep standing up, maybe they could sleep while walking too, and thus didn't even know.

First light was still hours away, and Jackson didn't realize they had reached Two Harbors until Whitney slowed her horse. They had just emerged from a small grove of trees, and the moonlight illuminated a collection of buildings a couple hundred yards ahead of them. To Jackson, they resembled a small ranch.

"Banning House Lodge," Whitney said.

"This our place?"

She nodded.

"And if there's no room in the inn?"

"We camp under the stars, cowboy."

They rode slightly closer, then dismounted. "Do I need a cover story?" Abby asked, handing her reins to Jackson.

"We were camping, got cold, is there a room?" Whitney said.

"I don't have much cash on me."

Whitney reached into her pocket and pulled out a wad of bills.

"Whoa, where'd you get that?" Jackson asked.

"I come prepared."

"How big of pockets do you have in that jacket?"

"Big ones, fortunately, since somebody packed up most of my stuff."

"You guys keep fighting," Abby said as she took the cash from Whitney. "I'll get us a room."

"I never did ask," Whitney said when Abby had disappeared into the shadows. "How did you get the Bible from Mats and Annika?"

"You ever catch reruns of *Welcome Back, Kotter* in Canada?"

"What is that, a TV show?"

"A long time ago."

Whitney shook her head. "Never even heard of it."

"Then the phrase 'up your nose with a rubber hose' won't mean much, I guess."

She shook her head some more. "The people you meet when you travel."

"Or in your case, when you look in the mirror."

Abby returned five minutes later. "Cliff House East," she said. "Off the main house, king bed and queen sofa." She handed the extra cash back to Whitney.

"Any trouble?"

Abby shook her head. "They were a little wary when I walked in at three-thirty in the morning, but they seemed to buy the cover story."

"Good," Jackson said. "Then let's get settled."

"What do we do with the horses?" Abby asked.

"Tether them," Whitney said.

"Or send them home," Jackson replied.

"Send them home?"

He nodded. "Horses can always find their way home." He looked into two quizzical faces. "Don't either of you ever watch Westerns?"

"We should pay the owners," Abby said. "We did steal them."

Jackson nodded at Whitney. "Stuff some Benjamins under your saddle."

"I paid for the room," she said. "Stuff your own cash under your own saddle."

Jackson sighed and reached into his wallet. He pulled out a slightly wet business card and tucked it inside the harness of his horse. "When the owner calls, I'll explain the Canadian government forced me to commandeer his horses."

"Good luck with that," Whitney said.

Jackson turned the horse around and gave it a pat on the rump, sending it back along the path. Reluctantly, Abby and Whitney followed suit and watched their horses gallop back toward the heart of the island.

"Now," Jackson said, "did the desk clerk say anything about where we can get some chow?"

*　　　　　*　　　　　*

7:44 a.m.

WHITNEY HAD offered that she and Abby would share the king bed, leaving the queen sofa for Jackson and maintaining some modicum of modesty. He had declined. No offense, but he didn't trust Whitney if both he and Abby were asleep. They'd take shifts, and he had let Abby sleep first. At six a.m., he'd woken her up and taken his turn. With dawn beginning to break, his body had been confused, but he'd managed to catch a few winks.

The running shower woke him up. Abby was on the sofa, the Bible on her lap. She looked exhausted.

Jackson rubbed his eyes and sat up on the edge of the bed. "Is it intact?"

"I think so," Abby answered.

"No FBI or CIA agents came to the door?"

"Nope."

He nodded toward the bathroom. "And she didn't try to slink off with it?"

Abby shook her head. She closed the Bible and set it aside, then pulled off latex gloves initially brought along so as not to leave fingerprints at Regina's. She leaned forward. "So we just wait all day?"

He nodded.

"I hope they have room service."

"Continental breakfast," Jackson said.

"Dare we show our faces?"

"Depends."

"On?"

He nodded at the TV. "You want to turn that on, see if we've made the news. I doubt word has reached the guests or staff here, but it wouldn't hurt to check."

"What are you doing?" she asked.

The water in the shower was still running, and he had bent to pick up Whitney's jacket from the floor. "Seeing what we're missing."

The pockets were empty.

"She took her money into the bathroom with her. That's rich."

Abby shrugged.

"She have anything else on her?"

"Her shoes," Abby said with a nod at a pair of cross-trainers by the door.

Jackson replaced the jacket on the floor as the water quit in the bathroom. "You mind?" he asked, nodding at the Bible.

"Go ahead."

Jackson donned a pair of gloves as Abby flipped on the television. Then he picked the Bible off the table and sat back on the bed.

"What day is it anymore?" Abby asked.

"Monday."

She began flipping channels in an effort to find a local news program while Jackson started turning pages. He was in no mood to try to crack Alec's personal code at the moment. But who knew, maybe something would jump out at him. His mom had always told him the answers never did that, but maybe just once . . .

After channel surfing for a few minutes, Abby settled on one of the national morning programs. Jackson turned to the New Testament. Whitney popped out of the bathroom, looking too refreshed for someone who'd slept less than four hours.

Just before the top of the hour, the local weather girl came on and promised more warm sunshine, strong breezes, and a chance of storms toward evening. Probably about the time the trio boarded the ferry back to the mainland. With a sigh, Jackson returned to the Bible. Alec appeared to have hardly touched the Gospels after quite a bit of note-taking in the Minor Prophets; it struck Jackson as odd. But then again, so did this whole thing.

". . . a very strange case overnight in Pacoima," the local news anchor reported, "where a drunk driver crashed into a Cadillac parked near the corner of S and Vaughn. When police arrived on the scene, they found three bodies in the trunk of the Cadillac. Police have identified one of the men as Desmond Vanderbilt, a local talent agent and son of the late renowned art collector Alec Vanderbilt. Identities of the other two men have not yet been determined."

Jackson lifted his eyes to Abby, whose face had turned into stone.

Chapter Twenty-Three

7:59 a.m.

"ABBY?" JACKSON SAID at length.

She didn't turn, didn't blink. "How . . . how can . . . how can that be?"

"I don't know. I . . . I'm sorry."

"He's . . . Desmond's dead?"

Whitney sat down on the edge of the bed and put her arm around Abby. "It could be a false report," she said.

"What?"

"A ploy to ferret us out."

Jackson stood up. "Tell me you aren't playing her right now."

"Of course not." Whitney popped to her feet. "I'm trying to give her hope. He could be alive."

Jackson sighed and looked down at Abby, who had turned her eyes to him. He'd been there before, hoping against hope—against reality—that his parents were alive, that he would turn around and see his brother. It was stupid. It was pathetic. It was only human. And now Whitney had just put Abby through that same emotional 180. And Jackson had to let her down.

He gently shook his head, hoping his eyes conveyed the compassion he felt.

Abby nodded and stood. "I'm, uh . . . I'm going to get us some food."

"I don't think that's a good idea," Whitney said.

"I'm starving," Abby replied. "If they've tracked us to Two Harbors, it won't be long before they find us anyhow."

"You want some company?" Jackson asked.

"No. I need to think."

"Okay."

Looking lifeless, Abby exited the room. No sooner had the door closed than Jackson turned to Whitney. "What do you think you're doing?"

"What?"

"Thirty seconds after she finds out her brother's dead you start throwing out conspiracy theories about his death being a fake news story?"

"Stepbrother," Whitney said, "who I thought was one of our enemies in this whole mess. And my theory makes sense."

"Right. The entire LAPD is after us because we stole a Bible from Swedish art thieves who stole it from an art collector who stole it from a former cartel informant."

"I'm sorry, were you there when we had to ride out of town like a trio of bandits?"

"Yeah, I just missed the part where we were such wanted criminals that the cops would leak a fake story to the press about the stepbrother of a woman who isn't even known to be working with us!"

Whitney's eyes blazed, but only for a moment. Then they cooled, like lava forming a cold, hard crust. "Well, in that case, the only other explanation is that your CIA agents killed him."

"My CIA agents? You were the one who first told me they were CIA."

"Didn't they confirm it?"

He looked away with a sigh.

"And I'm pretty sure CIA agents aren't allowed to kill U.S. citizens, especially on American soil," she continued. "Which means either they aren't really CIA or they've gone rogue, in which case we're in more trouble than we ever thought."

"So let's quit playing games and try to figure a way out of this."

"What do you think I've been doing all night long?"

"Playing a spy version of hard to get."

"I'm a government agent, Douglas. I can't tell you everything." She sighed aloud. "How many times do I have to repeat myself?"

"Until anything you say is actually a repeat."

"You know what, forget it, okay? Think whatever you want about me. I know the truth."

"Like finding a needle in a haystack, isn't it?"

Whitney sighed. "Would you hand me the Bible?"

"No."

"Really. Are you going to give me the silent treatment too?"

"No. But you're not touching that Bible."

"We have a deal."

"I'm breaking it. You should be familiar with that concept."

"You are interfering with a CSIS operation."

"An operation in the U.S.A. I consider it an act of patriotism."

Whitney's lava rocks began to melt with heat. "This is ridiculous," she said, moving toward the bed, where Jackson had set the Bible. "You have absolutely no r—"

He jumped into her path.

"Get out of my way."

"How about you get out of my country?"

They were inches apart, and neither moved for several long seconds. Then Whitney shrunk back.

It was a decoy move, and she made a sudden lunge toward the Bible. Jackson hadn't been fooled and hadn't relaxed, and he moved quickly to cut her off. He shouldered her away from the Bible, and she bounced off the bed and to the floor, rolling against the wall.

Whitney stood, her eyes practically smoking. Jackson moved the Bible to the nightstand and waited. She edged around the end of the bed, feinted left as if to attack, and then dove across the bed toward the Bible. He didn't know what she intended to do, unless it was somersault off the bed, grab the Bible while upside down, and keep rolling to the door. Whatever her plan, Jackson was again not fooled, and again dove to intercept her. Their heads just missed colliding, and instead, his shoulder plowed into hers, driving her into the headboard with a crack.

She emitted something between a groan and a scream, but quickly recovered, wrapping Jackson in a headlock. It wasn't a good one, and he pushed away and out of it. However, his foot failed to find purchase as the comforter on the bed gave way. Whitney pushed off the headboard, jumping onto his back and again wrapping him in a headlock, this one much tighter.

With her on his back, Jackson stood. She was latched on tight, and as he spun, she flailed around like a cape, nearly knocking the muted TV over. Jackson turned and backed into the wall with all his force, smooshing her between his body and the wall. He felt her grip loosen slightly. Before his oxygen gave out, Jackson slammed backward again, and this time Whitney's arms slipped from around his neck.

He stepped forward and turned around. Whitney dropped to the ground, gasping for air. She was in no position to resist as Jackson lifted her up and pushed her onto the bed, pinning her head down into the comforter with one hand. With his other, he twisted her arm behind her back.

She continued to gasp and wheeze until her breath returned. When she started to struggle, Jackson pushed her head a little harder.

"Okay," she said softly, still short on air. "Oh . . . kay. I give up."

He leaned down. "You suckerpunch me, and so help me, I don't care if you are a woman and maybe a federal agent, I will put you down, you got it?"

"Yes."

He released pressure and stood back. Whitney rose slowly, then sagged back against the wall, panting for air.

"Are you all right?" he asked.

"Oh, don't give me that."

"Give you what?"

"The big bad chauvinist act, like you're afraid you hurt me."

He walked toward her and her body tensed. "If I had wanted to hurt you," he said evenly, "I could have. I didn't because I didn't."

She took in several deep breaths, not answering.

"Now, are you okay?"

"I'm fine."

"Good. The Bible is in my possession. It is going to stay in my possession, and if you try to take it by force, I will want to hurt you."

She huffed in reply.

"And you try anything with Abby . . ."

"I won't," she said, rubbing her shoulder.

"Good." He backed away.

"This isn't over, Douglas. Remember, I have the weight of the CSIS behind me."

"You remember, I don't care."

She huffed again as he retreated to a sitting position on the bed, just as Abby returned. She stared at them and the bed for a minute, her eyes asking a question without her saying a word.

"I repelled a mutiny," Jackson said. His tone softened. "I don't mean to be cold, Abby, but did anyone notice you?"

"Not that I could tell." She set a large bowl of fruit and a plate of pastries on the table, next to the TV. Wordlessly, the trio ravenously ate breakfast. When they were finished, Whitney announced she had to make a call.

"No," Jackson said.

"What?"

"No. I don't trust you."

"I don't care."

"I do, and I'm running this ship now."

Her eyes radiated heat, and he thought she was ready to make another attack. He had meant every word of his threats a few minutes ago and had gained confidence over the years in his somewhat natural ability as a scrappy fighter, especially against someone he had in size, reach, and strength. But he still wasn't wild about hand-to-hand combat and decided diffusing the situation might be a smart play.

"I'll make you a deal, though. You give me your cell phone until we're off the island, and I let you look at the Bible while we wait."

"I don't need your permission to look at the Bible."

He said nothing, guessing her statement was a last-ditch effort at maintaining some semblance of control.

"Fine," she said after a half minute of glaring. She retrieved her phone from her jacket and tossed it to Jackson. He in turn nodded at the Bible, which she took to the sofa.

Jackson scooted over beside Abby. "How are you doing?"

"I don't know. He is my brother."

He said nothing.

"And two days ago, he kidnapped me. I've been so mad at him for so long . . ." She shook her head. "I'm numb."

"That's understandable." He put a hand on her back. "We'll get out of here this afternoon, we'll go home, and we'll take care of everything."

"I need to call Noah," she said.

Whitney flipped a page of the Bible.

"We'll take care of it," he said, something suddenly nagging at him. He pushed it aside. "In the meantime, why don't you rest a little? Try to sleep."

"I don't know if I can. And you should sleep. You didn't get much last night."

"I will after you. At least lay down and rest."

She nodded and lay down on the bed. Jackson walked over and sat down by Whitney.

"What, are my Scripture reading privileges being revoked again?"

"No, I actually came to call a truce."

She looked up skeptically. "A truce?"

"Yeah. Because I have this funny feeling we don't just walk down to the ferry dock at three and sail away."

"No?"

Jackson looked at Abby and continued to keep his voice low. "No. And we can't be at each other's throats—literally—if we're going to get off this rock."

"Okay," Whitney said. "Truce."

Jackson nodded.

"But as soon as we get to safety, we're back to where we are right now," she said. "How do we decide who gets to keep the Bible?"

"Flip to First Kings," he said.

"Solomon and the prostitutes?"

"If I tell you and her I'm going to cut the Bible in two, I'm guessing it's not you crying around my ankle."

"I don't think it mentions anything about them crying around Solomon's ankle."

"Creative interpretation."

"And that's different anyhow. The baby in First Kings wasn't an issue of national security."

"Okay. You found any Canadian secrets yet? RCMP uniform specifications? Syrup recipes? Maybe a strategy to beat the Canadian penalty kill in Sochi?"

"Does everyone in America have such little respect for Canadians, or are you just the guy who started the ugly American stereotype?"

"I was going to ask you the inverse question about the friendly, happy-go-lucky Canadian label."

Whitney smirked. "Well, that was a fun truce while it lasted."

Jackson returned the grin as he got up and paced. The sun was shining brightly outside, and it looked like a beautiful day. It was a shame to be cooped up inside, but Jackson consoled himself with the thought that if they could reach the ferry, they were home free.

Abby managed to sleep for a few hours, then Jackson took a turn. He had called Leroy and told him little, just letting him know that he was still working. Then he had scanned local TV channels with the sound off, hoping to find an update on Desmond. No luck.

He'd given orders to be awakened at one, but awoke on his own a little before noon. Abby had taken his place in front of the TV, eyes glazed over, while Whitney caught a nap on the sofa. After checking in with Abby, Jackson took a quick shower in the hopes of refreshing himself a little. It worked. A little. Then the trio had leftover pastries for lunch.

After killing a little more time, they finally checked out of their room shortly after two-thirty. It was a ten-minute walk to the pier, which gave them a little extra time to purchase tickets and board the ferry. From their vantage point atop a hill on the south side of Two Harbors, the small village looked like little more than a campground. And a sleepy one at that.

"This might be easy," Whitney said. She wore her hair down and loose, with her jacket around her waist. Abby's hair was pinned up, and she had changed into a spare shirt—blue instead of yellow. Jackson had also changed from the night before, and they had already made plans to split up when they reached the ferry. Jackson would go first, alone, and Abby and Whitney would follow a few minutes later. If anyone were looking for a trio or for a man and a woman matching Jackson and Whitney's descriptions, the ruse would hopefully throw them.

It never came to that.

Shortly before they reached the beach, Jackson spotted a policeman on patrol at the near end of the pier. Seconds later, Whitney pointed out a police car parked a few hundred feet down the beach. They quickly retreated to the shelter of the trees. Whitney pulled her binoculars from Jackson's backpack and studied the pier.

"I see two officers, one at the near end, another by the loading gate."

"Just two?"

"Yeah, but it looks like they're checking IDs."

"Super."

"What do we do?" Abby asked.

"I don't know. Think you can find some horses around?" Jackson asked Whitney.

"And ride where?"

"What are we going to do?" Abby asked again.

"This town's called Two Harbors, right?" Jackson asked.

Whitney looked at him.

"So where's the second harbor?"

She pointed over her shoulder. "Other side of the isthmus."

"Does the ferry load there too?" Abby asked.

"No," Whitney answered.

"So how does that help us?"

"We find somebody with a private boat," Whitney said, her eyes bright as she looked at Jackson. "There were a couple of power boats moored in the windward harbor, and there's three or four out here."

"So how do we find the captains?" Jackson asked.

Whitney grinned and turned over her shoulder. "Ask at the local watering hole."

It took three inquiries by Abby, the least recognizable of the group, but she got a name from a midday patron at a small cantina in the middle of town. Al Upton owned a pleasure cruiser, and if the price were right, he would provide taxi service. If he was in the mood. And sober.

Upton lived in a shanty on the west side of town, a five-minute walk from the cantina. "I take it you have a plan for this," Whitney said to Jackson as they walked.

"Me?"

"Being a private eye, I assume you deal with a lot of drunks and rednecks. How do you coerce them into helping you?"

"Dangle a good-looking female in front of them."

"Fine," Whitney said, fluffing her hair. "But I get my cell back as soon as we're on board."

"Agreed."

Shanty was being kind. Jackson expected a bunch of little African children to appear from around Upton's place, kicking a worn soccer ball down the dusty street. Instead, a tall, tanned, reasonably thin man in cutoffs and an Oakland Athletics tee opened the screen door as they approached the shack. He carried a bottle of beer in his right hand and a sandwich in the other, and he sat down in an old rocker on his front porch before acknowledging them.

"You all lost?" he asked in a gravelly voice. "Because I got no money to buy anything and I've already got religion."

"Then you're in luck," Whitney said as she took the first step up onto the porch, tossing her hair over her shoulder with a nod. "Because we're here to buy."

Upton regarded her with a stare, as if she'd committed a grave sin by stepping on his stairs. Then he took a huge bite of his sandwich, shards of lettuce and a thin piece of roast beef falling onto his lap. He ignored them. "Go on."

"We need a ride back to the mainland," Whitney said. "Marina del Rey."

"I don't do business with criminals."

"Do we look like criminals?"

"Else stupid. If you run, you can still make the three o'clock ferry, and it's a lot cheaper than I am," he said, tipping up his bottle.

"Her husband is looking for us," Whitney said with a nod at Abby. "He'll expect us to take the ferry."

"Husband?" Upton shook his head. "I don't get involved in love triangles either."

"It's nothing like that. We were camping, a little relationship building sort of a thing, trying to save our best friends' marriage. They had a fight, it got violent, and we had to run. It's a small island, and—"

Upton held up his hands. "I don't want no details. Five hundred dollars gets you to the mainland."

"Do you have a problem with fifties and twenties?"

Upton's boat was moored on the leeward side of the island, and he insisted on finishing his sandwich first. And his beer. Whitney then paid him two hundred dollars, the rest due when he picked them up at the windward port. A handshake sealed the deal, and Upton took off for one pier while Jackson, Abby, and Whitney headed for the other.

"Nice cover story," Jackson said. "Abusive husband."

Whitney shrugged. "I've got a handful at the ready. Any good agent does."

The cops did not think to stake out the much smaller dock on the windward cove, and as the sun began its descent in the western sky, the trio boarded Upton's cruiser—*The Albatross*—without hassle. He navigated the shallower waters of the inlet, then chugged around the northwestern tip of Santa Catalina Island.

When they hit the open ocean and started toward the mainland, Jackson let out a sigh of relief. He was stationed up front with Abby and Whitney, watching the bow cut through the choppy Pacific. The morning weather girl had been right; it was breezy, and it did appear that storms could be building.

Abby was still quiet, as she had been most of the day, while Jackson and Whitney again debated how they were going to handle possession of the Bible when they reached Los Angeles. Whitney insinuated that she would have to call her headquarters and Jackson told her good luck with that. Eventually, they gave up arguing, and Jackson turned his attention to Abby.

"I feel guilty," she said when he asked how she was holding up.

"Guilty?"

"For not feeling more sadness. Desmond is . . . was family. No matter how much I disliked him, he was Alec's son, and Alec loved him. I should be more upset."

"A friend once told me you can't trust your emotions in times like these. They're out of whack, especially right now when you're still in shock."

"You think I might feel something once it wears off?"

"I wouldn't doubt it," he said. Then he shrugged. "Besides, you can't control your emotions. They come and go whether you want them to or not. The trick is making sure they don't control you."

Abby smiled, almost laughed. "You sound like a greeting card."

"Sorry. I didn't mean to be trite."

"I know. And thanks."

He nodded.

"Do you think it was Andrews and Newton?" Abby asked a few minutes later. "That killed Desmond, I mean?"

"I don't know. It's awfully coincidental if they didn't. Pacoima's right next to Hansen Dam. If they really took Desmond and those other two in, what were they doing back there?"

"But why would the CIA kill him?"

"I don't think they would."

Abby frowned.

"I don't think they're CIA," Jackson said. "Or they could be, but there's another explanation. You said you thought Desmond was involved in criminal enterprises. Maybe it *was* just a coincidence. Once we get back, we'll find out."

She nodded.

The route from Two Harbors to Marina del Rey led them almost due north past Rancho Palos Verdes and various beachside communities. It was hard to believe it had been just more than twenty-four hours since they had traversed the same waters en route to Catalina. Then again, it also felt like months since the masquerade ball where everything had started. And now that night's host was dead.

"We got company!" Upton shouted from the helm.

Jackson, Abby, and Whitney all spun around. "What?"

He jerked over his shoulder with his thumb. "Speedboat astern, been honing in on us for several minutes."

Whitney beat Jackson to the starboard passageway leading to the stern. They both squinted into the late-afternoon sun at a speedboat several miles behind them and closing fast.

"What do we do?" Abby asked from behind them.

"Nothing," Jackson said. "It's just a boat."

"You really believe that?" Whitney asked.

"I mean, so far there's no threat. We wait."

Whitney looked up at Upton. "Will they catch us before we get to the harbor?"

He shrugged. "Maybe. But *they* definitely will." He gestured straight ahead with his binoculars, and the three passengers turned to see an oncoming cruiser about the same distance away as the speedboat.

"Who's that?" Abby asked.

"That would be the good old United States Coast Guard," Upton answered.

"Coming for us?"

Her question disappeared in a sudden gust of wind. When it passed, a distant thup-thup-thup-thup of a helicopter carried over the choppy ocean waters. All three again whipped their heads around, and Whitney spotted the chopper first. It was low on the horizon, coming at them from just east of south. The direction of Avalon.

Whitney turned to Jackson. "I think that constitutes a threat."

"That we definitely can't outrun," Upton called down.

Abby's face was slightly more panicked. "We're trapped!"

Chapter Twenty-Four

4:33 p.m.

THE SPEEDBOAT WAS no more than a couple miles behind them. As Upton pushed *The Albatross* northward, the Coast Guard cruiser continuously grew closer. And the helicopter likely bearing alleged CIA agents was closing fastest of all.

"I don't know what you folks are up to," Upton said, "but I got a feeling this ain't about an abusive husband. Unless he's the governor."

"What are we going to do?" Abby asked.

Jackson looked around, no solution forming in his mind.

"What kind of case did you put the Bible in?" Whitney asked.

"What?"

"What kind of case. Is it waterproof?"

"I don't know. It's what the Swedes had it in."

"What's it made of?"

He shrugged. "Some sort of plastic."

"Let me see."

"What?"

"Are you hard of hearing? Let me see it."

Reluctantly, Jackson slipped the satchel off his shoulder, the one he'd taken from Fred at Las Escaleras, the one into which he'd placed the Bible—having returned it to the pouch Fred and Katie had placed it in—before leaving Banning House Lodge. He unzipped the satchel and withdrew the plastic pouch, handing it to Whitney.

"Al, you got any plastic?"

"What kind of plastic?"

"Something to wrap this in. And some duct tape."

He frowned but nodded. A second later, he pitched a roll of duct tape down to them. "There's a tarp under that bench."

"What are you doing?" Jackson asked.

"I'll take the Bible and swim to shore."

"Nice try."

"You got a better plan?"

"It's at least a mile to shore."

"I'm a good swimmer. It's no problem," she said, already on her way to the bench. She lifted the seat and pulled out a tarp. "Knife?"

"What are you folks doing?"

"You'll get a bonus!" she shouted to Upton. A moment later, he dropped a pocketknife down to her. With a quick look at the closing boats, she began cutting a two-foot strip off the thin tarp.

"You're not leaving here with the Bible," Jackson said.

"Think about it. They'll be here in minutes. Either you give the Bible to them, or you give it to me."

He shook his head.

"I promise you," she said, "I'll wait for you."

"How can I trust you? How do I know you didn't call them?"

"You don't, but I give you my word."

Jackson looked to Abby. The chopper was a steady drone.

"I swear on the maple leaf," Whitney said, tearing the strip loose. "It's now or never."

Jackson sighed. "Fine." He extended the Bible in its pouch to Whitney.

"Duct tape the zipper, then wrap it and duct tape the seams. Tight."

He tore off a strip of duct tape, then handed the roll to Abby to tear off more while he covered the pouch's zipper. Then he wrapped it tightly in the strip of tarp, and, using lengths of duct tape Abby provided, bound it as well. He was confident the Bible would survive a quick dunking unscathed, but a mile swim in the ocean?

"This will work," Whitney said, seeming to read his doubts. "Their pouch looks waterproof. This is just a precaution."

He nodded.

She lifted up her shirt, almost to her bra. "Tape it to my stomach. Tight."

Jackson quickly bound the Bible to her midsection, wrapping the duct tape all around her. "Too tight?"

"Perfect." She twisted her hair into a makeshift knot as she kicked off her shoes. "I give you my word," she said as she pulled off her socks and then unzipped her pants. "I'll call you."

"Or spend your life running."

She nodded as she stepped out of her pants. She looked fore and aft. The speedboat was maybe a mile at most behind them. The Coast Guard cruiser was half that. Making eye contact once more with both Jackson and Abby, Whitney dove overboard. The waters were rough and as cold as they would be all year. Plus it would be dark soon. Jackson didn't like Katie Ledecky's chances, much less Whitney's. And to top it off, the helicopter was so loud he expected it to appear overhead any moment, and anyone aboard would easily be able to spot her as she swam to shore.

Jackson watched her take several powerful strokes as he stuffed her shed clothes into the backpack. He tossed the satchel overboard, then turned to Upton, who had watched the whole scene from the helm. His face registered disbelief.

"Can you veer a little west?" Jackson asked. "Take us away from her."

Upton nodded, and Jackson and Abby stashed the shreds of the tarp back in the bench.

"How do we play this?" she asked.

"Noncommittally," Jackson answered.

"Jackson, if they killed Desmond . . ."

"That's not happening. But if you get worried, come clean."

"What do they think is in that Bible?"

"Good question."

"We're being flagged down by the Coast Guard," Upton shouted. "I'm stopping."

"Drift as far west as you can."

Upton answered by shutting down the engines, allowing the waves to rock the boat as it gradually came to a stop. The cruiser pulled along the port side just moments before the speedboat caught them and idled to starboard. The helicopter, which had circled around from the southwest, timed its arrival, intentionally or otherwise, at the same moment. If anyone had noticed Whitney stroking through the surf, they weren't giving it away with their actions. Then again, the same choppy surf that would make her swim a challenge also served to conceal her as she swam.

The speedboat was piloted by a short man with a backward cap and fancy sunglasses. His passengers were two very attractive Swedes. Jackson didn't see any weapons, and he turned his eyes to the Coast Guard cruiser. A uniformed man with a bullhorn instructed Upton to follow them to the harbor. Jackson didn't spot any familiar faces aboard. He assumed that the helicopter contained Andrews and Newton.

The cruiser turned, and Upton revved his engines and followed it back toward the marina. The speedboat puttered along just out of their wake, with the low-flying chopper bringing up the rear of the procession. Jackson climbed up to the helm with Upton.

"Anything you want to tell me?" Upton asked, not taking his eyes off the cruiser in front of them.

"You a Bible-reading man?"

Upton laughed. "The Bible?"

Jackson nodded. "Ever read about Jonah?"

"I've heard the story."

"Well, consider us to have just thrown him overboard."

Upton chuckled but said nothing more.

The Coast Guard cruiser led them to a dock on the east side of the harbor. Leroy's houseboat was just across the channel as Jackson and Abby stepped off *The Albatross*. The speedboat had moored less than fifty feet away, and the helicopter had preceded them and landed in a nearby parking lot. In less than a minute, Fred/Mats and Katie/Annika (from the speedboat), Andrews and Newton (from the helicopter), and Regina and several Coast Guard officers had gathered around Jackson, Abby, and Upton. So too had Pablo Diaz, who had jumped off the cruiser after the officers.

"What are you doing here?" Jackson asked Pablo.

"Same thing as you, man."

"Oh. *You* see any dolphins?"

"Where is the Bible?" Regina asked.

"Mine's on the table beside my bed."

"That's not what I asked. Where is the Vanderbilt Bible?"

"Mr. Douglas, you're in a lot of trouble," Andrews said.

"I'm in trouble? You should talk."

"Be careful how you address an FBI agent, Mr. Douglas."

"Point one out to me and I will be."

A thick-armed Coast Guard officer stepped in between Jackson and Abby and the lynch mob. "Hold on here, folks. We'll get to the bottom of this, but let's stay calm."

"Officer . . . Duran," Andrews said, pausing to read his badge, "these two stole a Bible that rightly belongs to the FBI as a matter of national security."

"That Bible is mine!" Regina said. "It was stolen from my gala last night."

Duran held up his hand again. "You're FBI?"

"That's right," Andrews said, providing her badge.

"It's a fake," Jackson said.

"It looks authentic to me, sir," Duran said. He handed it to a second officer. "Verify this for me, Tom."

"Yes, sir."

Duran turned to Regina. "You claim this missing Bible is yours?"

"It is mine. It was on display when it was taken during a power outage."

"By these two?" Duran asked, gesturing at Jackson and Abby.

"No, by them," Regina said, pointing at Mats and Annika. "But he was there," she added, pointing now at Jackson. "With the other woman. Where is she?"

"Who?" Jackson asked.

"Her name is Robyn Pearson, A.K.A. Robbie Pierce," Andrews said. "She claims she's FBI."

"There's a lot of that going around," Jackson said.

Duran looked over the dock area. "Where is she?"

"That is a good question, Officer Duran," Andrews said. "She was last seen at the gala with him."

"But you claim these two stole the Bible?" he asked, looking at Regina but pointing at Mats and Annika.

"So I have been told."

"We attended the gala on our honeymoon," Mats said. "That Bible is a family heirloom, and it was stolen from us at our hotel last night. By him," he said, pointing at Jackson.

Duran regarded Jackson for a second before turning to Andrews. "And you said the Bible was stolen from you?"

"That is correct."

"By this man?"

"Yes."

"I've apparently been very busy," Jackson said. "Stealing the same Bible from two different people and all. And like I said, I don't have it."

"Do you mind if I search this backpack?"

"Please do." He swung it off his shoulders and handed it to Duran. While everyone watched, he put on a pair of latex gloves and sorted through the contents of the backpack. "You've got some pretty hi-tech gear in here."

"Is that a crime, Officer?"

"No. But it is suspicious."

"There's a lot of very interesting wildlife on the island," Jackson said, nodding at the binoculars.

"There is no Bible in here," Duran reported.

"Then it's still on the boat," Regina said.

"Or with the other woman," Andrews said.

"Do you know anything about this Robyn Pearson woman?" Duran asked Jackson and Abby.

He shook his head. "I don't know anyone by that name."

"You're lying!" Regina said.

Duran turned to Upton. "Sir, how many passengers today?"

"Two."

"What was the purpose of their trip?"

He shrugged. "They paid in cash. I didn't ask."

"May we search your boat for this Bible?"

Upton nodded and directed the remaining officers who had come ashore to check *The Albatross*. Upton went with them.

"Let me make sure I have this right," Duran said. "You claim that these two stole the Bible from you," he said, looking at Andrews but pointing at Jackson and Abby, "and so do you," he said to Mats and Annika, "but meanwhile you claim they took it from you?" he concluded by turning his eyes to Regina but his finger toward the Swedes.

They all nodded.

Duran turned to Jackson and Abby. "And you say you were on the island to watch wildlife?"

"We certainly didn't go to steal some Bible from these people," he said, motioning at Andrews and Newton, Mats, and Annika. "Like I said, I already have my own Bible."

"And how do you fit into this?" Duran asked Pablo.

"He's working for us," Annika piped up. "We hired him after the Bible was stolen from us. When we suspected it was aboard *The Albatross*, we instructed him to contact the Coast Guard."

"And he just happened to arrive at the Coast Guard station within minutes of Miss Archambeau?"

Annika and Pablo both shrugged.

At that moment, Tom returned with Andrews' ID. "It's legit," he said. "She's FBI."

Andrews nodded. "Thank you, Officer Duran. We'll take it from here."

"Not so fast," Regina said. "This isn't an FBI matter. That Bible was mine."

"It was ours," Annika said.

"That Bible is property of the United States government," Andrews said, her voice rising as she stepped forward.

This was getting out of hand. "Look, Officer," Jackson said. "We've been very cooperative, but we clearly don't have this Bible, and we're not interested in some jurisdictional spat. Can we go?"

Duran turned toward *The Albatross*, where another officer shook his head.

"This doesn't smell right," Duran said, "but I don't know that we have any reason to hold you." He nodded at Tom. "Make sure Officer Randolph has your contact information."

"We are in charge now," Andrews said, stepping in front of Duran. "And we still have questions for them."

"Then call our lawyers," Jackson said. "And call yours too, because we're going to have some questions about Desmond Vanderbilt's unlawful death." He withdrew a business card and handed it to Randolph. "You can reach us both through that number."

He took it with a nod.

Jackson took Abby by the arm. "Let's go." He pushed past Andrews and Newton and ignored Regina's spluttering questions. Another voice, however, called for him to halt. Jackson turned. It was Upton.

"You still owe me two hundred and fifty bucks. Second half on delivery."

Whitney had paid him the second installment as soon as he had picked them up at the windward harbor, but Jackson got Upton's meaning. Two-fifty was the price for his silence. Jackson reached for his wallet. "I need to hit the ATM. You want to come along?"

Upton nodded, disembarked, and hurriedly shuffled toward them.

"You're not just letting them go?" Regina said to Duran.

"They don't have the Bible, ma'am, and you yourself said these two took it from you. If any of you would like to swear out a complaint . . ."

She turned to Andrews and Newton. "What about you? Do something."

"Our investigation is ongoing," Andrews replied.

Jackson took the opportunity afforded by her reticence at the mention of Desmond and happily left the madness behind. He, Abby, and Upton set out in search of an ATM.

"This is really all about a Bible?" Upton asked as they entered a building housing a few restaurants, a knickknack shop, and public restrooms. And an ATM.

Jackson pulled out his debit card. "You've got to go back to your boat, past them all. You really want answers to their questions?"

"Now that you mention it, not really."

Jackson withdrew five hundred dollars, handing half of it to Upton. "Thanks."

"If you ever want to go camping again . . ."

Jackson grinned. Then he turned to Abby. "Let's get out of here before the rabble starts to think clearly."

The Granada was parked only a few hundred yards down, by the ferry dock, and they walked quickly before anyone back at the dock changed their mind.

"Why'd they let us go?" Abby asked as they drove out of the parking lot.

"The Coast Guard, because there was no evidence. Andrews and Newton, because they didn't want to talk about Desmond in front of witnesses. Mats and Annika . . . I don't know," he said with a glance in the mirror.

"Now you think Andrews and Newton killed Desmond?"

He looked at her. "I do."

"Why didn't you say something? Press the issue?"

"Because if they did kill him, they're at best dirty CIA agents and at worst something far more sinister. I wanted to get out of there while the getting was good."

She nodded as a distant rumble of thunder echoed across the sky. Jackson looked to the left, where the setting sun had receded behind a wall of bubbling clouds. It made for a pretty picture, with orange and pink streaking the sky above the clouds.

"What about Mats and Annika?" Abby asked. "Do you think Whitney was right about them?"

"Being Swedish art thieves? I don't know. It's possible."

"And hiring that P.I., Pablo? This is too crazy."

"It actually makes sense. If they're foreigners, they'd want a local to help them out. When they started chasing us from the island, they called him to bring in the Coast Guard. The old pincer movement."

"And so did Regina?"

"I guess. She must have come back to the mainland earlier. I don't know why."

Abby sat back. Jackson checked the mirror again. They appeared to have gotten away clear.

"Do you think Whitney made it?" Abby asked.

"It was a long swim in cold water, but I'm hoping she wouldn't have jumped overboard if she wasn't sure she could swim the distance."

"You think she'll keep her word?"

He looked over and made eye contact with Abby. "I do. Can't say why I trust her this time, and I won't be surprised if I'm wrong. But yeah, I think she'll contact us."

Abby nodded and sat back. "I just hope the Bible's okay."

"It was sealed up pretty good. Plus it was already in the case."

"So what do we do now? Just wait?"

"And eat," Jackson said.

"Good."

They returned to his place, where Jackson offered Abby his shower. She still had a change of clothes in the backpack, and while she showered, Jackson ordered pizza. When Abby was finished, he had a quick shower and shave. Feeling slightly better, he joined her downstairs as the pizza arrived. Several thick, cheesy slices hit the spot.

While they ate, they watched the news for any update on Desmond. There was none.

There was also no word from Whitney. As the evening wore on, Abby's nerves became palpable. Jackson called both Ashley and Maggie, fishing for information on Desmond's death. Neither had anything other than what the morning news had reported, but Maggie promised to look into it.

"Can you call Whitney?" Abby asked.

"Her phone was in her pants pocket," Jackson said. "Which means . . ."

"Do you think she'd go back to the hotel?"

Jackson rummaged through the backpack and pulled out Whitney's pants. "It's possible."

"I'm going to call," Abby said.

Jackson nodded. Whitney's cell was in the back pocket of her pants, and he searched through it. Everything was nondescript, nothing to validate or discredit her story that she was a CSIS agent. He scrolled through her address book, but none of the numbers had names attached to them. So he redialed a few of her recent calls, but none of them produced an answer either. Theoretically, that made sense, if she had been calling some main switchboard at CSIS headquarters in Ottawa, as it was after ten on the east coast.

"No one there by any of her names," Abby said. "I tried all three."

"Did you try the room number?"

"No, what was it?"

"Two-oh-four."

She dialed and asked to be connected to the room. Thirty seconds later, she hung up. "Still nothing."

"Give her time," Jackson said, as much for Abby as for himself. Frankly, he'd be glad to be rid of the Bible, but he had to do what was in his client's best interest. Besides, the thought of living the rest of his life with Whitney having pulled one over on him made his stomach churn.

To occupy their minds, Jackson got out his computer and searched several local news stations' websites. But he could find no mention of Desmond's death.

"That's strange," he said. "How does it get reported this morning, and now nobody has it?"

"Maybe Andrews and Newton had the story pulled."

He shook his head. "If they can hack the FBI's website, I suppose it's possible."

Abby glanced nervously at the clock. "It's almost eight."

"Yeah."

"What do we do?"

"Remember, she swam to shore with a Bible strapped to her stomach and no pants. Plus, she was probably exhausted. She'll want to get settled."

Abby sighed.

"Give her another hour," Jackson said. "If she still hasn't called, we'll go check out her place in Hermosa Beach."

Abby nodded.

"In the meantime, you look beat. Try and get some sleep."

"You look beat too," she said.

"I'll be all right."

She nodded and stretched out on the couch. Jackson stepped out onto the deck, where the air was charged with an oncoming thunderstorm. He tried calling Mouse but got Pam instead. She told him he was working until eleven and would be wasting his life at the computer after that. Jackson sarcastically thanked her and went back inside.

With nothing more to do at the moment, Jackson dropped into his rocker in front of a muted TV. The next thing he knew, his phone was ringing. Playing "Bad Moon Rising" to be more accurate.

He glanced at the time before answering: 9:24.

"Yeah, Maggie?"

"Ooh, bad time?"

"No, I'm fine. You find something?"

"Nothing, Jack. You sure about this Vanderbilt guy?"

"Positive. Saw it on KNBC this morning."

"Well, there's nothing on the wire."

He sighed. "Okay, thanks."

"Jack, are you doing all right?"

"Long weekend, Mags. I'll check in when things die down."

"Okay."

He closed his phone and looked at Abby, who yawned as she sat up on the couch. "Not Whitney?"

"No."

"What time—"

"Nine-thirty. Sorry, I dozed."

"Jackson, it's been almost five hours."

"I know." He fought off a yawn of his own. "Let's head to the beach."

Chapter Twenty-Five

10:12 p.m.

STORMS HAD MOVED through while Jackson and Abby had napped, and as they started out for Hermosa Beach, they saw distant lightning over the Santa Ana Mountains and not quite as distant lightning west over the Pacific. By the time they arrived at The Breakers at 16th and Beach in Hermosa Beach, the lightning flashed as often as it didn't, and a dull, continuous rumble of thunder echoed back and forth off the sky.

They had called Whitney's room again before leaving and again received no answer. Jackson had a sinking feeling, but he tried to buoy Abby's spirit. The problem was if something had delayed Whitney, there was a good chance it had also resulted in her losing the Bible.

Large drops of water began to pelt down on Jackson and Abby as they climbed to the second-story corridor at The Breakers. The drapes in Whitney's room were pulled, and no cracks of light peeked around them to suggest that she was inside. Still, Jackson knocked twice before resorting to picking the lock.

"Is that legal?" Abby asked.

He looked up at her. "Nope."

"Aren't you afraid of getting arrested?"

"Seriously, you ask that question *now*?"

Abby fought a sly grin.

"Besides, if she's Canadian, this is sort of counter-terrorism."

"If?"

Jackson shrugged as the lock clicked. He stood up and entered the room in front of Abby. As soon as he flipped on the light, he stopped.

"Whoa," Abby said.

The room had been turned upside down. The bed had been stripped, the sheets and comforter piled in the corner. The drawers of the entertainment center and dresser were stacked to the side or left hanging open. The heat register and air conditioner had both been taken apart, the grates and screws left lying on the floor. Even the Gideon Bible had been searched and was splayed on the floor at the foot of the bed.

Jackson stepped carefully over everything and checked out the bathroom. It had similarly been searched, with the lid of the toilet tank left leaning against the wall. He returned to the main room, where Abby stood staring in shock. He nodded behind her. "Better shut the door," he said as a louder peal of thunder shook the paintings on the walls. She obeyed.

"You think she was kidnapped?" Abby asked.

"No. I don't think she was here at the time. None of her stuff is. But somebody must have figured out she got off the boat with the Bible."

"Now what?"

"Now, we—"

Jackson's phone interrupted him. It was an unknown number, and he warily raised the phone to his ear. "Yeah?"

"Jackson?"

It was Whitney.

"Where are you?" he asked with a confirming nod at Abby.

"I'm in Long Beach. Where are you?"

"On our way to Long Beach," Jackson answered. "Where?"

"Casa del Sol," she replied. "Right on the beach."

"What room?"

"Call me at this number when you're five minutes out," she said. Before Jackson could answer, she hung up.

"What'd she say?" Abby asked.

"She's in Long Beach," Jackson said, heading for the door. "Let's go."

It took a little over thirty minutes to drive from Hermosa Beach to Long Beach, and while they drove, Jackson pondered Whitney, the CSIS agent. Something wasn't right, and he stared through the rain beading on his windows, trying to arrange the pieces in his head. As he turned off the Long Beach Freeway and crossed the Los Angeles River, he still didn't quite know what to think.

He called Whitney. She said she'd meet them in the lobby. Jackson asked if she'd be hiding behind a newspaper, and she again hung up on him.

Casa del Sol was a new property, with three levels of rooms above an open-air lobby that allowed the smell of the rain and the rumbles of thunder to rush in on the breeze. Colorful mosaic floor tiles, wicker furniture, and large potted palms added to a Caribbean vibe, as did the dark-skinned clerk in a floral shirt.

"Can I help you, please?" he asked.

"Uh, thanks, but we're meeting someone," Jackson said, scanning the room for Whitney. She was not in any of the chairs in little nooks around the lobby or at the darkened bar hidden in the recesses to Jackson's left. Nor descending the staircase leading to the mezzanine. He was about to call her again when she strolled in from behind them, off the beach.

Jackson clapped a few times. "Very Nancy Drew," he said. "What's going on?"

"My hotel in Hermosa was tossed, so I'm not taking chances. I had to make sure you weren't followed."

"You know, I knew those headlights were behind us way too long," Jackson said.

"Funny."

"Do you have the Bible?" Abby asked.

"It's safe," Whitney answered. "Follow me."

She led them up the stairs to the mezzanine level and down a hallway to the far eastern end of the hotel. Her suite had an ocean view and a balcony, and all the comforts and amenities of home. After she had bolted the door behind them, she offered them a drink from the mini-bar.

They both declined.

"So, how was your swim?" Jackson asked.

"Fine. A little cold." She poured a glass of soda over ice. "The tricky part was getting from the beach to the hotel without any pants."

"I see you managed," Jackson said.

"I walked. On the beach, from a distance, underwear and a swimsuit are indistinguishable."

"So why aren't you in Hermosa Beach?" Jackson asked, playing dumb. "Your place was searched?"

"'Searched.'" She huffed. "I got back around quarter to seven and found the place had been ransacked. I grabbed my stuff and got out of there."

"Why Long Beach?"

She shrugged. "Why not?"

Jackson sat down on a couch facing the window. Whitney hadn't turned on any lights—just a dim lamp in the entry, and through the glass, he could see the lightning heading toward San Diego.

"Where's the Bible?" he asked.

"It's safe."

"What's that mean?" Abby asked.

"We've been dodging the same people for three days," Whitney answered, sitting on the arm of a chair, drink in hand. "Your strategy, my strategy, our strategy has always been to keep the Bible with us. And they keep taking it from us again." She lifted her glass. "So I stashed it."

"Where?" Jackson and Abby asked at the same time.

Whitney swallowed and lowered the glass, ice cubes tinkling. "Somewhere safe."

"Let's try again," Jackson said. "Where is the Bible?"

"It's in a place where no one can get to it."

"Except you," Abby said.

Whitney bobbed her head as a concession.

"We had a deal," Jackson said, realizing the irony as he spoke.

"We've had several deals," Whitney replied evenly. "And I could have just run, never called you, stayed off the grid. But I'm a woman of my word."

Jackson did his very best to chortle.

Whitney huffed. "I'm a woman of my word," she repeated. "Until we can come to a lasting agreement of what we're going to do with the Bible, it stays where it is." She took another drink.

Jackson stood angrily and paced to the window.

"Tell me you wouldn't have done the same thing," Whitney said. "Or worse, just cut me out of the deal entirely."

Jackson gritted his teeth. "What sort of agreement?"

"I take it back to Ottawa," she answered. "I give you a receipt, and after the CSIS has sanitized it, it's yours. Or rather, Abby's."

"Forget it," Jackson said. "You leave the country with the Bible, it's never coming back."

"What happened to just looking at it?" Abby said.

"This isn't the deal we agreed to," Jackson said.

"Yeah, well, things changed when you lied to me, when you kept me from even looking at the Bible, and when I had to strap it to my belly and swim a mile to shore to keep it out of the hands of who knows who. So we'll do it my way."

Jackson turned as Whitney took another drink. He wanted to smack the glass out of her hand, but he refrained.

"We have a deal?" she asked as lightning flashed, momentarily casting half of her face in shadow.

Jackson glared at her.

"What," she said, setting the glass on the table and taking a few steps toward him, "you want to try to beat it out of me?" She stood just inches from him, her jaw firmly set.

"It's tempting."

"Well, go ahead and try, tough guy. But know this, I'm as tough as I am stubborn." If possible, she moved even closer. Her eyes never left his. "And I don't think you have it in you."

"You haven't read my file."

"Guys," Abby said.

Neither flinched.

"Can we think about it?" she asked. "Your terms?"

"Think all you want, but they're not changing," Whitney answered without moving her eyes.

"Jackson," Abby said. He slowly broke his stare and backed down. "We'll sleep on it," Abby said to Whitney. "Let you know in the morning?"

Whitney shrugged. "Fine. I'm not going anywhere."

Jackson huffed. "We're supposed to believe that?"

Whitney wandered over to a stand by the door. She picked a set of rental keys out of a bowl. "Here, take these."

"What, because you couldn't possibly take a cab?"

"If I was going to run with the Bible, why would I call you, tell you where I was, give you keys to my car, and then take a cab and start all over?"

Jackson shook his head. "I don't know. But if I could figure you out, I wouldn't be standing here right now."

"Take 'em or leave 'em," she said. "You know my terms, and you know where to find me."

He held out his hand, and she tossed him the keys.

"I checked with the clerk about half an hour ago, and the suite right next door is vacant. Sleep on my offer, and we can meet tomorrow for breakfast. Say nine? I could use a good night's sleep."

Jackson was fuming, but he realized he had no choice but to play Whitney's game. No choice, that is, but to try to physically beat the location from her. And as mad as he was at her and as much as it might feel good to wring her neck, the idea of actually beating her up was not appealing. Not to mention, had their earlier fight not occurred in a closed in space with walls against which he could crush her, she might have taken him. So he nodded, realizing if he had to do things her way, it'd go the most smoothly if he did so with some sense of compliance. "Let's go, Abby."

She turned away from Whitney and followed Jackson.

"Oh," he said, stopping. He reached into his pocket. "Left this in your pants," he said, pulling out her phone. She held out her hand, but he withdrew the phone. "Collateral."

She shrugged. "It's fine. I bought another burner."

Jackson nodded.

"You keeping my pants as collateral too?"

"No, I just left them at my place. I didn't know we'd be chasing all around the county tonight."

"Fine." Whitney followed them to the door. "Nine?"

"Whatever you say, *Alias*," Jackson replied.

The door closed with a little added emphasis, and he and Abby stood in the hall for a moment.

"What do you think she's done with it?" Abby asked.

Jackson guided her a few doors down. "A locker somewhere, probably at the airport."

"What are we going to do?"

"I'm working on it. In the meantime, let's get you checked in."

"Me checked in?"

Jackson held up Whitney's phone. "I've got a few things to do."

*   *   *

Tuesday, January 22
8:45 a.m.

JACKSON FOUGHT to open his eyelids as he turned his head toward the clock that was beeping beside him. He reached out a hand and fumbled around until he found a button that would silence the cacophony. He forced his eyes to open and focus and take in the time. It meant nothing to him because he couldn't remember when he had fallen asleep, other than not long enough ago.

The door to the bedroom was closed. Jackson got off the foldout couch and staggered to his half bath. Splashing some water on his face helped, and as he brushed his teeth, the evening and night started to come back to him.

After leaving Whitney's suite, they had checked into the one next door, and then run to a nearby Wal-Mart to buy a few things they would need overnight. Because they could, he had taken Whitney's car.

Jackson had then dropped Abby off and gone to see Mouse. He'd asked him to run a reverse search on the numbers in Whitney's phone. They were names and places that didn't make sense, scattered across the country from Los Angeles to Salt Lake City to Denver to Des Moines to Washington, D.C. There were none in Canada, but there had been two Mouse hadn't been able to trace, with area codes completely unfamiliar to him, and not belonging to any state or province in North America.

The night still coming back in fragments, Jackson changed his underwear, socks, and shirt, then tousled his hair and let some body spray cover his lack of shower. When he emerged from the bathroom, Abby was heading for the sliding glass doors to the deck. Theirs was an exact replica of Whitney's suite, only facing the other way, and had afforded Abby a private room to sleep in. She appeared to have made good use of it.

"Morning," she called, turning back to Jackson. She held a cup of coffee in her hand.

"Is there more of that?"

She nodded at the pot on the table, and he helped himself.

"What time did you get back in?" she asked, looking out the window at a clear blue sky.

"I don't remember. The night was a blur."

"Did you go somewhere beside Mouse's?"

He slid open the door and stepped onto the deck, squinting into the morning sun. Abby followed him.

"No," he answered. "I just know I didn't sleep well."

"Probably the bed," she said.

"No, the woman in the next suite over," he said, gesturing with his thumb.

"What are we going to do?" Abby asked.

"Play along and stall," he replied. "We're not letting her take that Bible to Canada."

"Jackson," Abby said, putting her hand on his arm. "Please don't do anything . . . crazy."

"Crazy?" He took a long pull on the coffee. It wasn't nearly hot or strong enough, but it was something.

"What did you mean last night when you said, 'You haven't read my file'?"

"A bluff, mostly. Don't worry, as tempting as it is to grab Whitney and shake her like a maraca, I'll restrain myself."

Abby took a drink. "So what then?"

"That, I'm working on."

A scream interrupted his next drink of coffee, and Jackson realized it was coming from Whitney's room. He hesitated for just a second, wondering if he should jump the railing to her balcony or go back inside. He chose the former, depositing his coffee cup on the railing before he hurdled it.

Whitney's sliding door was closed, but Jackson could see through the glass. Two men held Whitney, one grabbing each arm, carrying her against her will toward the door. They were joined by the dark, lithe frame of Regina Archambeau.

Jackson banged on the glass, which drew everyone's attention. Whitney screamed again, and one of the men manhandled her to the floor. He picked her up in a chokehold, while the other hurried ahead of them and opened the door.

Once again, Jackson thought about going back inside to chase them through the hallway. But there was a fire door at the end of the hallway, and they would be gone before he got back. So closing his eyes and covering his face as best he could, Jackson rammed his shoulder into the glass.

It splintered and shattered, and he crashed into the room. As he rose to his feet, he saw Whitney's captor haul her out the door, with Regina on his heels. The other man backed after them. Just in time, Jackson saw the gun in his right hand. He dove to the floor and the cover of the couch as two silenced bullets spat over his head into the wall.

Chapter Twenty-Six

8:59 a.m.

JACKSON STAYED DOWN. No more bullets flew his way, and when he did finally peek around the couch, the shooter was gone.

To avoid the shards of glass on the floor, Jackson returned to his and Abby's suite via the hallway. She was waiting wide-eyed.

"What happened?"

"Regina just kidnapped Whitney," Jackson said, quickly stepping into his shoes.

Abby did likewise. "You're bleeding."

He looked down at a red stain forming on his right shoulder, where he had crashed through the window. Now that she mentioned it, he could feel the cut. But it beat a bullet hole. He knew.

"It's fine," he said, grabbing yesterday's shirt off the floor and scooping his keys, wallet, and phone off the table. "Come on."

Abby followed him into the hallway, which was clear. Whitney's car was parked behind the building, away from the beach, with all the other vehicles. Since Jackson didn't want to take the time to explain things in the lobby, and since the emergency bells were already clanging, he used the fire door.

Down the external staircase, they made a sharp turn, followed by a quick sprint along a hedgerow, leading them to the parking lot. They were just in time to see a burgundy Cadillac Escalade tear out of the lot, almost on two wheels.

"That's got to be them," Jackson said as he ran toward Whitney's rented Chevy Cobalt. He and Abby quickly strapped themselves in, and he punched the accelerator to the floor.

"You think she was lying about the Bible?" Abby asked as he turned out of the parking lot.

He made another quick turn, amid blaring car horns, onto Ocean Boulevard before answering. "No. I think . . ." He zoomed around a pair of slow(er)-moving vehicles. "She might be leading them to it."

"You think she'll actually take them to it, though?"

Jackson zipped around another car, then cut in front of it to avoid running into the back end of a pickup. He was sure he was drawing curses and inappropriate gestures, but it was L.A.——people expected to encounter at least one incident of road rage per day.

His latest maneuver brought him in sight of the burgundy Escalade, and he relaxed his pace a little. There was no need for Regina and her crew to know he was behind them.

"Depends how nice they are in asking," he finally answered.

"You mean how not nice, don't you?"

Jackson nodded.

Abby sighed and sat back. "How did Regina find us?"

"Beats me. I think everyone must be tapped into CIA satellites and tracking systems except us."

At the light at Shoreline Drive—which led to the aquarium, arena and convention center, and harbor—Jackson pulled up one car behind the Escalade. They were in the center lane, headed straight, likely to the interstate. He said as much to Abby.

"Then where?"

He shrugged. "Anywhere. With Whitney, a wild baboon throwing darts is as good a guess as anybody."

"What do we do when we get there?"

"That's a good question. Depends where there is." He looked over at her. "They have a gun. I should have said something, but I was in a hurry. If you want to bow out . . . we do. This Bible can't be worth getting killed over."

"What about Whitney?"

"Her either. Just kidding," he said before Abby could chastise him. "We call the cops, let them handle it."

Abby shook her head. "I'm not giving up. Not now."

"Okay."

"But I also can't ask you to risk your life for me. So if you want to bow out . . ."

Jackson turned onto Golden Avenue, which would lead to the Long Beach Freeway. He was a few hundred yards behind the Escalade. "I'm kind of mad about getting shot at," he said. "Besides, I'd like to expose Regina for who she apparently really is."

She nodded. "Okay then."

"All that being said," Jackson said, "if at any time you want out, just say so."

"Same for you."

He nodded. Then pulled out his phone. He handed it to her. "We might still want to call the cops."

"Me?"

"I need to focus on driving," he said as they crossed the Los Angeles River. They joined with the Long Beach Freeway just north of the Port of Long Beach, and Jackson closed the gap as traffic immediately thickened. Half a mile and a pair of interchanges later, traffic on the northbound lanes was at a standstill. So too, apparently, was 9-1-1, as Abby was on hold.

"How can 9-1-1 be on hold?" Jackson asked.

She shrugged.

Traffic inched along until Abby finally was able to talk to an operator. As Jackson began to increase his speed slightly, she reported that a woman had been kidnapped at gunpoint from the Casa del Sol in Long Beach and forced into a burgundy Escalade last seen heading north on the Long Beach Freeway at West Pacific Coast Highway. She gave a good description but, per Jackson's instructions, left out the part about them being in pursuit.

"Good job," he said when she closed and handed back his phone.

"So what happens when the police show up and find us involved again?"

"Yesterday was the Coast Guard," he said.

"Don't they communicate?"

"Maybe. But we'll worry about that then."

They continued to stay several car lengths behind the Escalade, which was easy because traffic still wasn't going anywhere. As they slowly neared the intersection with the 405, it came to a complete standstill once again.

"Oh my gosh," Abby said. "This is terrible."

"Slowest chase since O.J."

While they puttered along, Jackson kept his mind busy. Where would he have stashed the Bible if he were Whitney? She had come ashore near the airport (if she'd swum in a straight line), walked to her hotel in Hermosa Beach, rented a car, and driven to Long Beach. Jackson figured she would have picked a location off that path, and judging by the fact that the Escalade was making no attempt to leave the Long Beach Freeway at the 405, that guess seemed accurate. Unless Abby was right and Whitney was leading them astray.

Jackson also pondered Abby's other question. How had Regina found them? How did Andrews and Newton, Mats and Annika, Cortez, Desmond, and everyone else who had been tracking the Bible keep finding it? Did they all have Mouses they relied on for help, or were they all working for or with national intelligence agencies? And if so, who was working for which agency? All he knew was Pablo Diaz certainly wasn't providing any measure of valuable assistance to anyone.

Traffic didn't improve much once they cleared the 405, and it reminded Jackson of Saturday afternoon when he and Whitney had been headed for The Exquisite Hotel. Back then, Whitney had been Roberta Pierce, FBI. This after a stint as Robyn Pearson, also FBI. Now it was Whitney Raines, CSIS, and Jackson was having his doubts about that. But it didn't matter right now. She was the only link they had to the Bible, and she was in danger.

Traffic remained slow past the Gardena Freeway and all the way to the 105, where it finally began to move at a decent pace, without an explanation as to why it had been stalled for so long. Typical. It had been close to an hour, and they had traveled less than ten miles. These weren't great conditions for making a getaway, but then again, they weren't real ideal for a police chase either.

"Where are we going?" Abby asked as they continued northward.

"Downtown?" Jackson guessed. He shrugged. "She could have put it anywhere." He shrugged again. "We'll find out in a few minutes. Either they take I-5 toward downtown, or else they're headed to San Bernardino."

Traffic once again slowed as they climbed over a BNSF freight yard.

"Are we coming to I-5?" Abby asked.

"No."

"So why the slowdown?"

"That," Jackson said, pointing up ahead at flashing red and blue lights just around a slight bend in the freeway.

Abby strained against her seatbelt. "What is that?"

"Either a major accident or a roadblock."

Traffic had come to a crawl, with Jackson managing to get a little closer to the Escalade in case it exited the freeway. But as they drew nearer, he realized the roadblock was set up before the exit ramp.

"They're trapped," Abby said.

"Don't bet on it. Whitney probably dyed her hair and pulled a CTU badge out of her underwear and will claim she's Tara Baxter and she commandeered the vehicle for national sec . . . ur . . ."

The side door of the Escalade flew open, and Whitney jumped out. She was followed by Regina.

"Or that," Jackson said. He watched in astonishment as Whitney and Regina jumped over the guardrail and clambered down the side of a hill into an industrial district.

"Now what?" Abby asked.

Jackson reached into the back for his spare T-shirt. "Here, can you make this look like an unborn baby?"

"What?"

"Under your shirt," he said, rolling his finger.

"What are you doing?"

"We wait, we lose them," he said, honking the horn. He cut to the side of the road and veered around several cars, nearly scraping mirrors with the Escalade.

"Jackson, what—"

"Just pad your stomach as best you can," he said, tooting the horn again. "And put some water on your face," he added, nodding at a bottle of water Whitney had left in the car the day before. "You should be sweating."

"Jackson, this is crazy."

"You can do it. Just breathe heavy."

Jackson continued to honk as he passed a dozen more vehicles in line for the roadblock. He received angry honks back as a red-faced California Highway Patrol officer approached his window. Jackson lowered it and cut off the officer. "My girlfriend's going into labor," he said. "Two months early. She's had complications."

The officer took one peek inside, where Abby had managed to make Jackson's extra T-shirt resemble a baby bump. Sort of. She had wiped some of the water on her face and took a drink from the remaining liquid while holding her hand over the shirt and pretending to suffer a contraction. Like Jackson had said, a natural grifter.

The officer's face relaxed from a frown into an anxious nod. "Go ahead, go ahead," he said, waving them through.

"Thank you," Jackson said, and sped through a narrow opening leading to the exit ramp. He turned to Abby. "That was good."

"You're crazy."

"Yeah, maybe."

"Why girlfriend and not wife?"

"Huh?"

"You called me your girlfriend."

"No ring." He nodded out the window. "You see them anywhere?"

"No," Abby said, pulling Jackson's shirt out from under hers.

They were stopped at a light at Washington Boulevard. Straight ahead, a dead-end street led to a junkyard. Beyond it was a two-lane street that ran beside the freight yard. Jackson doubted Regina and Whitney would hop a freight car, so when the light turned green, he turned left and headed east toward a part of town that seemed more amenable to locating a cab. That, he guessed, would be Regina's next move.

Regina was wearing khaki pants and a dark pullover. Whitney was decked in jeans and a plaid button-down. Neither would stand out in a crowd, although there weren't any crowds along Washington Boulevard—not yet. But the industrial district was about to change into a commercial district, and Washington was about to intersect with Atlantic Boulevard.

"Cover your side," Jackson instructed Abby. "You see them?"

"No."

Jackson willed his eyes to spot Regina and Whitney ahead and to the left. He calculated it had been four or five minutes since they had jumped from the Escalade. They could have walked a few blocks, about where Jackson and Abby were now. Unless they had gone south or west.

"Nothing," Abby said.

Jackson reported the same as he turned right onto Atlantic. A minute later, Abby nearly jumped out of her seat. "There!" she yelled, pointing across the street to the parking lot of a Taco Bell. It was in front of a small shopping center that was just stirring to life. The Taco Bell lot was still empty, save for a yellow taxicab that two women were ducking into. Regina and Whitney.

Jackson jerked the wheel on the Cobalt hard left, careening into the parking lot just ahead of an oncoming semi. By the time he maneuvered around a small landscaping island, the cab was already heading for the exit. Jackson had to pause to allow two female pedestrians to cross in front of him, then wait for several northbound vehicles on Atlantic.

The cab had crossed into the left lane and turned onto westbound Washington. Jackson followed, turning through a yellow arrow that turned red. He received several horn honks for his action. He also drew the attention of someone in the cab, because it almost immediately veered onto a northbound side street. Jackson followed into a compact residential neighborhood, and for several minutes, chased the cab along narrow streets. The cab driver raced along like a madman, while Jackson drove a little more carefully, considering the neighborhood.

They looped back around until they were headed south on Atlantic, and this time the cabbie turned through a red arrow, onto eastbound Washington. Oncoming traffic was already in the intersection, leaving Jackson no option but to wait as the cab disappeared.

When the light finally turned, Jackson did as well, but the wait had been several minutes, and the cab was gone. Jackson took the next street south, heading back toward Atlantic. His plan was to follow it to the next major intersection, hoping to luckily run into the cab.

Atlantic passed under the railroad tracks and intersected with Bandini Boulevard near the freeway. Jackson waited for a few seconds before the light turned, but saw no cabs, either on Bandini or turning onto Atlantic, or headed for the freeway.

"Now what?" Abby asked. It was becoming a familiar refrain.

Jackson picked up his phone, hoping Mouse was at home. And awake.

"Hey, dude."

"Mouse, I need a favor."

"What is it?"

"I need you to hack into the server of a Pill Cab Company. They just picked up a fare at a Taco Bell at Washington and Atlantic in Commerce. I need to know the destination."

"Pill Cab Company?" Mouse asked.

"Yeah."

"Never heard of them."

"That matter?"

"Just saying, they might not have a high-tech dispatch system."

"It's the twenty-tens, Mouse. Everybody's high-tech."

"You should talk."

"Call me when you get something."

"This urgent?"

"Yeah."

"I'm on it."

Jackson clapped the phone shut. Bandini Boulevard ran west through rows and rows of warehouses and past the BNSF yard. At the next major intersection, Jackson turned north.

"How do you know they're going north?" Abby asked.

"I don't. But if they had intended to go predominantly west, they would have gotten off the freeway voluntarily before the roadblock."

"How do you think of this stuff so quickly?"

He shrugged. "It just comes to me."

His phone began playing the James Bond theme, and he quickly slapped it open. "Yeah?"

"Okay, they have an electronic system, but not much of one," Mouse said. "Not even a firewall."

"You find a destination?"

"Yeah. Two passengers picked up at ten-oh-three, headed to Union Station on North Alameda."

"Thanks, Mouse. I don't suppose they have a GPS monitoring the cab's location?"

Mouse laughed.

"Didn't think so. Thanks."

"Union Station?" Abby asked when Jackson had told her the destination. "You don't think they're getting on a train, do you?"

"No. Whitney probably stashed the Bible in a locker." He punched the accelerator. "They've got a few minutes on us, which is all it takes to go in and grab a Bible from a locker." He looked over at Abby. "And once they do—"

"The Bible's gone," she said.

"Yeah. And maybe Whitney too."

Chapter Twenty-Seven

10:16 a.m.

LOS ANGELES UNION Station was located southeast of downtown, just north of the Santa Ana Freeway—the 101 to locals. Opened in 1939, the Spanish Mission Style structure with its distinctive clock tower and surrounding tall, skinny palms—known as sky dusters—was a throwback to yesteryear, to the Golden Age of Railroading and streamliner diesel locomotives.

Jackson had been to the station once before when his mom and brother had taken the Amtrak from San Diego to Fresno to see his aunt, uncle, and baby cousin. That had been twenty-plus years ago, so his memory was somewhat faded. He just remembered it was big and imposing, and everything inside was a shade of brown.

Exiting the 101 onto Alameda, Jackson almost immediately spotted a familiar yellow cab a block in front of them. It was turning at the entrance to the station, and Jackson zoomed around a delivery truck that had suddenly veered into his lane. He darted back into the right lane just in time to make the turn.

The cab was parked right outside the front entrance, and Regina and Whitney were getting out. Jackson pulled to the side of the drive. "You jump out and keep an eye on them," he said. "Don't get too close; just see where they go. I'll park and come find you."

"And then what?"

"We'll figure that out," he said. "Go."

Abby hurriedly got out, and Jackson waited for the cab to pull away from the curb before continuing on to the parking lot. It took a couple of minutes to find a parking spot and quickly change out of his blood-stained shirt, and he ran back to the station. Abby was waiting just inside the entrance by an information center. To their left was the old, now abandoned ticket area.

Directly ahead was the high-ceilinged waiting room, buzzing with activity. A quick glance around the room suggested a train was about to depart.

"You got them?" Jackson asked, slightly out of breath.

"Over there," Abby said, nodding to the far side of the waiting room. Regina and Whitney were standing next to an Amtrak ticket kiosk. "They're buying tickets," she said. "That's why they came to the train station." She turned to face Jackson. "So where's the Bible?"

"Still here, I'm betting."

"I guess that makes a convenient getaway."

Jackson shook his head. "I don't think so. Come on, they're moving." He led the way into the waiting area and pretended to watch a departure screen while keeping an eye on Regina and Whitney.

"Don't we need tickets?" Abby asked.

"No." He nodded. "They're heading for the lockers."

"The Bible."

He nodded again, and they switched vantage points again.

"So they're not getting on a train?" Abby asked. "I'm confused."

"I don't think the train's a getaway."

Jackson watched as Whitney procured a small case from a locker. It was not the case Mats and Annika had been using, the one Whitney had strapped to her stomach before jumping off *The Albatross* the day before. It was a simple pouch with a zipper, very nondescript. Jackson didn't see Regina holding a weapon of any kind, and he concluded she must have found a different means of coercion because Whitney made no attempt to get away. She merely took the case out of the locker and handed it to Regina. Then the two of them turned back to the waiting room.

Jackson and Abby quickly ducked back behind a rack of postcards. Regina and Whitney walked very calmly to the nearest pair of seats and sat down, their backs to Jackson and Abby. He motioned toward empty chairs, and the duo sat down as well.

"Jackson, what is going on? Why are they sitting there?"

"Waiting for the train to leave," he said.

"I thought you said you didn't think it was a getaway."

"I don't. I think Regina's putting Whitney on the train."

"What? Why?"

"Now that Regina has the Bible, all she wants to do is make a clean getaway, right?"

"Right."

"And as far as she knows, she lost us in the cab. So she just has to get rid of Whitney."

Abby nodded.

"So she puts Whitney on a train, and even if it's just till the next station, it's plenty of time for Regina to take a cab to anywhere. By the time Whitney gets off the train, Regina will be long gone. And even if she thinks we somehow did track her to the station, the last thing she'd want to do is box herself in on a train with a passenger manifest, cameras confirming her departure, and the like. She'll find a more discreet way to disappear."

"So what do we do?"

He reached into his pocket. "Go get the car," he said, handing her the keys. "It's in the north lot. Bring it around and park behind all the cabs as far south as you can. When Regina comes out, I'll come to you, and we'll tail her again."

"Are you sure?"

"I'm sure."

"What if she gets on a train?"

He shrugged. "If she does, it will be at the last minute. By the time we know which train she's on, it will be too late to get a ticket, and we'll need to follow in the car anyhow."

Abby's eyes were far from convinced, but she nodded and took the keys. "Okay."

He watched her leave, then turned his attention back to Regina and Whitney. They were seated casually as if they were a mother and daughter waiting for a wine-and-cheese rail cruise. Regina's hands had to be burning with desire to open the case and verify the Bible. Whitney had to be itching for a fight. But from Jackson's vantage point, everything was calm.

He used the down time to study the inside of the station a little more. He was looking for exits, hiding spots, security or police, and taking in human traffic patterns and movements. But he also couldn't help noticing the elegant architecture, from the terra cotta floors to the marble and tile walls to the art deco lanterns hanging from the raftered ceiling. Massive arches spanned the doorways and latticed windows on opposite sides of the waiting room allowed in plenty of Southern California sunshine, both adding to the grand, nostalgic aura.

A boarding announcement echoed through the waiting room. Jackson turned his head as a dozen or more passengers stood and began to make their way to the tunnel leading to the train platform. They passed in front of Regina and Whitney at the same time as Regina took a phone call. Jackson glanced up at the clock—10:21—and when he looked back, Whitney had lunged at Regina.

She had her hands around Regina's neck, and Jackson stood along with several other passengers. A few moved in to break up the fight; Jackson moved over to get a better look. It appeared as if Whitney could have mauled Regina had she wanted to, but instead, she left her with a bloody nose and began ransacking her purse.

Jackson took a few steps farther to the right, his thoughts on the case containing the Bible. It had fallen to the floor, several feet away from the fracas, and he thought about running and grabbing it. But something stopped him—it was still too close to Whitney and Regina, and Whitney was more focused on the contents of Regina's purse than the Bible, which made him question if it was the real Bible. Whatever the reason, he hesitated.

Several passengers finally broke up the fight, pulling Whitney away from Regina and her purse. They helped Regina back into her seat and checked on her, while a couple of them looked around the waiting room, presumably for security or police officers. In the commotion, one of them accidentally kicked the case, and a passerby picked it off the floor and set it on the armrest of a chair. Done hesitating, Jackson decided to circle around, grab the Bible, and make a run for it.

He didn't get the chance.

While everyone's attention was still on Whitney and Regina, a woman in stylish jeans and a fitted San Francisco 49ers tee snatched the Bible in a smooth, hardly noticeable motion and kept on walking toward the underpass to the boarding platform. Had Jackson not been looking at the Bible, he never would have noticed her, what with her luxurious blond hair pinned up behind her head. And had he not noticed her, he wouldn't have noticed the handsome, chiseled man next to the ticket counter who made brief eye contact with the woman.

Mats and Annika, also known as honeymooners Fred and Katie.

They had just scooped the Bible. Literally.

Two security guards rushed over and joined the group of people who had broken up the tussle between Whitney and Regina. Jackson could see a major commotion was about to start, sorting out who was who (or at least who claimed to be who), who had started the fight, what it was about, etcetera. He tried to circumvent it all and follow the Bible, but the crowd made it difficult to get around. When he was finally clear, he had to sprint through the tunnel to the platform and was just in time to see Mats boarding a train.

Before he could get close enough to identify the number of the train, it started to pull away. Jackson turned around, dodged a porter, and raced back through the tunnel and into the station. He scanned the list of departures and spotted a 10:25. The *Coast Starlight*.

The ticket counter to his right had a long line, but Amtrak's information center didn't. He hurried over, just beating an old woman with a walker. It was completely legit.

"Can I help you?" an old guy with a handlebar mustache asked from behind the counter.

"Any trains other than the *Coast Starlight* leave within the last two minutes?"

"Metrolink just left a minute ago," he said with a glance at his pocket watch. The guy was apparently from the same time period as the station itself.

"No, this was an Amtrak."

"Then the *Coast Starlight* is the only one. Next departure's the *Surfliner South* at quarter of."

"Where's the *Starlight* go?" Jackson asked.

The man handed him a brochure. "All the way to Seattle. Twenty-nine stops in between."

Jackson opened the brochure, which contained a complete schedule for the train. He offered a quick, "Thanks," and avoided running over the woman with the walker as he turned around.

He looked next for Whitney and Regina. He spotted Regina, her nose still dripping blood, surrounded by a couple of concerned passengers and the security guards. She was temporarily out of commission. Whitney, as had become her custom, had disappeared.

Jackson didn't care. The Bible had switched hands yet again, and now his quarry was a pair of Swedish art thieves on a train bound for Seattle.

Chapter Twenty-Eight

10:30 a.m.

"DRIVE!" JACKSON SAID as he opened the door of the car.

"Where?"

"Get back on the freeway," he said, sitting down and slamming the door. "Westbound, then north."

"What happened?"

"I'll explain. Just drive."

He buckled his seatbelt as Abby peeled away from the curb. She crossed Alameda, and immediately bit her lip. "I think I wanted to turn there."

"This loops back around," Jackson said. "There." He pointed at a sign on the left. "Freeway entrance."

Abby stomped on the brakes, then floored the accelerator after a series of cars in the opposite lane flew by. The curving onramp led them into a short tunnel and then merged with the 101.

"Where are we going?" Abby asked. "What happened?"

Jackson opened the *Coast Starlight* brochure. "Uh . . . Van Nuys," he said, realizing they could never make the train's first stop, Burbank, in time. "Stay on the 101 for now."

"What's in Van Nuys?"

"Besides used car dealers, the next stop."

"We're chasing a train? Who's on it?"

"The Bible," he said. "Can I have your phone?"

Abby frowned but handed it to him.

"Thanks. And you might want to step on it. We've only got about twenty minutes."

She drove, and he thumbed his way to directions to the Van Nuys Amtrak Station. "Stay on this till it joins with the Ventura Freeway," he said.

She nodded. "You want to tell me what's going on?"

He sighed. "After you left, Whitney attacked Regina."

"What?"

"Just went off on her. Not sure why. Or rather, why then. It looked like she was after something in her purse."

"What about the Bible?"

"It fell to the floor and got lost in the shuffle. I was on my way to grab it when Mats and Annika beat me to it."

"Mats and Annika?"

He nodded. "They hopped on the *Coast Starlight* just before it pulled out of the station. Next stop, Van Nuys."

"Then what?"

"If they get off, we tail them. If they stay on, we join them."

"Oh my gosh, this is crazy."

"You think?"

Abby shook her head. "I don't get it. Why would Whitney suddenly attack Regina? Why not way back when they left the car on the freeway? Why'd she get into the cab with her?"

"Regina had a gun then. She must have pocketed it before entering the station. But why Whitney waited until she did . . ."

A phone started ringing. Jackson confirmed it wasn't Abby's, then answered his own. "Hello?"

"Jackson? It's Whitney."

"Where are you?"

"On the *Coast Starlight*. Mats and Annika have the Bible."

"What? You're on the train?"

"I saw them take it and chased after them."

"So did I. I never saw you."

"I was right behind you," she said. "You guys followed me all the way to the station?"

"More or less. Why didn't you say something?"

"There wasn't time. I had to catch the train."

Jackson shook his head.

"Look, I can't explain now. But I'm here keeping my eye on them. I've got to go."

Before Jackson could utter a reply, she hung up. With a growl, he lowered his phone, then relayed the conversation to Abby.

"So what happens when we catch the train?" she asked. "Do you have a plan for getting the Bible back from them?"

"Maybe we should try just asking."

"I'm serious."

"So am I," Jackson said. "We know nothing about them, except who Whitney said they were. Maybe we can reason with them."

"You really think so?"

Jackson sighed and looked out the window at passing L.A. neighborhoods. For one of the few times in his life, he kind of envied the regular guy, the nine-to-fiver who didn't chase Bibles and women with Multiple Personality Disorder around the city for a living.

The 101 took them through East Hollywood, Hollywood, and the Hollywood Hills neighborhoods, the latter of which was scattered across the eastern end of the Santa Monica Mountains. Once north of the mountains in the San Fernando Valley, they journeyed west on the Ventura Freeway (still the 101) for several miles before exiting at Van Nuys Boulevard. Despite Abby's less than aggressive driving, they made good time on the freeway. But now on Van Nuys, they seemed to catch every red light.

Jackson held both his and Abby's phones, using hers for directions and time while contemplating calling Whitney back on his. He didn't.

They arrived at the station at five minutes to eleven, right as the *Coast Starlight* was scheduled to depart Van Nuys. As Abby navigated the parking lot and approached the entrance to the station, Jackson spotted a westbound Amtrak train beginning to pull out.

"Is that it?" Abby asked.

"It's the only one at the station. It has to be."

"Where's the next station?" she asked, already maneuvering a U-turn.

Jackson whipped out the brochure he'd picked up at Union Station. "Uh, Simi Valley, but we'll never make that. It departs Oxnard next at 11:52."

"Oxnard? We don't even know that they're still on the train."

"I'll call Whitney," Jackson said, at the same time scouring the parking lot for any sign of Mats or Annika. There were only a couple of people moving about, none matching the last-known appearance of the alleged Swedes.

"Back to the freeway?" Abby asked, waiting to turn onto Van Nuys Boulevard. To their right, the last car of the *Coast Starlight* was crossing the highway overpass.

"Uh, yeah," Jackson said, using her phone again for directions. "No, wait. Take Sherman to the 405. That will get us to the 101, which will take us to Oxnard."

As Abby drove, Jackson tried calling Whitney, who didn't answer her phone. So he sat back and made sure Abby knew where to turn. She did, and once they were on the highway, there was nothing to do but watch the time.

Abby was right—there was no way to confirm that Mats and Annika were still on the train. They could have gotten off in Burbank or Van Nuys before Jackson and Abby arrived, or could get off in Simi Valley. If so, Whitney was again their only hope.

The 101 continued west out of the valley and wound through the foothills of the Santa Monica Mountains, cutting through such towns as Calabasas, Agoura Hills, and Thousand Oaks. Hillary lived in Thousand Oaks, and Jackson hoped he didn't have to involve her in this case again. Or in anything, for that matter. Despite reaching something of a truce—or at least a ceasefire—in the wake of what happened in Nevada, they weren't exactly pals.

After trying Whitney again, still with no luck, Jackson used Abby's phone to locate the train station. It was in the middle of town, and as Jackson and Abby entered Oxnard from the east on Highway 34, they spotted the *Coast Starlight* rolling through a small freight yard.

"Okay," Jackson said, handing Abby her phone back, "when we get there, I'll get out and look for them in case they've gotten off. You go buy tickets in case they haven't."

"For how far? The train goes all the way to Seattle."

"I quit at the state line," he said. "Seriously, San Jose or Oakland. Just in case."

Abby sighed. "My expenses are rising. I should have just paid the lawyers."

"We quit anytime you want," Jackson said.

"I know, I know." She turned onto Meta Street and then into the parking lot a moment later. The Amtrak locomotive was just making the corner and approaching the station.

It wasn't as fancy as Union Station, but the Oxnard Transportation Center was a very fashionable brick building. Green roof, arched carport, and a clock tower of its own. The tracks ran at an angle on the north and east sides of the building, and buses and a few cabs were lined up on the west. The parking lot, mostly empty, was on the southeast side, and Jackson hopped out before Abby had a chance to bring the vehicle to a stop.

Jackson hurried inside and confirmed the arrival as the *Coast Starlight*. Like in Van Nuys, it was the only train at the station. He had to wait two minutes, and then a steady stream of people entered the station. He kept his eyes peeled for a red 49ers shirt or the light blue polo Mats had been wearing.

They almost fooled him. Annika had donned a black pullover that obscured the 49ers tee. But there was no mistaking the long blond hair that she had unfurled. She pulled a small rolling suitcase behind her, and Mats— now wearing a San Francisco Giants cap—carried a duffel over his shoulder. Jackson didn't see the case with the Bible but assumed it was in one of their bags.

Using other passengers as a shield, he followed them toward the exit, at the same time looking for Abby so he could signal her to forget the train tickets. He also pondered the 49ers and Giants paraphernalia the Swedes were wearing. Coincidence, or did they have a connection to the City by the Bay?

Mats and Annika headed outside and turned toward a row of cabs. Abby had the keys to Whitney's car, so Jackson would have to take another cab to follow them unless he could get a hold of her. He whipped out his phone and started to dial when another thought struck him. Looking around, he spotted a porter doing nothing. Jackson hurried over to him.

"Excuse me," Jackson said. "He has my bag."

The porter, a wrinkle-faced man with graying hair, looked up at Jackson. "What's that?"

"That man," Jackson said as he pointed at Mats, "he took my bag by mistake."

"Are you sure?"

"I'm positive. Can you help me?"

The porter didn't look thrilled but began ambling after Mats and Annika. "Sir," he called. He cleared his throat and called again. Mats looked up just before getting into a taxi. If he recognized Jackson, he didn't immediately show it. And Jackson stayed in the shadows as long as possible.

"Sir, I'm sorry, but this gentleman says you took his bag by mistake."

Mats' eyes honed in on Jackson and turned a shade darker. So did Annika's. "That's not possible," he said.

"Do you have any way of identifying the bag as yours?" the porter asked.

"Uh, no, it's brand new."

"My Bible's in there," Jackson said. "At the bottom. It has my name in it. It'll prove it's mine."

Mats attempted to slice Jackson in half with his eyes. Jackson didn't dare turn his gaze to Annika.

"I'm very sorry, sir," the porter said. "But may I search your bag?"

"No."

"Absolutely not," Annika said, which relieved Jackson. It had been a fifty-fifty shot as to whose bag contained the Bible, and he'd guessed that Mats would be the one to carry it, just as he had been when fleeing from Las Escaleras. Even thieves had chivalry, right? And Annika's unwillingness to comply indicated Jackson had hit on the right bag.

"I'm terribly sorry for the inconvenience," the porter continued, "but the only way to resolve this issue is to verify which of you is the actual owner of the bag in question. Unless you have some other way to do so, I suggest you allow me to look in the bag for the Bible. I promise I will be discreet."

Mats looked to Annika, who did not have another way. So he reluctantly agreed.

"Sir, what's your name?" the porter asked Jackson. "If I find the Bible."

"Alec Vanderbilt," Jackson answered.

Annika opened her mouth to protest but said nothing. The porter reached out his hand, and Mats thrust the duffel bag at him. He set it down on the ground and knelt down to unzip the bag. Jackson's phone rang. He quickly fished it from his pocket. "Hello?"

"It's Abby. I've got two tickets. Where are you?"

"I think I found my bag," he answered, hoping she understood the code. "Any sign of your sister?"

"My sister? Jackson, what's going on? Do you mean Whitney?"

"That she is."

"No, I don't see her."

"Okay, I'll call you back in a little while."

The porter removed several shirts, a pair of blue jeans, and a toiletry bag. He pushed aside some socks and underwear, then lifted out a pair of shoes. He looked up. "I'm sorry, sir, no Bible."

Jackson frowned and glanced at Mats and Annika. Both of them were wide-eyed. It was all he needed to see.

"I don't get it," he said. "I thought . . . Well, my mistake. Sorry to be a hassle."

Phone still in hand, he turned and ran back toward the station. He paused as he opened the door and speed-dialed Whitney. She didn't answer, and Jackson found Abby and pulled her toward the platform.

"What's going on?" she asked.

"They didn't have it," he said as he snapped his phone shut.

"What?"

"Whitney must have it. And she's not answering."

"You think she's still on the train?"

"Since they just got off, my guess is yes."

"I don't get it."

"Neither do I," he said, urging her onto the platform. The conductor was calling all aboard, and Jackson and Abby presented their tickets just in time to clamber onto the train. They turned left into the car and found their seats, on the left side of the train.

Jackson dropped into the window seat and peered out at the platform, expecting to see Mats and Annika racing toward the train. He didn't spot them, but just before the train started rolling, he saw a tall, thin woman in a dark shirt and khaki pants board the car in front of them.

Regina Archambeau.

Chapter Twenty-Nine

11:53 a.m.

THE *COAST STARLIGHT* was about a dozen cars in length—Jackson hadn't taken the time to count. He did know they were on the third car from the front, on the lower level in the coach section, facing forward. A solitary man seated opposite them hadn't yet looked up from his tablet. Across the aisle, a family of two parents and two teenagers seemed focused on their own conversation. He and Abby were as close to having privacy as was possible aboard a train.

"Did Whitney say where she was?" Abby asked.

"No," Jackson said, reaching for his phone again. He tried calling Whitney for the fourth time since she had called him, leaving his second voicemail when she didn't answer. He'd known some frustrating women in his time, but Whitney was quickly climbing to the top of the list.

"So it's just us and her?" Abby asked.

"No. Regina's here."

"What?"

"She boarded the next car at the last second."

"How?"

He shrugged. "And you can be sure Mats and Annika will be waiting at the station in Santa Barbara."

"Is that the next stop?"

"Yeah. In about an hour."

"That should give us time to search for Whitney."

"Yeah." He took a quick peek at Oxnard out his window. "As far as I could tell, Regina got on alone. She hasn't come this way, so she's in front of us. So I say we start with the back half of the train."

Abby nodded.

"You take the upper level," Jackson said. "Walk fast, like you're going somewhere, not like you're looking for somebody. But keep your eyes peeled."

Abby nodded again.

"And don't assume she's a passenger," Jackson said. "She could be anyone."

"Okay."

"When you get to the back of the train, wait for me. We'll switch levels and then work our way forward."

Another nod.

"Whenever you're ready," Jackson said. Abby stood and started for the back of the car. Jackson took another look forward, just to see if by chance Regina was coming his way. She wasn't. He glanced out the window again, saw they were crossing a river that was more sandbar than river, and then stood himself.

The car directly behind them was the same as theirs, but immediately thereafter, Jackson's plan fell apart. The fifth car wasn't accessible from the lower level, and he had to backtrack to the stairs in the middle of the fourth car. He didn't see Abby and assumed she was well ahead of him.

A corridor ran between sleeping rooms that doubled as seats in the daytime, and Jackson strode toward the back of the car, as if he had nothing on his mind but keeping his balance. He managed to scan most of the forward facing passengers, none of whom were Whitney.

The next car—the fifth—was split in half, with stairs again in the middle. The front half housed bedroom suites that took up most of the width of the train, with just a narrow hallway running beside them. Toilet facilities and stairs were in the middle, and the back half of the car was split in half, with a central walkway separating roomettes—seats that converted into curtained off beds for sleeping. He took the stairs to the lower level, which was partitioned similarly. He couldn't search the bedrooms and didn't spot Whitney in any of the roomette seats.

The fifth car didn't connect to the sixth car at the lower level, so he again climbed the stairs to move from car to car. He had to repeat the procedure all the way to the back of the train. Even though the lower levels didn't have as much space, to accommodate for the car's wheels, all the up and down slowed him down.

Jackson counted cars and totaled ten before the dining car. It was lunchtime, and the car was full of passengers. Whitney wasn't one of them, nor was she working the bar or dressed as a waitress or busser. Jackson elbowed his way through the crowd to the final car of the train. It was a lounge car, and he quickly found out it was reserved for those passengers with sleeping car tickets. Without one, Jackson was forced to turn around. He was convinced that, somehow, Whitney was in there watching the scenery roll by.

It had improved. They had left Oxnard and Ventura and were cruising along the Pacific Coast on a small strip of land between the pounding surf and the 101. It was a spectacular view, but Jackson had other things on his mind.

He saw no sign of Abby in the dining car, and after waiting several minutes, he began to work his way back toward the front of the train, where Abby was waiting for him in their seats.

"Any luck?" she asked.

"No. You?"

"No. And I must not have been too discreet. A conductor forced me back to my seat. I only made it to the eighth car."

He nodded, then briefly recounted his up-and-down search. "No sign of her." He shrugged. "Unless she was moving around too, she isn't behind us. Unless she's in the bathroom, or a private bedroom, or the lounge car. She could be anywhere."

"You didn't search the lounge car?"

"Couldn't," he said. "Not with—"

An object out the window distracted him. He turned his head and saw it was a helicopter, flying low over the ocean, keeping perfect speed with the train.

"I don't believe it," he said, sitting back.

"What?"

He nodded at the window. "I'll bet you your expenses for this case that's our FBI-slash-CIA friends Andrews and Newton."

Abby leaned forward. "Oh my gosh. No way."

"It's starting to get ridiculous," Jackson said.

"Now what?"

"We check the forward cars. You take the lower level; I'll go upstairs."

"Okay."

Jackson climbed to the second level and looked to see the helicopter still beside them. Only the Pacific Coast Highway separated them from the ocean. On the other side, the 101 still ran parallel to the tracks. Beyond it, the Ventura Hills rose up toward a clear blue sky.

Jackson made it to the gangway between the second and first car, at which point he spotted Regina just a few seats ahead of him in the first car. Not wanting to alert her to his presence, he quickly scanned the car, still not seeing Whitney. It was possible to miss her with just a quick glance, but a chance he'd have to take. He returned to his seat and waited for Abby, who returned a moment later. "What'd you find?" he asked.

"Nothing. What if she got off back in Oxnard?"

"It's possible." He looked outside and saw the chopper, then told her about seeing Regina.

"What do we do?"

"I guess we wait until the station, then look for her again." He consulted his brochure. "We've got five minutes between arrival and departure, so that gives us time to get off. See your phone?"

She handed it over, and a minute's worth of research revealed the platform at the Santa Barbara station was on the right side of the train. According to the time on her phone, they were about fifteen to twenty minutes out. So they spent a few minutes plotting strategy and then sat back for the rest of the ride.

Jackson kept an eye out the window, tracking the helicopter that continued to hover a few hundred feet above the ocean. Eventually, it flew on ahead of them, his first indication that they were nearing Santa Barbara. When the tracks left the coast and the ocean was replaced out the window by fancy seaside residences, he knew they were close.

The train began to slow, and Jackson and Abby stood and made their way toward the gangway. He instructed her to go left, toward the front of the train, and said he would take the rear. They both agreed not to get back on the train, as the next stop wasn't for almost three hours, and the conductors weren't likely to let them make a detailed compartment to compartment search for Whitney.

Santa Barbara was known for, among other things, its prominence of Mission Style buildings. Stucco walls, clay tile shingles, arches everywhere.

The Santa Barbara Amtrak Station was no different. A couple dozen passengers stood on the platform or back in the shade of a portico that spanned most of the length of the station. It shouldn't be too hard to spot Whitney if she got off.

Jackson and Abby were among the first off the train, and he immediately turned east, toward the back half of the train. There were quite a few passengers—more than he had expected—disembarking, and he kept his head on a swivel looking for Whitney. He didn't spot her, and he drifted back toward the middle of the train.

"Abby?" he asked, his phone to his ear. He had called her phone before they got off so they could use their phones like walkie-talkies.

"Yeah. Nothing."

"Me either. I'm—"

"What is it?"

Jackson's eyes focused on an upper-level window near the front of the car. Whitney peered out at him, a placid smile on her face.

"Jackson?"

"I got her. Car . . . seven. Where are you?"

"Car two."

"Get back on and head toward the back, upper level. We'll meet up."

"Will do."

Jackson lowered his phone and boarded the train again, climbing to the second level. He knew it was coming but still growled in anger when Whitney wasn't there. She could have retreated farther back while he'd been boarding, could have ducked into a bedroom compartment, or could have moved forward to the next car. Jackson hoped for the latter as he moved toward car six. Maybe he and Abby could trap her.

On the sixth car, Jackson hurried through the roomettes and stopped by the stairs to peek out onto the platform. Most of the passengers had either boarded or exited the train, and the commotion on the platform was dwindling.

Not spotting Whitney, Jackson turned to continue forward. He nearly ran into Andrews and Newton.

They looked at each other for a second. Then, before they tried to arrest him or accost him in some way, Jackson cut in front of them and hurried down the corridor to the next car. He couldn't believe his eyes as he searched the platform again for Whitney. He didn't see her, but he did spot Mats and Annika running toward the train. Might as well make it a party.

Jackson raised his phone as he pushed through the roomettes at the back of the fifth car. "Abby?"

"I'm on car four. I just saw Regina."

"Still on the train?"

"Yeah. Whitney?"

"Not yet. I'm on five. Keep coming."

"Okay."

He stopped in the middle of the car again, directly above the lower-level door, and scanned the platform. Andrews and Newton ignored him and continued down the corridor. Jackson was about to follow when there was a small jerk and the train began to inch forward. The movement caused him to stop and sweep his eyes across the platform one more time. A few people stood waving to departing passengers and several others pulled luggage toward the station.

And then, as the train rolled a little farther down the tracks, Jackson saw a woman with strawberry blond hair at the edge of the platform. The trademark ponytail was there, and so were cunning blue-green eyes that swept over the train without locking onto him.

Then Whitney turned and headed for the station.

Chapter Thirty

AT THE END of the car, Newton swore as he too spotted Whitney on the platform. The Holy Spirit reined in Jackson's tongue and kept him from following suit.

She had lured him back onto the train so that she could jump off it and make a clean getaway, and he was mad. This was the last straw of last straws. There were no more deals. If he saw her again—which at the moment, he doubted he would—he would punch her right in the esophagus, take the Bible, and hand her over to the FBI or NSA or KGB or whatever legitimate government agency he found next. But that was a big if because they were stuck on the train all the way to San Luis Obispo some eighty miles northwest of Santa Barbara. By then, Whitney could be anywhere.

Jackson raised his phone. "Abby, you there? . . . Abby?"

"Yeah, I'm here."

"She got off."

"What?"

"Last second. I'm headed back to our seats."

With a heavy sigh, Jackson closed his phone. Before a quietly conversing Andrews and Newton could decide to detain him, he pushed past them and returned to his and Abby's seats near the back of the third car. She was already there, staring listlessly out at the blur of Santa Barbara.

"How?" she asked when Jackson sat down.

"She played us," Jackson said. "She knew we'd be looking for her on the platform, so she lured us back on the train." He shrugged. "It was smart. We had to get back on or risk letting her get away on the train. We couldn't afford to call her bluff." He shook his head. "Maybe I should have . . . I don't know, done something to keep her contained."

"Did she have the Bible?"

"She had a bag over her shoulder."

Abby leaned forward and massaged her temples. "Where are we headed next?"

Jackson sighed. "San Luis Obispo. Three-ish hours."

She looked up. "Three hours?"

"Afraid so."

"San Luis Obispo isn't that far away."

"Not as the crow flies, but we curve around the coastline most of the way. Probably have to slow for a lot of the curves and hills."

He sighed. Abby moaned.

"The southbound train leaves twenty minutes before we arrive," Jackson said, "so we'll have to rent a car, get back to L.A. this evening, and then . . ."

"Quit," Abby said.

Jackson looked at her.

"Right? She'll be long gone, won't she? A six-hour head start?"

"Yeah. Unless Andrews and Newton or Mats and Annika or Regina has someone on the outside who can slow her down. But I doubt it."

"So Andrews and Newton are on the train?"

"Yep."

"And Mats and Annika?"

"They were running for it, but I don't know if they made it. Probably."

"This is unbelievable."

"You're telling me."

She sat back. "What about that Pablo guy? He was working for Mats and Annika, right? Maybe he's still out there, on the outside."

"Even if he was, which is doubtful, he's no match for Whitney."

She sighed. A moment later, she rolled her head toward him. "I think I need a drink. You?"

"I don't drink, remember?"

"I thought maybe this could change your mind."

He shook his head. "You want company?"

"No. I need to think."

"All right."

Jackson watched the scenery. The Amtrak line continued to hug the 101—*El Camino Real*—The King's Highway. But that was out the opposite window. Out his, more of Santa Barbara rolled by. He'd never been a big fan of the town. There was a great ice cream joint he knew of, and *Psych* called it home, but all that ever came to mind when he thought of Santa Barbara was Hillary. She'd attended UCSB before Pepperdine Law, and well . . . There were plenty of other good beachside towns in SoCal.

Jackson felt an adjustment to his headrest and thought Abby had returned. But when he turned his head, he saw Agent Newton leaning against the headrest. Agent Andrews stood sternly beside him.

"What would you say to a drink?" Newton asked with his trademark smirk.

Jackson tried to think of a good Norm Peterson line, but it had been a while since his last *Cheers* rerun. So he simply replied, "No thanks."

"We need to talk to you," Andrews said, sans smirk.

Jackson did smirk. "Same answer."

"We weren't really asking," Newton said. He nodded toward the rear of the train. "Join us in the Parlour Car."

Jackson sighed. "Why not."

He slowly got up and walked between Andrews and Newton all the way back to the rear of the train. They had sleeper car privileges and thus were able to get into the Pacific Parlour Car, the first-class lounge car that offered spectacular views through its abundant windows. With a bar, food service, and plenty of comfortable seats, the Pacific Parlour Car was the ideal way to enjoy a train ride. Unless one was accompanied by iffy CIA operatives posing as FBI agents.

Jackson dropped into an armchair at the back of the car, where he, Andrews, and Newton had privacy. He flopped his left ankle onto his right knee and put on a cocky smile. "Okay, talk."

"We're done dancing," Andrews said. "We've had enough of all your games. We need the Bible."

"Not sure what kind of strange vantage point you had in the chopper, but I don't have the Bible."

"We know. But you can help us get it back."

"Help you?"

"Yes. You're an American citizen, and this is a matter of national security."

"So I keep hearing."

"Look," Newton said, leaning forward. Buddy to buddy. "I know we haven't really hit it off here, but we're on the same side. If you knew what was in that Bible, you wouldn't want it getting in the wrong hands any more than we do."

"Problem is," Jackson said, leaning forward so he was in Newton's face, "I don't know whose hands are the 'wrong hands.'"

Newton stared at him for a moment and then sat back.

"What are you, one of them?" Andrews asked.

Jackson slowly turned his eyes to her. "Them?"

"The conspiracy theorists, the 'true patriots' who think the CIA started the drug wars in South America and injected AIDS into America's inner cities."

Jackson shook his head. "No more than I believe they murder people and stuff them into the trunk of Cadillacs." He feigned sudden inspiration. "Oh, wait a minute!"

Andrews was not amused.

Jackson sat back. "What exactly do you want?"

"Anything and everything you know," she said. "Particularly about 'Whitney.'" She used her fingers as quotation marks as if her tone didn't convey the concept.

"Okay," Jackson said. "But you first."

"This is not up for debate."

"Then if you don't mind, I'm going to head back to my seat and watch the ocean." He started to rise.

"Sit."

He stood anyhow. "I'm sick of dancing too," he said. "And I have been jerked left and right across all of Los Angeles County by you guys, Whitney, Mats and Annika—everybody. So if you want my help, you give me yours first. That's the deal. Take it, leave it, or haul me off to a safe house where you can beat the truth out of me."

Andrews looked at Newton and sighed. "Sit down."

"Do we have a deal?"

She sighed again. "What do you want to know?"

"Start with who you really are."

Andrews looked around. They were still alone. "Like we told you before, we're with the Central Intelligence Agency."

He looked at her for a long few seconds. "Okay, suppose I buy that. You're still sticking to the 'the CIA scares people' reason for posing as FBI agents?"

"We also knew that Alec Vanderbilt's ties to the CIA were well-known. If we showed up claiming to be with the CIA, it could cause associates of his to go underground."

"Associates? What exactly was he up to?"

"We don't know."

"You don't know?"

Andrews looked down for a moment, fidgeting with her hands. "Alec Vanderbilt worked for the CIA until 1994. The last seventeen years of that career were off the books. Alec was an expert in covert operations and a top-of-the-line intelligence gatherer, and the circle of people who knew he was still with the Agency was minuscule. All his work during that time was classified, and with two changes of director and massive staff turnover, the only person who knew everything Alec knew was Alec."

"And you think he put all of that knowledge into his Bible?"

She nodded. "Unfortunately, the CIA did not learn about the Bible until shortly before his death. By then, it had disappeared."

Jackson took a peek out the window. They were back by the ocean, rolling through the California countryside. He looked back into her cobalt eyes. "Still, we're talking almost twenty years ago. Exactly what could he have written that is so important today?"

"Alec retired twenty years ago, but he could have written in the Bible until the day he died," she said. "And without knowing what he wrote, there is no way to tell how important it is. That's why we need the Bible, to study it, try to crack the code. If it turns out to be harmless, so be it. But we have to know."

"What about these associates you mentioned?"

"Theoretical," Andrews said with a shrug.

"So you don't know that anyone else is or was working with Alec?"

"No."

"What do you know about all the players in this game of ours?"

"We know all about you," she said. "A rookie private investigator, unmarried, family deceased, who got himself into hot water with just about every branch of the U.S. government and armed forces last fall, but generally competent."

"Very succinct. Abby?"

"She is Alec's stepdaughter, an artist. Of everyone, her motives seem to be the purest."

"Except yours, of course."

Andrews and Newton both glared at him.

"Now how about you answer some of our questions," Newton said.

"In a minute. But if you're CIA, then you have to have the resources to know who everybody else is, right?"

"Like who?" Andrews asked.

"Mats and Annika."

"Who?"

"The good-looking couple, tall, blond, should be at a Speedo photo shoot in the Keys."

"What'd you call them, Mats and Annika?" Newton asked.

Jackson nodded. "Whitney said they were Mats Bjorn-something and Annika Danielsson, a couple of renowned Swedish art thieves."

Andrews suppressed a laugh. Newton smirked from ear to ear.

"What, let me guess, FBI?"

"Hardly," Andrews replied, returning to a stone face. "They're former Russian KGB agents named Vladimir Lapidus and Svetlana Kublanov."

"We think they're after the Bible for Mother Russia," Newton tossed in.

"What? Russia?"

"You have to remember, for the majority of Alec's time in the CIA, the United States and the Soviet Union were locked in the Cold War."

"But it's over. Why does Russia care?"

"Most Americans think that after the Berlin Wall fell, Russia just went away into poverty and bread lines and political chaos," Newton said. "The country's still thriving, and trust me, the Russian government would love to know what Alec Vanderbilt knew about them."

"And more importantly, what he knew about the U.S. government," Andrews said.

"Russians?" Jackson asked with a wince. "They're too good looking to be Russians."

Andrews sighed. "Are you through?"

"Almost. What about Whitney?"

Andrews shook her head. "She is a blank slate."

"She claims she's with the CSIS—Canadian Secret Intelligence Service, I think."

Newton shook his head.

"No?"

"No," Andrews answered. "Trust me, we would know. There may be foreign agents we're not aware of, but not from our closest and nearest ally. Especially not operating on U.S. soil so brazenly. If she was CSIS, we would know about it."

Jackson sighed. It confirmed his hunches. "Well, who then?"

"We don't know. We have no record of her, her aliases, or anyone matching her description. Best guess, she's some sort of private contractor working for the highest bidder."

"Whoever that may be," Newton said.

"That's why we want to know anything you know about her," Andrews added. "We're in the dark as to who she really is or who she's working for."

"We've answered your questions," Newton said. "Now how about you answer ours?"

"One more," Jackson said. "Desmond."

Andrews shook her head. "What about him?"

"I leave him in your custody, and the next morning I find out he's dead. Is that how 'the Company' typically operates?"

"We did not kill Mr. Vanderbilt," Newton said.

"Then who?"

Andrews shrugged. "We don't know. The CIA had no use for him, so we turned him over to LAPD." She shrugged again. "Maybe they cut him loose, maybe his lawyer got him off. We have no idea. But we did not kill him."

Jackson stared into her dark blue eyes again. Her story was convincing, but then again, he'd heard a lot of convincing stories in recent days. He still wasn't sold that they were legitimate CIA agents, or that, even if they were, they hadn't killed Desmond. But they certainly weren't going to cop to it. Neither was he going to give them anything too secretive.

So he told them the basics about Whitney, her aliases, her lies, her explanations. He told them Abby's story, which he believed to be the truth and which he didn't think would get her into any trouble. And he told them everything he knew about Mats/Vladimir and Annika/Svetlana, as well as Regina and Cortez. But he didn't really know any of them and said as much.

"But Whitney has the Bible now?" Andrews asked.

He nodded.

"You're sure of it?"

"As sure—"

He stopped as his phone rang. The caller ID was a familiar one: Whitney's burn phone.

"Who is it?" Andrews asked.

"The missus." He snapped open the phone. "Hello?"

"Jackson?"

"Yeah. Who's this?"

"It's Whitney."

"Oh, hi," he said. "It's been a while."

The frown was evident in her tone. "Where are you?"

"You remember that old Kenny Rogers tune about a gambler on a train?"

"So you're still on the train?"

"I'm working on a case."

"Jackson, is there someone else with you?"

"Yeah."

"Who? Abby?"

"No, we broke up."

"Andrews and Newton?"

"Yeah, they're still together."

"What about Mats and Annika or Regina?"

Jackson grinned. "I saw them not too long ago, actually."

"So everyone's on the train?"

"Like one big happy family."

"Okay, listen carefully."

He flicked his eyes to Andrews and Newton, whose expressions gave nothing away. He decided to keep up what he hoped was a clever ruse.

"Your next stop should be San Luis Obispo," Whitney said.

"That's what I hear."

"Get off the train, act dejected, act like you're giving up. Three blocks northwest of the station in SLO is a little square called Mitchell Park. I'll meet you there."

"Oh, why's that?"

"Just trust me, okay?"

"You've got to be kidding."

"I'm serious, Jackson. I'll explain everything."

He forced a chuckle for his audience. "That's a good one."

"Just make sure you aren't followed. Sell that you've quit and are bummed and stuck in town or something, okay?"

"Yeah, sure. We'll talk another time."

"Mitchell Park."

"Okay, bye." He closed the phone.

"Who was that?" Andrews asked.

Jackson looked at her for a moment, trying to determine her level of suspicion. Not too high. He nodded as he stuffed the phone back into his pocket. "Old friend."

She nodded.

"Anything else you want to know? Otherwise, I should find Abby."

"You tell us," she said. "Is there anything you haven't told us?"

"Nothing relevant."

She nodded, and Jackson stood. "It's been real."

"I trust you're done pursuing the Bible," Andrews said.

He remembered Whitney's instructions on the phone, and for a reason he couldn't comprehend, decided to trust her. One bonus last straw. "I'm out," he said. "Whitney's been playing hard to get since the beginning, and I've decided to quit chasing. As soon as I can get off this stupid train, I want nothing more than a good club sandwich and a cold drink."

Andrews nodded. "Good."

Jackson gave them a goodbye nod and trekked back to his seat. Abby was waiting for him and asked where he had gone.

"I was debriefed," he said.

"By whom?"

"Andrews and Newton." He gave her a rundown, then relayed Whitney's call.

Abby huffed. "Do you believe her?"

"Not necessarily. But she did have the Bible last."

"What about Andrews and Newton? Do you trust them? Do you believe what they said about Desmond?"

Jackson shook his head. "No. It's plausible, but right now, I don't trust or believe anybody—Whitney, them, the Swedish Russians."

"Me?"

He made eye contact. "You are the one person I do believe."

Abby smiled. "I feel like I keep asking this, but what do we do?"

"Right now, we've got nothing to lose by going along with Whitney. In her defense, if she was lying, why would she keep calling us? Just to toy with us?"

"Would you put it past her?"

He huffed. "No, not really. But it doesn't hurt us to see if she shows."

The 101 curved inland, but the *Coast Starlight* followed the coast west to Point Concepcion, then journeyed north, with the Pacific still out the left windows. Jackson and Abby watched the scenery, acting for all the world as if they were out of the chase. It didn't matter—they didn't see any of the other players for the rest of the ride.

San Luis Obispo was located a dozen miles inland, in a valley west of the Santa Lucia Mountains that was divided by a chain of hills called the Nine Sisters. The Amtrak station was on the east edge of town, built in the Mission Style of Union Station, albeit much smaller.

Jackson and Abby disembarked and trudged south toward a café. Jackson spied Andrews and Newton hurrying for a cab and the alleged ex-KGB agents Vladimir Lapidus and Svetlana Kublanov wandering aimlessly. If any of them paid more than a second of attention to Jackson and Abby as they headed for the café, they hid it well.

Instead of entering the café, Jackson and Abby circled around it and started northwest on Santa Barbara Street, which became Osos Street as it neared Mitchell Park.

"What if she doesn't show?" Abby asked.

"Then you get your pick of a plane, train, or automobile back to L.A.," Jackson answered.

"And the Bible?"

"Let's just see if she shows."

Mitchell Park filled a city block, with sidewalks cutting diagonally across the lawn to a central gazebo. A variety of trees cast plenty of shade over the grass and sidewalks, and Jackson was happy to find a bench in the shade and relax for a minute. He'd spent plenty of time seated on the train, but sitting on a moving object was different. It wasn't quite relaxing. Then again, neither was a wood bench, but . . .

Jackson didn't get to sit for long. A silver Nissan Altima rolled up to the curb twenty feet from the bench. Whitney lowered the passenger window and leaned over. "Get in."

"Nice to see you too," Jackson said.

"Come on. We're in a hurry."

"Answers first. What are you up to?"

"I don't have time to explain now. Just trust me."

Jackson shook his head with a smile.

"Where's the Bible?" Abby asked.

"On the train. Now come on!"

Chapter Thirty-One

4:01 p.m.

BEFORE JACKSON HAD closed his door, Whitney pushed the gas pedal to the floor. Bracing himself with one hand, Jackson reached for his seatbelt with the other. "Where's the fire?"

"Paso Robles," Whitney called over her shoulder.

"What?"

"Where's the Bible?" Abby asked from the front seat.

"Just let me get back on the highway first."

Whitney drove maniacally, and in two minutes, they were northbound on the 101. She glanced over her shoulder at Jackson. "Thanks for meeting me."

"Where's the Bible?" Abby asked.

"What she said," Jackson said.

"It's on the train."

"You have an accomplice?"

"No. I hid it."

"Where?"

"Let me start from the beginning."

"By all means," he said, sitting back.

"I got on the train in L.A. just behind Mats and Annika and stayed out of sight. We made a whistle stop in Burbank, and they checked both of their bags. The only reason I could figure for them checking their bags then and not in L.A. was because they had put the Bible in one of them. Then it was just a matter of removing it."

"That easy?"

"Well, I had to pose as an attendant to get unhindered access to the baggage car in Van Nuys, but . . ."

"But you're rather adept at role-playing," Jackson said snidely.

She winced at him in the rearview mirror.

"So why did you stay on the train?" Abby asked.

"I was going to get off in Oxnard, but then I saw they were getting off. I thought the train would make a good getaway since I was alone. Then I saw Regina and you guys, and—"

"You saw us?"

"I was still dressed as an attendant, just to be safe, hair up under a cap," she said, pulling up her ponytail with one hand. She dropped it to use both hands to swerve into the left lane and whip past a minivan. Jackson glanced at the speedometer. They were pushing eighty. What'd it matter, a Canadian secret agent could surely beat a speeding ticket. He checked his *Coast Starlight* brochure, still in his pocket, as Whitney continued talking. The train was due in Paso Robles by four-thirty.

"I realized the chase wasn't going to end unless somebody changed the status quo," Whitney said. "I figured everybody was following me, so I got off in Santa Barbara. That would leave a three-hour ride for you all to stew, then get off and try to chase me."

"And yet you followed the train to SLO," Jackson said. "Why?"

"And where is the Bible?" Abby asked, her voice giving away her frustration.

"On the train," Jackson answered in sync with Whitney. "Where?"

"I'll show you."

"Show me?"

"When we get back on in Paso Robles. All my plan."

"How genius."

Whitney glared at him in the mirror. "I don't see you being all that brilliant."

He sighed. "I assume Regina bought you your ticket."

"Yeah. She drugged me with something, said if I tried anything, I wouldn't get the anecdote. It was her way of keeping me in line until she could get me on the train."

"And you believed her?"

"Couldn't risk it. Her needle was very convincing."

"So then why'd you go postal?"

"I figured she had to have the anecdote on her if it existed. I saw an opening and attacked."

"In her purse," Jackson said.

Whitney looked up at him in the mirror.

"I saw you going for it instead of wailing on her."

"I take it back. You are sort of brilliant. You see me pop the pill too?"

Jackson shook his head. "Why didn't you tell us any of this?"

"Because I was afraid if I told you where the Bible was, you'd take it and disappear. I needed to keep you hooked."

"I'm starting to get chafed from the leash around my neck," he mumbled.

"So stop straining against it." She swerved around a semi, then nearly cut him off to move back into the right lane and avoid an oncoming car.

"Assuming we make it to Paso Robles in one piece, then what's your plan? The next stop is Salinas."

"It's up to you," Whitney said over her shoulder. "One of you can take this car to Salinas, and one of you can ride the train with me."

"And then we'll do our little dance over who gets to keep the Bible?"

"Something like that."

Jackson sat back, bracing himself for the inevitable crash.

"So tell me," Whitney asked when they had a clear stretch of highway, "what did Andrews and Newton have to say?"

"Same story," Jackson answered. "We need the Bible this, national security that."

"I see."

"They said Mats and Annika aren't actually art thieves but ex-KGB agents named Lapidus and Kublanov."

"Ex-KGB?"

"Funny, your CSIS intel didn't turn that up."

"I told you, HQ couldn't be sure without a photograph."

"Right." Jackson looked out the window for a moment. "They also had a few thoughts on you."

"Oh?"

"They said they'd never heard of you."

Whitney's eyes flitted up to the mirror.

"Of course, if they're not really CIA . . ." Jackson said.

Whitney was quiet for a change as they climbed toward Paso Robles. When they arrived at the station, she handed the keys to her Nissan to Abby. Both Jackson and Abby had agreed that he would ride with Whitney aboard the *Coast Starlight*. He would be better prepared if Whitney tried to pull a fast one, and he had some more things to discuss with her.

"Just stay on the 101," Whitney said. "Take the Main Street exit in Salinas. The station's just off Main on Railroad."

Abby nodded.

Whitney looked up at Jackson. "Ready?"

He nodded and turned to Abby. "See you in Salinas."

They sat in Jackson and Abby's seats, leaving Whitney's seat a car ahead of them in coach vacant. The sun was low in the sky as they rolled out of Paso Robles and through central California farm fields. Jackson waited five minutes before he asked. "Where's the Bible?"

"Car seven."

"What's it doing in car seven?"

"Hiding."

"With whom?"

"Empty seat."

"So what are we doing here?"

"Waiting for the conductor."

"As what, an escort?"

"Just the opposite," she said. "I've got their pattern down, so just trust me."

"You know, every time you say that, I get a pain right here," Jackson said, pointing to his temple.

"You're cute, you know that?"

"Thank you."

In two minutes, Whitney gave the all clear. She led the way back through several cars, dodging conductors like they were warehouse guards in a shoot 'em up video game. She stopped when they reached the roomettes in car seven. "Um . . . someone's in the seat."

"I thought it was an empty seat."

"It was when I stashed the Bible. Somebody must have taken that seat in Santa Barbara or San Luis Obispo."

Jackson sighed.

"It's okay," she said. "I've got this. Just follow my lead."

"Why not."

Whitney approached a single man in a shirt and tie sitting in the roomette car. The tie was loosened, his shoes were off, and he appeared set until dinner, if not longer.

"Excuse me, sir," Whitney said. "I'm Agent Fry with the ATF." She flashed a badge so quickly if the guy had blinked he would have missed it. "This is Agent Long, NTSB. I'm afraid we have a problem."

The creases in his face deepened. "What's wrong?"

"It's a bit complicated," she said in a voice just above a whisper. "But last week this seat was occupied by a Guillermo Salazar, a member of the Salazar Cartel. We believe he was smuggling heroin and cocaine, using the *Coast Starlight* as his conduit between Tijuana and Portland."

If the creases got any deeper, the man's face was going to divide.

"Here's our problem," Whitney continued. "The FBI supposedly searched his seat for any illicit drugs, but they're a bit understaffed and, frankly, under-competent."

"What are you saying?"

"I'm terribly sorry, but we need to search this area again."

"What, now? You said it was a week ago that this . . ."

"Guillermo Salazar."

"That he was on the train."

"Yes, sir, and I'm terribly sorry, but Salazar is being held right now in Portland, and if we can't produce evidence in the next two hours, a judge is going to let him walk. If he's released from custody, there's a good chance we'll never see him again, and our chance at taking down the cartel goes from slim to none."

The man sighed heavily, his forehead muscles working overtime to furrow his brow further yet.

Whitney reached into her pocket. "I've arranged for a credit for you in the Pacific Parlour Car," she said, extending a plastic card to him. "For your troubles. It shouldn't take us more than half an hour."

The man grumbled and mumbled something under his breath. But then he slid his feet into his shoes. He stood, took his coat, computer case, and coffee cup. Still angry, he accepted the card from Whitney and trudged for the stairs.

"I'm not even going to ask," Jackson said.

"When I was an attendant, I filched a few comp cards, just in case."

"Of course."

"Here, stand back," Whitney said. Jackson gave her room and watched while she pulled a latch that unlocked the two seats, allowing them to fold down into a bed. In the process, the back of the seat came away from the wall. She reached in behind it and pulled out a hardcover case—a small ZERO Halliburton suitcase or briefcase.

"That's it?" Jackson asked.

She nodded.

"Prove it."

"Really?"

Jackson raised his eyebrows.

"Not here," she said.

"Where?"

"We've got a couple of hours. I'm hungry."

"Fine." He followed her back to the dining car, wondering what happened when the cranky guy with creases in his head left the lounge car and found them poring over the Scriptures while downing cheeseburgers. But he decided to let Agent Fry handle that one.

They sat in opposite sides of a booth on the right side of the train. Out the window, rolling California hills were bathed in an orange glow from the setting sun. It was beautiful, but Jackson wasn't in the mood for scenery. He nodded at the case.

Whitney placed it on the table and opened it, revealing the Bible.

Jackson didn't have gloves, so he settled for wiping his hands on his pants. At this point, they were past white-glove treatment, he figured. He took a few minutes to verify it was indeed the Vanderbilt Bible and not a fake. Satisfied, he nodded, and Whitney closed the case. Jackson extended his foot under the table, connecting with her shin.

"Ow," she said, flinching slightly. In doing so, she released her grip on the case, and he grabbed it and set it on the booth beside him.

"Sorry, clumsy feet."

Whitney gave him a quasi-evil eye. "Fine, hold onto it. But you're not taking it to the bathroom."

They ordered sandwiches and drinks and sat back to wait for their food. Jackson watched the hills roll by for a moment, then exhaled. "So who are you?"

"I beg your pardon?"

"You're not Canadian Secret Intelligence or whatever you claim to be."

"I'm not?"

"No."

Whitney leaned forward onto the table. "You want to tell me why not?"

"A lot of reasons, none of them meaning much on their own, but together . . ."

The waiter returned with drinks, and Whitney took a sip of water. "Like what?"

"For starters, Andrews and Newton have no idea who you are."

"So you believe them?"

"I believe that whoever they are, they'd know a CSIS agent."

"Even an undercover agent?"

He nodded.

"And they'd tell you?"

"It was a very open conversation."

Whitney took another drink. "What else?"

"When you first said you were CSIS, you came up with a very good story about Alec and some French woman named Amelia Forte—"

"Amélie Fournier."

"Whomever. It was all very convincing, especially made up on the spot."

"It was true, and it wasn't made up on the spot."

"Just like that Guillermo Salazar bit?"

Whitney looked down.

"Back on Catalina, you measured the distance to Two Harbors in miles, not kilometers."

"That's because I was with Americans."

"Mm-hmm. What about your Iowa sweatshirt, naming our aliases just now after legendary Hawkeye players and coaches, or the fact that your computer password is the Hawkeyes' mascot."

"How do you know that?"

"Brilliant, remember? But the thing that first made me question you— aside from you being you, of course—was back on the ferry. In addition to being familiar with U.S. and California sentencing guidelines, which I guess could be explainable if you were just really thorough, you casually referred to the Clinton administration. That struck me as a little odd for a Canadian. I certainly don't measure time based on Canadian prime ministers."

Whitney took another drink, looking at Jackson over her glass.

"So I ask again," he said, leaning in, "who are you? I don't really know why I ask because there's no reason to believe you'll tell me the truth this time. But I'm just curious what agency you'll think of next. Or country, for that matter. Czech Intelligence? Australian Ministry of Defense? Maybe South African Secret Police?"

"None of the above," Whitney said quietly.

He looked at her, waiting.

She blinked and sighed. "My name is Zoey Paragon. And I don't work for anybody."

"Zoey Paragon? And you're what, a lady hotel detective from the '40s?"

"I'm a private contractor," she answered.

"What's that mean?"

"It means I work for whoever pays me."

"Who's paying you?"

She turned her head slightly to the side. "I can't tell you that."

"Of course."

"Would you tell me who your client was?"

He raised his chin. "Work how?"

"It depends. I find people. Find things. Run security. A little bit of everything."

"So you're a mercenary?"

"No."

He nodded without conviction.

"There's a difference," she said.

"Oh yeah, what's that?"

"Mercenaries . . . Mercenaries don't draw lines."

Jackson bit his tongue.

"I know you don't have any reason to believe me, and . . . I'm sorry I misled you. I really am. But . . . I'm just sorry."

Jackson sat back. How did he stay angry at an apology?

"Look," he said, "what's done is done. What are we going to do now?"

"I don't know," she said. "How are you at arm wrestling?"

"Better than rock, paper, scissors."

Chapter Thirty-Two

Twenty-three years ago . . .
Saturday, July 21
7:34 p.m.

"JACK, GET IN the car," David Douglas said. His voice was at the same time calm but firm. Jackson didn't make a habit of disobeying direct orders from his dad, and he especially knew to heed *that* voice. So without delay, he pulled open the passenger door of the family Taurus and got in, careful not to get his ice cream cone caught in the automatic seatbelt.

Through the windshield, Jackson looked past his father at the stranger who had approached them as they were exiting Dairy Queen. The man was gruff, with a long, scraggly beard that was mostly gray but a little brown, and almost a greenish yellow color around his mouth. It reminded Jackson of the way Grant's face used to look when he ate mashed squash as a baby. The man had deep and dark eyes, shielded from the evening sunlight by a blue Chargers hat. It covered messy and stringy hair that went in every direction.

The man was big, although not as big as Jackson's dad. He wore an old T-shirt with pictures of people Jackson didn't recognize in front of different colored boxes on the front. Blue jeans and a pair of sneakers. Nikes. Jackson always recognized the Swoosh, which always made him wish his mom would buy him name-brand shoes.

A drip of ice cream turned Jackson's attention from the man to his cone. When he looked back up after licking away the drip, David was getting into the car while the man turned and walked away.

"Dad?"

"Hmm?" David asked as he started the car and backed out of the parking spot, looking over his shoulder through the rear windshield. On their way back to the front, his eyes settled on Jackson for a second, and he smiled.

Jackson wondered how his dad did it, how he backed up a car and turned the wheel, all with one hand, while the other held an ice cream cone that seemed immune to drips.

"You had a question?" David asked.

"Why was he asking for money?"

"I don't know his exact reason. But there are a lot of people who do that."

"Beggars?"

"That's one word for them."

Jackson licked for a few seconds, lest his ice cream turn to slop.

"Did you give him any?" he asked.

"No, Son, I didn't."

"How come?"

David pursed his lips.

"Doesn't the Bible say we're supposed to help those in need, help the poor?"

"Yes it does."

"So what gives?"

David turned his head, and a small smile formed when he saw Jackson hadn't used those words disrespectfully.

"Some people ask for money or for food or for help because they are really in need, because they have nowhere else to go. And some people ask for things because it's easier than working for them, or because they know they can take advantage of people."

"You think he was trying to take advantage of us? You think he wasn't really in need?"

David nodded.

"Why's that?"

"Several things. For one, he didn't ask for food or money for food; he just asked for money. That's always something of a concern."

Jackson repeated the same question as before.

"Because if I were to give him money, I don't know what he'd do with it. He might buy food, but I had suspicions he'd use it for something else."

"Like what?"

"Did you notice the discoloration around his mouth?"

"Uh-huh."

"That's a nicotine stain, evidence of prolonged cigarette smoking."

"So you don't give him money because he smokes?"

"Not just that. His breath also smelled of liquor. That tells me that he's using his money to buy alcohol and cigarettes."

"Instead of food?"

David nodded. "He also had brand new sneakers." He shrugged. "They could have been a gift, he could have found them, I suppose, but they made me suspicious of whether or not he was really and truly in need."

"Hmm."

"And did you notice his arms?"

"What about them?"

"They were strong. The man was in good shape. He clearly wasn't malnourished or in dire need of food. Based on all of that, I decided my priority was taking you home before your ice cream melted," he said with a wink.

Jackson turned his attention back to his ice cream for a few minutes.

"So the guy was lying?" he asked.

"I don't know for sure," David said. "I suspect he might have been being deceitful, which is very similar."

Jackson sighed.

"What's the matter?"

"So what if you're not a genius code-breaker like you? How do I know if someone's trustworthy or not?"

"Do you remember the story of Joshua and the Gibeonites?" David asked.

"Were they the ones with the moldy bread and old shoes?"

"That's right. God had given the Israelites great victories, making the kings of other nations afraid. Most of them decided to band together and attack Israel, but the people of Gibeon decided to trick Joshua and the Israelites into making a truce with them."

"Meaning they couldn't attack each other, right?"

"Right. So they sent men in old clothes and sandals and with worn out and beat up luggage, and with dry and moldy food, all to make Joshua think they had come from a long way away and weren't a threat to Israel. And Joshua fell for their trick."

"Guess he should have had a dad in the Navy too, huh?"

David chuckled. "Joshua should have prayed and asked God what to do."

"Is that the answer? Is that how I know who's lying to me?"

"It's a start. God won't always tell you everything. You also have to learn to observe and think critically." He reached over and ruffled Jackson's hair. "You're young yet, kiddo. You have plenty of time to learn."

"So what happened anyhow?"

"To Joshua? The Israelites had to live with the consequences of making a truce they shouldn't have."

"No, I mean the Gibeonites. Shouldn't they have gotten in trouble for lying and deceiving?"

"Yes, and they did. The Israelites forced the Gibeonites to work for them for the rest of their lives. They made them cut wood and carry water for the house of God."

"Let them off easy, it sounds like."

David grinned.

"So you get punished for being deceitful and for falling for it?"

"Not for falling for deception so much as for not seeking God's direction. People are always going to try to trick you and lie to you, Jack."

"They are?"

"Unfortunately. And sometimes, despite your best efforts, you're going to fall for it. But that's why you need to pray and why it's important to know what the Bible says—what God has told us—so that you know if someone is lying. Knowing what the Bible says won't help you know if a person asking for money is really in need or not, maybe, but you will know that if someone says something that disagrees with what God has said in the Bible, they aren't telling the truth. No matter what the situation is, you can always trust God's Word to be right."

Jackson caught up on his cone.

"That all make sense?" David asked.

"Yeah."

"Good."

"I can trust you too, right Dad?"

David smiled. "Yes. Your mother and I are very careful to make sure that what we say and do agrees with what God says." He nodded. "You can always trust us."

*   *   *

Tuesday, January 22
6:35 p.m.

DARKNESS HAD fallen over central California by the time the *Coast Starlight* pulled into the station in Salinas. Jackson and Whitney—er, Zoey—had spent the last hour in their coach seats, not saying much. He had tried to come up with a flaw in her "Zoey Paragon" identity, just to see if she had another one in the bag. But he didn't have enough knowledge about Zoey to discredit her, which meant he also didn't have sufficient evidence to believe it was anything more than a fast cover story.

Jackson carried the ZERO Halliburton case with the Bible in it as they got off the train. Zoey carried the key. A cool breeze blew inland off Monterey Bay, only half a dozen miles west, as they headed around the station. The platform was deserted, and the darkness seemed darker than it should have for six-thirty at night. Jackson half expected fog to float out from under the parked *Coast Starlight*. Or from under the restored steam locomotive and caboose residing inside a chain-link fence at the eastern end of the platform.

"You think Abby'll be mad?" Zoey asked.

"You mean that you're not who you said you were? Again." He tipped his head. "Maybe, until she sees the Bible."

"Maybe you should tell her."

"What, Zoey's shy and timid?"

"I'm just trying to keep the peace," she said.

"Wow, this is a different you."

Zoey glared at him as they turned and walked in front of the old locomotive. "How long are you going to keep this up?"

"Funny, I was going to ask you the same thing."

She huffed.

"You're on your fourth persona in four days. Five if you count Bianca the bantering bloodsucker. Quite a while yet."

"I don't do it on purpose, you know."

"What, antagonize me?"

"Switch identities. It's all part of—"

Two men appeared in front of them. Not casually, as if they were trying to make the train. But intentionally, blocking Jackson and Zoey's path to the parking lot. The man on the left was tall, black, with a smooth, no-nonsense face and a receding hairline. The man on the right was shorter but not short, white, a few pounds heavier, with plenty of wavy brown hair. He was not in the mood for nonsense either.

The one on the left spoke first. "Jackson Douglas?"

"Who's asking?"

He reached into his overcoat. Strange, Jackson thought, because although it was cool, it wasn't that cool. He pulled out a badge. "I'm Agent Dwayne Harris, and this is Agent Vance Stockton, NSA." He returned the badge to his coat. "We have reason to believe you are in possession of the Vanderbilt Bible." He eyed the ZERO Halliburton.

"Let me see that badge again," Jackson said.

"Certainly." Harris withdrew it and extended it for Jackson to scrutinize. He looked at Zoey, who shrugged.

"Is that the Bible, Mr. Douglas?" he asked, again eyeing the case.

"I don't know where the NSA got its intel, but if it was any good, there'd be no reason to believe I have the Bible. This," he said, holding the case slightly higher, "is private property."

"We're going to need to see the contents of the case, sir."

"On what grounds?"

"It's a matter of national security, sir."

"Do you have a warrant?"

Harris turned to Stockton and nodded, and Stockton reached into his overcoat and produced a folded document. He handed it to Jackson, who snapped it open with one hand and attempted to read it in very dim light. He didn't know a lot about federal warrants, but he was able to make out that the warrant gave Agents Harris and Stockton the right to search him and any property he was carrying.

Jackson handed the warrant back to Stockton. "There are two problems, gentlemen."

"What's that, sir?" Harris asked.

"One, I have no way of knowing if this is real. It's pitch black out here, and in the last four days I've seen more fake badges and IDs and heard more stories than you can shake a stick at. And two, this isn't my case. It's hers. I'm simply being a guy and carrying it for her."

"That's very convenient," Stockton said, his voice gruff to match his face.

"So unless you have a search warrant for her as well—"

Stockton reached into his pocket and pulled out a second document, which he practically thrust at Jackson. A search warrant for Zoey Paragon and any personal property on her.

Jackson sighed. "Of all your names, they pick the right one."

"We also have warrants for Whitney Raines, Roberta Pierce, and Robyn Pearson," Harris said.

"You happen to have any other identities?" Jackson asked.

Zoey shook her head as she scanned the warrant.

"Please, sir, open the case."

"No," Zoey said.

"Ma'am, that's a federal search warrant, and this is a matter of national security. You are legally bound to comply, and we're—"

"You guys must be liberals, huh?" Zoey said.

"Excuse me?" Stockton said.

"I assume that because you're ignoring the Constitution, in particular, the Bill of Rights, and in particular the Fourth Amendment. '*The right of the people to be secure in their persons, houses, papers, and effects, against unreasonable searches and seizures, shall not be violated, and no Warrants shall issue, but upon probable cause, supported by Oath or affirmation, and* particularly describing *the place to be searched,* and *the persons or* things to be seized.' Emphasis added." Her recitation finished, she looked all three men in the eyes and shook her head. Holding up the warrant, she said, "This is vague and does not particularly describe the things to be seized." She flung it back at Stockton. "Go back to the judge."

She turned to walk away from them, but he grabbed her by the arm.

"Hey!" she said.

Jackson stepped forward and was stopped in his tracks by a firm hand to the chest from Harris. "Open the case," he said to Zoey.

"No, now unhan—"

Stockton spun her around, pushing his leg into the back of her knee, dropping her to her knees. With leverage, he easily pushed her to the ground.

Jackson swung his arm up and around, throwing Harris's arm back and lunging toward Stockton. He never made it. He felt himself jerked back and spun around, and before he knew it, he was staring at the pavement from an inch away, his arms behind his back and a knee in the small of his back.

Somewhere in between being grabbed and flipped, he'd dropped the case in his right hand.

He was able to turn his head, and he saw Stockton straddling Zoey, his hand pushing her head into the ground. "Where is the key?"

"Wouldn't you like to know," she said.

"Miss Paragon, do not play games with us," Harris said.

"Violation of constitutional rights is not a game."

"We're going to find it," Stockton said.

Jackson turned his head, looking toward the train, hoping someone else had gotten off, then toward the parking lot in the hopes that someone was watching. He saw no one, not even Abby in the silver Nissan, but they were partially hidden by the locomotive. He was drawn back to Zoey when she literally began screaming, "Bloody murder!"

Stockton bounced her head off the pavement.

"Ow!"

"Hey!" Jackson said. Harris responded by firmly pushing his head against the concrete.

"The key," Stockton growled.

"You want it, you're going to have to strip-search me right here."

In one smooth motion, Stockton stood and jerked her up, still facing away from him. Grabbing her plaid button-down shirt by the collar, he yanked it back, ripping the buttons and pulling it down her arms, leaving her in a tank top. Holding her hands bound in the shirt with one hand, Stockton began patting her down, working his way down her legs. Then he stood and started up from her waist. She struggled against him, but the more she did, the tighter he held her.

Still holding her arms, Stockton looked back at Harris. A moment later, he reached for Zoey's tank top and began to lift it up. She wriggled and wrestled and tried to get free, but was no match for Stockton, who continued to undress her.

"It's in her shoe," Jackson said.

Harris at first pressed his head down, then released it when he realized what Jackson was saying. Stockton let go of Zoey's tank top and looked at her. "Take them off."

"No."

He spun her around, and with more resistance this time, again pushed her to her knees. He then dropped his weight onto the back of her legs, holding her arms with one hand while prying off her shoes with the other. A small key tinkled to the pavement when he removed her left shoe, its sound magnified by the silence around them and, perhaps more so, by its significance.

Palming the key, Stockton quickly stood, leaving Zoey off balance, and she fell awkwardly to the pavement. At the same time, Harris released Jackson. Harris picked up the suitcase and tipped it on its side, turning the front toward Stockton.

As they opened the case, Jackson stood as nonthreateningly as possible and helped Zoey up.

"Let go of me," she said, ripping her arm from him.

"Are you okay?" he asked.

She didn't answer, instead shooting daggers at the two men with her eyes.

With a click, the case opened, and both men looked into it. They spent less than a minute verifying the Bible was legitimate, then locked the case. Harris turned toward them. "Thank you both for your cooperation," he said. "On behalf of the United States gov—"

"Save it," Jackson said. "Just get out of here."

Harris held out his hands, and the two alleged NSA agents disappeared into the darkness.

"Are you—"

"I'm fine," Zoey barked. "Why did you tell them where the key was?"

"Because I didn't think you really wanted to be strip-searched in the parking lot."

"It beats letting them have the Bible."

"You really think they wouldn't have checked your shoe? That's kind of Spook Hiding Spots 101."

Zoey swiped some hair off her forehead with her free hand. The other was still wound up in her plaid shirt, which hung to the ground beside her. "Do you see Abby?"

"No."

"How did they find us? How!"

"Spy on the train?"

"Who followed you to the park and followed us to the station and directed them all the way to Salinas?"

Jackson shrugged. "Better question, how'd they know to pull the Zoey warrant first? And how did they know all your other aliases?"

Zoey glared at him.

"Hey, if they're legit, at least it lends credence to your claim that you're her."

Without a word, she turned and strode toward the parking lot.

Chapter Thirty-Three

6:48 p.m.

ABBY HAD ACTUALLY parked in a smaller lot on the other side of the station. She stood leaning against the side of the Nissan, and her shoulders dropped with relief when she saw Jackson and Zoey. Then, seeing Zoey's hair askew and her outer shirt in her hand, she frowned. "What happened? Where's the Bible?"

"Gone," Zoey said flatly.

"Gone?" Abby turned to Jackson. "What does she mean, gone?"

"The NSA just took it from us," Zoey said. "Keys?"

Abby opened her fist and tossed the keys to her. "The NSA?" she asked Jackson.

"So they claimed," he said as he opened the door for her.

She got in, mumbling, "NSA?" under her breath.

Jackson looked up as Zoey circled the car and approached the trunk. "What are you doing?"

She lifted the trunk liner that covered the spare tire and reached under it to pull out a small leather case.

"Zoey?"

She handed him the keys. "You can drive."

He nodded at the case. "What's that?"

"I'll explain as we drive. Let's go."

With a sigh, Jackson circled around her and got in the driver's seat.

"What do you mean by 'so they claimed'?" Abby asked as he closed the door behind him.

"You said 'if they're legit' a minute ago too," Zoey said. "What are you thinking?"

"I'm thinking I'm suspicious of any federal agents right now. I'm especially suspicious of agents who would grope a key off a woman in a parking lot."

"I gave them guff," she said.

"Still, why didn't they pull a gun? Why the strong-arm tactics?"

"Don't know."

"You think they were legit?" Abby asked over her shoulder.

"Seemed to be," Zoey said.

"What about their unconstitutional warrant?" Jackson asked.

"What?" Abby asked.

"It was probably slapped together in ten minutes. An oversight. It doesn't mean they were frauds."

"Was that actually the Fourth Amendment you quoted?" Jackson asked.

"Yes, will you drive?"

"You have the Bill of Rights memorized or something?"

"Don't you?" She met his eyes in the rearview mirror. "Drive."

He obeyed.

"So that's it?" Abby asked as he exited the parking lot. "It's over?"

"It's not over," Zoey said.

Abby turned around. "Why not?"

"First," Jackson said, "you should probably know she's no longer Whitney."

Abby's head jerked back. "What?"

"Meet Zoey Paragon," he said with a movie trailer narrator's voice.

"What?"

"She's a private contractor."

"You're not Canadian Intelligence?"

"I'm from Iowa."

Abby was dumbfounded. "You're Zoey . . ."

"Paragon," Jackson answered. "Name's kind of ironic, isn't it?"

Abby shook her head. "Okay, whoever you are, how is this not over?"

Zoey leaned forward and extended her arms between the seats. She opened the leather case and pulled out a small electronic device. "Yesterday afternoon, after I swam to shore and saw that my hotel in Hermosa Beach had been tossed, I took out a little insurance policy."

"What kind of insurance policy?"

"I implanted a tiny tracking device inside the binding of the Bible." She held up the device from the leather case. "This will enable us to track it."

"Unless they find it," Jackson said.

"Trust me, they won't find it. Short of ripping the cover off the Bible."

"Can they jam it?"

"Only if they know it's there. Or by accident."

"What's the range?"

"Oh, about a thousand miles," Zoey answered. "It runs off a satellite."

"So which way?" Jackson asked.

"Give me a minute."

"Do we have time to get something to eat?" Abby asked. "I didn't think to grab anything."

"We should also top off the gas tank," Zoey said. "I filled up in Santa Maria, but once we determine which way they're headed, we may want to drive for a while."

Jackson started the car. "Might also want to figure out a plan. Unless it's to hijack the NSA on the highway and take the Bible back, which, given our last interaction with them, doesn't strike me as overly promising."

They stopped at a Valero station close to the highway, and while Jackson filled up the tank, Abby and Zoey went inside to buy snacks and drinks. Pocketing the car keys, Jackson quickly used the restroom, then joined the women back at the car.

Zoey flipped on her device, which resembled an old-fashioned cell phone, without all the buttons. A tiny screen showed a crude map with a blinking light that, Jackson assumed, represented Harris and Stockton.

"High-tech," he said, looking from the display to Zoey. "What's that, an IBM 2?"

"I'm sorry, should we use your tracking device?"

"South?" he asked.

"They're almost to Soledad. Better get moving."

Salinas and nearby Monterey both had airports capable of landing private jets. The nearest major commercial airport was in San Jose to the north. Since Harris and Stockton were headed south, it meant they weren't flying. And there was nothing of note south this side of L.A.

Jackson, Abby, and Zoey ate and discussed their strategy for recovering the Bible. Zoey agreed they couldn't do anything while it was in transit, but said they should stay close. Not that they really had a plan for when Harris and Stockton stopped at wherever it was they were going. They also had to deal with the legality and wisdom of trying to take the Bible from NSA agents. But if Harris and Stockton were indeed bound for L.A., they had four and a half hours to figure it all out.

Jackson closed to about ten miles behind Harris and Stockton and held the position. They were driving at the speed limit, still proceeding south on U.S. 101.

As they drove, Jackson questioned Zoey some more about her identity, about all of her cunning and conniving the last few days, and about what they would do if they recovered the Bible—how they would keep from losing it again and how they would determine whether Abby or Zoey kept it. It was another iteration of the same old debate, and they once again failed to settle on a satisfactory answer. Zoey began to get annoyed with Jackson's pestering questions, and he once again grew frustrated with her dodges and deceptions. By the time they jogged east through the mountains on Highway 46, they had given up talking to each other at all.

Still about ten miles behind Harris and Stockton, Jackson followed them onto southbound I-5 northwest of Bakersfield. Ten minutes later, Zoey announced the Bible was stopping. "Looks like there's a rest area."

Jackson said nothing.

"Don't you want to maybe slow down?"

"No. Even if we do catch up to them, they won't recognize the vehicle, and we can track them just as well from ahead as behind."

"What if they turn off?"

"You mean if they're having a secret rendezvous in the desert or something?"

Zoey sighed. "Stranger things have happened."

"Guys," Abby said, rejoining the realm of the conscious, "if it means anything, I have to use the bathroom."

"There's an exit just past the rest area," Zoey said. "We can stop there, use a gas station or something. That way they should ultimately stay ahead of us."

Jackson consented, figuring he could use the stop to stretch his legs.

By the time they reached the rest area, Zoey's device indicated that Harris and Stockton were already back on the highway. Jackson pulled off the interstate anyhow, and as Abby headed inside to use the restroom, he and Zoey got out of the car and stretched.

"Maybe we should get out," he said across the hood.

"Get out of what?" Zoey asked. She still held the receiver, keeping an eye on the NSA agents' progress.

"The chase."

She shrugged. "Go ahead."

"I mean it. This isn't going to end. There's always going to be somebody else to steal the Bible from us."

"Not if we come up with a plan."

"Which we haven't been able to yet."

"So you want to quit?"

"I was shot at this morning," he said. "You were kidnapped and drugged. Abby was kidnapped. Her brother's dead. We've avoided being arrested—or worse—by various government agencies—or worse. Maybe it's time to quit while we're ahead."

"So quit," she said. "I'm still in."

He squinted. "Who are you working for, anyhow?"

"A man by the name of—Hey, you almost tricked me."

Jackson made a face. "Fine. But next time you get kidnapped, don't expect me to chase you."

"Like you would have if I didn't have the Bible."

"You're not arguing again, are you?" Abby asked as she walked back to the car.

"Jackson wants out," Zoey said.

"You do?"

"I'm just saying, we've made it through quite a bit. Sooner or later, we won't be able to dodge the bullet—literal or figurative."

"I'm not giving up, Jackson. You can bail, but I want the Bible. I don't care if it's FBI, CIA, NSA, or whoever. They don't have a right to take what belongs to me."

"We should get moving," Zoey said. She held up the receiver. "They were quick. They're almost fifteen miles ahead of us."

They got back into the car—Abby now in back so she could stretch out and sleep some more. Jackson and Zoey said nothing as they continued south. To him, it felt like it was the middle of the night. In reality, it was only a few minutes after ten.

They drove in silence for half an hour, until Highway 99 from Bakersfield merged with I-5 and the road curved to a more due south bearing. They were nearing the Tejon Pass, on the other side of which were the northern suburbs of the Greater Los Angeles Area. Traffic thickened, then slowed, unusual for the time of night and location. Normally, it was a desolate drive.

"What's going on?" Abby asked groggily from the backseat as Jackson applied the brakes. Ahead of him as far as he could see, cars were slowing or had already stopped, blocking all four southbound lanes of I-5.

"I don't know. Some sort of traffic jam."

"It looks like the Bible's stopped too," Zoey reported.

They were just past the unincorporated town of Grapevine, where the interstate split as it ascended into the Tehachapi Mountains. It was too late to exit the interstate, and Grapevine consisted of little more than hotels, restaurants, and service stations—and no road leading anywhere. So they coasted along for another quarter of a mile, Jackson switching lanes once and then settling in behind a hatchback full of college kids and bumper stickers. There was time to read them because traffic stopped completely a short distance up into the hills.

"Well this is great," Zoey said after a few minutes.

"What would cause this?" Abby asked. "An accident?"

"It'd have to be a pretty bad one to shut down four lanes of traffic," Jackson said. "Nobody's moving." He gave it a couple more minutes and then shut off the engine. "Bible?" he asked.

"Stopped," Zoey replied. "Less than a mile ahead."

Jackson yawned. "So we wait. Mind if I nap?"

"Nap?"

"We can't go anywhere. If traffic moves, wake me up."

Zoey raised her eyebrows. "Sure, why not."

Jackson reclined his seat and closed his eyes. He hadn't slept much of late—too little on Friday night, none Saturday night, hardly any Sunday night, and poorly and too little Monday night. Now it was Tuesday night, and morning felt like it was a week ago. He had basically become accustomed to being tired, and now with an opportunity, he couldn't force himself to drift away. Somehow, having Zoey sitting beside him kept him from being able to relax.

Tuesday night. Had it really only been four days since he had dressed as a pirate and taken the Bible from the Vanderbilt mansion during Desmond's masquerade ball? And since then, Zoey took the Bible from him and Abby,

FBI/CIA Agents Andrews and Newton took it from her, Luis Cortez took it from them, Regina took it from him, Mats and Annika (or were they Vladimir and Svetlana?) took it from her, Jackson and Abby and Zoey took it from them, Zoey hid it, Regina forced her to retrieve it, Mats and Annika recovered it during the fracas at the train station, Zoey stole it back from them on the train and hid it until she and Jackson reclaimed it, only to have Harris and Stockton of the NSA—presumably—take it back one more time. No wonder he was tired.

Zoey tapped his knee, and Jackson realized that maybe he had drifted off for a moment or two—at least halfway. "Yeah?" he said.

"The Bible's moving."

"What?"

"It's flying. Sixty, seventy miles per hour."

Jackson rubbed his hands over his face, driving away any hints of sleep that remained. "How can that be?"

"I don't know, but it's moving."

"What's happening?" Abby asked.

Zoey answered while Jackson got out of the car and stood, trying to see what was happening up ahead of them. All he saw were taillights upon taillights, wrapped around a curve as I-5 hugged the side of the hills. A quarter of a mile to the east, traffic in the northbound lanes was humming along.

The night air was refreshing, and Jackson really didn't feel like getting back into the car. Especially since they weren't going anywhere. But he did.

"I rebooted the receiver," Zoey announced as he sat down. "Just in case something was wonky with it."

"And?"

She shook her head. "The Bible's still on the move."

"Maybe traffic's thinning," Abby said.

"Maybe."

Traffic was not thinning. They sat in place for another half hour, by which time the beacon on Zoey's device indicated the Bible was almost to Santa Clarita. Finally, traffic began to inch its way along. It was still incredibly slow as four lanes of stalled traffic merged into one over the next half mile. Amid the glow of hundreds of taillights, Jackson also discerned the pulsing red and blue lights of the California Highway Patrol.

"They got off on 210," Zoey said. "They aren't headed for the airport."

"At least not LAX."

They were herded over to the far right side of the pavement, technically on the shoulder. In single file, traffic continued to plod around the curves of I-5. Rain began to fall, first just a mist, then heavy enough that Jackson had to turn on the wipers. It also caused just enough interference that they couldn't make out the cause of the traffic jam until they were almost upon it.

A semi had jackknifed and tipped over, blocking three and a half lanes of traffic and spilling its cargo—electronics components, it appeared—all over the road.

"Whoa, what would cause that?" Abby asked. "It isn't raining that hard."

"And it just started," Zoey said.

They closed in on the semi and saw that it wasn't alone. In addition to half a dozen emergency vehicles, a black SUV was also parked by the overturned semi's cab. Several people stood around the SUV, and Jackson suddenly had one of those feelings.

In another thirty seconds, the stream of single file cars brought Jackson, Abby, and Zoey even with the SUV and semi cab, and Jackson saw that the SUV wasn't parked—it had crashed into the overturned cab. Its front end was pretty badly smashed, and one of the tires was flat.

"Isn't that . . ." Zoey asked, leaning over to see through the raindrops on Jackson's window.

"Yep," he said, his eyes focused on a black man in an overcoat. He was talking on a cell phone and surveying the damage to the SUV while holding some sort of cloth to his head.

"Who?" Abby asked.

"NSA Agent Dwayne Harris," Jackson said. "The man who *had* the Bible."

Chapter Thirty-Four

11:58 p.m.

IMMEDIATELY PAST THE overturned semi, traffic spread back to four lanes and resumed at normal highway speed. Jackson turned to Zoey. "So, how'd you pull that off?"

"Me? You're the one who talked about hijacking the NSA on the highway."

"I also said it wasn't a promising idea. Oh me of little faith."

"I didn't see Stockton," she said, looking over her shoulder, even though they were more than a mile away by now. "Maybe he has it."

"And what, double-crossed Harris?"

Zoey shrugged. "Is anything too unbelievable right now?"

"Fair point."

"So wait," Abby said, "you're saying somebody staged an accident to steal the Bible?"

Jackson nodded.

"Oh my gosh. Oh. My. Gosh."

Zoey turned to look at her.

"She says that a lot."

"What the heck is a gosh anyhow?" Zoey asked.

"What?" Abby asked.

"'Oh my gosh.' Who or what is gosh?"

"I don't know. It's . . . Really, that's what you're asking right now?"

"I mean, if you want to cuss, cuss, but what is a gosh?"

Abby looked at Jackson. He shrugged. So did Zoey when he turned her way.

"Who would have done this?" Abby asked a moment later.

"Take your pick," Jackson said.

"I'm betting Andrews and Newton," Zoey said. "Regina doesn't have the horses to pull this off, and neither do Mats and Annika."

"Unless they are ex-KGB like Andrews and Newton said."

"Or all working together," Abby said.

"I don't think so," Zoey said with a laugh.

"The enemy of my enemy is my friend."

"Kind of like the three of us," Jackson said. He leaned over to peer at Zoey's receiver. "Where's the Bible?"

"North of Pasadena, still on the 210."

"They're circumventing L.A.," Jackson said. "Heading east?"

"Looks that way."

"How do you force a semi to crash?" Abby asked.

"Not too easily," Jackson said at the same time as Zoey mumbled, "Easy." They looked at each other.

"Put an IED in the road," she said. "Shoot out the tires, an RPG."

"But to know the truck would come along at just the right time, ahead of Harris and Stockton, and to get it to block four lanes of traffic?" Abby asked.

"Blocking traffic might have been an unintended consequence," Zoey said. "All they really had to do was cause Harris and Stockton to crash. Or they could have blocked traffic and waited for the right vehicle to come along and triggered it to crash too. They might have even stolen the truck themselves." She shrugged. "Easy."

"Still," Jackson said, "it requires some pretty good timing either way, dealing with a lot of witnesses, *CHiPs* getting there and making Bible-pilfering tricky. Not to mention dealing with two big, strong NSA ag—"

"They've turned," Zoey said. "This can't be."

"What?" Jackson and Abby asked at the same time.

"It looks like they're headed up into the mountains." She turned the screen so he could see. "They're on Highway 2."

"What's up that way?"

"Nothing. It's the Angeles Crest Highway, but . . ."

"Where does it come out?" Abby asked.

"Between Palmdale and Apple Valley. But there's no way they'd take that route if that's where they were going. They'd head around the north side of the mountains."

"Maybe they thought they were being followed," Abby said.

"So they take a desolate road? No way."

Jackson kept his eyes on the interstate, trying to make sense of it all. It wasn't really that hard to figure. The cycle just kept repeating itself.

As they descended out of the mountains south of the Tejon Pass, the lights of Santa Clarita and the surrounding towns represented the start of Los Angeles sprawl. It felt to Jackson as if they had been gone for days.

"I'm out," he said.

"What?"

"I'm done. Forgive the *Groundhog Day* rip-off, but we have been shot at, kidnapped, interrogated, threatened, nearly hijacked on the highway, people have been killed. I've had enough. This is never going to end."

"Come on, Jackson," Abby said, sitting forward to lean between the seats. "You can't give up."

"They're still in the San Gabriels," Zoey said. "They're trapped."

"Trapped? We're a private investigator, an artist, and a schizophrenic up against people capable of overturning semis on I-5 to stage a hijacking. They may be trapped, but we're outgunned, and they have the high ground."

"So we'll think of something."

"No."

"Think about it at least," Abby said. "Sleep on it."

"I'd like to, but it will be two a.m. before I get to bed. Sorry, but I'm done. I'll drop myself off at home and get my car tomorrow."

"Jackson . . ." Abby said, slouching back. "I can't believe it."

He turned over his shoulder. "You should get out too. Before something actually happens to you."

"I'm not getting out."

"What would Alec want you to do?"

"Don't bring him into this."

"Bring him into it? This is supposed to be all about him, about knowing him. His son is dead because of this Bible. Do you think he'd want you to give your life too?"

"You have no idea what he would want," Abby said. "You want out, fine. You're out. I'll send you a check. But don't tell me what to do!"

"Buick," Zoey said, and Jackson hit the brakes, then moved over to pass a Verano.

They drove in silence from then on, with Zoey continuing to track the Bible and only announcing when it stopped, high up in the San Gabriel Mountains. Jackson took the 405, which for once wasn't clogged with traffic, back to his neck of the woods and pulled into his driveway at one-thirty a.m.

"Abby, are you sure you won't reconsider?" he asked as he got out.

"I'm not quitting. Not now."

"I know you miss your father, but—"

"You're fired, Jackson, okay? Thanks for your help, but we'll take it from here."

He nodded as he got out.

Zoey circled the front of the car and met him by his front door. "Are you sure *you* won't reconsider?" she asked. "We know where they are, and we aren't making a move tonight, either. Just think about it."

Jackson shook his head. "No thanks. I plan to sleep till noon, make a sandwich, and go back to bed. You guys can keep playing king of the mountain with half a dozen agencies and governments. Just remember, they're playing for keeps."

Zoey nodded. "I guess this is goodbye, then."

"I guess."

"If you change your mind . . ."

"It'll be too late. You'll be someone else by then, and I'll have no way to track you."

Zoey gave him an evil eye. "Under different circumstances . . ."

"Yeah?"

"I might *really* dislike you."

"Yeah, but under different circumstances, you wouldn't even be you. So I guess the more things change . . ."

*   *   *

Wednesday, January 23
8:03 a.m.

JACKSON HAD seriously not intended to get up before noon. But the repeated ringing of his doorbell not only woke him up but also shooed away his sleepiness. Grumbling about the early hour, he stood and looked down to see what he was wearing. He hadn't bothered to take off anything but his shoes before going to bed, so he was fully dressed. He trudged down the stairs, running a hand through his hair and thinking about that line in *Independence Day* about hanging up the phone if it wasn't an insanely beautiful woman.

It was not an insanely beautiful woman. It was NSA Agent Dwayne Harris, sans overcoat, with a bandage spanning the corner of his eye socket. Agent Vance Stockton stood behind him and wore the overcoat, as well as several facial bruises. A cold blast of air whipped in through the open door, and Jackson guessed it was in the mid-forties, a drastic change from the recent balmy weather.

"I don't have it," he said. "And if you try to strip search me for it, one of us is going to end up dead."

"Sir, may we come in?" Harris asked.

"No. Not unless you have a warrant, and it had better have all the I's crossed and T's dotted."

Harris looked blankly at him.

"I meant that the other way around. It's early. What do you want?"

"We'd like to talk with you, preferably indoors."

"Why, you don't want any witnesses when you throw me to the ground?"

"I took you down because you made a move toward Agent Stockton."

"I'm not talking about you and me."

"Miss Paragon resisted a federal warrant," Harris said. "We acted by the book."

"Public strip-searches are by the book?"

"It was Miss Paragon's suggestion. And finding that Bible is an urgent matter of national security."

"Right." He shook his head. "I don't know anything anymore, or care. But if you want to waste your time, come on in."

He turned and paced into the living room.

"Thank you, sir," Harris said, maintaining at least the appearance of professional decorum.

Jackson turned around. "So, how was your drive down from Salinas? Run into much traffic?"

"I'll come to the point, Mr. Douglas. The NSA—"

"You're still NSA?"

Harris frowned. "Yes, sir."

"Wow, two days in a row. That's a record for this little escapade."

Harris cleared his throat. "As I was saying, the NSA believes that two Russian intelligence agents were responsible for the ambush on Interstate 5 last night."

"Russian intelligence?"

"Yes. Members of the SVR, the successor of the KGB's foreign operations and intelligence agency."

"By any chance are their names Vladimir Lapidus and Svetlana Kublanov?"

Harris frowned and exchanged a look with Stockton. "No, sir. We believe they are Agent Stanislav Nenasheva and Agent Elena Andreev. They may have been masking themselves as FBI Agents Stanley Newton and Ellen Andrews."

"Andrews and Newton are KGB?" Jackson asked.

"SVR, technically," Harris answered. "But yes, we believe so."

"And you think they're the ones who flipped a semi on I-5 last night and stole the Bible from you?"

"That's right. You mentioned a Lapidus and Kublanov?"

"That's who Andrews and Newton told me they were. I've also been told they were Swedish art thieves named Mats Bjornstad and Annika Danielsson. For all I know, they're actually newlyweds named Fred and Katie."

Harris nodded at Stockton, and Stockton—with some apparent discomfort—procured a tablet from his coat pocket. He tapped it a few times and handed it to Harris, who in turn passed it to Jackson. "These two?"

"That's them."

"Fredrick Lindholm and Kirsten Ahlström, with the Swedish KSI."

"KSI?"

"*Kontoret för Särskild Inhämtning*, Sweden's Office for Special Collection. They liaise with foreign intelligence."

"And steal Bibles?" Jackson asked, handing back the tablet.

"We can't verify that, but it would explain their presence in the area."

"What about Robyn-Roberta-Whitney-Zoey? You got a real name for her?"

"No," Harris said. "We know all of the names you mentioned as aliases, but her real identity is a mystery."

"To the NSA?"

"Unfortunately, sir, yes."

Jackson sighed. "What do you want from me?"

"We need to know anything you know," Harris said. "Anything that could help us find the Bible."

"You're with the NSA, you just told me who all the players really are, and you want my help?"

"You've been in this since the beginning. You know how Nenasheva and Andreev have been thinking and working. And you know where Miss Paragon and Miss Vanderbilt are."

"No, I don't. We got back last night, and I bowed out."

"Excuse me, sir?"

"I quit. I'm done chasing the Bible. I've got my own upstairs. I'm sick of putting my neck on the line. I'm done."

"I appreciate that, Mr. Douglas, but if there's anything at all you can tell us . . ."

"All I can tell you is that I never trusted Andrews and Newton or Andrev and Nenasheeva or whoever they are. They first said they were FBI, then CIA, but I think they killed Desmond Vanderbilt. Beyond that, I have no idea where Abby and Zoey are or, for that matter, if you're really NSA agents who go a little too far or MI6 trying to get the Bible because you fear it has secrets about what's really hidden in the Tower of London or who killed Princes Di or a really good recipe for Yorkshire pudding. And unless you're about to haul me off to McGarrett's windowless blue room, I don't care."

Harris was practically dumbfounded as he looked at Jackson. Stockton furrowed his brow in anger.

"Look," Jackson said. "Zoey had a room at the Casa del Sol in Long Beach Monday night, but I doubt she's there anymore. I'd be shocked, in fact. And that is really all I know."

It wasn't quite all, but he wasn't giving them anything that could possibly set them on Abby and Zoey's path, such as the last-known general whereabouts of the Bible. And Harris seemed to buy it.

"Now, if you don't mind, I'm a little tired and, like I said, really sick of this whole Bible business. Do you mind?"

"No, sir, thank you for your time."

Jackson followed them to the door.

Harris reached into his suit jacket pocket and withdrew a business card. "If you think of anything else, please give me a call. Day or night."

"Right."

"Recovering that Bible is a matter of national security," he said. "If you do know anything else . . ."

"Goodbye, Agent Harris."

"Uh, and for what it's worth, I do apologize for the, um, inconvenience last night."

"I'm not the one who's owed an apology," he said, shutting the door on the NSA agents. Through the peephole, he watched them leave, then thought seriously about going back to bed. But as tired as he was, he wasn't sleepy. So he crashed on the couch and flipped on *SportsCenter*. He'd been so busy that he didn't even know who was playing Green Bay in the Super Bowl in a few weeks.

As he watched highlights of NBA and NHL games, Jackson couldn't help but think about Agents Harris and Stockton (he was about two-thirds certain they were indeed NSA, albeit rough around the edges), or about Elena Andreev and Stanislav Nenasheva, or Fredrick Lindholm and Kirsten Ahlström—or whoever any of them really were. It was all a mess, and his client—former client—was caught in the middle of it. And even though he had warned her, he sort of felt guilty about letting her run off with Zoey.

For one thing, he didn't know who Zoey really was. Even the NSA didn't know. For another, if Andrews and Newton really were Russian intelligence agents Andreev and Nenasheva, then they likely had killed Desmond and wouldn't hesitate to kill another Vanderbilt if the situation called for it. Then there were the Swedish KSI agents unless the NSA was wrong about Andreev and Nenasheva who had then been right about Mats and Annika being ex-KGB. Either way, Russian agents were involved. And somewhere, Regina and Cortez were still on the loose.

Abby was bound and determined to get the Bible, regardless of the risks. And Zoey was, well, equally motivated. Whether they continued to work together or not, he didn't see Zoey's involvement making things any better for Abby. He had been the only one really looking out for her, and now he had quit.

Jackson sighed heavily as a pretty ESPN reporter interviewed Tom Brady after practice. So it was a Patriots-Packers Super Bowl. Two of the NFL's all-time franchises battling for a world championship. Jackson couldn't wait.

He just hoped, as he reached for his phone to try calling Abby, that he would survive to see it.

Chapter Thirty-Five

JACKSON PACED AROUND his living room for fifteen minutes, stealing glances now and again at the TV. Luis Cortez had not been heard from since the shooting at his place that left him wounded and Amir Assar dead, so Jackson assumed he was out of the race—a pawn that had served its purpose. That left four parties in addition to Abby and Zoey: Regina Archambeau, Elena Andreev and Stanislav Nenesheva of the Russian SVR, Fredrick Lindholm and Kirsten Ahlström of the Swedish KSI, and Dwayne Harris and Vance Stockton from the NSA. Of all of them, he found the NSA agents, despite their somewhat brutish behavior in Salinas, to be the most credible, so he was working off their profile of the other parties. But at this stage in the game, nothing would surprise him about anyone's identities.

It left him not sure who to trust or how to go about protecting Abby and helping her recover the Bible. Neither she nor Zoey had answered their phones when he had called a little while ago. Maybe they were sleeping in. Or maybe they were ignoring him. Or maybe they were stuffed in a trunk of a Cadillac in Pacoima. Jackson just knew that on TV, nobody ever didn't answer their phone for a *good* reason.

Jackson decided to call his usual sounding board, Reggie. Then he felt a rumble in his stomach and decided to go see him in person instead. After a quick shower and change of clothes, Jackson remembered he didn't have a car. The Granada was still at the hotel in Long Beach. So he gave Reggie a call after all. He wasn't working that morning and agreed to give Jackson a lift to the south side of L.A. But first, they swung by Cameron's for some breakfast.

"So this is what you've been doing for four days?" Reggie asked after Jackson had given him the rundown of events. It had taken the length of the drive from his house to Cameron's and also spanned the wait for their food to arrive.

"Pretty much," Jackson said.

"And now you're out of it?"

"Was. Until the NSA visited me again this morning."

Reggie shook his head, then rubbed it with a meaty hand. "So now you feel like you got to go save the girl again?"

"It's the classic P.I. story," Jackson said. "Client hires P.I.; client disobeys P.I.'s warning and gets in trouble; P.I. reluctantly risks his life to save the client."

"Got to hand it to you, man. I'd have quit a long time ago."

"I'm like Hook," Jackson said. "I have indefatigable good form."

"So what do you need from me?" Reggie asked. He sat back as a waitress named Lori delivered steaming skillets of eggs, meat, hash browns, and plenty of cheese.

Jackson refilled his coffee before answering. "Right now, just a ride and some advice."

"Advice about what?"

"Who to trust?"

"That's easy, man. Nobody."

Jackson stirred his skillet. "Nobody?"

He nodded. "From what you say, it seems this Vanderbilt guy retired in '94, right?"

"That's the story."

"Think about what's happened in the world since '94. Half a dozen small wars in Europe and Africa, 9/11, Iraq, Afghanistan, the death of Osama bin Laden."

"Long shorts for basketball players."

"That was a little before, I think," Reggie said. "But in '94, nobody knew who al-Qaeda was. We all thought Saddam was done, and Afghanistan was a place to buy those knit blankets."

"Afghans. So what are you saying, Hoss?"

"I have trouble believing all these agencies are all aflutter about twenty-year-old intel."

"So who are all these people?"

"I don't know. But they want that Bible for something."

"The NSA I get," Jackson said. "They're obsessive about not letting anything leak out. And the Russians I buy too because they want anything they can have on America. But the Swedes?"

"Didn't you say somebody told you they were art thieves?"

"Yeah."

"That'd make more sense, man," Reggie said, lifting a bite to his mouth.

Jackson frowned. "But that means the NSA agents lied to me about them, and about the Russian agents who also lied to me about the Swedes. You see why I wanted out?"

Reggie nodded.

Jackson concentrated on his skillet for a while. Piping hot and spicy, it was what he needed to give him some pep.

"What about this Zoey Paragon?" Reggie asked. "Sounds like she should be Jell-O wrestling at the Forum on Saturday nights."

"So that's why you're busy on Saturdays."

Reggie grinned. "Seriously, man. You say she told you she's a private contractor?"

"That's the latest story."

"And nobody else knows who she is?"

"No."

"So who's she working with? Or for?"

"I don't know."

Reggie pointed with his fork. "Might be the key, man."

Jackson replayed the last four days, trying to think of times when Zoey or one of her aliases could have been working with any of the other parties. There were several, but just as many occasions that proved her loyalty to Jackson and Abby—or at least, her disloyalty to anyone else.

He sighed. "I don't know, Reg. This is like *The Mole*. I don't have a clue who's on which side."

Reggie shrugged. "So take some time, man."

"I can't. Abby and Zoey are probably chasing up into the mountains as we speak."

"So what are you doing here?"

"Trying to figure out a way not to go into this blind. Besides, unless I can get a hold of Abby and Zoey, I don't know where specifically the Bible is. It stopped somewhere in the San Gabriels last night, but I don't know where. And that was last night."

"So you have to team up with somebody else, and you need to know who?"

"That's about the size of it."

Reggie took a slow, thoughtful bite. "What are the Swedes' names again?"

"Depends who you ask." He sighed. "Fredrick Lindholm and Kirsten Ahlström."

"I'd try them."

"You would?"

He nodded. "I still don't buy the CIA and NSA legitimately being all over this thing." He rubbed his close-shaved head. "I don't know, man, maybe that's just me. But I think it's far more likely this is about a quarter-million dollars' worth of old, old Bible than it is about national security."

"So why are all these agencies involved?"

"Exactly. And until I know that, I'm not trusting them."

Jackson shrugged. "Okay, but why choose the Swedes? Why not Regina in that case?"

"Can she help you?"

"She seems to be connected."

"Yeah, with former cartel snitches who set off a bomb in a tunnel and Iranian thieves who shot said snitch in his own home."

"We don't know he was Iranian, but fair point."

"And because the Swedes are the only ones in this thing who've never lied to you."

"They said they were honeymooners."

"Maybe they are."

"Fredrick-Fred and Kirsten-Katie." He shrugged.

"Even if they are KSI agents, there's no hostility between the U.S. and Sweden. You need an ally; they seem like the best bet."

"I gotta get out of this business," Jackson said with a sigh. "You by any chance in need of a new sous chef?"

*   *   *

12:04 p.m.

AFTER PICKING up his Granada at Casa del Sol in Long Beach, Jackson drove home and did some research. If the *Kontoret för Särskild Inhämtning* had a website, Jackson couldn't find it. Probably all in Swedish anyhow.

He also didn't find anything to suggest that there had ever been a pair of Swedish art thieves named Mats Bjornstad and Annika Danielsson. That lent credence to the NSA's claims that they were really Fredrick Lindholm and Kirsten Ahlström with the KSI, which lent credence to the NSA's claims that they were indeed NSA. Then again, not being Mats and Annika didn't make the Swedes Fredrick and Kirsten any more than it made them Vladimir and Svetlana or art-loving honeymooners or Speedo supermodels after all.

Still, he liked Reggie's advice to call the Swedes. He hadn't trusted Andrews and Newton before they became Andreev and Nenasheva, so he certainly wasn't going to trust them now. And while his gut told him Harris and Stockton were really NSA, he was getting sick of the agency runaround. Besides, they hadn't given him the feeling they were willing to work with him, and until somebody could offer him more than the phrase "national security," his obligation was to his client (assuming she'd have him back again). And it wasn't about the Bible, anyhow; it was about Abby's safety. For whatever reason, it felt like she was Jackson's responsibility. And he liked his chances of protecting her better with the Swedes than with any other government agency. If that made him a traitor, so be it.

Shortly after noon, Jackson called the Swedish embassy. He got passed around and put on hold for fifteen minutes, then was regarded suspiciously when he finally asked to speak to two persons with the KSI.

"I am sorry, sir, but no such persons exist," a woman told him. She was the fourth person he had spoken with at the embassy, and her accent and tone convinced Jackson she had graying blond hair in a bun so tight it pulled the wrinkles out of her face.

"Look, I understand if you can't tell me anything," Jackson said. "But this is important. So if Lindholm and Ahlström are real, can you please find a way to get them a message? Let them know Jackson Douglas is looking for them. I'll give you my cell, and they can call me. If I'm barking up the wrong tree, then just humor me and tear up the message."

No answer.

"Please? It's important."

Still nothing. Jackson gave her the number, repeated it, and again stressed it was urgent that he spoke with Lindholm and Ahlström. No promises were made, and he closed his phone without much hope.

Needing some air, he wandered out onto the deck. The temperature hadn't warmed up much, and the wind was still whipping off the ocean. The sky was white, but not a bright white that suggested the sun was about to break through. If there was such a thing as a dark, foreboding white, this was it.

He thought about trying Abby and Zoey again. He'd already called each of their cells three times, leaving a message once. He could only guess where they were or what they were up to.

He also thought about what he would do if the Swedes didn't call back. Driving into the San Gabriel Mountains and looking for a silver Nissan was getting even odds with booting up the Xbox.

His phone rang. An unknown number. Could it be?

"Hello?" he said.

"Jackson Douglas?"

"Yeah."

"This is Fredrick Lindholm. I understand you called?"

"Yeah. Can we meet somewhere?"

"Why?"

"I've got a deal for you."

"I'm listening."

"I'd rather discuss it in person. Do Swedes eat tacos?"

"Some do."

"There's a Taco Bell on Lincoln and Pacific in Santa Monica. How soon can you be there?"

Fredrick's reply was muffled, and not until he heard a female voice in the background did Jackson realize Fredrick was asking Kirsten. "One o'clock," Fredrick answered a moment later.

"Okay. Thank you."

Jackson arrived early and ordered a few chalupas, even though he wasn't really that hungry. Fredrick and Kirsten arrived promptly at one, dressed casually. Both of them still looked like models. Bypassing the counter, they joined Jackson at a table by the window.

"You're not hungry?" he asked.

"We're not the taco-eating kind of Swedes," Fredrick said lightheartedly. A foreign agent with a sense of humor? Back to art thieves as their most likely identities.

Jackson nodded. "First, I'm sorry about pulling down your pants at the pool, but all's fair in love and when chasing Bibles across the state."

Fredrick raised an eyebrow.

"That aside, I assume since you're here that you don't know where the Bible is."

Fredrick and Kirsten exchanged a quick glance. "No," he said.

"But you still want it?" Jackson asked before taking a bite of his second chalupa.

"We do."

"Okay, here's the deal," Jackson said as he swallowed. "I know roughly where it is. Or at least, where it was. And I think I know who has it. I also know that Abby and Zoey are still after it, and my concern in this is their safety."

"What are you saying?"

"I'll tell you everything I know, on the level. You help me find Abby and Zoey and make sure they're safe, and the Bible's yours."

"Just like that?" Kirsten asked.

"As long as you make Abby and Zoey's safety the first priority."

"Are they in imminent danger?" Fredrick asked.

"I don't know. I haven't been able to get a hold of them all morning, and last night they were still raring to go." He shook his head. "Abby's stepbrother has already been killed, I think because of the Bible. Abby and Zoey have both been held against their will. I was shot at yesterday. I don't know what's in that Bible, but it isn't worth it."

The Swedes exchanged glances again, and Jackson took the opportunity to stuff the remainder of the chalupa in his mouth.

"Why are you coming to us now?" Kirsten asked. Her eyes were cutting, boring into Jackson the way only a beautiful woman's could. It was hard to believe this was the face of a government agent. A *Glamour* cover girl, maybe.

"Because I have nowhere else to turn."

"What about your own government?" Fredrick asked.

"I don't know who my own government is. Is it the NSA agents who forcefully took the Bible from us last night in Salinas, or is it the people they claim are Russian agents but who claim they're actually CIA posing as FBI? Who, by the way, claim you're Russian agents."

Kirsten raised her eyebrows.

"I never believed that, for the record," Jackson said. "You're both too good looking. That whole Russians are hot thing has never panned out in my experience."

"Are you serious?" Kirsten asked.

"Yeah. I mean, Maria Sharapova's not bad, but that's about the—"

"I mean are you serious that you're convinced we're legitimate because of our looks?"

"Not entirely. I wasn't fully convinced until you called back."

"You said you know where the Bible is?" Fredrick asked.

"I know where it was last night. Approximately. I'm hoping you have a way to pinpoint it."

"How would we do that?" Kirsten asked.

Jackson shrugged. "I figure the Swedish government must have some sort of cutting-edge technology. At the very least a satellite you can task."

"To what?"

"I'll tell you that once we have a deal."

Kirsten exhaled, beauty's version of a huff.

"So what happens if you lead us to this Bible and Abby and Zoey are nowhere to be found?" Fredrick asked.

"Unless we find evidence to suggest something has happened to them, we shake hands, and you have the Bible."

"And if there is evidence?"

"You help me make sure they're safe. Whatever that entails. I know it's a little open-ended, but that's the deal. Take it or leave it."

Fredrick looked at Kirsten. Then Jackson. "Give us a minute."

"I'll hit the head," Jackson said. He got up and returned three minutes later, after stopping to fill up his soda. Fredrick and Kirsten studied him as he sat down.

"We have some terms," Fredrick said.

"Shoot."

"We call the shots. Abby and Zoey are the priority, like you said, but we do it our way."

"That's fair."

"And if we find out you're anything less than truthful or if you double-cross us in any way, the deal's off, and you become expendable."

"I can live with that. Anything else?"

They looked at each other one more time. "We have a deal," Fredrick said.

Jackson extended his hand.

Fredrick laughed. "Just like in American cinema." Then he reached out and shook Jackson's hand.

Chapter Thirty-Six

2:03 p.m.

JACKSON MET FREDRICK and Kirsten at their hotel in Rancho Park, just east of the intersection of the Santa Monica and San Diego Freeways. He was pretty sure they knew where he lived but didn't want to take the chance of meeting there just in case. If things went south, he wanted to be able to go home.

Jackson wore blue jeans and a sweatshirt over a long-sleeved tee. They were headed into the mountains where, rumor had it, snow was falling. Fredrick and Kirsten, not knowing their destination yet, were dressed for warmer weather. Then again, they made their home on the tundra.

Fredrick admitted Jackson to their room, and they got down to business.

"After Zoey swam to shore from the boat on Monday," Jackson explained, "she put a tracking device in the spine of the Bible. She didn't tell us about it until after we got off the train last night, by which time the NSA was in possession of the Bible."

"And they have it now?" Kirsten asked.

"No. We tracked the Bible back toward L.A., but north of the pass, we ran into a traffic jam, held up by a tipped over semi, which was actually an ambush to steal the Bible from them. Zoey's tracker indicated the Bible continued toward L.A. while the NSA agents were still stuck in traffic. Turns out, they had crashed, and someone had used the opportunity to lift the Bible from them. When the NSA agents stopped by my house this morning, they told me they believed Russian SVR agents named Elena Andreev and Stanislav Nenasheva were the culprits."

"Andreev and Nenasheva," Fredrick said.

"A.K.A. Andrews and Newton of the CIA or FBI, depending on who and when you ask."

"We know them."

"Where are they?" Kirsten asked. Beautiful but impatient.

Jackson took an anxious breath before playing his trump card. Then again, he'd come this far. . .

"Zoey tracked them along Highway 2 into the San Gabriel Mountains. I don't know the exact location, but there aren't many roads that intersect with Highway 2, and it just climbs into the mountains and then comes down the other side. There are better ways around the mountains if that's all they wanted."

"So you think they took it to some place in the mountains," Fredrick said.

"That's my guess. I figure they have some sort of safe house up there, well off the beaten path."

Kirsten shook her head. "That's still a lot of area. How are we supposed to know where they are?"

Jackson shrugged. "Can't you get your government to ping phones or replay satellite footage or something? Match vehicles that were at the traffic jam in Grapevine to those that drove up into the hills a few hours later?"

Fredrick grinned. "You watch too much TV."

"All I know is TV," Jackson said. "You guys are the special agents."

Kirsten pursed her lips.

"Make the call," Fredrick said.

She opened her cell and dialed, pacing to the corner of the room. Fredrick opened his laptop. Jackson dug his hands into his pockets and waited. While the Swedes weren't exactly Eric and Nell in Ops, they did manage to pinpoint a believed location within ten minutes.

"There are approximately twenty-five residences along the Angeles Crest Highway beyond this point," Fredrick said, pointing at his laptop screen. The point in question was an estimate of where the Bible had been when Jackson had last seen Zoey's receiver. "Of those twenty-five," Fredrick continued, "six had a discernible heat signature increase between midnight last night and eight a.m. today according to thermal imaging from our satellite."

Jackson offered a slight smile. "Not bad."

"Of those six," Kirsten said, "we were only able to identify the owners of three of them. But one of those three belongs to a company called Aloha Enterprises. Aloha is a front for JNF Corporation, which has ties to several Russian businessmen."

"That's good," Jackson said.

"This," Fredrick said, switching the image on the screen, "is a satellite photo from a little over six hours ago, showing a Buick Regal." He enhanced the image. "We can only see a partial license, but it matches a plate a Caltrans traffic camera at Hubbard Street and Foothill Boulevard—just off Interstate 210 in Sylmar—caught a little before midnight last night. It matches the time and route you say Andreev and Nenasheva would have been on had they taken the Bible from the NSA agents."

"That is very good," Jackson said. "I don't know how you got access to Caltrans, but I'll take it."

Kirsten's cell chirped, and she whipped it to her ear. *"Ja?"* She paced back to the corner and unleashed a torrent of Swedish a moment later. Jackson had to give it to all of these agents. They'd come a long way. In the movies, foreign agents always had an accent. But everyone he'd been dealing with could switch in and out of languages and accents like Frank Caliendo.

"Unfortunately, this is the only angle we have," Fredrick said to Jackson. "It looks like there's a garage or an outbuilding of some sort over here, but we don't know how many cars are there or how many people have come and gone."

"What about heat signatures?" Jackson asked.

"We were able to pick up an increase, but it's too fuzzy from this distance to know if it increased from two to four or from four to six. Or because someone came into a cold house and turned up the heat or it self-adjusted for morning."

Kirsten continued to talk in rapid Swedish.

"And we can't see if anyone has come or gone since eight this morning?" Jackson asked.

"Satellite's out of range now."

"Of course it is," Jackson said, jamming his hands into his pockets. "So what you're telling me is we're going in blind."

"Not blind," Kirsten said, rejoining them. "I just spoke with Sörensen, and he confirmed Andreev and Nenasheva's identities. They are Russian *Sluzhba Vneshney Razvedki*. SVR."

"You two have weapons?"

"We do," Fredrick answered. "You?"

"Glock," Kirsten said. "Nine millimeter."

Jackson turned around to where she held his pistol. His eyes flitted up to the taunting, teasing look on her face, to the gun, and back to her. "Nice lift." He held out his palm, and she slapped the gun back into it. He checked the magazine and safety before returning the gun to the back waistband of his jeans.

"So the question is," Fredrick said, "what are Andreev and Nenasheva doing in the hills north of Los Angeles?"

"Laying low," Jackson said. "If the NSA fingered them, airports, seaports, everybody'd be on the lookout for them."

Kirsten's mouth formed a thin smile. "Wouldn't stop us."

"Yeah, but you're Swedish. They're only Russian."

"True."

"One other thing," Fredrick said. "The satellite passed out of range just after eight this morning, so it's like I told you, we don't know if Andreev and Nenasheva are still there or if anyone else joined them. Including Abby and Zoey." His eyes cut to Kirsten and back to Jackson. "If we show up and they aren't there . . ."

"Then you're welcome for the intel and kindly drop me off back here on your way back to Stockholm with the Bible."

"If it's that easy," Fredrick said.

"He means if we run into opposition, will you still be willing to help us?" Kirsten asked.

Jackson nodded.

"Why? What's your motivation?"

"It's the price I pay for your help."

"How do we know you won't back out?"

"Same way I know you won't shoot the three of us in the back and run with the Bible."

The Swedes looked at each other.

Jackson shrugged. "And because I shook Sinatra's hand."

"What?"

"Nothing. Daylight's burning. You guys ready?"

Fredrick threw on a sweater and Kirsten ducked into the bathroom to change shirts. She added a windbreaker vest and a stocking cap that made her look an awful lot like a mature Alex Mack, and then the Swedes grabbed their gear and led the way down to a rented Ford Escape.

The air was still cool and the sky gray, with a strong wind gusting up toward the San Gabriels to the northeast. It felt like it might snow in L.A., let alone at altitude. Thoughts of a gunfight in snowy mountains filled Jackson's head with images from *Red Dawn* as the trio headed for the freeway.

"So why does the Kingdom of Sweden want a Dutch Bible?" he asked from the middle of the backseat.

Kirsten smirked back at him.

"What?" he asked. "I mean, I get why all the U.S. agencies want to keep old CIA secrets close to the vest, and the Russians have obvious reasons. But what does Sweden care? Aren't we allies? I mean, our biggest beef with you is the '92 Olympics."

"What happened in the '92 Olympics?" Fredrick asked.

Jackson looked out the window. "We tied in a round robin hockey game."

"And you're upset about that twenty years later?" Kirsten asked.

"We led three nothing after two periods," Jackson said. "And we had this goalie—Ray Leblanc—who got hot."

"Did you medal?"

"Fourth," Jackson said. "Lost to the Czechs."

Kirsten shook her head. "I don't get it."

"Have you ever blown a 3-0 lead in the third period? It stinks."

"I didn't take you for a hockey fan," Fredrick said.

"I'm not really, but I was ten, and it was the Olympics." He leaned forward. "But that's my point. That's the only bone I can think of to pick with Sweden. Do you really think some former CIA operative and art collector has the goods on you guys?"

They exchanged looks another time.

"What? What's that mean? Something I don't know about?"

"There are rumors," Kirsten said.

"Rumors of what?"

They both looked straight ahead.

"Fine. But still, shouldn't you be more worried about the Russian version of Alec Vanderbilt or Finland's power play or something?"

"Why don't you let us worry about what we should be worried about?" Kirsten said.

He sat back. "Fine."

Jackson expected a couple of Swedes to tune the radio to some weird techno station, but except for a few brief traffic checks, Fredrick and Kirsten kept the radio off. L.A.'s web of freeways didn't provide an ideal route to Highway 2 at the base of the San Gabriel Mountains, but Fredrick found his way. As they started to climb into the mountains along the winding Angeles Crest Highway, Kirsten turned over her shoulder and gave Jackson advice on what to expect when they arrived at the house and how to proceed. She treated him as if he was a rookie meter cop about to join SWAT on a raid of a terrorist compound, and had she not been so cute in her charcoal stocking cap and had he not been flashing back to afternoons sneaking away from the family to watch Nickelodeon, Jackson might have been insulted.

Snow started falling shortly after they entered the mountains, enormous white flakes that began to accumulate faster and faster. By the time they crossed the "divide" separating the south side of the San Gabriel range from the north side, the road was covered in snow, and Fredrick had to take it slow in a top-heavy SUV.

"You're used to this, right?" Jackson asked as Fredrick braked around a hairpin curve.

"Our last assignment was in Australia," Kirsten replied.

"Stockholm's actually pretty mild," Fredrick said. "Sweden isn't all snow and ice."

"Well, you know Americans, we have to stereotype everyone."

"We know," Kirsten said. She turned her attention to the vehicle's GPS and guided Fredrick. They were only half a mile from the driveway where Andreev and Nenasheva's vehicle had been spotted, and Jackson tensed, preparing for potential action.

Fredrick drove past the driveway without slowing, continuing for another half mile before finding a place to turn around. The initial surveillance hadn't revealed anything—just a driveway leading into the trees.

"We'll park by the road and walk in," Fredrick said.

Jackson and Kirsten both assented. Fredrick parked at the edge of the road, just past the driveway, and the trio got out. Giant white flakes continued to flutter toward the ground, and the wet snow crunched under Jackson's feet as he followed the two Swedes to the driveway.

"Tracks," Kirsten pointed out.

"Pretty wide," Fredrick said. "SUV, maybe a pickup."

"Not the car we saw on satellite."

"Great," Jackson said. "It's a party."

The house was about fifty yards off the road, set slightly lower along the hillside. Satellite images had revealed it was big, several thousand square feet per floor, and at least two stories tall, with a large deck wrapping around the back of the house and hanging over a small cliff. But that was about all they knew, other than about the existence of the outbuilding in the front and off to the right of the house.

Large ponderosa pines towered over the driveway and blocked out much of the late afternoon light without shielding the snow. They also provided cover as Jackson and the two KSI agents approached the house. When it was in sight, Fredrick put his back against a tree while Jackson and Kirsten crouched behind several bushes.

Two vehicles were parked in front of the garage. The closer of the two was a dark, new model pickup. A thin layering of fresh snowflakes frosted the paint and windows. The other was a car, likely a four-door. It was covered in a blanket of snow, obscuring the make and model as far as Jackson could tell. Could have been the Buick Regal identified on satellite, could have been Zoey's Nissan.

Fredrick checked his weapon. "Okay, we go in quick."

Kirsten looked at Jackson. "No shooting unless necessary. We know Americans are quick-triggered too."

"I follow your lead," Jackson said.

"Okay," Fredrick said. "Let's go."

They crept out from behind their hiding places and hurried across an open driveway, taking cover behind the snow-covered car. Jackson reached a hand out to brush snow off the license plate.

"That's not a Buick Regal," Kirsten whispered.

"No, it's Zoey's car."

"So where is Andreev and Nenasheva's?"

"Maybe in the garage," Jackson said.

"Or gone with the Bible."

Fredrick nodded. "Come on."

On his signal, the trio scampered from behind the car to a small porch in front of the house. It was so quiet that Jackson could almost hear the snow falling. There were no lights on in the house—nothing to indicate anyone was there. So where were Abby and Zoey? Or the driver of the pickup? And Andreev and Nenasheva?

With Kirsten behind him and Jackson on the other side of the doorway, Fredrick tried the doorknob. It was unlocked, and he pushed the front door open a few inches and waited. Then he shoved it all the way, revealing a dark interior.

Fredrick made eye contact with Jackson and Kirsten before entering the house. She followed right behind him, and Jackson brought up the rear. Late in the afternoon, in the woods, on an overcast day, the house was dark. It was also massive. There was a powder room on the right, then a short hallway to the kitchen. A split staircase was straight ahead, and beside it, a hallway leading to a living room on the back of the house. Another hall led left, toward a den or bedroom, it appeared. Everything was dark.

Kirsten peeked into the powder room, and then Fredrick motioned for her to head into the kitchen. Meanwhile, he and Jackson moved toward the living room.

It was spacious, two stories high, with a vaulted ceiling spanning the entire back half of the house. The north wall was filled with windows that looked out onto the deck and the snow-covered trees beyond. Overhead, roughly hewn wood rafters extending from a loft to the far wall and a chandelier made of deer antlers gave the room a rustic, woodsman's cabin feel. It was offset by the plush furniture situated around a flat screen TV and full entertainment system on the left half of the room. A second, more intimately arranged set of furniture faced a tall stone fireplace on the other side of the room. If Jackson didn't know better, he'd think he had arrived at a ski lodge just before everyone returned from a day on the slopes.

Until he saw the leg.

Jeans and a socked foot, extending from the other side of one of two chairs perpendicular to the fireplace.

Jackson grabbed Fredrick's arm and pointed. Fredrick tensed, and he and Jackson both gave the room a second look before entering. Fredrick went right, Jackson left. He circled a couch and peeked behind a couple of chairs. No legs were sticking out from behind any of them.

Suddenly feeling a draft, Jackson glanced through an open sliding-glass door out to where the snow continued to flutter onto the deck. He saw a set of very faint footprints, almost wiped away by the additional snow. They were too obscure for him to tell if they were coming or going.

He turned to Fredrick's half of the room and saw embers dying in the fireplace. Combined with the draft from the door, the sight of them made him shiver. But it wasn't the draft that made his blood run cold; it was a second leg—this one upside down and partially hidden behind another chair.

Jackson looked up at Fredrick, then down at the body in front of the chair on his right. Jeans, dark socks, a pullover that was stained with blood. Blond hair, wide open blue eyes, and a mole above the lip. Elena Andreev.

He knew she was dead, but he checked her pulse anyway. Then he turned to the other leg, behind the opposite chair. It belonged to Stanislav Nenasheva. Three bullet holes in the chest and stomach. His eyes were shut, and a check of his pulse revealed he was just as dead as his partner.

Jackson looked up at Fredrick and shook his head. Kirsten had arrived beside him, and she stared at the bodies wide-eyed. She looked to Fredrick, then Jackson, then back to the bodies. Her face asked the obvious question: Who?

Jackson had several ideas, but before he could process any of them, a bullet spat into the coffee table in front of him, causing him to dive for cover behind the chair.

Chapter Thirty-Seven

4:48 p.m.

JACKSON SCRAMBLED TO get fully behind the chair, at the same time reaching for his Glock. He heard several more shots on different trajectories, fired by Fredrick or Kirsten, and then a bullet shattered the window behind him.

Jackson waited until he heard more return shots from the Swedes, and used them for cover to peek out. He got his first glimpse of the loft overlooking the living room. Two rooms—probably bedrooms—sat on either end of the loft. Between them, a wide wooden railing spanned the remaining distance. Jackson didn't see a shooter, but a muzzle flash caused him to duck back behind the chair.

"Jackson!" Kirsten hollered.

"Yeah."

"What do you see?"

"Shooter upstairs."

More bullets rained down on the chair, and Jackson waited for one of them to penetrate through the chair and into his flesh.

"Cover me," Fredrick called, and Kirsten opened fire. At the same time, Jackson used her cover to again get a bead on the shooter upstairs. He fired several shots at shapes, then ducked back behind the chair. Their combined barrage gave Fredrick enough time to scurry through the living room and take up residence behind a chair on the other side of the room. He and Jackson now had varying angles on the upstairs shooter.

"You okay?" Fredrick asked.

"Yeah. You?"

"Fine. We—"

Several bullets tore into the chair Fredrick was hiding behind, and Jackson rose up and shot into the loft. The gunman turned his way, and

Jackson ducked back down. Immediately, Fredrick rose up and fired, and a sickening groan indicated he'd hit his target. That was followed by a clunk as a body fell hard against the loft railing.

"Shooter down," Fredrick said, tentatively rising from behind his chair. Jackson stood too, and Kirsten joined them in the middle of the room.

"You get an ID?" she asked.

"No. You stay here, keep an eye on him. Jackson and I will clear the upstairs."

Jackson checked his rounds—nine remaining—and followed Fredrick back into the entryway and up the stairs. He'd been in shootouts before, and in situations scarier than this. Even so, his legs felt wobbly as they climbed the staircase that opened into a spacious loft tucked in between a pair of bedrooms and overlooking the living room.

Jackson kept watch while Fredrick approached the body. He kicked the gun away and nodded back at Jackson. It was a dead body.

They did a quick sweep of three bedrooms and three bathrooms, all of which were empty. Returning to the loft, Fredrick peeked over the railing to Kirsten. "All clear," he said, clicking the safety on his gun and holstering his weapon.

"Who is it?" she asked.

Fredrick used his foot to turn the body over to the supine position. "You know him?" Fredrick asked.

Jackson studied the face and hid his shock. "Yeah. His name's Luis Cortez. Former member of the North Coast Cartel in Cartagena, Colombia. Also a former CIA informant."

"What's he doing here?"

"The story I've gotten is he thinks the Bible could incriminate him with his old cartel members."

Kirsten climbed the stairs. "How do you read this?" she asked Fredrick. "Andreev and Nenasheva had the Bible, Cortez shot them, then we came in before he could find the Bible?"

Fredrick nodded. "But how did he take them by surprise?" he asked. "They would have had to hear his truck pull in."

"Maybe not," Kirsten said. "I saw footprints on the deck. Maybe he sneaked around back and surprised them."

"And where are Abby and Zoey?" Jackson asked. "Their car's here too."

"So where's the Bible?" she asked. "I can't believe they were just sitting and watching a fire."

"If they were waiting for someone, maybe," Fredrick said.

"Maybe this Cortez guy, and things went wrong?"

"I don't know. You clear the kitchen?"

"And dining room. But there were stairs to a basement or wine cellar."

"Plus bedrooms up and presumably down."

"Let's split up and look. It has to be here."

"Most likely long-term hiding places would be in the closets or a wall safe or some kind of secret hiding space," Fredrick said. "Unless they had it with them, heard the truck, and stashed it somewhere quick."

"Cortez killed them, and before he could find it, we showed up, so he took the high ground. That makes sense."

"I agree. Either way, it's got to be here. We'll take the place apart if we have to."

She nodded her agreement.

"I'll take the bedrooms up here," he said. "You want to check the others downstairs?"

Kirsten nodded again and hurried downstairs.

"I'll check the basement," Jackson said, thinking it was the most likely place to find Abby and Zoey. He followed Kirsten downstairs, and as she ducked into the hallway branching away from the kitchen off the main hallway, he headed toward the kitchen. He briefly stuck his head into a laundry room that doubled as a utility closet. Then, with gun drawn, he opened a door across the hall. Figuring all the shooting had blown the element of surprise, he flipped on the light switch before starting down.

The basement was only half the size of the upstairs and was unfinished. Metal shelves lined one of the walls, and several wooden crates were stacked beside them. A quick investigation revealed nonperishable food items, some clothes of various sizes and styles in an armoire against the side wall, and guns and ammunition in the crates. The Russian safe house angle was looking good, and Jackson made a mental note to tip off a certain female police detective when he returned home.

After taking another minute to make sure there weren't any secret chambers or compartments where Abby and Zoey could have been stashed, Jackson returned upstairs. He checked a small pantry off the kitchen and then entered the dining room that connected it to the spacious living room. It extended from the east end of the house with windows opening to look over a chasm to the north and the garage to the south.

The garage.

Jackson poked his head into the living room and listened for Fredrick or Kirsten. Hearing nothing, he ventured back through the dining room. There was a side entrance to the house off the laundry facilities, and if he was lucky, a garage key or garage door opener sitting on a shelf.

He stopped.

A drawer in the dining room credenza was ajar. Not open, but not tightly shut either. He stepped back, listened again, and pulled open the drawer.

Sitting on top of some long candles and a butane lighter was a King James Bible. Just sitting in the dining room credenza. It fit with Fredrick's theory that it had been hastily hidden.

Jackson wiped his hands on his pants and lifted the Bible out. He took a moment to confirm that it was indeed the Vanderbilt Bible. Then he lifted up his sweatshirt and tucked the Bible into the front of his jeans. It was a tight fit that made walking around awkward, and it was certainly an ignoble way to transport the Word of God—especially an ancient version worth hundreds of thousands of dollars. But he had the sudden desire not to leave the Bible where Fredrick and Kirsten could find it and abscond with it. In his mind, they had broken their deal, abandoning any search for Abby and Zoey after finding Andreev and Nenasheva and killing Cortez. He decided having a bargaining chip might not be a bad idea.

He closed the drawer tight, stopped again to listen for either of the Swedes, and then exited through the laundry door as quietly as possible.

The snow was still falling steadily as he stole across the grounds to the garage. There were two windows on the northwest side, but they were too high for him to look through. So he used the key he'd found on a peg in the laundry room and unlocked the door. Gun drawn, he stepped into the blackness.

He heard an intake of air and knew he wasn't alone. He crouched for several seconds, waiting until his eyes adjusted to the light and he could make out the shapes of two vehicles parked side by side. The nearest was a car, probably a Buick Regal. The other was bigger, an SUV or truck.

"J-J-Jackson?"

He whipped his head to the side, gun leading the way. He squinted and saw two people seated under the windows. "Abby?"

"Y-yeah."

"Are you all right?"

"We're p-p-peachy," Zoey called. "Now get over here and unt-t-tie us."

Jackson walked toward their voices and knelt down in front of them. They were both shivering constantly, and he realized the garage wasn't heated. "How long have you been out here?" he asked.

"Th-that depends on wh-what time it i-i-i-is," Abby said.

"Since about t-ten o'cl-clock," Zoey answered. "What ha-happened? We h-heard sh-shots."

"Long story," he said, looking behind her. Their wrists were duct taped behind their backs, with more tape wrapped around their arms, binding them to the wall of the garage. It took Jackson several minutes to peel loose the tape and free them both. While he worked, he explained that Andreev and Nenasheva were dead, Cortez was too, and Fred/Mats/Vladimir and Katie/Annika/Svetlana were actually Fredrick Lindholm and Kirsten Ahlström, Swedish government agents who were searching the house for the Bible.

"They haven't found it yet?" Zoey asked.

"No. I have it."

"You h-h-have it?" Abby asked.

Jackson took off his sweatshirt, revealing the Bible in his waistband. He gave the sweatshirt to Abby, and she struggled against cold, stiff limbs to put it on. He doffed his stocking cap and gave it to Zoey.

"L-let's get out of h-here," Abby said.

"You have the keys for your car?"

"No," Zoey answered. "The Russians took them. But I can hotwire it."

"I have a better idea," Jackson said. "If you two can walk, the Swedes are parked at the end of the driveway."

"What difference does it make?"

"A, they have all-wheel drive; B, they have keys to that car but not yours; and C, they'll be wondering where I am at any minute."

"So your p-partnership with them is over?"

"Yeah. We had a deal, you guys before the Bible. They violated that, so they can explain to the cops all the dead bodies inside. Come on."

Jackson peeked out the door, saw nothing, and pointed at the bushes he and Kirsten had hidden behind not long ago. With him keeping watch, Abby and Zoey ran for cover, and then he joined them. There was still no sign of movement from the house. Fredrick and Kirsten were probably so consumed by the search for the Bible that they hadn't even noticed Jackson's absence. He could only hope.

"The SUV's just west of the driveway," Jackson said. "I'm pretty sure they didn't lock it."

"Wh-what are you doing?" Abby asked.

"If they should happen to come out, they could see our footprints and figure out where we are. I'll lay down some cover," Jackson said. "Don't worry, I'll be—"

He stopped as headlights illuminated the snowy ground of the driveway. Jackson quickly tackled Abby and Zoey back into the brush as a silver SUV rolled past and parked just behind Zoey's Nissan. Two men got out and looked at each other for a moment. Harris and Stockton.

Jackson feared the NSA agents would spot their footprints leading from the garage, but their focus was on the house. He waited until they started for the front door, then motioned for Abby and Zoey to start up the driveway. "Quietly," he whispered.

Once Harris and Stockton had entered the house, Jackson backed up after Abby and Zoey. When he could no longer see the front door through the trees and around the slight bend in the driveway, he turned and ran after them.

Both driver's side doors of the Escape were open. Abby was climbing in the backseat, and Zoey was laying half in and half out of the front, on her back, reaching up under the steering column. Jackson took the Bible out of his waistband, brushed some snow off the cover, and handed it to Abby. "Here, hang onto this."

She nodded, and he closed the door. "Got it?" he asked Zoey.

"Just a second. If I could feel my fingers . . ."

Hotwiring was not a private investigator skill Jackson had picked up, so he kept watch, expecting a contingency of domestic and foreign government agents to spill out of the driveway at any second. Instead, he heard a sparking sound and then the rev of the engine as the vehicle started.

He turned around. "I'll drive." He handed his gun to Zoey. "In case we're followed."

She nodded, crawling across to the passenger seat. Jackson got in, took one look in the rearview mirror, and put the SUV in gear. There were at least three inches of snow on the road, and it took him a few minutes to get comfortable steering a vehicle so much different than the Granada in conditions he wasn't accustomed to. He also kept one eye on the rearview mirror, waiting to see headlights. Beside him, Zoey cranked the heat, then used the butt of Jackson's gun to smash in the GPS unit on the console.

"Are you both all right?" Jackson asked.

"J-just c-cold," Abby said. "And hungry."

"You want to explain everything?" Zoey asked, settling back into her seat. She held her hands out toward the dashboard vents, warming them as if over a fire. "In a little more detail this time. I thought you were 'out.'"

"I will," he said. "But first we need a plan."

"A plan for what?" Abby asked.

"For ending this," he said. "They should keep each other occupied for a while back there, but they'll be coming for the Bible again. And this is quickly turning into *And Then There Were None*. I'm willing to die for the Bible, but not like this."

"Okay, so what's the plan?" Zoey asked, taking off Jackson's stocking cap and tossing it in his lap.

"I'm still working on the details," Jackson said. "Part one is getting to the bottom of the hill without turning this thing into a bobsled."

Chapter Thirty-Eight

JACKSON, ABBY, AND Zoey walked up to the front door of the First Santa Monica Bank building at 10th and Montana. Southern California was again bathed in warm sunshine, and the cold and gray and mountain snow of the day before were a distant memory. The dead Russian SVR agents and Luis Cortez were not. Nor were Harris and Stockton of the NSA or Lindholm and Ahlström of the Swedish KSI. But Jackson had a plan.

After coming down out of the San Gabriel Mountains the night before, the trio had ditched Fredrick and Kirsten's Ford Escape and checked into a hotel room. They had bought some food and some changes of clothes, and Jackson had laid out the first details of his still-forming plan. Somewhat hesitantly, Abby and Zoey had both agreed to it. So after getting a reasonably good night's sleep, they had checked out and driven a newly rented Chevy Cruze first to Jackson's house to pick up his safe deposit box key and then to his bank.

It was three minutes after opening, and they were the first patrons. A very prim woman named Jennifer was manning the safe deposit box desk and looked at the trio dubiously as they approached. "Good morning," she said with a smile that was more cursory than genuine.

"Good morning," Jackson replied. "I need to get into my safe deposit box."

"Of course. Your name?"

"Jackson Douglas. Box 3417."

Jennifer entered something into her computer, then placed a small electronic device on the counter. "Please place your hand here, Mr. Douglas."

He placed his hand on the device, which scanned his palm print.

"Thank you," Jennifer said. He lifted his hand, and she drew the device back.

"They'll both be accompanying me," he said. "They're not on the account."

Jennifer didn't seem to like this, but after another moment at her keyboard, she forced another smile and edged the same device forward, along with a stylus. "I'll need you both to sign here, please."

Abby and Zoey did so, and Jennifer entered one more thing into her computer. "Do you have your key, Mr. Douglas?"

He held it up.

"Right this way then."

She led them back around a corner and into a vault. Safe deposit boxes of every size were built into the left and far walls. On the right, several booths were available for private viewings of box contents. Fluorescent lights reflected off all the metal and created a sickly green color that felt almost clinical. Jackson couldn't help but wonder how many millions of dollars of valuables were stashed in the room.

Jennifer used her key like a divining rod, stopping halfway along the wall. "Three-four-one-seven," she said. "If you would please insert your key here, Mr. Douglas."

He did so, she placed her key into the slot beside it, and they both turned their keys. After a quiet click, she pulled the door open. "There you go."

Jackson took his box by the handle and slid it out. Two feet long, a foot wide, and three and a half inches deep, the box was plenty big enough to hold the Bible.

Jennifer motioned them over to the nearest booth, pulling back the curtain to admit the three of them. "Take all the time you need," she said, sans smile, and then drew the curtain behind them.

"You two mind?" Jackson asked. "There's some sort of personal stuff in here."

Zoey eyed him.

"Don't worry," he said. "Houdini couldn't make the Bible disappear in here."

She nodded and closed her eyes, while Abby turned away. Jackson lifted the lid and looked down at several stacks of cash—part of Hillary's winnings in a Las Vegas poker game when the two of them had been undercover. That was before things had gone sideways. Jackson's passport and birth certificate, the deed to his house, and the title to his car, along with several other important papers were also in the box, and he took a moment to rearrange things so that there was room for the Bible.

"I'll take it now," he said to Abby. Without looking, she handed him the Bible, and he placed it in the box. He closed the lid and tapped Zoey's elbow. "Satisfied?" he asked, holding out his hands.

"Ish."

Jackson lifted the box off the table and opened the curtain. He returned the box to its slot, and he and Jennifer both closed and locked the door. She led them out of the vault, Jackson thanked her, and the trio left the bank. In the parking lot, Jackson held his key out to Zoey.

"If you disappear with this, I am going to be really mad."

"Why would I do that?"

"I don't know. But I'm going out on a limb here."

"You're going out on a limb? The Bible's in your safe deposit box."

"Which I can't get into without the key, and you can't get into without my hand."

"Doesn't give me much motivation to confiscate the key, does it?"

"I can't begin to understand your motivations."

She gave him a look that was half frustrated sigh and half grin. "So now what?"

"Now I get the ball rolling. Lay low, and I'll call you on your burn phone."

"Promise?"

"I can't do it without you," he said. "I promise."

"Well, you want to drop me at a hotel, or do I have to take a cab?"

He unhooked his car keys from his chain and flipped them to her. "Take it. We've got other arrangements."

"You're sure?"

"I'm sure."

Zoey's eyes were skeptical, but she pocketed the keys. "I'll be waiting for your call."

He nodded and watched her walk over to the car and drive away.

"Are you sure about this, Jackson?" Abby asked.

"Yes. I told you, I have a plan."

"When are you going to tell me what it is?"

"In time."

She sighed.

"Do you trust me?" he asked.

Abby bit her lip.

"Do you?"

She nodded.

"Okay. I promise, if everything goes to plan, when this is all said and done, the Bible will be yours free and clear."

*　　　　　*　　　　　*

12:24 p.m.

THE WAREHOUSE was on Cannery Street, a block from the Los Angeles Harbor. It had been abandoned for several years and was scheduled for demolition next month. Mouse had used his hacking skills to find the warehouse and learn about its state of neglect, and also to discover that it was no longer protected by BJK Securities out of Compton. It was perfect.

Having stashed Abby at a beachside motel where she could relax, make some arrangements for Desmond's funeral, and stay safe and out of sight, Jackson and Reggie headed to the port to check out the warehouse in person. Picking the lock was easy, and with no observers but a flock of seagulls sorting through trash in the parking lot, they entered the warehouse.

It was cavernous, its skeleton made of steel support columns and beams that crisscrossed some twenty-five feet over Jackson and Reggie's heads. The walls were aluminum, with broken and cracked—and in some cases, boarded up—windows letting in a little bit of light. Most of them were too dirty to afford someone on the outside a view in. Dirt and dust covered the floor, and aside from the remnants of a few wooden shelves and a dozen or so broken, half-rotten pallets in the corner, the warehouse was completely empty.

"It'll work, I guess," Reggie said. His deep voice echoed around the room. "Might need some lights."

"Yeah. And chairs, a table."

"You got bay doors on the west side," Reggie said, rubbing his head with his palm. "Another door on the north. Looks like there used to be an office in that corner."

Jackson nodded. "I'm thinking we set it up over here," he said, pointing toward the corner with the bay doors. He started walking that direction. "We

323

make them enter where we came in, and that can be Mouse and Zoey's door," he said.

"You really think she'll do it?" Reggie asked.

"I don't know. She's a hard one to read, but I think so."

Reggie rubbed his head again. "So what's the plan for the bay doors, emergency escape?"

Jackson looked at his friend. "Yeah."

"Great."

"We're going to need another man for security, too. I don't trust these people to show up alone. We can't have any sore losers calling in reinforcements."

"I can find somebody," Reggie said.

"Actually, I've got somebody in mind if he's free. But it might not hurt to have a backup."

Reggie nodded. "I can score you the chairs and table from Cam's. I don't know what you're going to do about lights."

"You know anybody who works road construction maybe?"

"I know a guy at SMPW. I can give him a call."

"Great," Jackson said and started walking toward the door through which they'd entered the warehouse.

"So what's next, man?"

Jackson grinned. "I send out invitations."

*   *   *

1:52 p.m.

JACKSON USED Reggie's private office in the basement of Cameron's to make his calls. He kept the TV on but muted, in case news about the goings on at the Russian safe house in the San Gabriels broke or the NSA issued a warrant for his arrest or something. Mostly it was just news about Syria and a shooting at a mall outside Oklahoma City.

Jackson's first call went to Fredrick. He didn't answer, and Jackson decided to try again later as opposed to leaving a voicemail. So he moved on to call number two.

"This is Regina."

"Regina, it's Jackson Douglas."

Silence.

"I have the Bible," he said.

She hesitated. "Why are you calling me?"

"Because I'm selling it," he said. "I've had enough of people trying to kill me, so I'm getting rid of it."

"What's your price?"

"To be determined."

"Why don't you stop beating around the bush?"

"Why don't you let me dictate terms?" Jackson said. "Considering I had the courtesy to include you in my little auction."

"An auction?"

"That's right. Tomorrow at noon. High bidder gets the Bible, end of story. You'll come alone, no weapons, and you will be searched. If you don't like the terms, then you can try your luck with the Book of Mormon."

Regina swore.

"What's that, you aren't interested and I should hang up?"

Her response sounded like a teeth-clenched growl. "Where?"

"I'll call you tomorrow with the location."

He disconnected the call, cutting her off mid-sentence. That brought a smile to his face as he tried Fredrick's phone again, only to have Kirsten answer with a bored-sounding "Hello?"

"Agent Ahlström."

"Who's this?"

"Jackson Douglas."

She responded the same as Regina, with silence. Then, "What do you want?"

"I'm auctioning off the Bible. You and Freddie are invited."

"What kind of stunt is this?"

"No stunt. Noon tomorrow, just the two of you, no weapons and I mean no weapons. I'll call you in the morning with the location."

Her voice was icier than a Swedish winter. "You had better know what you're doing."

"You had better exchange your kronas for Benjamins. I'll call you tomorrow."

Two for two. The third call scared Jackson, and he thought about calling his lawyer first. But right now, she scared him more, so he took a deep breath and dialed.

"This is Agent Harris."

"Agent Harris, it's Jackson Douglas."

"Mr. Douglas, we've been wanting to talk to you."

"I found the Bible," Jackson said.

"I thought you might have."

"And I'm selling it."

"That Bible belongs to the United States government."

"Not according to the front flyleaf, and I've got a judge and a court order that agree with me," he bluffed. "But that's beside the point because I'm getting rid of it. Tomorrow at noon, an auction. Uncle Sam can put his money where his mouth is."

"After all your country has done for you?"

"I pay my taxes, Agent Harris. My country and I are even."

"You really think you'll get away with this?"

"I'm not getting away with anything. I have something a lot of people want, and I'm being a capitalist. That's still legal in this country, isn't it?"

Harris sighed. "Who else is coming to this auction?"

"The regular gang," Jackson said. "Maybe a few ringers."

"What are your terms?"

"No weapons, just you and Stockton, and if you think about calling in SWAT or the National Guard or the 4th Army, know I have a contingency and you'll never see the Bible again."

"And you'll never see the light of day again."

"Not according to my judge," Jackson said, adding more cockiness to outduel the butterflies in his stomach. "I'll call you tomorrow with the location."

"Fine, play this your way," Harris said.

"I will," Jackson said, clapping his phone shut. Then he sank back into Reggie's couch. He waited for his breathing to regulate and the anxiety to subside. He planned to call Pablo, maybe the Russian embassy, and anyone else he could think of. He wanted as many people at the auction as possible, for several reasons. One, the more people who attended, the more credence the auction had. Two, more bidders meant more bad blood and bickering which would keep the parties focused on each other and not him. And three, he didn't want to exclude anyone. The last thing he needed was some additional party not getting word that he'd sold the Bible and coming after him (or worse, Abby) somewhere down the line.

But first, Jackson called Zoey. He'd been on the phone all day, and his ear was getting sore. But he had to keep her on a short leash.

"Yeah?"

"It's Jackson. Meet me at the bank tomorrow at ten. We'll get the Bible out then."

"What's the plan?"

"Still working on it. I'll call you later when things are finalized."

"Okay."

"You aren't on the way to Juarez with my key, are you?"

"No, I thought I'd actually try Canada out."

"That's funny."

"I'll wait for your call."

"Right."

Jackson closed his phone and sighed. He needed a nap, but he didn't have the time. There was too much work to do.

*   *   *

Friday, January 25
11:44 a.m.

METAL FOLDING chairs had been arranged in two short rows, split by an aisle down the middle, in front of a sturdy card table. A flat screen TV sat on the table, plugged into Jackson's laptop. Borrowed construction lights bathed the area in a soft glow and left the rest of the warehouse eerily black. Two webcams monitored the street out front of the warehouse and the parking lot and entrance on the south side. Both were also wirelessly connected to the laptop. Mouse had set up all the electronics and was now with Zoey in a rented U-Haul truck a block west on Seaside Avenue.

Reggie had taken care of most of the physical setup and now remained with Jackson and Abby in the warehouse. He was in grunt mode, dressed in black, guns—both mechanical and muscular—on full display. Brady Kane, a reformed and still reforming wife-beater, was manning the door. Jackson had run into Brady and his wife Stephanie the past summer and intervened in a domestic assault. Jackson had temporarily taken Stephanie in, then hidden her at Sam's for several months while forcing Brady to get help with his violent temper. They were now back together, expecting a child, and Jackson kept in contact with Brady. All signs were positive, and Jackson hoped a one-day stint as a security guard/bouncer wouldn't cause Brady to relapse. But he needed the muscle.

At a quarter to, Jackson activated the small communications device in his ear. "Brady, you copy?"

"Yeah. All clear."

"Zoey?"

"We're set."

"Okay, stand by," Jackson said.

"Jackson, are you sure about this?" Abby asked from beside him.

He looked to Reggie before answering. "No."

"You promised—"

"I know," he said. "Trust me."

She nodded.

"Jackson," Brady said, "I've got a silver SUV turning into the lot off Tuna."

"Copy." He turned to Abby, who was not on comms. "They're here."

He had called everyone just after leaving the bank that morning, telling them where the auction was and how to proceed when they arrived. He had also laid out the rules a second time, making sure nobody tried anything funny. He had called the NSA agents last of all, not wanting to give them any extra time to mobilize some sort of assault. They were the wildcard. If they called his bluff and brought in a SWAT team or just decided to arrest him, then everything would fall apart. If not, his plan had a chance. Besides, he'd brushed up on his Fourth Amendment knowledge and the particulars of what a warrant covered and didn't cover, and he had a contingency plan. And a good-looking blond lawyer on speed dial.

Agents Harris and Stockton entered the warehouse as Brady announced in Jackson's ear that they were clean—no weapons. Jackson checked the laptop and saw their SUV in the parking lot. The Cannery Street camera showed nothing.

Jackson regarded the NSA agents with a nod, and they took front row seats without a word. Regina arrived a few minutes later, followed closely by Pablo Diaz. Regina sat on the opposite side as Harris and Stockton, and Pablo shook his head at Jackson and sat in the middle of the back row. "Man, what are you doing, man?"

Jackson said nothing, and his comm squawked. "Jackson, I have a Pavel Kredlenko here."

"Let him in," Jackson said.

Kredlenko—presumably sent by the Russian embassy in place of Andreev and Nenasheva—sat behind Regina. A few minutes later, a short Latino man with a goatee entered the building. Javier Cota, Luis Cortez's brother-in-law and the owner of the van that had ambushed Andreev and Nenasheva in the Figueroa Street Tunnels. He sat on the other side of Pablo, leaving the front middle available for Fredrick and Kirsten when they arrived.

"Is that everyone?" Brady asked after admitting them a minute later.

"Should be. Proceed as planned."

"Check," Brady said, and left his post temporarily to make a sweep of the building.

Jackson looked out at the eight faces in front of him. "Ladies and gentlemen, thank you for coming. Shall we get down to business?"

Chapter Thirty-Nine

12:02 p.m.

REGGIE USED A remote control to turn on the TV, and Jackson tapped a sequence of keys on the laptop that sent the image he saw to the TV screen. In the U-Haul a block away, Mouse used a small camera to film Zoey as she displayed the Bible to the prospective bidders. She stood in front of a black drop cloth, with small portable lights illuminating her and the Bible without revealing that they were inside of a U-Haul.

"The Vanderbilt Bible," Jackson said, stepping to the side of the table. "Most of you recognize Miss Paragon. She is working with me for a one-third cut of the proceeds, so please bid generously."

He smirked. His audience did not.

"Here are the brass tacks. For obvious reasons, the Bible is not here at the warehouse. It is close, which is all I'll say, and it will stay close until after the bidding."

"You expect us to pay you without authenticating the Bible?" Regina asked.

"You will have every opportunity to authenticate the Bible," Jackson said. "Once everyone is satisfied that Miss Paragon is holding the genuine article, I will take silent bids. After everyone has had an opportunity to bid, I will announce the high dollar amount. Consider this a mulligan for those of you who are unaware of the stakes at the head table. I will then take a second round of silent bids. The high bidder is the winner, and my security force is here to ensure that there are no sore losers."

He looked over the stern faces as Brady sounded in Jackson's ear, reporting a clear perimeter sweep and announcing he was back at his post.

"The winning bidder will then initiate a wire transfer to a specific account. While the transfer is taking place, Miss Paragon will bring the Bible here. When she arrives, she will hand over the Bible. If it is unsatisfactory, the

330

winner can cancel the transfer. If the Bible passes muster, the winning bidder will wait until the wire transfer is complete, at which time our transaction will be finished. Any parties coming in low on the second bid will have to remain through the duration of the proceedings and for a brief period while the winning party is allowed to leave unencumbered. It wouldn't do to have them ambushed on the way out. Are there any questions?"

There were none.

"Good," Jackson said. He turned toward the TV. "Miss Paragon, kindly display the Bible."

Jackson then stepped back while Mouse zoomed in on the Bible. Zoey showed the front cover, including the nick in the leather edging at the bottom. She opened it and turned through the first several pages, showing Alec's handwritten notes (or perhaps codes) that were in such high demand. She showed the dedication page, and then flipped to a few other pages, making sure to point out the notes in the margins.

When she was finished, Jackson turned back to his audience. "Any questions?"

"How do we know that Miss Paragon is live and this is not some staged production?" Kredlenko asked.

"Have her turn to the dedication page," Regina said. "The one Abby claims was written to her."

Jackson instructed Zoey, she obeyed, and Mouse zoomed in and allowed the camera to focus. He held it in place for almost a minute, allowing Regina and the other bidders to read the text on the page.

"Satisfied?" Jackson asked.

"No," Kredlenko said. "For all I know, she is in on it," he said, shooting a glare at Regina.

"Have her open the Bible to the Gospel of John," Agent Harris said.

Again, Zoey complied with Jackson's instructions.

"Have her show me three fingers," Kredlenko said.

"You care which hand?" Jackson asked.

Kredlenko didn't smile.

"Miss Paragon, three fingers," Jackson said.

Zoey held out her left hand, three fingers raised.

"Anyone else?" Jackson asked.

Nobody spoke.

"Good," Jackson said as he returned to the computer. He toggled off the feed to the TV. "You'll find two notecards taped under your seats. Remove them, write your bid and name on one of them. Fold it over and give it to my associate," he said, nodding at Reggie.

The would-be bidders reached under their chairs, and for several minutes conferred and scratched out numbers on the notecards. It was rather low-tech, but to avoid them surreptitiously texting the location or other details to associates, Jackson had had Brady confiscate all electronic devices upon entry. In theory, Harris and Stockton could have called in backup or Regina a new host of Cortezes before entering the warehouse, but this was a low-budget, ad hoc plan if ever there was one.

Jackson watched the group. He wasn't sure if Harris and Stockton would actually bid; or if Pablo would bid on his own, for the Swedes, or not at all; or if Cota had any interest in the Bible. He was the closest relative to Cortez and a former business partner, so if anyone related to the late cartel member wanted the Bible, Jackson figured it would be Cota.

Reggie collected five total bids, which he brought to Jackson. He took just a moment to see who had bid how much before looking up at his gallery. A less honest, less fearful man—one who was in it for the money—would have doubled the total, just to raise the final price, knowing they could have all lowballed in the first round to keep the price down. But Jackson knew when not to push the envelope

"High bid is twenty-five thousand, American," he said. "I'll now give you five minutes to submit your final bid."

Jackson glanced down at the laptop, still showing the feed of the U-Haul. Mouse and Zoey had not moved. The webcams outside the warehouse were still clear. Turning away from the bidders, Jackson whispered just loudly enough for his comm to pick it up. "Brady?"

"All clear. You want me to make a second sweep?"

"Yes."

Jackson turned back and watched as Fredrick and Kirsten whispered to each other again. Harris and Stockton also shared a brief conversation. Regina, the high bidder in the first round, stared a hole through Jackson. Pablo looked confused, which wasn't anything new. Kredlenko scratched away on his notecard. Only Cota, who had not submitted a bid the first time, seemed calm. If he hadn't come to bid, why had he come at all?

"Still clear," Brady reported, alleviating a few of Jackson's fears. All the parties seemed to be playing by his rules.

"One minute," he announced.

Harris and Stockton had been the cheapest in the first round, which wasn't a surprise. Jackson expected them to up the ante this time. Pablo and Fredrick and Kirsten had been within five grand of each other, likely working together. Then Kredlenko and finally Regina, five grand over the Russian's bid. Of all the parties, she knew the Bible's artistic worth and was clearly lowballing Jackson. But he didn't care—he just wanted to finish his auction.

Five bids came in again, most of them in the neighborhood of fifty to seventy-five thousand dollars. One, however, was a significant outlier. Jackson had to suppress a grin. He couldn't have asked for a better outcome.

With a nod at Reggie to make sure the big man was ready, Jackson spoke into his comm again. "Mr. White, come on over."

He looked down at seven expectant faces and one that was very smug. "Another of my associates," Jackson said. "He's a technology expert and will oversee the funds transfer. As mentioned, once the transfer is initiated, Miss Paragon will bring the Bible to the warehouse."

He cleared his throat for dramatic effect. "The winning bid, in the amount of one hundred fifty thousand dollars, belongs to Mr. Kredlenko. Congratulations."

Regina swore.

Pablo let out a wide-eyed, "Whoa."

Fredrick and Kirsten scowled, but only half as sternly as Harris and Stockton.

Cota wore a detached stare.

And Pavel Kredlenko grinned as he stood.

"Mr. Kredlenko, please come up to the table, and we'll initiate the transfer. The rest of you, I ask that you remain in your seats."

Several loud sighs and another muffled curse from Regina sounded, but nobody moved. Mouse entered through the Cannery Street entrance two minutes later. He gave Jackson a nod as he took his place beside him at the table.

Jackson reached into his pocket and withdrew a folded slip of paper. He extended it to Kredlenko. "Please wire the funds to this account," he said. "Mr. White will make sure everything goes as planned."

The account was from a bank in the Cayman Islands, with no name attached to it. Mouse had opened the account that morning and would handle any transfers out of it. But for the time being, his role was to make sure that Kredlenko's wire transfer was genuine. He handed a tablet to Kredlenko, with which he could make the transfer, then sat at Jackson's computer. A few seconds after Kredlenko initiated the transfer, Mouse nodded at Jackson. "It's underway. Should take about five minutes."

Jackson nodded. "Miss Paragon, bring the Bible."

She didn't reply.

"Miss Paragon, do you copy?" he asked, pressing his finger on the comm in his ear.

Still nothing.

Jackson reached for his cell phone.

"What is going on?" Kredlenko asked.

Jackson ignored him and dialed Zoey's number. He gave it five rings before snapping the phone shut. "Mr. Gray, do you have a visual on Zoey?"

"Uh . . ." Brady said.

"Yes or no?"

"No. The U-Haul is in place."

Jackson turned to Mouse. "Bring up the camera."

"I demand to know what is happening," Kredlenko said. "Where is the Bible?"

Mouse's fingers raced over the keys, and he looked up at Jackson.

"What?"

"It's been deactivated."

"I am canceling the transfer," Kredlenko said, raising the tablet.

Jackson glanced at Reggie, who cast a wary eye at the seven people still sitting in the folding chairs.

"Zoey, do you copy?" Jackson asked again, not expecting an answer. "Zoey?" he asked again, looking from the angry Russian to a worried Dutch woman beside him. He tried to convey reassurance with his eyes but wasn't sure the message got through.

"It is canceled," Kredlenko announced with a snarl. Mouse confirmed with a nod. "Now what is the meaning of this?" the Russian demanded, pulling a gun from his waistband. Brady was officially fired as bouncer.

"Don't think about it," Reggie said, just as quickly drawing his SIG Sauer P220. He briefly turned to make sure everyone else remained in their seats.

His eyes came back to the Russian. "You pull that trigger, you're dead before the hammer hits."

Kredlenko was undeterred. "What is your game?"

"No game," Jackson said. "She double-crossed me too."

"I do not believe you."

"Why would I stage this?" Jackson asked. "To make you angry before I auction it again, or to make you angry before I sell it to somebody else?" He shook his head as he looked at the laptop. "I'm not getting any money. You canceled the transfer."

Kredlenko didn't blink.

"He's right," Harris said. "It's the woman."

"How about you lower the weapon?" Reggie said.

"Where is she?" Kredlenko asked.

"I don't know."

"Where!"

"Okay, okay, stay calm. She was in a U-Haul a block west on Sea—"

"Jackson, I've got her," Brady said into Jackson's earpiece.

"What?"

"What?" Kredlenko echoed. "Who is that?"

"Mr. Gray, come again."

"Zoey's on foot, headed for the oil depot."

"On foot?"

Kredlenko thrust the gun forward. "Where is she?"

"She's on foot," Jackson said. "Headed for the oil depot."

Lowering the gun, Kredlenko turned and ran for the exit. Fredrick and Kirsten exchanged a quick look and jumped up to chase after him.

"Paragon has the Bible?" Harris asked.

Jackson nodded.

"That was a legit feed?"

"There's no way to fake what you saw."

"We're going to want to talk to you later," he said as he and Stockton headed for the exit. Regina was on their tail.

"Jackson, what's going on?" Abby asked.

"I don't know."

"She's too smart to take the U-Haul," Reggie said.

"Where's she going to go when she gets to the oil depot?" Jackson asked.

"Swim again," Abby said. "Come on!"

Before Jackson could stop her, she was chasing after Kredlenko, the NSA agents, the Swedes, Regina, and Cota and Pablo, who had also joined in on the pursuit.

"Stay here," Jackson said to Reggie. "Get this stuff packed up, and you and Mouse get out of here."

"You sure?"

"I'm sure. I'll take Brady. Go."

Jackson sprinted toward the exit and burst out into broad daylight. The sun was almost blinding, and he squinted toward the western half of the parking lot. Fredrick had almost caught up to the lanky Kredlenko. Kirsten was in the Swedes' vehicle, racing across the parking lot, while Harris and Stockton's SUV squealed as they turned in pursuit. Abby was left to run across the parking lot well behind Regina, Cota, and Pablo.

"What's going—" Brady started.

"Come on."

"What about the guns and phones?"

"Where are they?" Jackson said, pausing.

"In the safe by the door."

"Key?"

Brady held it out. Jackson took it, tossed it toward the safe, and pulled on Brady's arm.

The parking lot ran all the way to the end of the block, where a bunch of rusting containers were stacked next to a pile of crates and a small shed. Across the street was the oil depot, a triangular manmade peninsula of land, and beyond that, a thousand-foot channel of water. If Zoey could swim across it, she would reach a marina with an ample supply of cars to hotwire or boats to steal.

Jackson and Brady closed ground on Abby as she neared the containers. That was also the time when the first gunshot sounded.

"Abby, get down!" Jackson yelled.

She didn't listen, and he pushed himself onward. He caught her and made a flying tackle as they reached the street just short of the oil depot. More gunshots echoed through the giant oil storage tanks across the street, and Jackson pinned Abby to the pavement.

"Jackson!" she yelled, then cried.

"That Bible is not worth getting killed over," he said.

Abby squirmed, beating him with her fists, but Jackson didn't let her up. Two more shots sounded in the distance, and Brady took up a shielding position between Jackson and Abby and the shooting.

"Jackson," Abby cried, giving up on getting loose. "She's going to get away."

"I know," he said. They sat up, and he pulled her into a hug.

"I trusted you," she said, pushing him, sobbing, and then falling back against his chest. "I trusted you, and you let her get away."

Brady watched awkwardly for a moment, then extended a hand to Jackson. "We should probably get out of here. The shooting will draw a crowd."

Jackson nodded and helped Abby to her feet. He put an arm around her, but she wriggled free. "No. Let me go." She pushed away and started back toward the warehouse, leaving Jackson and Brady to trudge after her.

Chapter Forty

IT HAD TAKEN some doing for Jackson to get Abby to show up for dinner at Cameron's. It was a beautiful, unseasonably warm day, and he had used his pull with the owner to reserve the entire upstairs deck, consisting of half a dozen tables. Reggie's caveat had been that Jackson at least pay for his dinner. A fair trade.

The sun had just set as Abby arrived at the table, wearing jeans with a teal blouse under a light sweater, her hair pulled back. She also wore the expression of someone who was learning to smile again after a tragedy, and she regarded Jackson warmly.

"Thanks for coming," he said, standing as she sat down.

"I'm sorry about last week," she said. "I made a complete fool of myself."

"No," Jackson said, "you didn't. I asked you to trust me and didn't provide you with enough collateral. I'm sorry about that."

Abby nodded.

"And I'm sorry about Desmond too. I know you two weren't close, but I'm sorry just the same."

"Thank you."

The funeral had been Tuesday and had marked the official end of the quest for the Vanderbilt Bible. Zoey had gotten away the previous Friday—Jackson didn't know how. Hid in the oil depot? Swam to safety? Had someone from whatever group she really worked for ferry her away? Jackson didn't know and didn't care. The only thing that mattered was that she got away. He had monitored the news Friday afternoon and evening and all day Saturday, looking for any mention of her or the Bible. There had been none.

Agents Harris and Stockton had stopped by on Saturday, and Jackson had given them the same story. He was sick of the chase, decided to sell the Bible, and had talked Abby and Zoey each into a one-third cut. Zoey had double-crossed him—again—and was in parts unknown. They had grilled him pretty hard and tossed out phrases like "obstruction of justice." But eventually, they had let him go with nothing more than an oral slap on the wrist. He was seventy-five percent sure they were legit.

Pavel Kredlenko and the Russian contingent, Javier Cota, Regina Archambeau, and Frederick and Kirsten and their lapdog Pablo Diaz had either given up or were busy chasing Zoey around the world. None of them had bothered Jackson, and after a week, he was convinced he was in the clear. They weren't interested in settling petty scores; they wanted what was in the Bible.

To that end, Jackson still didn't know if it contained CIA secrets, insights and lessons Alec had pulled from the Scriptures, or the incoherent ramblings of a doddering old man. And frankly, he didn't much care. He was more concerned about his client.

"So, you said you had something important to tell me," Abby said.

Jackson nodded. "I did. And I do."

"Are you going to tell me what it is?" she asked as a waiter poured two glasses of water.

"I am. But you need to trust me until after dinner."

She sighed and thanked the waiter for her menu.

"I promise, it will be worth it," Jackson said.

"Okay."

They settled down to the business at hand and ordered, and while waiting for dinner and nibbling on appetizers, Abby told Jackson about the funeral. It had been sad, despite her and Desmond's jaded past, but there had been some good to come from it too. "I got to see Noah again," she said. "It had been years, and we talked for a quite a while."

"Is he still living in Europe?"

"Amsterdam. He flew back yesterday."

"Was he staying with you?"

"No. He actually spent yesterday in Las Vegas. He'd never been. Seemed like kind of a strange time for sightseeing, but what do I know?"

"Hmm."

"What?" she asked, reaching for a slice of fresh-baked bread.

"I don't know," he said, suddenly feeling something was amiss. Noah, Amsterdam, sightseeing—he couldn't place it. Maybe it was just a reference to Las Vegas, even after all these months, that triggered anxiety.

"It's nothing," he said, brushing away the feeling.

Their dinners arrived—a steak for Jackson, a seafood platter for Abby—and they ate while enjoying the last rays of daylight over the Pacific. Abby talked about work, and what she would be doing next in the new chapter of her life. Post-Alec, post-Bible. Jackson had no prospective cases and wasn't sure what his future held. After all, he had gone through in the past couple of years and the close calls of the last few weeks, he would be happy to have some downtime.

"So is this being added to the expense list?" Abby asked when they were almost finished. "You are going to bill me for what I still owe, aren't you?"

"I am," Jackson said. "I didn't think the timing was quite right, what with the funeral and so forth."

"I appreciate that."

"And the dinner's on me. It's the least I can do."

"That's very kind."

Jackson signaled toward the waiter, who had just emerged from the doorway. He disappeared back inside, and less than two minutes later, Reggie sauntered onto the deck. He was dressed in dark blue jeans and a white button-down shirt, about as dressed up as he ever got. Still, it was quite a change from his bodyguard persona of a week ago.

"How was everything?" he asked.

"Excellent, as always," Jackson said.

"Very good," Abby said. "Thank you."

"In that case, you ready for dessert?"

"I couldn't," Abby said. "Dinner was too good. I'm stuffed."

Reggie grinned. "That's all right. I was speaking metaphorically anyhow."

Abby frowned. "What?"

Reggie's smile only widened. "Come with me. I'll show you."

*   *   *

Twenty months ago . . .
Friday, May 6
4:11 p.m.

"COME ON, Reg. What's the holdup?"

"It's weird, man. Two dudes?"

"I'm not asking you to try on pants with me, man," Jackson said. "It'll take half an hour, and you'll probably never need to go back."

Reggie flipped a sheet of paper. He was reading a résumé, or "curriculum vitae," as an entrepreneurial businessman should refer to it. He was hiring a waitress who he'd pay five bucks an hour, Jackson argued. Call it an application. But that wasn't the sticking point.

"Come on, Hoss."

Reggie finally looked up. "Why? When are we ever going to need it?"

"I don't know."

"You really think this sort of Machiavellian tactic will ever be necessary?"

"What are you, a word-of-the-day calendar or something?"

"Look, man, I get that you're eager, but you just got your license, what, three days ago? And you've still got goodbye cupcake frosting on your lip, man. Aren't you taking this a little fast?"

Jackson wiped the back of his hand over his mouth, then realized Reggie was speaking metaphorically. And that no one at Bauer & Bauer had thought to bring cupcakes for his last day. He shifted his weight. "Maybe, but there's no time like the present. And I'd hate to put it off until after I need it."

Reggie sighed. "Just let me finish looking over this résumé, okay?"

"Don't you mean 'curriculum vitae'?"

Reggie took ten minutes, then they headed for Jackson's Granada. "She a yes, no, or maybe?" Jackson asked.

"Yes," Reggie said.

"Is she cute?"

"What difference does that make?"

"Can help with tips."

Reggie shook his head.

"What? Cute waitress, playful smile, I probably tip better than if it's Anjelica Huston or Sandra Bernhard. I'm also more likely to come back."

"And you're still single, huh?"

"I know, right?"

"It's also why you aren't in the restaurant business, bro." Reggie grimaced as he touched the hot metal handle on the Granada and grumbled as he got in and sat on leather seats. "Man, when are you going to get a new car?"

"After my first big kidnapping case."

"Ha."

Jackson pulled out of the parking lot and onto the Pacific Coast Highway.

"So tell me again the rationale for this," Reggie asked.

"I don't know."

"Good start."

"Being prepared," Jackson said. "You never know when I'll need to pull a pizza parlor sort of deal."

"You already picking up trade lingo or you making this stuff up?"

"A little of each."

"And, man, why you planning on being conniving? I thought you wanted to be a P.I. to do the world some good."

"I do. But sometimes it gets messy. Besides, Jesus told His disciples to be as shrewd as snakes."

"And innocent as doves," Reggie said.

"Or what about that shrewd manager in the parable?"

"You mean the dishonest manager who acted shrewdly because he was too lazy to work?"

"So now you're a New Testament scholar too? Besides, you're missing the point."

"Uh-huh," Reggie said with a nod.

"Didn't Paul write something about being crafty and using trickery? Or read through the Old Testament. Those guys were all sly and devious."

"They also had nine wives and more concubines than you can shake a stick at. But at least you've done your homework."

"This can work both ways, you know," Jackson said. "You never know when this might come in handy for you too."

"Whatever you say, man, whatever you say."

A few minutes later, Reggie changed the subject to baseball and the slumping Dodgers. By the time Jackson could explain away their losing streak, blaming it on bad luck, injuries, and the probabilities of a one hundred sixty-two-game season, they had arrived at the bank. A middle-aged woman named Sarah greeted them with a wide smile and asked how she could be of help.

"We'd like to open a joint safe deposit box," Jackson said.

"Of course. Have a seat, and I'll get the paperwork."

Jackson raised an eyebrow. "I'm telling you, Reg, someday this is going to pay off."

* * *

Thursday, January 24
9:21 a.m.

"REG, IT'S Jackson."

"Hey, man. You get your Bible back?"

"Uh, sort of," Jackson said, glancing at Abby. The two of them were standing outside the bank, waiting for a bus that would take them to a hotel, where Abby could safely hide out for the day. "I need your help, Hoss."

"Name it."

"I need you to go to the bank and retrieve the Bible out of our safe deposit box."

"You for real?"

"I am," he said, flitting his eyes to Abby again. They said, "Trust me."

"All right," Reggie said. "What do you want me to do with it?"

"I'm sending someone to pick it up later this morning. You may want to hurry."

"Who?"

"You'll know her when you see her."

Reggie laughed. "Whatever you say, J."

"Also, there's a little transmitter hidden in the binding, near the top. It's tiny, but it's there. If you open the Bible all the way and shine a flashlight at it, you should be able to see a little gray dot. That's the transmitter. I'm going to need you to remove it and leave it behind in the box."

"A transmitter?"

"Without damaging the Bible," he said with a wink at Abby. "It is, after all, worth thousands."

"Great."

"You'll probably need a tweezers or something to get it out."

Reggie sighed. "Whatever you say," he repeated.

"Oh, and be discreet. Don't walk out with the Bible under your arm or something."

"Right."

"And maybe wear gloves. It's worth—"

"Thousands. So I shouldn't put it on the table with my ketchup and fries?"

"You got anything pressing for the next few days?"

"Why, you need me to be your personal banker for a while?"

"More like wingman."

"Yeah, I can rearrange my schedule, man. Just tell me what you need."

"For now, the Bible. I'll be in touch."

"You got it, J."

"Thanks." Jackson closed his phone and turned to Abby.

"What is going on?" she asked.

"Just trust me, okay? I promise this will all make sense in the end."

"What are you planning?"

"We've known it for several days now," Jackson said. "Getting the Bible isn't the end because someone else is always going to be coming for it. So we have to find a way to end the chase."

"And you've got a way?"

"I think so."

"Think?"

"Abby, just tr—"

"Trust you, I know."

He nodded. "Bus is here. Let's go."

*   *   *

Friday, February 1
6:23 p.m.

"WHERE ARE we going?" Abby asked as she and Jackson got up from dinner to follow Reggie.

"Trust me one last time."

"I don't . . ." She shook her head.

"Come on," he said, guiding her arm. Reggie led them inside to the private elevators the staff used to bring food from the kitchen to the upstairs dining room. Once on the lower level, they took a back hallway that circumvented the entry stairway and led to Reggie's office.

"Have a seat," Reggie said, closing the door behind them. He motioned toward his couch, and while Jackson and Abby sat down, he walked around his desk to his safe.

"Jackson, what in the world is going on?" Abby asked.

"I told you to trust me, didn't I?"

"Yes."

Jackson looked at Reggie as he spun the combination and pulled the handle on the safe. He withdrew a small backpack and brought it over and set it on the coffee table in front of Abby.

She looked up expectantly at Jackson. "What . . ."

"Open it."

With trembling fingers, she unzipped the backpack.

"Oh my gosh!" She jumped back. "Is it?"

Jackson nodded.

Abby reached into the backpack and pulled out a clothbound rectangle. She quickly lifted back the cloth to reveal a leather-bound King James Bible. Brown, worn cover, nick on the bottom, engraved "Holy Bible" on the cover that had faded from gold to white.

"This can't be," she said.

"It is," Jackson said.

"But . . ." She looked up to Reggie, who was beaming, and back down at the Bible. "How?" She turned to Jackson. "How did you do it?"

Chapter Forty-One

THE CAB DROPPED Jackson at Gideon's Books at quarter after nine. For some reason, he still had *Independence Day* on his brain and was expecting Jeff Goldblum's dad, right on down to his colorful Yiddish phrases and cigar. But Gideon Kaplan was younger and sprier. He did have the graying, thinning hair and reading glasses perched on the end of his nose, but no cigar, and a genial, toothy smile instead of a scowl. It got toothier when Jackson handed him a crisp hundred-dollar bill.

"Come in, come in," he said. "I think I've found what you're looking for."

Jackson followed him back through a small, quaint, somewhat dated bookstore and down a narrow hallway lit only by lantern-like sconces on the walls, to a back office that had recently been tossed by burglars. Or else subjected to a tornado. Books were stacked everywhere—including, in a few instances, on shelves. They flowed over desks, a spare chair, atop what appeared to be a roll of carpet, and on the floor itself. Only one desk was free of books, and that was a computer desk against the far wall. It housed an ancient desktop computer and was only free of books because there was no room for them amidst the piles of CD cases, user manuals, printouts, old 3.5-inch floppy disks, and approximately one-third of a tuna salad on whole wheat sandwich.

Gideon pressed a button on the computer, and it seemed to grunt before starting to hum. That was followed by a chirp, and the monitor screen flickered to life.

"Your e-mail was very specific," Gideon said as the computer slowly booted. "The Bible you sent photos of is nearly four hundred years old and

346

incredibly rare. An original, even if I could find one, would cost you five figures, and that would be one that had been tossed around and used as a coaster and stored in an attic or garage."

Jackson nodded, finding it odd that a man with an office as messy as Gideon's would deign to criticize anyone's book storage protocols.

"However, about two hundred years ago, Kingsworth Press in London printed a King James Version that, I believe, is almost identical."

"And that's the five-hundred-dollar-version?" Jackson asked.

"Yes."

Windows XP loaded, the machine grinding and humming some more while the cursor wheel spun. Gideon broke several minutes of anxious waiting with a, "Here we are," as all his desktop icons finally appeared. He double-clicked one, a shortcut to a web page. When it loaded after several seconds, it displayed a picture of a Bible that, on first glance, could have passed for the Vanderbilt Bible.

"Now, it's not a perfect match," Gideon said. "It obviously doesn't have the same wear and tear marks, same fraying pages, etcetera. And there were slight changes in the various spellings of words, the sort of thing you'd expect between the seventeenth and nineteenth centuries. Everything else was replicated as thoroughly as possible, down to the typeface, margins, flyleaves, binding, and cover."

"And you can get this for me? This isn't in a private collection or something?"

"I spoke to the owner this afternoon, and the price is five hundred. He guarantees its condition as stated on the website," he said, nodding at the screen.

"That actually seems cheap for a Bible that old."

Gideon shrugged.

"How soon can he get it here?"

"If you're willing to pay, by opening tomorrow. Nine o'clock," he added before Jackson could ask.

"Where's he live?"

"Belgrade."

"Serbia?"

"Montana." Gideon shrugged again. "I asked, anticipating you'd want it fast, and he said he could have it here by then."

"How? You know what, I don't care. Do it, whatever the charge."

"And then my fee is two-fifty."

"On top of the five hundred and the shipping?"

Gideon nodded.

"You take cash?"

"Everyone takes cash."

Jackson reached for his wallet, hoping Abby was good for all these expenses. "Here you go."

"Pleasure doing business with you. I'll call you the moment it's in."

Jackson thanked him and returned to his waiting cab. On the ride back to the hotel, with a scheduled stop to pick up take-out, he pulled out his phone.

"Hello?" a woman's voice said.

"Hillary?" he asked with a frown. Wrong McKenzie.

"Jackson?"

"Girl's night out?"

"What?"

"I hear sounds of the city in the background, and you answered Heather's phone."

"Oh, you're quite the crack P.I., you know that? The sounds of the city are Tim's TV."

"So are you double dating, or is this a sister-sister version of *Freaky Friday*?"

"What do you want, Jackson?"

"I need to talk to Heather. Is she there?"

"Just a minute."

Jackson shook his head. Why was every conversation with a member of the McKenzie family like pulling teeth?

"This is Heather."

"Heather, it's Jackson. I need a favor."

"What kind of favor?"

"First, tell Hillary to quit rolling her eyes."

She giggled. "He says to quit rolling your eyes," she said, her voice muffled as she turned away from the phone. Jackson heard but didn't understand Hillary's voice in the background, then Heather came back on. "She said to quit forking your tongue."

Jackson searched for a comeback but found nothing.

"This favor?"

"You still a modeler?"

"I still do some detail work on 3-D models, yeah."

"Are you better than you were three years ago?"

"You have an odd way of asking for a favor, you know that?"

"I didn't say you were bad three years ago."

"Jackson, we were just sitting down to dinner. Can you stumble to the point a little faster?"

"Sorry. If I showed you a very old book, could you recreate it?"

"Recreate it how?"

"With another book. Could you make a new book look like a four-hundred-year-old book, exactly, if they were essentially the same to start with? Replicate nicks and scratches and wear and tear?"

"Maybe. I'd have to see it. It would have to be a really close match to begin with."

"Okay. You happen to be free tomorrow?"

She hesitated.

"I'm willing to pay for this favor, Heather."

"I work in the morning," she said, "but I can make my afternoon free."

"Okay. I have to arrange some details. Can I get back to you?"

"Sure."

"Thanks. Could I talk to Hillary again?"

"She's right here. He wants to talk to you," she added, her voice fading.

"What is it?" Hillary asked.

"I need a favor."

"Is Holly in on this too?"

"That's very clever, Hill. Please?"

"What do you need?"

"I need you to pick up something—actually two things—for me tomorrow morning and get them to Heather."

"I have to be in court tomorrow."

"And you're out partying tonight?"

"Heather was right, you do have a funny way of asking for help."

"What time is court?"

"Nine."

"Till?"

"Ten, ten-thirty."

"Perfect. You can make the pickups after that, and Heather works in the morning, so as long as they get to her by the time she gets home . . . Please, Hill. You know I wouldn't be asking you if—"

"If you could find anyone else to do it?"

He sighed. "Please."

"On one condition."

Full of dread, Jackson said, "Name it."

*   *   *

Friday, February 1
6:32 p.m.

"SO THAT'S why it took you so long to get dinner Wednesday night?" Abby asked.

Jackson nodded.

"Where'd you find this guy, Gideon?"

"Monday, after you checked in at the Casa del Sol, in addition to visiting Mouse, I made a ton of calls and checked on the internet, looking for anybody who dealt in old books."

"Monday already?"

"I was starting to think we could maybe use a duplicate to make an exit strategy, if we could find one and if we could get the Bible. Anyhow, I put out some feelers and finally heard back from him Wednesday, just after I quit, got interrogated by the NSA, and decided to get back in. I sent him some pics of the real thing, and when we got to the motel, found I had a voicemail."

"Which is why you were so insistent on being the one to go get dinner instead of just having it delivered."

"I suppose I could have had Zoey or whatever her name was then go get dinner, and I buy clothes, but I figured this was best."

Abby frowned and shook her head. "Why didn't you just tell us?"

"I didn't want to burden you with it," Jackson said.

"Burden me? It would have been a relief."

He shook his head. "It's hard to pull off a con. I figured it'd be easier for you not to have to act if you thought the Bible we were auctioning off was real. The downside was you thought the Bible was lost, and I'm sorry about that."

"Now that I have it again, it's fine," Abby said. "And you did tell me to trust you."

"I stretched the boundaries of good faith a little."

"So you had Hillary pick up the real Bible from Reggie too?"

"Yeah, after picking up the fake one from Gideon, while Mouse and I were looking for warehouses. Then Reggie and I checked the warehouse out in person, and after that, I met with Heather."

"And she recreated the fake?"

Jackson nodded. "She does detail work on 3-D models for some company, and for art, I think. She's actually really good."

"But . . . when Zoey showed the Bible at the auction . . ." Abby shook her head. "It had all of Alec's notes inside, even the dedication to me. How?"

Chapter Forty-Two

Thursday, January 24
4:27 p.m.

"ARE YOU ALWAYS this impatient?" Heather asked. She wore blue jeans with huge holes in the knees and a loose cotton shirt that was spattered with various artistic substances. Her hair was piled into a wad yet, despite it all, she was still beautiful.

"I've got . . . a date tonight."

"Don't hassle him, Heather, he probably had to pay for it."

Jackson turned to Hillary, who sat with legs crossed on the counter beside Heather's work table. Her shortened work day done, she wore a business suit, no shoes, her hair elegantly styled behind her head. Even with the smirk—or perhaps because of it—she too was beautiful.

"You're watching your sister detail a fake four-hundred-year-old Bible, and you're running down my social calendar?"

Hillary narrowed her eyes, then stuck out her tongue—her version of touché. Or so Jackson assumed—he had seldom if ever landed the final blow in one of their verbal sparring matches.

"Okay, I'm done," Heather said, putting down what looked like a scalpel. "What do you think?"

Jackson picked the Bible off the desk and studied it for a minute, glancing several times at the Vanderbilt Bible. "I can't tell them apart."

Heather smiled.

Jackson glanced at the clock on the wall. "Four hours at the discounted 'we were almost family once' rate of fifty an hour, comes to two bills."

"Hillary told me why you were doing this," Heather said.

"Did she?" he said, turning his eyes to Hillary. She stared at him while she took a drink of whatever libation was in her glass. "Who told her?"

"Reggie, apparently."

"Chatty Cathy. Well, it's not like you thought this was my form of entertainment, did you?"

"It's on the house," Heather said.

"What?"

She shrugged and stuck her hands in her pockets. "I'm a sucker for a sweet story."

"You're serious?" Jackson looked from sister to sister. "This isn't going to come back to bite me someday?"

Heather smiled, and Jackson was convinced the room brightened. "No strings," she said. "As far as I'm concerned, I'll always owe you for saving Hillary."

"Careful, he'll call you on that," Hillary said.

Jackson gave her a quick evil eye before smiling at Heather. "Thank you." He put both Bibles into protective cases and then into a backpack. "I do need to run."

"Give me a call, let me know how it goes," Heather said.

"I will."

"I'll walk you out," Hillary said, gracefully sliding off the counter. She led him down the stairs from Heather's studio apartment and out onto the small patio. "That condition I mentioned on the phone."

Jackson noticeably let his shoulders drop.

"We're having a couples shower—"

"No," he interrupted.

"For Tim and Heather."

"No."

Hillary scrunched her face. "You going to back out on a deal, is that it?"

"Yes, absolutely, with no shame. You don't want me there any more than I want to be there. You just want me to turn on the spit. Forget it, Hill. I'd rather pay Heather's fee."

She grinned. "You win. But that's not the favor."

"What is?"

"Are you seeing anyone?"

He studied her for a moment. Her poker face gave nothing away.

Hillary raised her eyebrows, waiting for a response.

"I'm sorry, but I'm trying to figure out what I'm walking into here."

"Nothing. I was just going to invite you over for dinner sometime, and thought I'd extend the courtesy to your girlfriend, if you had one."

"Dinner?"

She shrugged, almost appearing reticent. "After everything we've been through. . . . And Brian would like to meet you."

Jackson nodded as the other shoe fell.

"If you don't want to, I understand, but I thought I'd ask."

"Let me think about it, okay? And I do have to run."

"Sure. You know my number."

"I do. And I'll call you."

"Okay. Bye, Jackson."

He waved in response and headed for the car, spending a few moments contemplating Hillary's invitation. Then all the balls he had in the air commanded his attention.

Traffic was a mess, and it took him almost an hour to make it to Sam's apartment. She answered the door immediately, still in hospital scrubs. "I just got home," she said. "Come on in."

Jackson followed her up to her apartment and set a pizza (also part of the reason for his long commute) on the table.

"Smells great," she said.

"Just don't get grease stains on the Bible."

She grinned. "I'm going to change. Go ahead and get started."

While they dined, Jackson gave her a full recap of events leading up to his urgent request for help. Sam had the best penmanship he had ever seen, and in a rare moment of mischief once, had shown an uncanny knack for imitating Reggie's signature. She was a far better forger than Jackson, despite his many efforts as a teenager to duplicate Grant's signature and send his childhood crush Megan Halladay a love letter.

"Okay, what do I need to copy?" Sam asked after they had finished eating, washed their hands, and donned surgical gloves.

Jackson opened the real Bible—the Vanderbilt Bible. "Pretty much everything. Front flyleaves, back, this dedication page especially. I'd recommend anything on the first page of any book, anything else that seems prominent."

"You weren't kidding about this taking all night."

Jackson looked around. "You weren't kidding about the apartment needing cleaning."

Sam gave him an evil glare. "I've been working seventy hours a week, Buster."

"Which is why I appreciate you so much more for doing this."

Sam rolled her eyes. "Save it."

"You think you can duplicate it?"

"I think so. It's distinctive, but not over the top."

"And remember, we don't want an exact translation."

"Run that part past me again."

"If the Bible does contain national secrets, I don't want them getting out. If you start transcribing letters and numbers here and there, and maybe some words and phrases in the more obscure parts, it should be a safeguard against that."

"And you don't think anyone will notice?"

"Nobody's had it long enough to memorize it, and none of the paragraphs has any sort of cogent thought to them such that changes will stand out. As long as the first few lines are the same and your changes are subtle, we should be good."

"Okay," Sam said with a shrug. "Let me grab my pens. Help yourself to something to drink. I wouldn't want you to get dehydrated cleaning the apartment."

Jackson sighed but got to work. His deal had been simple. She would copy Alec's notes until she dropped, and he would clean the "so dirty" apartment she had been complaining about of late. Knowing Sam, he had figured it probably meant a missed spider web in the corner and determined he would be getting the better end of the deal. He wasn't wrong, despite his earlier jibe.

They broke at ten for snacks and at midnight for a walk outside in the cool night air. It was invigorating, and they returned to work around twelve-thirty. By two, he had finished with the apartment, including cleaning Sam's light fixtures, the inside of her toilet tank, and everything short of her unmentionables drawer. She, meanwhile, continued to write.

"How's it going?" he asked.

"Good. I had to power through a little writer's cramp, but . . ."

"Can I help?"

"No." She nodded at the couch. "You should lie down, try to sleep. From what I hear, you've got a big day tomorrow."

"Yeah. You'll wake me if you need anything?"

"I will."

She turned back to her work, and Jackson watched her for a few minutes. The lone light above the dining room table created a halo atop her golden blond hair, and at that moment, Jackson found it entirely apropos. He thought about giving her a peck on the cheek or a shoulder massage but didn't want to run the risk of causing her pen to jump. So he settled onto the couch, falling asleep within minutes.

*   *   *

Friday, February 1
6:37 p.m.

"SHE STAYED up all night?" Abby asked.

"She's a nurse; she's used to it."

Reggie shook his head at Jackson.

"And she copied every single word Alec wrote?"

"Seventy-five, eighty percent. Once we got away from the front and back flyleaves, I let her freestyle a little."

Abby shook her head. "Still . . ."

"I put the phony Bible in the safe deposit box Friday morning," Reggie said, "just before you all met Zoey at the bank."

"And put Zoey's tracker inside the binding," Jackson said.

"So where was the real Bible?"

"In my safe since last Friday morning," Reggie said.

"How . . . how did you know that everyone would buy it?"

"I didn't. But I figured with all the chasing around, no one had had much time to examine anything in detail."

"Or take pictures," Reggie said.

"Admittedly, I didn't think of that. But once they bought that the Bible was legit, they wouldn't bother checking any pictures."

"You hoped," Reggie said.

He shrugged. "Sam did good work. I figured our odds were pretty good."

"I hope you reimbursed her."

"I cleaned her apartment."

"So no," Reggie said.

Abby shook her head some more. "What about Harris and Stockton? What if they'd have served you another warrant?"

"I wasn't in possession of the Bible, so it would have been null. And Whitn—Zoey was right unless it *'particularly'* described *'the place to be searched, and the persons or things to be seized,'* it would be invalid. And there was no way for them to know the place to be searched. And, technically, *'the thing to be seized'* was in Reggie's safe, so . . ."

"Had they chosen to bust you for selling government secrets to the Russians, on the other hand . . ." Reggie said.

"I never sold them secrets. I sold them a dummy Bible."

"With some secrets unaltered by Sam."

"But secrets they couldn't prove in court were secrets to begin with."

"So you say."

"So did you know about this?" Abby asked Reggie.

"He briefed me in stages," Reggie said. "I told him he was crazy."

Jackson shrugged. "It worked."

"So was Zoey in on any of it?"

"Sort of."

"Sort of?"

"It's like Captain Jack Sparrow said in *Pirates of the Caribbean*, about always being able to trust a dishonest person to be dishonest. I figured if I left her alone with the Bible, she'd run."

Abby's eyes widened. "You planned on her running?"

"I banked on it. I never intended for the transfer to go through. I just had to string her along and time her disappearance."

"What? How?"

"I told her the plan, that she and Mouse would video the Bible as proof of possession and that he would then come over to the warehouse to oversee the transfer. I knew she'd realize she'd have a couple of minutes to get away without having to knock Mouse out or give him the slip. And I figured she'd take the easy way."

"Hard part was getting Mouse to go along with it," Reggie said with a laugh.

"I didn't tell him I expected Zoey to double-cross us. And the real hard part was getting Zoey to go along with the sale in the first place."

"How did you?"

"I had to plant the seed early that she could get away with stealing the Bible. She never would have gone for it for just one-third of the sale, especially if . . ."

"If what?"

"She was working for someone who wanted the Bible."

Abby frowned.

"If it was about money, a third would be worse than the whole wad but better than nothing. And if it was just about the code . . ." He shook his head. "But if somebody else wanted the Bible . . ." He stared at the wall, urging his mind to put the final piece of the puzzle together. A piece he wasn't even sure was missing.

"Jackson?"

"Yeah, sorry." He shrugged. "She said something about working for whoever pays her, but I can't remember. She changed stories faster than Johnny Cash switched harmonicas."

"So you planned everything, just as it went down?"

"Well, I didn't plan on Brady missing Kredlenko's gun, but otherwise, yeah. I couldn't have scripted it better."

"And we're in the clear legally?"

He nodded. "Harris and Stockton lectured me a little, but I came away unscathed."

"What about everyone else?"

"They're all chasing Zoey, wherever she is. And it's been a week, so if things were going to hit the fan, I expect they would have by now. Just don't go advertising that you have the Bible or reading it on Venice Beach or something."

Abby grinned. "I can't thank you enough. I can't believe . . ." She grinned even wider, which in turn caused Jackson to grin. "If you want," she said, "I still want to crack Alec's code and figure out what he really wrote in here. If it is something important, I'll give it to the FBI or whoever, but I could use some help."

"If it's all the same to you, I think I've had enough of this particular Bible. I'll pass."

"I understand," she said. She put the Bible down and leaned over to give Jackson a hug. "Thank you so much."

"Just do me one favor," he said as they separated.

"Anything."

He nodded at the Bible. "Don't just hold onto that as a link to Alec. Read it. It will be worth your while. Trust me one more time."

Chapter Forty-Three

IT WAS ONE of those lethargic days that was so enviable while chasing across town in cabs and buses and rental cars or shooting at shadows in a loft but was actually quite boring when it arrived. Reggie was at his other L.A. Cameron's locale in Newport Beach for the day, Mouse was into some new online role-playing game that Jackson found lame, and Maggie and Sam were both busy with work. It left Jackson alone with his virtual Trojans and Rams, competing for Rose Bowls and Super Bowls, respectively.

As he ran out the fourth quarter against another hapless foe, his thoughts turned to Abby and her Bible. There were a lot of loose ends that had been left untied. But that could be the case when dealing with governments both foreign and domestic and when creating an exit strategy as opposed to a resolution. Besides, Jackson wasn't bothered by frayed yarn.

But one thing continued to nag at him—had for days.

Zoey.

Who was she really, and who was she working for?

It didn't really matter, but it still bugged him. Especially since he felt like somewhere in the recesses of his brain, he knew the answer. Or at least, part of it.

His third-team running back fumbled, and Jackson turned the defense over to autopilot. It was 42-10, and he didn't really care.

Suddenly he could feel it was close. He stood and paced through the living room. Things Zoey had said and done came flooding back to him. About her knowing about the Bible by "working sources." Or the way she had flinched when . . .

Something on the TV distracted Jackson, and he looked to see that his game was finished. While his progress saved to the hard drive, he went to get his mail. The air was cool despite the sun, and he hoped some fresh air would help him think.

All he had was a plea for money from some eco group and a postcard with a photo on the front of a stone bridge over a canal. It looked oddly familiar. Clooney and Pitt in *Ocean's Twelve?*

He turned the postcard over, wondering who was sending him mysterious mail now. It was postmarked in Amsterdam, and suddenly the tumblers clicked.

Noah Vanderbilt.

He was Zoey's employer.

No wonder Jackson's subconscious had started making a racket whenever his name was mentioned. How could he have overlooked Noah, the other brother—the one Zoey had immediately disregarded when Jackson told her Abby's brother had kidnapped her? She'd right away jumped to Desmond, and at the time, Jackson had figured she was just making the logical conclusion that the black sheep of the family was responsible. But had she tipped her hand? Had she jumped to Desmond because she knew it wasn't Noah?

Along with Abby and Regina, and maybe their lawyers, Noah was the only other private citizen who would have known about the Bible to begin with, who would have also known about the masquerade ball, who would have known Desmond's thought processes with regard to revealing it there, and who would have had any reason to hire a "private contractor" to retrieve it. Now it all made sense.

He looked back to the postcard. A hastily written note was scrawled in tiny black letters under a description of the image on the front of the card.

Jackson,

I felt I owed you an explanation. My real name is Robyn Davis. I work for a private company, and what I told you as Zoey was true. We find people and retrieve things no one else can. Noah hired me to get his father's Bible, which is why I couldn't split the money with you. I brought it to him here in Amsterdam, and in case you're nuts enough to chase us around the world, Noah's moving and by the time you get this, I'll be on a beach somewhere.

Anyhow, I wanted you to know I got away safely. I told you I could swim. ☺ I'm sorry I had to mislead you so often, and I'm sorry about the way things turned out. But you know what they say, all's fair . . .

-Robbie

Jackson read the postcard twice.

And grinned.

Wide.

There was something sort of gratifying in pulling a good con. It maybe wasn't terribly Christ-like, but setting everything in motion and then bringing it home was rewarding. And when the person you conned thought they had pulled a fast one on you . . . Well, Jackson had to laugh.

It was just too bad he couldn't send her an explanatory postcard in return.

Acknowledgements

I WOULD LIKE to list all the people who have crossed my path and been instruments of God, teaching me His ways and showing me how to walk in them. But the list would be too long, and I'm sure I would leave someone out by accident. That said, please know, if you fit into that group, I am indebted beyond words for all the little things (and the big ones too) that have pointed and still point me to Him.

I am also grateful to the usual cast of characters for their help bringing this manuscript to publication. Sierra, I couldn't continue if I didn't have your unwavering support. The words of encouragement do matter. Mom and Dad, your belief continues to inspire me. Thanks for the proofing too. Tiffani and Mark, thanks for the edits and ideas and the dialogue, and for always being there for me. Chris, thanks for giving my writing your attention and critique, and for your enthusiastic help.

I keep writing the same words—encouragement, support, proofing, edits. All have been needed in abundance over the last year. So too have been the words and comments from you, the readers. They motivate me to keep writing, so keep them coming!

Despite all my work and that of the people above, I still haven't caught the wind. I'm sure there are still some holes in my plots and typos on my pages. I take full responsibility for them, and hope they don't take away from the story.

If you like what you read, I'd love a review on Amazon. I'd also love to hear back from you, as I mentioned above. Please visit www.nathanbirr.com to learn more about my books, what I have in the works, to see what I'm blogging about these days, or to find ways to interact with me.

Lastly, if you've come this far, you clearly like to read. I've got a recommendation for you: the Bible. Like Jackson told Abby, it will be worth your while.

www.ingramcontent.com/pod-product-compliance
Lightning Source LLC
Chambersburg PA
CBHW022145010726
47493CB00002B/343